CHERRY-ROSE
Blood & Wishes

Styrofoam Media

Any references to historical events, real people, or real places are used fictitiously. Names, characters, and places are products of the author's imagination.

First Styrofoam edition 2024.

Edited by Jennia Herold D'Lima: https://jenniaedits.com

Front cover image by Giselle C. at Gigi Creatives

www. jeffwiederkehr.com

ISBN 979-8-3507-3415-7

Library of Congress Control Number: 2024914074

CHERRY-ROSE
Blood & Wishes

Jeffery C. Wiederkehr

Styrofoam Media

For Luna & Oz

I

Ju Ju Hand

Once there was a time when the Blue Fairy's magic flowed through the earth and the sky, the mountains and the rivers, the trees and the ivy. It flowed through the wolves and the weeds, and the bears and the bushes; every beast, every bird, every person, everywhere. Here, even here there was magic, even here in this humble cottage so far beyond the village that it has been forgotten by most, so deep in the forest that it is part of the forest. Even here where long long ago a woodworker and his wife dreamt of a quiet happily-ever-after and called the Blue Fairy to help make one last wish come true.

A Father's Wish

"A BOY, just a boy." A humble wish mumbled into work-hardened hands. *A boy, just a boy.* Tinkering with his paints and clocks and wooden soldiers until she whispered, "It's time."

A boy, that isn't too much to ask, as she pushed and pushed, her labored breath becoming moan, moan giving way to silence and silence to a soft sad smile, until that smile gave way to tears.

"My darling ... my love, tell me ... is something wrong?" he asked when he knew that it was.

"What can I ..." He didn't finish his question because he knew there was nothing to be done.

"Too ... too much ... too much blood," when he saw that there was ...

"I don't know if I can," when he didn't know if he could. When he knew he couldn't.

He looked up with eyes full of fear, arms full of red and a writhing child. His eyes found her eyes—his love, his true love, bleeding out before the hearth—as the echoes of their last shared wish faded out from the cottage to the clearing to the forest ... *A boy, just a boy.*

He offered his wife a view of their child. She managed a last, soft, peaceful smile. She had always wanted a daughter.

＊ ＊ ＊

This funeral-birthday brought new wishes.

If only we had more time. If only I had another chance. I'd give anything to do it all over.

New wishes and old wishes in new ways.

If only I could do something, anything …

A boy? … A boy. Just a boy.

Even here there was magic.

＊ ＊ ＊

For thirteen years these funeral-birthday wishes seeped into the cottage's frame and floor and mixed with the bloodstains hidden beneath the living room rug. For thirteen years they colored everything within the cottage's walls. For thirteen years he passed most of his days doing that which brought him pleasure. He mourned and he shaped wood and he tried to make something—a tribute, a toy, a boy, a son—something worthy of his wife's life and their last shared wish.

And for thirteen years the daughter who made up the latter half of the funeral-birthday grew up in a cottage with a ghost of a mother, a ghost of a father, and thirteen years' worth of wooden almost-brothers.

Thirteen years of his trial and error, thirteen years of shaping almost-sons. A wish … wishes and wishes. *Just a boy.* Pure and true. Almost perfect. Almost. Until the day the Blue Fairy decided it *was* perfect. Until *She* came to close the circle on the wish his wife was unable to fulfill. Until the Blue Fairy gave him the son his wife never could.

How could he have known that their wish would require him to say goodbye to the daughter his wife had given him?

Funny how for those thirteen years, no one but the forest and his long-buried wife even knew he had a daughter. Funny how no one, not even the forest, cared. Funny how, if this story had a cricket, it might chirp, "Funny how no one wants what they have." Or perhaps it'd say, "Funny how a happily-ever-after is never enough."

However, this story doesn't have a cricket. If it did, it might suggest that perhaps some wishes shouldn't be answered.

"My darling child, I won't be long, I promise," said the father.

Funny how well-intended promises become lies. Funny how *I won't be long* can turn into goodbye forever.

* * *

Just outside the cottage, in place of a father, a little girl inherited a huge wall of almost-brothers. A disformed and disfigured wall of unruly, unfinished, unrealized wooden-boy parts and pieces. A wall of wood stacked high with blocks that might be legs, might be arms, and might be feet— might-be-brothers, never-could-be-fathers. Blocks with twigs that might be a head with a nose; half-shaped torsos cracked and broken, twisted and split, all lying about with their cousin sticks and stumps. A wall. A lifetime of wood, a monument of mistakes. A wall of wooden almost-somethings that almost got to live again. A wall that rattled with want and possibility; that shook with the desire to embrace their almost-sister; that begged for the return of their almost-father; that quaked with the haunt of all of their almosts and shook with the ghost of all their maker's unanswered Blue Fairy wishes.

How could she know that this wall was a tribute, a smothering crown of sorrows that multiplied daily in honor of a shared wish? How could she know that it was carefully stacked piece by piece, each failure a promise to try again? How could she know that each *almost* was lovingly laid upon her mother's grave to demonstrate that he hadn't forgotten? How could she know, when her father never told her so?

It was difficult to speak of such things, father to daughter, daughter to father, dead to the living. So, for those thirteen years while her father carved his clocks and toys and boys from wood, the daughter made what she could with what she had. For those thirteen years while her father built his wall of almost-sons, she gave the ghost of her mother form as she stitched together echoes, pieces, and imagined memories from that which lay about the cottage. There wasn't much, but she had just enough: *her* garden, *her* record collection, *her* spinning wheel, *her* books and bureau full of cloth and rags, yards of fabric, and a small book of simple spells. However, what she loved most of all were the mother things her father kept hidden in the shed.

The shed, just beyond the wall of almost-brothers, was not for daughter eyes, daughter thoughts, nor daughter hands. It was his. Not hers. *His*. And because this was the way of things, there would be no discussion. The rules were for following, and the shed, it was for hurt and loss and mourning, for keeping, for hiding, for secrets, for fathers.

No discussion? Didn't matter. Her words were hidden behind a mouth that choked on sin and shame and drowned in a flood of inadequacy. Silence in service to the great ghost of guilt and fatherly rules. Were the rules ever spoken? She could never quite remember. Whatever the case, they were always there, just behind the door, somewhere in the shed: daggers in the watery gleam of a fatherly eye; a twitch in the lie of his smile; rage in a lonely sigh by a fire; buried beneath the crushing stroke of a gentle fatherly hand. He didn't ever have to speak the rules because all of *it*, all of *this*, was lingering, living, thriving, coloring the aura of everything under the sky, looming its haunting doom throughout the cottage, scratching hard at the base of her spine, begging to be spoken. Never had so silly a rule so desperately desired to be broken.

When one's life is colored with words that are too difficult to speak, imagination rules the day. Pretending becomes a way of life. The shed? In spite of the scratch and itch of the rule, she pretended there was nothing to discuss. She pretended not to care, not to notice, not to be driven mad by the want to run straight into the shed and set it alight just to quiet all those unspoken everythings. What's more, she pretended that she never never disobeyed … and most of all, she pretended not to know that within its walls, there were secrets worth knowing.

She pretended that she did not know that the shed swam with the heavy must of dried marigold, that there were inverted bouquets dying over the door, wilting over windows, and rotting from rafters. She never mentioned the shelf filled with tiny boxes of mother-made lilac soap that sat just above dozens and dozens of mother-made juniper candles. She pretended that she never knew that beneath a shelf of polished yet-to-be-brother-faces, there were hidden boxes of dead-mother dresses, mother- needles and mother-pins, buttons, and patches. Each box sealed with a ribbon, each ribbon tied into a bow, each bow binding a bouquet of dried marigold; and beneath the boxes of clothes, and bows, and buttons, there were other books, older, larger books. Each book tied so intricately she dared not disturb them. Books wound and bound with horse hair and twine all knotted with delicate bouquets of her mother's favorite orange blossom. Knots wishing to be cut, marigold crying to be crushed, books dying to be read.

She never mentioned that the only rule she never broke was to never speak of the dead. She never mentioned how much she needed the shed. That it was both her greatest joy and her greatest sorrow. She never mentioned the shed at all because there were rules and he could never know what she didn't quite know what to say. *The shed helped to fill the space where the scent of a mother should be.*

So, it is with a twisted smile and only the slightest mist in the eyes that she recalls the day her father yielded his secrets and released her mother's. On that day, on that last day, seated beside her on the hearth, taking in the morning fire, he waited until she had finished writing out her night's dream before he spoke. "I'll be back soon, my child. Tomorrow ... Certainly tomorrow," he said as if he weren't quite sure it would be so—lilac candles to cleanse the air. "Tomorrow at the latest. No, no, don't cry. Don't worry. You will be safe. Just stay inside. Don't leave the cottage ... Tomorrow night at the latest," he said as he stood—juniper soap to cleanse the body. "You understand, don't you?" He looked back as he opened the door. "If you were lost, wouldn't you want me to find you?" He didn't wait for the answer—fire to cleanse the soul.

She stood and pressed her face against the window to watch him disappear into the forest. And she felt, but wasn't quite equipped to say, *I am here right now, lost, lonely, sad, and you haven't come looking for me.*

On the morning when his promises became lies, when she knew he was never coming back, that morning, she sat at the hearth and wrote out the words to the lesson she learned. "Fathers don't always tell the truth. Fathers … they never, never, tell the truth. Never!" She set down her pen, picked up the seam-ripper, and ran for the shed. Wooden heads rolled, boxes with clothes slid, and lids flew until the books she never dared touch for fear of being discovered were sitting in her lap.

With a shaking hand, she took seam-ripper to knot and watched the flowers crumble.

If ever something was meant to be, inside the cover of the first book, *Darkest Dreams & Moon Magic*, she found what she was sure was her mother's flowing hand. A single finger traced oval loops in black ink as she read the words. Tears fell as she imagined her mother's hand gliding over the page, giving her the very words that she'd often heard her father whisper while shaping his wood: "Everything begins with a wish."

* * *

As she came to understand her mother's magic, she began to see motherly echoes in fatherly ways. Each night after dinner, he would weave his magic. The rocking chair. The pipe. The fire. That cruel smile. A glass of gin. A book. Maybe a photograph. A gentle pat on the head. A letter written. A letter burned. Lyrics sung. Scribbles in a notebook. A melody. Eyes, mustache, mouth reaching for something beyond the ceiling. More fire. More music. More gin and those orange blooms that he dried in the shed.

This spell, it wasn't in any of the books, but she knew what it was. It was a fatherly-mourning-spell.

On those mourning-spell nights, as she read by the light of the fire, he'd play *her* records to summon the ghost of his wife. A block of wood resting on his lap, an almost-boy hidden within its grains. With Julie London, Ella Fitzgerald, and Connie Francis crooning for a ghost; with their last shared wish—*just a boy*—echoing out from the bloodstain beneath the rug, he'd wish their wishes all over again.

She could see it now; it was all there in the books. When the music played and the fire roared, his wife was there somewhere between the words, somewhere beneath the flames, somewhere behind that echo, somewhere in the shadow that she cast on the rug. Her mother, his wife. He was calling *her*, to show her that he could make their last wish come true.

A boy, just a boy. As always, as ever, for thirteen years, over and over and over until it was just right. No. Until it was perfect. Until it was so perfect that it shook the moon from the sky.

Mourning frenzy. Mother music, a fire, the clang of clocks, an almost-son, a wooden boy —a frenzy to make the Blue Fairy magic. This time, like the time before, and the time before that ... like every time, like every other time, only this time, in the small hours of the morning, the cottage shook with a pale-blue light that breathed life into a lifeless wooden shell. No mother, no blood, no heart, no strings.

A boy ... just a boy.

* * *

From the furthest corner of the cottage, from the soft edge of slumber, she could sense the change, for these morning sounds were not her morning sounds. The mornings she knew, with their almost-silent song, suggested by the distant call of some warbling bird and the soft crackle of dying coals, were entirely shattered. On this morning, the cottage was in frenzy. Music was blaring, the windows were rattling, and the cupboards were creaking, and the floor was thumping, pounding, pulsing up into the walls, shaking out a lifetime of dust that rained down from the rafters.

She *knew* ...

There was singing. *Father and another voice.*

She knew.

There was dancing. *Father and someone new.*

Father and ...

Despite the singing and dancing, and the dust as sky falling, she decided that the morning shouldn't change. That it wouldn't. Dream journal in hand, she slid from her bed to the floor, from the floor to the door. Still rubbing the sleep from her eyes. She entered the frenzy, intent on performing *Daughter as Ever, falling feather, unbreakable even when thrown by the chaos of the wind.* So, she made her way, like every morning for as long as she could remember—bed, floor, door—heading for the hearth to take in the soft orange glow of the dying coals where she would write out her night's dream.

Beyond her door, she did not waver when churning gusts pushed and pressed to toss her about.

The wind pushed. "Come … join us … come dance."

Upon the hearth, she did not break character when assailed by the persistent breeze who drove to unseat her.

The breeze pressed. "Come … come sing,"

She closed her eyes and scooted away at the touch of the breeze, and the retreating breeze began to reason for her, "She is still heavy with sleep, after all. And it is so early, after all. And we've had so many mornings together, after all. And surely we will have so many more, after all."

Cross-legged at the edge of the hearth, she sat to write out her night's dream. It seemed, however, that in spite of her performance, the morning was working against her. The beat of the music, the thump of the floor, the call of that new voice, it all worked in concert to chase her dream away. As the night's dream spilled out of the girl, the rage of this morning's wind rushed in; and because there was no dream to write, because something had to be done before she blew away entirely, something new made its way onto the paper.

A wish of fire, of fury, and of fangs.

As soon as the wish was written, she felt shame for knowing that her father wouldn't understand. She tore the page, leaned in, and offered it to the morning's coals.

Girl, dreamer, wish-maker, feather fluttering with that rushing rage, she watched the embers turn her words black and drift and float and fly out the chimney to meet the morning moon.

Her wish, so pure, so true, it did not need thirteen years to be answered. Hours? Days? A week? Too long … whatever, the wooden boy was soon gone.

Gone so soon she couldn't even recall his name …

How could she have known that her wish would also take her father?

The Funeral Birthday

Gone, everyone gone. Everything but the forest. Didn't he say that the forest was the best teacher of all?

When the days were lonely and the nights were long, Forest did what it could to offer comfort. "So your father is gone, so your mother is dead," Forest said. "Consider the bear. Consider the deer. Consider the raven. Where are their fathers? Where are their mothers?"

In time, she realized she had everything she needed. Needle and fabric, a spinning wheel and thread; a home, a garden; Forest and fire—more, more, more than she needed because now the shed was hers; the shed and all its secrets, all its magic, everything, everything she needed to make her nights a little less lonely.

* * *

Stained fingers sift through the morning's ash. Beneath the gray and black, the seamstress retrieves a pair of eyes shaped by the fire; and, when her doll is stuffed just so, she presses them tight into place. She completes the form with a small stitch of red thread just below the hairline at the base of the neck. She ties the knot. She bites the thread. She kisses each cheek as she imagines a mother might, and she says, "Won't you make a lovely daughter?"

And for a time, she is a little less lonely.

* * *

On this very morning, with the cottage teeming with life of all sorts, the seamstress hardly felt lonely at all. What's more, considering the progress she made on her latest doll, its completion perfectly timed with the impending dead moon, there was little to feel lonely about. Assuming she didn't stay dead, the next day would be her daughter's funeral-birthday.

The cottage was in chaos. Twelve magical mannequins all sewn up, stitched up, and knotted up into fully grown almost-daughters were busy making funeral-birthday preparations. Daughters who were dolls, dolls who were once dead, the dead who were once vermin, bird, or beast, sang and danced and decorated the cottage as the seamstress knotted the last knot on her latest daughter-doll. It was almost impossible to be lonely these days.

"Girls, girls, gather 'round, she's just about ready," said the seamstress, returning pins to cushion. "Violent-Joy, Shy-Blue … Peaches, Mojave … girls, all of you, isn't she perfect?" The seamstress took a step back, placed a hand on her chin, and began to nod as she circled the form on the table.

"Remember, girls, if we make our wishes just so, tomorrow, just before the sun rises, you will have a brand-new sister."

Twelve ragdoll mannequin-somethings moved in a wild knot as they swarmed to see their almost-sister dressed up and displayed in her funeral-birthday best, a black-collared birthday dress, decorated in a flower pyre of marigold blossoms and pale candlelight, swimming in the thick thick stench of heady musk. A doll, who was hardly more than a shell, lay ready—quiet, still … dead … dying somewhere. After all, it was her funeral-birthday.

"What shall we name your newest sister?" The seamstress dodged elbows, knees, and hips, barely finishing her words before she was overrun by a deluge of daughter-dolls.

"Ivy, for the color of her skin," said Sprinkles as her hand ran up a lifeless arm.

"Diana!" added Mojave, jiggling a lifeless leg.

"You and your Wonder Woman comics," laughed Violent-Joy as she snatched the arm away from Sprinkles. "How about ..." she said, drawing out the *about* as she thrust the arm toward the ceiling, "Luna for ... you know ... the moon!"

The naming game went on this way for minutes until, in near but not quite perfect unison, a dozen father-clocks rang out to silence the frenzy. As the last hum of the last bell in the last clock gave way to silence, Shy-Blue spoke. "Cherry-Rose."

"Cherry-Rose?" repeated Jasmine, turning the name up into a question.

Shy-Blue stretched the cold lips of her almost-sister into a wide smile. "Yes, Cherry-Rose for her lips. They look like summer rose petals, but darker and deeper, like wild blood cherries. Lips like a dark red rose, but a cherry-red rose. As if there were a Cherry-Rose."

"Yes, yes," the cottage howled.

"Yes, yes" the seamstress echoed. "Cherry-Rose."

* * *

There she was ... almost. A lifeless form dead to the world, displayed for all to see. Supine on the table like a funeral ornament. These witnesses, however, would shed no tears. They would not mourn what the thief of time took too soon. They would not wail over a wasted beauty displayed in the early stages of rot, nor choke on stories of who she was, nor sniffle at who she would never become. This coming night, this very funeral-birthday eve, they would celebrate an awakening. A new life, or at least a life in a new way, and if their mother's mother's magic did its work, if their wishes were made just so, the next morning these almost-sisters would find that something had to die so that something could be born.

A funeral. A birthday. A funeral in reverse. Some magic. A wish, a shell, a souvenir. A funeral-birthday.

As twilight died, the forest whispered the last of the day's songs to set the stage. A million tiny forms—beetles chirping, grasshoppers singing, rats, roaches, and snakes all sounded their twilight goodbye beneath the ivy.

In the cottage, candlelight shook and swayed and threw dancing daughter shadows on each wall. The candlelight moved with the heavy scent of manifold forest blooms. Flowers of every kind decorated every corner and every daughter-doll, and on the funeral-birthday table—marigold and a Cherry-Rose. Marigold because as Mother's books described, from a time before dolls had memories, the flower of the funeral-birthday altar was marigold. Every almost-funeral, every almost-birthday, every funeral-birthday eve, for every almost-girl— marigold.

Just as the books described, the seamstress placed marigold upon the altar to call wandering spirits. It called to those who might not be through with this plane, to those who might have more to see, to those who might be too broken or shocked to move beyond whatever separated them from their previous form. The bloom whispered softly, a crumb trail for a wandering soul, and with the cottage full of its musky scent, if dolls and wishes were made just so …

Cherry-Rose.

Almost.

* * *

"We need fire, flowers, and the music to carry our wishes to the stars and the moon. The bigger the frenzy," the seamstress quoted from her mother-books, "the farther our wishes will fly."

To make the frenzy, some decorated scraps of fabric and paper and fat ribbons with Blue Fairy runes. They hung them from the mantel, the windows, and the animal-faced clocks. While some busied themselves with ribbons and bows, others … decorated Cherry-Rose. They wound a crown of marigold blossoms and placed it upon her head. Then they covered her eyes, throat, and breast. Last, a line down her belly ending at the V where her legs met.

While the others put the finishing touches on the decorations, Violent-Joy ran to the turntable.

"Yes, my Violent-Joy, music for Cherry-Rose." The seamstress rocked in her chair and moved a hand as if she were conducting an orchestra.

Violent-Joy lowered the needle onto her favorite song, and when the record sounded the *click-click-click* of "Uncontrollable Urge," it was as if she cast a spell. The song snapped everyone out of whatever they were doing, right there wherever they were, with whoever they were doing it with, and they danced a violent funeral-birthday dance. The seamstress and all the living-mannequin ghost-dolls were singing, dancing, jumping, and jerking about without anything to hold them down—screaming all their "yeah, yeah, yeah's," as if to wake Cherry-Rose.

The frenzy ran long into the night. Fae formed a queue at the record player. She wanted to sway with *Let's Dance*; Betty waited to play *The Idiot*; Apple cued *Easter*; Daisy, *The Fine Art of Surfacing*. Others, when legs became heavy from dance, decided to lay about in other worlds, faces full of prose and poetry. Rey-Rey was deep in *Twenty Love Poems and a Song of Despair*; Jasmine upon *The Golden Sutra*; Mojave under *The Song of Wandering Aengus*.

If they weren't singing and dancing, or daydreaming while reading, they were writing poetry for Cherry-Rose. Scarlet liked to recite. She wrote and spat and sang her lines and cast them into the fire with a stomp …

> Cherry-Rose, of full red lips
> *Stomp
> And Jupiter eyes
> *Stomp *Stomp
> Your carcass is out there
> *Stomp *Stomp *Stomp
> ALL FULL OF FLIES
> *spit *wad *throw *burn

Funeral-birthday eve went on and on until the seamstress fell asleep in her rocking chair. On and on until most of the mannequin-girls too, were lost to sleep and scattered upon the floor. On and on until the haze of dawn began to crawl over the hills and its light slipped softly between the trees. On and on until the last gaggle of ghost-girls—Violent-Joy, Shy-Blue, Sprinkles, and Peaches—sat arm-in-arm at the hearth, refusing to sleep until they met Cherry-Rose. So, with a decorated corpse of a doll on the table and a room littered with sleeping bodies, the last four kept the funeral-birthday fire. They swayed and they sang with Patti Smith. "Because the Night," all mad-eyed and wild. They too begged to be touched—on and on until they sang that last chorus, mumbling and improvising as the song faded out, and then softly chanting with "Ghost Dance" as the next song faded in.

On and on until Cherry-Rose sat up to say, "What's all this?"

On and on until in imperfect unison, the four shouted, "Happy birthday, Cherry-Rose!" Over and over, "Happy birthday!"

The birthday calls did their job and quickly swept the cottage up into a renewed Bacchanalia of the sewn and the stitched—dolls and dance, and song and screams, mannequin and seamstress—everyone awake belting out the birthday song.

When the birthday song finally faded, it was time for the funeral-birthday dance. Violent-Joy dropped the needle again to hear Elvis twang "Power of My Love."

"Shall we dance?" The seamstress extended her arm toward the newest living-ghost mannequin-daughter whose grip on the table suggested she was still feeling more lifeless-doll than not. Not waiting for an answer, the seamstress swept Cherry-Rose off the table and spun her in the middle of the room. Cherry-Rose swung with heavy legs, feeling wet and water-logged. She danced with legs that dragged and tumbled, with arms and head that flailed and bobbed, with limbs wanting the support of strings.

"Hello, beauty ..." *spin ...

"You are Cherry-Rose ..." *spin ...

"I am your mother ..." *spin ...

"These are your sisters ..." *spin ...

"We are one ..." *spin ...
"big" *spin
"happy" *spin
"family."

* * *

Cherry-Rose and her twelve sisters were the result of years of trial and error. Each new doll, the seamstress would tell you, inched closer and closer to perfect Blue Fairy form. The first doll that she created as a lonely thirteen-year-old girl was a tiny ragdoll (long gone now, forest rest her soul). Ragdolls were the easiest to shape, with their mitten hands and button eyes. But, as the years passed, the seamstress honed her craft blending sewing, wishes, and magic. Month by month, year by year, each shell began to look more and more real. Ragdoll became doll. Doll became daughter.

Each of the ghost-girls a spirit loosed from some other form. Violent-Joy was a scrub jay bludgeoned by the cottage window. Peaches, a racoon torn open at the edge of the clearing. Mojave, a snake stomped under hoof, skull crushed, oozing wet jelly all full of ants. Apple, a little girl who floated face down in a river far far from home and so on for each daughter-doll. Each a seamstress-sized mannequin-plaything that with a little magic was almost ... *almost* ... real. Too real, almost perfect, but yet never real enough. At least not yet. Not yet quite perfectly perfect enough to earn a visit from the Blue Fairy herself.

Could Cherry-Rose be the one? the seamstress wondered.

Yes, yes, she is perfectly perfect, she thought as she spun her newest daughter across the cottage floor. *She has to be. There are so many Blue Fairy wishes to wish.*

* * *

Cherry-Rose was indeed perfect, so perfect that even if Cherry-Rose weren't standing there breathing into the seamstress's neck, even if she were propped up against a wall posing a perfect doll-like pose, someone might mistake her for real, that is, until one looked close enough to examine the almost imperceptible seams that shaped her form and the fine, fine, finest stitching that held her together.

Yes, so real, one might even believe she were someone's actual daughter, until they looked close enough to see that she was a peculiar, but astonishingly beautiful, sort of mannequin-ghost girl.

Until they saw that she was made of cloth, a mesmerizing shade of the lightest faded green.

Until they pulled her thread.

Until they split her seams.

Until they discovered that the hair that fell to her breast, darker than a raven's neck, was stolen from a horse's tail; her eyes, that swam like Jupiter and all his moons, was just magic and glass once tied with runes.

Until they discovered that her lips, for which she was named, that hung like midsummer double cherries, ripe and fat, were too too perfectly blood-red to be real at all: redder than her maker's moon-day cloth, redder than ritual marriage sheets, red, red, redder than any rose. Until they came to find the loose thread which would surely unwind all their wonder. She just couldn't be real when even roses cried to be this red.

We Were All Something Else

THE SEAMSTRESS was glowing with motherly pride as she danced Cherry-Rose about the center of the room. But the night was long and the morning full, and the seamstress *had* given all of herself to ensure that the mannequin form was ready to meet spirit on this dead-moon night. Almost as soon as she took Cherry-Rose in her arms, seamstress twirls slowed until they had wound down to a gentle sway.

"Shy-Blue, my pet," the seamstress said as she held out Cherry-Rose's hand. "Mother needs her rest."

Shy-Blue appeared from beneath a tangle of sisters to meet the waiting hand.

"Cherry-Rose," Shy-Blue said with a slight curtsey, "So lovely to meet you. I am Shy-Blue."

As Cherry-Rose would eventually learn from Mojave days later when they found each other lying beneath the funeral-birthday, breakfast, lunch, and dinner table, Shy-Blue's name should have been Sky-Blue had Fae not misheard Mojave. Mojave recalled the story with a notable tinge of resentment. "It was Fae. She started it with her 'Yes, Shy-Blue! Shy-Blue. It's perfect because it isn't.' Blah, blah, blah. Ridiculous. But everyone started clapping and hooting, so Shy it is."

Shy-Blue, made some thirty-six moons ago, could have been the seamstress's younger sister. More than a moonlight echo, the resemblance was uncanny; a mirrored image, a ghost-girl reflection, Narcissus in cottage-pond, dancing here in fabric. She had an elfish form, a long, thin neck, with arms and legs to match; long, blonde hair, and blue, blue magical eyes. Eyes not unlike those of the seamstress, but all the same, the eyes were what set them apart. Shy-Blue's eyes were indeed blue like her mother's, but somehow, beyond. They were oddly blue, coldly blue, the bluest after-a-storm, empty-void-of-the-sky blue. Absolutely perfectly pure, the purest, pure sky-blue.

Exhausted, the seamstress sank into her rocker positioned in the corner by the hearth and thought of father things. When her chair was father's chair. When all of this, the tiny father-made table tucked in the corner by the rocker and the father-made dolls sitting beneath the tick-tick-ticking of all those animal-faced father-made clocks, were his. When everything, even the magic—even the wishes—were his.

As the first of a dozen plus three clocks clanged the seamstress out of her father-made daze, she smiled with satisfaction and watched Shy-Blue twirl Cherry-Rose about the room. Smiling, nodding, humming—the seamstress sang a quiet song to herself.

> *If* that *wooden boy,*
> *If* his *wooden boy,*
> *Can bring the Blue Fairy*
> *Can bring the Blue Fairy ...*

* * *

Just when Cherry-Rose wondered if she could spin another spin, Shy-Blue spun her to the edge of the family room.

"My sweetest, sweet, my Cherriest Cherry-Rose. Come, let's take a tour of your new home. Let me introduce you to everyone." Shy-Blue slid her arm around Cherry-Rose's waist.

Cherry-Rose gave a small, almost imperceptible nod at the sister supporting her shaking newborn legs.

Shy-Blue slowly turned Cherry-Rose around, bowed, and posed with left hand outstretched, palm to the ceiling.

"This is our bedroom," Shy-Blue began. "We all sleep here, although I suppose we could sleep anywhere."

She whispered with a smile behind the back of a hand, "We could, you know? After all, we are made of the stuff that stuffs mattresses."

Shy-Blue slid behind Cherry-Rose, clasping both hands around her waist to speak over her shoulder. "Now, here … this is Mother's room."

Cherry-Rose felt a gentle tug and followed Shy-Blue's lead, turning toward the chair that rocked near the fireplace. "You've met Mother."

"Hello, beauty. Welcome home."

"Th … thank you," Cherry-Rose stuttered with a voice, a language, and words that seemed foreign, that came up and out from a place she couldn't quite understand.

The words, the motion, the twirling welcome-dance were all spinning in her head. Eyes and laughter, *spinning*, new hands and feet, *spinning*, the heavy scent of marigold must, *spinning*.

Cherry-Rose began to quiver. She began to feel like the cottage itself was starting to shake. She closed her eyes to hold herself steady and saw hooves and forest and moss and tufts of grass and bright blue-sky flashing like lightning behind her eyes. A bolt of fear ran through her seams; a blur of trees, something fell … she fell …

Her mouth was full of grass, dead leaves, and dirt.

Cherry-Rose opened her wet, shaking eyes, looked down, and held tight to the arms still wrapped around her waist.

Eyes wide open, blind to the cottage. She was given visions. Claws tearing into her abdomen with a hot, wet rip, and she could feel sharp teeth on her liver that cut like the flashes of the bright blue sky that burst behind her eyes.

Legs began to falter. Shy-Blue held her steady.

Cherry-Rose tasted the metal and the salt of her own blood as it filled her throat, nose, and mouth. Metal and salt came with each violent kiss: neck, fang, fang, deeper, deeper, darker, darker, darkly.

Cherry-Rose swayed and found the floor. Knees, hands, on all fours, looking more beast than doll. *Fang, fang,* she heard her heart exploding with one last long kiss.

Dead eyes watched a wolf devour her tongue.

She smelled the marigold. She smelled her blood mixing with the soil, mixing with the dead leaves, feeding the reaching ivy on the forest floor. She smelled the stench of new death rising with the morning mist, the wet, cold scent that marked the end of something. Her own death filled her snout.

But here … here in this room, swaying with the ebb and flow of candle-light, swimming in the stench of death-bloom marigold blossom, the room smelled too much like forest; like fear, death, murder, like blood and soil, and piss and dirt and dry leaves … and marigold, and mannequin-somethings, and a woman swaying in a chair. And like the hungry forest, the room was full of teeth and eyes; wide, smiling teeth and wide-wide glaring eyes. Everywhere, all at once, even with her new hands covering her welling eyes, still, it all bled in; the forest death scene, the cottage vision spinning; everyone descending upon her; death, birth, living, dying—life seemed entirely made up of hungry teeth and hungry eyes.

Cherry-Rose melted between Shy-Blue's arms and settled on the floor.

Here in this room, these eyes weren't chasing, full of want for flesh, nor lusting for want of other things, and the teeth weren't grinding, and the fangs weren't biting. And all the sister-dolls who she'd never seen before, never known before this very morning, like the words she had never spoken before, they weren't hers, but somehow … they were.

Weren't they?

They were hers, these sisters who smiled and reached with their soft hands, who stroked her hair as if it had never been any other way. They were hers, these strange sisters with their strange mother who spoke in a strange tongue that she strangely understood. They were hers, these sisters who lived behind the glass that held back the forest.

They were hers.

Shy-Blue sat quietly next to Cherry-Rose and took her hand. She stroked and patted and whispered, "It will pass. We were all something else before we came here, weren't we?"

Shy-Blue blinked and nodded to her sisters scattered all about the cottage—each mannequin-ghost girl quietly seated, watching Cherry-Rose from wherever they fell—decorating the floor, the rug, propped up against a wall, the record player, the bookcase.

"All of us." Shy-Blue nodded to Cherry-Rose and then back to the watching room.

"Vi, scrub jay. Sprinkles, hare. Scarlet, mouse."

Scarlet, looking annoyed, stomped loudly and said, "Rat!"

"Yes, my deary dear, rat," Shy-Blue corrected, "apologies to you and your kind.

"Jasmine, owl. Rey-Rey, magpie. Mojave, snake. Daisy, opossum. Siouxsie, woodpecker. Apple, human. Fae, hawk. Peaches, racoon. And me, a fox."

Cherry-Rose's eyes drifted toward the rocking chair.

"Oh, Mother? She was also something else. She was like us. She was a daughter. Isn't that right, Mother?"

"Another life, my sweet. Another life."

None of this registered for Cherry-Rose, maybe because none of this made sense.

Her eyes were wet and wide, and they blurred the room. She swooned and leaned forward, falling on all fours. Hands under shoulders, knees under hips, she shook like a dripping jellied calf that just slid out of its host. Her stomach was wrenching, her stitches were tight and straining, her eyes were lost behind those dark lids, spinning in the vines of her mind. Her mouth hung open, her throat was bleating, stretching out guttural newborn moans …

"Huuuuuugh, huuuuuuugh, uh-huuuuuuugh."

"Breathe, baby, breathe"—the chair rocked—"breathe."

Cherry-Rose tried, but she was still lost, still in shock. She was breathing, it just felt like she wasn't. She heaved hard and heavy and wet dripped from her eyes, nose, and open mouth as she moaned, "Huuuuughhh, huuuuughhh, huppphhhh," low and deep, her belly distended, her back arched, convulsions ripping through her body. She moaned like a beast that knows it is about to die.

It came again. From beyond the sky, Cherry-Rose could feel the crimson warmth flowing out onto the forest floor. She could see a red heart beating inside a soft brown carcass. She could see that carcass split open beneath a bough of waiting black birds. As if in a dream, slower, slower, until her shakes subsided, until she could manage to lift her head, until she could manage to shake out soft, scared, pleading words.

"Where ... am I?"

Huuughhh.

"Who ...

"Who ... who am I?"

Huuughhh, huuughhh.

"Breathe, baby, breathe." The chair rocked and rocked.

Dying all over again ... it made breathing difficult. On the rug, on her hands and knees, before the hearth, beneath the window of this modest cottage, she tried to breathe, but she couldn't. Cherry-Rose lost the world behind her eyelids and melted into the floor, and as she slipped back into her wolf-blood bleating and beating heart dream, Peaches covered her in a funeral-birthday quilt. "We made this for you. Happy birthday, Cherry-Rose," she said softly, almost apologetically, as she patted the blanket.

Hours passed this way, Cherry-Rose under the quilt, her legs pumping wildly in a dream.

She dreamt of ivy crawling over the empty shell of a deer and a strange voice singing, whispering, chirping in her ear. It was her voice. *It was, wasn't it?* The voice belonged to the Cherry-Rose who watched her death scene from high above those black birds who sat, patiently waiting to peck out her eyes. Beyond the dream of death, that Cherry-Rose whispered and chirped and sang, *run ... run ... run ...*

And while Cherry-Rose dreamt of wolves and death and crows, the cottage carried on with its celebration. Records played, sister-dolls sang and danced, candles made marigold shadows, and the seamstress rocked in her rocking chair, because this was how funeral-birthdays were made.

Another hour passed, maybe two. The winds shifted and pushed beneath the front door and through the cottage's great many cracks. Cherry-Rose began to stir. Even with her eyes closed, she could feel that the light in the room had changed. The room now wore the weight of twilight. She sniffed at the air, and behind the chaos of cottage potpourri, she found the familiar scent of the impending forest night riding the breeze.

Honeysuckle filled the room.

She allowed one eye to open just enough to see a herd of feet twirling across the floor. She could hear music pounding, flowing up through the rug. She could feel the wool pressing its pattern into her face, music pressing into her ears. Two eyes opened to see Sprinkles, Fae, and Mojave shaking to the beat pumping through the floor. She sat up with her legs swept to the side. She could feel the air in the room change—all of the eyes in the room upon her, and Cherry-Rose melted into soft sobs and slow, full convulsions. Peaches turned down the music and the cottage went silent. Again, very quietly, very sweetly, ever so apologetically, Peaches said, "Happy birthday, Cherry-Rose."

"Happy birthday," Shy-Blue whispered as she moved in to stroke Cherry-Rose's hair.

Just then, a soft chorus of "happy birthdays" began to trickle in from all directions when Cherry-Rose interrupted. "But ..." Cherry-Rose stammered, "But ...

"But I died. Didn't I?"

The Knowing

CHERRY-ROSE backed herself against the wall—beneath the window, just next to the rocking chair, spilling a stack of books held by a pair of wooden soldiers. Still not far enough away. Into the corner. Next to the hearth. She tucked her knees into her chest, wrapped her arms around her knees, and watched and breathed. Rey-Rey danced at the record player, Violent-Joy brushed Peaches' hair, Mojave sang, Scarlet stomped out more poetry, and the seamstress smiled a wide smile as she made her way to the door that held back the forest and the blinding blue.

"Rey-Rey," Shy-Blue shouted across the room, "could you be a dear."

Rey-Rey picked up the needle, and Shy-Blue announced, "Girls, girls, gather 'round. Mother is leaving to hunt."

Cherry-Rose, still in her corner, watched her mannequin-sisters gather near the door, each leaning in to kiss their mother's cheek. With the twelfth kiss, the seamstress tied her cape and pulled on her hood. The seamstress stood on toes, seemingly searching for her thirteenth kiss, but Cherry-Rose couldn't be further away—motionless in the corner, all wrapped up in herself.

"Oh, my Cherry-Rose, my baby-doll, my pretty pet, don't be scared," she sang. "This old thing"—she tugged on the front of her hood and further shadowed her eyes—"it helps keep me safe out there. The forest can be such a dangerous place."

Beneath the cape's hood, the seamstress did seem to become something entirely new. The hood gave her ears, pointed and gray, edged in white, and a snout that ran long to its black tip. A snout where hung an upper row of sharp, sharp, sharper teeth. Above and below her fangs, two wolf eyes, two mother eyes.

Cherry-Rose shivered in the corner like electricity was running down her seams.

"Don't worry, my darling-darling Cherry-Rose, Mother is never long," the seamstress said, seemingly misreading the expression on her newest daughter's face. "Shy-Blue will care for you while I'm gone. Won't you, my deary-dear, my baby Shy-Baby-Blue."

"Of course, Mother."

Shy-Blue echoed her mother's saccharine tone.

The cottage door opened with a flood of light. There it was, the forest Cherry-Rose had seen behind her eyes, but as soon as it was there, it was gone. The clearing that sat silently before a wall of trees was obscured by a shadow that blew a kiss to the room. "Back soon, my sweetest sweets," spoke the shadow as it disappeared on the other side of the door.

"Cherry-Rose, my dear," said Shy-Blue just as her maker might, "shall we resume our tour?" Not waiting for a response, Shy-Blue took Cherry-Rose's hand and helped her up from the floor.

"This ..."—moving to the window and spinning wheel, her hand gliding over balls of thread, scissors, and cushions with pins—"is where Mother spins her thread. And that out there"—motioning out the window—"is Mother's shed. It's where she keeps supplies and other silly trinkets. And that wall of wood, for the fire. It's our pile of almost-boys ... almost-brothers?" Shy-Blue turned her words up into a question.

"Uncles!" Mojave corrected. "Wave hello to your almost-uncles, everyone!" Mojave laughed, and a dozen arms lifted and waved silly waves to the shivering woodpile.

"Yes, almost-uncles. Right," Shy-Blue continued. "And there, the sky where we keep the sun and the moon. And ... hmm, I'm realizing now that I've never given this tour before. Rey-Rey, how am I doing?" Shy-Blue whispered with a wink at Cherry-Rose, "This is my first go as tour guide."

Rey-Rey jumped in. "These are grandfather's clocks." Her hand circled around her head at the cottage full of clocks. "Grandfather's? Well, ours now, I suppose." She turned to face Cherry-Rose, rubbing her chin pensively. "Yes, ours now. I believe he lives at the bottom of the sea these days with that boy of his. Isn't that right? Bottom of the sea? Yes?"

"Yes, that is how Mother tells it," added Scarlet. "The bottom of the sea with his waterlogged boy."

"Bottom of the sea," Sprinkles laughed as she twirled her dress, "bottom of the sea," pointing and naming, "The fireplace, the hearth, the sink, a bed, a Jasmine, an Apple, our clocks, our books, and our records." Sprinkles, still twirling, "Do it, Apple, put a record on."

Apple put on Louis and Keely's *The Call of the Wildest,* and Peaches handed out the gin. "Just a touch, deary." Peaches handed a glass to Cherry-Rose, and by the time Louis was shouting about having the world on a string, Cherry-Rose had found her legs and lost herself to the gin. She looked as natural as any mannequin-ghost girl could, dancing about in a cottage full of mad-mannequin-ghost girls.

Hours passed and records were played and runout grooves ran. Empty glasses clinked and *just a touch, a touch more, baby doll,* and a deluge of mannequin-sister tales were told. Tricks for learning seamstress magic flooded over Cherry-Rose. They poured from twelve separate mouths, seemingly all at once: When the seamstress went to market, what was market? What was found at market, where the gin was made, how to drink it, "Back bent, thumbs up, head between your legs," joked Scarlet, imitating the seamstress's tone while completely dismantling the "pinkies up" tea-sipping ritual.

The lessons continued to flow: how to write runes just so, how to make pure wishes for the Blue Fairy, who was the Blue Fairy? How to cast those wishes into the fire, how to spit and curse at the flames—"Piss. Shit. Fuck!" shouted Violent-Joy into the midday flames; how to spin thread, to bind and sew, "also pinkies up." Sprinkles smiled, demonstrating the form as she took a needle to a loose patch on her dress.

"Best for last, Cherry-Rose," Mojave said, opening the door with her back to the outside world. "This, my dear, is the door to all those other worlds: the forest, the market, the shed, whatever else, everything else," and she slammed the door shut.

"That's all of it," said Shy-Blue.

"Market? Forest? Everything else?" Cherry-Rose pressed her face against the window by the door. She let the cool of the glass tame the heat of the forest dream that was still running up her stitches. "What's in the forest?" Cherry-Rose watched her breath turn to fog on the glass as she stared full and hard into the green.

"Beasts, fangs, and claws," said Fae.

"And claws," repeated Apple, scrunching up her face. Her fingers flexed and bent, slashed to tear the flesh of the cottage air.

"But us, all of us, … we *were* of the forest," added Scarlet.

"But now, we are of the cottage," Betty finished.

"Yes, yes, but we *were* all of the forest," continued Scarlet.

"Anywaysssssss," Betty said, drawing out her "s" while shooting big eyes at Scarlet, "the forest is full of bears, wolves, birds, and people. All sorts of dangerous things."

Fae turned to Cherry-Rose. "But we don't really know what's *in* the forest." Fae held a finger over her lips and lowered her voice. "We can only see its edges and what comes into the clearing from behind these windows. We are forbidden to …"

Fae went silent as the porch outside the door began to creak.

"Forbidden, Fae? Is that so?" asked the seamstress as she opened the door, making a face that looked as though she was waiting for a reply, with eyes of the *I can wait* mother-eye. The eyes that seemed to say, *I'll wait for your response*, although judging by the tilt of her head and the turn of her lip, it seemed to Cherry-Rose that the seamstress knew one would never come.

There was a long silence that marked a change in the room. Nothing to hear but the runout groove clicking. A dozen father-clocks ticking. Mouths hanging. Cicada chirping.

The seamstress removed her hood. Wolf snout, ears, and eyes slid down to rest on her shoulders.

"Girls, girls. My lovelies. My daughters. My dolls. My baby dolls. My truest of true loves, no, no, no, no, no. No, that isn't quite right," she insisted as she hung her cape by the door.

"Yes, yes," agreed Apple, as if she realized the seamstress must have been listening through the door. "It isn't that we are forbidden; it's that our kind can't live beyond the door."

"Mother tells us we wouldn't want to anyway," Violent-Joy offered to Cherry-Rose.

"Girls, we've been through this. It is out of my hands. My magic, the magic that gives you life, only extends so far. Besides, it's dangerous out there. Bugs who bite, bees who sting, snakes to choke you, wolves that are always hungry and love to eat up little girls, and bears ... clever, clever bears. And worse, dirty foul roaches crawling everywhere, and rodents, the rodents who claw and tear and bite. And worse, the men and women— always hungry, hungrier, and clever, the most clever, too clever, and they are so dirty, the dirtiest. They are all full of foul lies, just as you are full of stuffing. All of them bursting at their seams with their liar liar lies," said the seamstress as she moved to her rocking chair.

The seamstress paused and reached for the pitcher resting on the table between her rocking chair and spinning wheel. She filled her mug, and just as she was about to continue, Mojave pointed at the mug excitedly. "That's it, that's it. How'd we miss it?" The mug read "Hollywood," arched over searchlights against a backdrop of stars on one side and "Norma" in bold black block letters on the Mojave-facing side.

"Is that it?" asked Mojave. "Norma! That must be it. Norma, Norma!"

The seamstress smiled a wide smile and laughed, turning the mug to read the name in bold black letters. "Norma?" she repeated, seeming surprised to find a name at all. "I am sure this *was* Norma's, but it isn't hers any longer. Perhaps it was Norma who sold it to me at the last moon market. It sure would be silly of me to ruin our game by bringing home a mug with my name on it, wouldn't it? I'd never deprive all of you of the fun of guessing. Never, never, never."

The seamstress paused to take a sip from Norma. "You are a little early for our bedtime game, aren't you, Mojave? Are you sure you want this to be tonight's guess?"

Mojave was indeed early. The guessing of Mother's name became a game exclusive to and woven into the bedtime ritual. Each night, the seamstress would tuck them into bed, and each night, one by one, her daughters would take turns making a new guess, for she promised to let them know if they ever got it right—she crossed her heart and said things about needles and pins. Violent-Joy made sure of it.

* * *

No, the seamstress's name was not Norma, nor Hollywood. Nor Madeline, Matilda, Miki, nor Maheya.

On the eve before Cherry-Rose's funeral-birthday-eve, the game went like this …

"Goodnight, Scarlet."

"Wendy," squeaked Scarlet's upturned voice.

"Goodnight, my dear Fae."

"Lynnie," Fae guessed.

"Goo …" started Peaches, as if not knowing what to guess.

"RUTH!" interrupted Mojave.

"Ruth?" laughed Violent-Joy. "Come on, Mojave, Sprinx guessed that last night." "Bob," said Violent-Joy, not waiting for Mojave to recover. "It's Bob, isn't it?" Violent-Joy rocked her head from left to right with each word, "Bob, Bob, Bob," as her sisters, all but Mojave, erupted into laughter.

Each night, when the girls were tucked up into bed, the names and laughs and giggles would fly, and each night when they invariably got it wrong, the seamstress would smile and say, "A mother must have her secrets. You may call me Mother." On and on every night, for many moons now—ever since Shy-Blue discovered that *Mother* was not Mother's name.

* * *

So, the seamstress, who was Mother—not Hollywood, Norma, Ruth, nor Bob, Bob, Bob—rocked in her chair and sipped her gin out of Norma's mug and said, "Mojave, let us save our game for bedtime," then she lowered her head and winked as if it were only for Mojave. "And no, it isn't Norma."

The seamstress angled her chair to face the center of the room. "Girls, girls, gather 'round; it is time for Cherry-Rose's Knowing story."

The girls sat on the rug, forming a loose crescent moon around the seamstress, Cherry-Rose positioned in the center. Again, the seamstress sipped her gin, and said, "But first, my Cherry-Rose, so you understand … the forest is full of danger. The forest is a taker. Even in the light of day, the forest is a scary, dark, dark place. The forest is so deep and dark."

Cherry-Rose shuddered as the seamstress dropped her voice to a breathy whisper— "Darker, darker, darkly, darkly, and full of death and secrets so dark that if you managed to find yourself in the forest, even for a moment, you'd wish you never left the cottage."

The chair rocked. The seamstress sipped.

"My lovelies, do you not have everything you need here?" The seamstress paused and smiled at Cherry-Rose. "You will find that you do, my darling," she said with a nod. "Remember, my sweets, out there is where I found you all dead and lifeless, all full of flies and their wiggling children, with torn-out necks and faces with pecked-out eyes. Every one of you, every one of us, was broken by the forest." The seamstress waved Norma toward the window that held the shed, the woodpile, and the trees.

"Are we not safe here? Do I not keep the beasts at bay? Do I not brave the moon nights for you so that we all might be safe? There are no teeth to bite you inside these walls. There is no one to pull you apart inside this cottage," she said, sipping at the gin in her mug. "You get to be. To dance and sing and play. Is that not enough?"

Cherry-Rose knew that she wasn't long in this form, and the uncertainty that her new cottage situation provided gave her enough doubt to keep her silent. However, still able to feel the cold fresh air of the forest rush in under the door, she wasn't sure that the offer to dance and sing and play was enough. Even in her brief new life, her forest visions and funeral-birthday party had given her perspective. She knew that some might choose this place; she could sense that some beasts might be willing to bludgeon themselves against the door for want of entry, for want of warmth, to hide from the cold stare of circling, hunting beasts. But the weight of *this*, always *this*, the too much of the saccharine-sweet safety, the too much of Mother hovering, circling, rocking; the too much of desire hidden behind fabric and stitch and wood and glass, just might be too much.

When the last sip of the gin was sipped, when the eyes in the rocking chair landed on the dancing fire and drifted a million miles away, when those eyes softened and fell back on the hearth, Shy-Blue asked, "Mother, Cherry-Rose? What did you find?"

"Yes, yes. Cherry-Rose. I found you. I did, baby doll, I did." Waving her mug at the nearest mannequin form, "More gin, please. Daisy, Daisy, darling Daisy, this story needs gin," she said, shaking her Norma mug.

When her mug was full and her lips were as wet as her eyes, she resumed. "It was ghastly. My dear Cherry-Rose, I am sorry to say that it seems you were taken by wolves" … *sip* … "belly torn open" … *sip* … "to take your liver" … *gulp* … "Throat torn open to taste your tongue" … *sip* … she waved the empty mug toward Daisy… "I believe the crows took your eyes … so many crows."

This story echoed in Cherry-Rose's chest. It pulled at her joints, and pushed through her eyes to release fat tears behind her pressing palms.

"By the time I arrived," she said, softening her tone, "all that remained was the corpse of a gutted doe, so empty it was already sinking into the ivy.

But it was a good death, my darling." Her lips were pursed and their edges were turned down, all timed with a slight motherly nod. After a short pause, she drew in a large breath and smiled as if there was nothing to be sad about at all. "Of course it was a good death, darling; it brought you home to us."

Cherry-Rose twisted under the weight of the story and shuddered at the stab of that confusing smile. The knowing was too much for Cherry-Rose, so much that in that moment, she might have tried to run out the front door if she weren't all tangled up in Shy-Blue and Fae, if Peaches weren't sitting behind her stroking her hair, if she didn't have her forest-death vision playing every time she closed her eyes, if she wasn't beginning to see the benefits of living behind glass and wood, if she couldn't still feel those fangs and those claws.

It took the seamstress a moment to register Cherry-Rose's discomfort, but when she did, the smile gave way to a more serious tone.

"I am truly sorry, Cherry-Rose, but you are here now and all the better for it. No one will hurt you here. No one will ever hurt you again." She paused to take another sip from her mug. "Did I mention you had the cutest antlers? You must have been the loveliest doe, Cherry-Rose. So rare to see a doe with antlers."

The words began to drift with the seamstress's descending gaze: "So rare."

The room was silent as the seamstress stared into her mug.

"Cherry-Rose, you must know. The night, the song, the marigold, they all helped to channel your spirit to this cottage. They helped you leap from forest shell to your new form ... and that is all it was, my sweet, just a shell, a doe of a shell ... but yes, the marigold helped you leap from that form to this. But you won't be able to stay here long without a little magical knot to tie you up. I have to work a spell over you or by morning your spirit may be gone forever. Forever, Cherry-Rose."

The seamstress made a horrible face and repeated the word whose meaning seemed too big to understand.

"Forever."

Cherry-Rose could feel every eye in the room upon her. It was as if they were waiting for something, as if they were waiting for her to *do* something. Cherry-Rose was confused by the Knowing. It didn't soothe her stitches; it set them ablaze. The wolf-hunting dream burned and howled inside her skin as hooves beat a running beat—faster, faster—in her chest. She could still feel those teeth around her neck, even now sitting on the rug before the seamstress, even now under the gaze of all those sister eyes, she still felt more doe than mannequin-girl.

In the wash of hurt and loss, the Cherry-Rose from beyond the forest vision filled in the silence. That Cherry-Rose reminded this Cherry-Rose that there was life, beyond the cottage door.

That Cherry-Rose whispered "run" while the other weighed the seamstress's story.

Run?

This Cherry-Rose silently considered the Other, thinking, *But there is nowhere to run.*

Cherry-Rose recalled her maker's words. *Gone? Gone forever? Forever?*

Whatever forever is, thought this Cherry-Rose, *it is scarier than fangs and claws.*

The Cherry-Rose on the rug asked the Other,

What is there to do when a forest of beasts lies just beyond the door? When I can still feel their fangs? What is there to do?

Forever. It just feels like too much? And it is warm inside the cottage. So warm.

It is warm, answered the Other.

So many soft eyes. Warm eyes.

They are soft.

And no fangs,

No.

And no claws.

None.

And no forever.

Whatever forever is, it isn't here.

Just a Prick

CHERRY-ROSE felt the moment of silence beneath the gaze of all of those sister-eyes, under the weight of the pounding and pressing tick, tick, ticks of just as many, more, father-grandfather-clocks, pass just as it had when, as doe, the first claw swept through her abdomen. The moment was marked with a confusion so profound that it stopped both time and pain, fang and blood, life and death. She didn't know what it was, but the Cherry-Rose beyond the vision told her that somewhere on the other side of this silence, there was a price to pay.

"My dearest Cherry-Rose," said the seamstress. "Would you please consent to stay?" The seamstress slid out of her rocking chair to join her daughters on the rug, leaning forward to take Cherry-Rose's hand. "Cherry-Rose, no one inside these walls will ever hurt you. I promise."

The Cherry-Rose beyond the vision whispered Forest promises.

Promises are what the hawk makes to the snake, the fox to the rabbit, the wolf to the doe.

Cherry-Rose looked from side to side. *Magic? Knots? Pain and promises? Forever?*

Cherry-Rose could feel pressure building with each passing *tick-tick-tick*. She knew everyone was waiting for her to do or say something, but the moment seemed too much for action—too much for words.

The seamstress gave her a slow nod and her hand a gentle squeeze.

Just when she wasn't sure she'd ever move or speak again, a low sister-whisper grew, coming first from her left, "Stay, Cherry-Rose," and then from her right, "stay, stay," then back again, "Pretty please." Then all at once, from all sides, building until the words lost meaning to the chaos of too many voices. Until Violent-Joy stood and waved her arms. "Girls, girls," said Violent-Joy, pushing against the air to calm the room. "It'll be alright, Cherry-Rose," she said, crouching at eye level. "We are all here because we said, 'Yes.'"

Cherry-Rose looked around the room and found nodding sisters with hopeful eyes.

"It isn't so bad, Cherry-Rose," said Shy-Blue. "I mean, if you think about it, you're already dead. How could it get any worse?" Shy-Blue laughed like it was the most normal thing in the world. "Stay with us for a while, won't you?"

The seamstress stroked Cherry-Rose's hand as Shy-Blue continued her plea.

"I'd really love it if you stayed."

Cherry-Rose lowered her head as tears welled and spilled onto the seamstress's hand. Again, the seamstress gave a gentle squeeze. Cherry-Rose didn't know why, but with a slight nod of her head, first to the seamstress, then to Violent-Joy, and last to Shy-Blue—the wait was over. Cherry-Rose consented.

"When you are ready, Cherry-Rose." The seamstress wiped her tear-stained hand as she rose and motioned to the funeral-birthday table. "Lie face down, darling. And don't you worry; this won't hurt much, I promise."

Cherry-Rose nodded again, and Shy-Blue led her to the table where she made like a snake, belly crawling until she was squarely centered on the table.

"Girls," said the seamstress, "let's have a song while Mother works her magic. And remember, now is dead moon time. We will be waxing soon, and the next thing you know, the full moon will be upon us. Read your spells, read your poetry, write your runes, write your wishes, write your dreams, and perhaps the Blue Fairy will visit to make all our wishes come true."

The seamstress twirled across the floor to the table full of marigolds and Cherry-Rose. "And Daisy darling"—she stroked Cherry-Rose's hair— "when you have a moment, please fill Mother's cup, and my Violent-Joy, music, we must have music."

"'Ju Ju Hand!'" demanded Scarlet.

The needle dug into the groove, and they all jumped and twisted and banshee cried like Sam the Sham. They growled and howled through the wood of the floors, into the earth, through the stained and bubbled glass of the windows, into the green of the forest, and into the blue of the sky. And while they danced and played, the seamstress readied herself over Cherry-Rose.

"Now, Cherry-Rose, Mother will need to hold you still for a moment." She gathered Cherry-Rose's hair and laid it to one side. "Yes, yes." She began to hum and her words poured out in strange song. "You will have to … play dead … darling. Just for a song … or two. Can't have you wiggling about. Just a little prick, darling. Nothing more. Just a tiny tiny prick, nothing more."

The seamstress released the button on the collar of Cherry-Rose's dress and opened the back down to the base of her spine. "Don't be nervous, darling. We just need to …"—she lowered her voice as if speaking to herself—"make a little room for …"—adjusting the fabric to find bare naked shoulders—"for Mother."

"Ju Ju Hand" blared as soft mother-hands slid over naked seams and measured the space between opposing shoulder blades. Cherry-Rose could hear the seamstress mumble words for knots and anchors and collars and chains. She could feel those mother-lips mumble words into her body, kiss them into the back of her neck.

She could see mother-hands sprinkle salt around the edges of the altar; she could feel the seamstress blow warm smoke over her spine. She could hear the crunch of dried flowers before they fell on the back of her head.

When Cherry-Rose thought it might be all over, she felt two hands press into the fabric of her shoulders. The hands began to sink and settle, warm and warmer with a building pressure. Deeper, harder, hot, too … just when the heat became almost unbearable, the seamstress released and began to breathe: *sniff, sniff, sigh … sniff, sniff, sigh … sniff, sniff, sigh.*

Cherry-Rose found playing dead was harder than it sounded. She tried to play dead for the seamstress; she wanted to play dead for her sisters. So, she lay perfectly still, trying to push her worries out from behind tightly closed eyes, but the pinecone that was her heart itched and scratched and pounded, and the nest that was her womb pulled at her organs, twisting all her insides into knots. Just when she thought it might be best to scratch the itch that was worming out from her insides, the worry, the itch, the pounding, the knots, they doubled when she realized she couldn't move her arm; they became fire when she realized she couldn't speak.

Something invisible had taken her voice and tied her limbs to the table. She was alive, but anchored, weighed, tied, frozen, the side of her face pressed into the wood of the altar.

Cherry-Rose heard the words again as the needle pierced her skin.

"Just … a little … prick … dar … ling."

Her eyes began to spill. Unspeaking, unblinking, she watched her mannequin-sisters dance over a pool of tears.

It was just a prick; then mumbly words followed by a song of hums, and another prick. And another. *Prick, prick, prick.* And another, and another, and one thousand pricks of sharp pain that released a thousand silent screams behind pouring eyes.

When the pain became too much, the pool of tears gave her its vision.

A doe bursting through the forest behind clouds of breath pulsing from snout. Hooves over ivy. Darting through trees.

The snap of snout and warm breath on her heels became hot breath on her neck, became smoke … became fangs and the juniper of gin. Fingernails. Needle. Prick, prick … prick, prick, prick. And while she ran where she could, behind tightly closed eyes, the Cherry-Rose who watched beyond her visions measured the meaning of mother-words against the pain of the needle.

There are no teeth to bite you inside these walls, prick. There is no one to pull you apart inside this cottage, prick. "Just a prick?" *Prick.*

No one will ever hurt me *again?* Cherry-Rose wondered at her mother's words.

Prick.

    Prick.

        Prick.

"I promise."

The Keeping Spell

THE SEAMSTRESS could sense the spirit of the deer running within Cherry-Rose. She felt it in a shivery rattle that emanated from within her form. The seamstress had seen this before. Over time, she had come to think of each of her daughters' spirits as a sort of moth caught in a jar. When shaken, to some degree or another, the spirit would tap and bang against its new walls, generating a little warmth as it fluttered. In most daughter-dolls, the moth who sang the dream of their last life quieted rather quickly; in others, the spirit settled consistently over time. However, in those like Apple, Rey-Rey, Peaches, and Violent-Joy, whose spirits seemed to run wild, they had vivid and dangerously persistent dream-life recollections. In fact, the strongest in spirit did not seem to lose their essence at all in the shift. The dream of life, death, and life again all ran on into the next form without a seam.

All signs indicated that Cherry-Rose was indeed special. Fortunately for the seamstress, her mother left her spells to manage this very inconvenience.

So, the seamstress stroked Cherry-Rose's spine and blew more smoke and mumbled her words to take the fire that burned in Cherry-Rose's belly.

"Don't you worry, my darling darling, it won't be much longer."

As the seamstress penned the last of the ink into Cherry-Rose, she recalled the days before she learned this magic, before she learned to seal a spirit in a new host.

The forest was green and full of life, but it was also a place of balance. Life was never without its partner. For all the green, there was always something dying, rotting, decaying on the forest floor. Just as life was exchanged for death, so too were moonlight and starlight exchanged for spirit. Each night, the stars and the moon gave what they could, and with each death, so too did the forest reciprocate. In a pact made before dolls had mothers, and wooden boys fathers, each death released its light— bird, bear, wolf, deer, ancient tree, mother—all into the night. All sent home to the Blue Fairy.

The seamstress learned, often by the third day of a visit, without ceremony, without the compassion and empathy befitting their brief but meaningful connection, somehow each spirit would lose its hold on the earth and slip through the glass of a window, the wood of the rafters, or drift out with the flames that fed the chimney. Her father always told her not to worry about them, that they were just going home. Those words, however, lost all meaning when he left the cottage for good. It was easy to see that he didn't worry about the proper things, about the creatures that needed worrying over most of all. It was easy to see they too needed someone, anyone, to care for them.

She was sure they would stay if only they could. She was sure they were lost. She was sure they needed a home.

Probably lonely.

Certainly alone.

Definitely lonely.

And if there were a way, shouldn't they be looked after by someone who knows what it means to be alone … what it means to be lonely?

Without a mother, without a father, without the sealing spell, the daughter felt the all too familiar crush of abandonment press hard into her heart. Everyone, everything, even the dead, abandoned her.

* * *

More smoke, more mumbly words, and two cool hands moved over Cherry-Rose.

"All done, my dear," the seamstress whispered.

More smoke, more mumbly words, and Cherry-Rose could feel the release of the playing-dead spell.

The seamstress stepped back with her hand to chin, her head tilted ever so slightly. "Girls, girls, girls, Cherry-Rose is ready."

No longer in pain, nor bound by invisible hands, but heavy, so heavy with an overwhelming need to sleep, Cherry-Rose didn't move. She couldn't, but now it was the crush of impending sleep that held her still. Too tired to move, helpless, she watched her sisters gather around the funeral-birthday table. She could feel Shy-Blue stroking her hair, Daisy's hand moving over her legs, and Violent-Joy tracing the image etched in her skin.

"Antlers," whispered Violent-Joy. "Beautiful, just beautiful."

I Put a Spell on You, Because ...

IN THE EARLY days, cottage life for Cherry-Rose was a blur. Reading and writing with Violent-Joy, Fae, Daisy, and Siouxsie; singing with Scarlet, Daisy, Apple, and Peaches; dancing with Shy-Blue, Rey-Rey, Jasmine, and Mojave; and all the in-between moments with the seamstress. As with all the daughter-dolls, the seamstress took personal pride in her mother's legacy. She taught Cherry-Rose to sew and spin thread, to write intricate Blue Fairy runes, and if all the daughter-chores were done, the seamstress made time to teach her some of the magic found in her mother's books: spells for winding clocks, for pulling thread, and those for moving needles through fabric. Tiny spells, simple spells, daughter-spells. There was much to learn.

The seamstress and her mannequin-daughters taught Cherry-Rose how to mark the sacred days, and more importantly, how to observe the sacred nights. They taught her about fire and song, the stars and the moon, and they taught her about the mother of the night, the Blue Fairy who watches over everyone: beast, bird, seamstress, mannequin-girl. They taught her how to speak to *her* ... if your wishes are made just so ... But when all the moons and all the birthdays had cycled through, when the Harvest Moon came around again, when all the runes were written and all the words were whispered and all the daughter-lessons were taught, Cherry-Rose found that time had slowed. In a cottage full of clocks, and walls, and windows with latches, and doors with locks, Cherry-Rose began to feel the tick of every hour like the needle that had once sealed her skin.

For when all the books had been read, and read, and read again; and all the records had been played and all their songs were sung; and all the legs danced all their dances; and all the mother-wishes were made; and when all the other sister-dolls were content on doing it all again; Cherry-Rose would close her eyes to feel the forest.

Hooves on moss and night on fur.

When her forest visions faded too quickly, Cherry-Rose would sit by the window to take in the world beyond the cottage. With her hand on the glass, her eyes traced the edge of the clearing, the edge of the forest, and the edge of the sky. On these days, while her sisters played and danced and sang, Cherry-Rose would drift and watch her mother tend to her chores on the other side of the glass. She watched her hoe the ivy, tend to the garden, burn the fat green leaves under the light of the moon, and disappear inside the shed for hours. With great longing, Cherry-Rose watched the seamstress live without limits.

Cherry-Rose had her forest visions to help give shape to the world beyond the veil of trees, but the world behind the woodpile, inside the shed, was a mystery. As was custom, with each full moon came a village-moon market. Prior to each moon market, the seamstress would disappear for a time inside the shed, and as was custom, each time the seamstress returned, Cherry-Rose would prod her for answers.

"Mother …"

It never helped to ask.

"What keeps you so long in the shed this day?"

Without fail, every moon market, every shed visit, Cherry-Rose waited to ask the seamstress a version of that very question.

Replies came sugar-coated, so sweet, so so sweet that Cherry-Rose felt them sting her teeth.

"Oh, my pet. My sweetest sweet ..."

"My darling, darling, darling ..."

"Oh, my Cherry-Rose, my deary dear ..." each reply began.

Like the beginnings, the endings left Cherry-Rose wanting.

"Every mother has her secrets. Be a good girl and play with your sisters. Mother must ready for market."

* * *

The seamstress could feel eyes upon her as she made for the door. Wanting eyes. Dreaming eyes. Daughter eyes. Jupiter eyes. She remembered her very own wanting eyes as she watched her father sneak away into *his* shed. She could feel those Cherry-Rose eyes follow as she made way through the garden. She knew, if she bothered to look back this time, that there would be two hands and a face with cherry-red lips pressed against the window.

How could Cherry-Rose ever understand? She couldn't, she told herself as she escaped into the secret side of the shed. *There are things a parent must keep from a child.*

The shed ... *as any mother would do,* the seamstress often told herself, as she imagined her mother would have done, as her father did; the shed was a place for keeping things safe. To hide small gifts for the girls— solstice treats, dead-moon gifts, full moon gifts, and little funeral-birthday presents—but the shed was also for work: for gin, for juniper berries, coriander seed, and licorice root. It was for drying flowers—baby's breath, globe thistle, and marigold. Most of all, the shed was for dolls and magic.

We mustn't tell the girls. No, no, no.

The seamstress could have set the boundary of her mannequin-sealing magic anywhere —just outside the cottage at the porch to let them take in the full night sky; at the edge of the clearing to let her daughters dance with her beneath the moon. Never mind removing the limits entirely, but outside of the cottage, there was too much to chance standing too close to the trees, and there was just too much to explain beyond the cottage walls.

The seamstress often reasoned while she worked. *Parents aren't made for explaining. And ragdoll-mannequin children certainly aren't made for understanding.*

Too much trouble explaining why beasts stalk the woodpile on full moon nights. Too much trouble explaining how beasts make the frenzy to call the Blue Fairy. Too much trouble explaining the ritual table behind the woodpile. Too much trouble explaining the ritual. Too much the shock of knowing things they just don't need to know.

And, of course, all daughters should know some magic, yes, but no daughters should know all magic. Not even Cherry-Rose.

Too much trouble explaining all the things found inside Mother's books.

"Cherry-Rose just wouldn't understand," said the seamstress as she lifted the heavy books that kept the lid tight on her basket full of tiny wiggling rag-dolls.

"All there?" the seamstress asked while peeking inside the basket.

Tiny rag-doll vermin squirmed beneath the lid.

"Good morning, good morning, my lovelies. Don't you worry, soon we will be off to market."

Where do we get the money for candles and comics—Her finger pressed into the ragdoll reaching up for the edge of the basket. *Books and records, meat and fabric?*

No, no, no. Her finger thwarted another at the edge.

Never once have they wondered. She shook the basket to topple the climbing ragdolls.

Down! She closed the lid, latched the latch, and tied the lid with green ribbon.

Too much trouble explaining how Mother goes to market to sell tiny rag-dolls of beetle, worm, and roach.

Too much trouble explaining how Mother sells her tiny dolls.

Too much trouble explaining how the children flock to see them dance without strings to hold them up.

Oh, the children with their mothers, and the children with their fathers, and the children with their mothers and fathers ... Oh, how the children are so full of want and need. The children want the doll and the parents want the story.

The girls could never understand, she thought as she replayed her latest visit to market.

"Darling, darling, sweetie, my sweet, dolly needs your magic to live," the seamstress would say, crouching to darling-darling eye level. "You believe in the Blue Fairy, don't you? ... Good, good ... if you are a good little child, your doll may live, but if you are wicked, in three days' time, the Blue Fairy will come to take your baby's spirit."

On her way home, the seamstress would recount her latest sale for the benefit of Forest.

"Oh, those market mothers and fathers," she said. "Oh, how they love that yarn. But, alas, three days is such a long time for any child." She would often laugh and pause to lean on a tree. "Much too long without being wicked." She'd push off the tree and head down the path. "Being children, of course, those little beasts will eventually show their fangs; and the dolls, being unsealed, will eventually unwind." She'd pause at the edge of the clearing to finish the story before bidding Forest goodnight. "Such a poetic way to get the best out of children for a few days ... and for the parents, such a small price for three days' rest."

No, no. Daughter-dolls could never understand these things. Too much trouble, all of this. Mannequin-girls are made for singing and dancing, not understanding.

Too much the shock of seeing their ragdoll cousins sold and traded.

Too, too much the shock of knowing this ragdoll secret, she'd remind herself.

While the ragdoll secret might be difficult to explain, of all the secrets the seamstress kept in the shed, perhaps the greatest secret of all was how she made anchor with the daughter-sealing spell.

Sealed. On the wall. A nail for each daughter. A tuft of fur, a claw, a lock of hair and a ribbon, a white-tipped tail, a jawbone, a wing, a feather, feathers, a paw, a lucky rabbit's foot, the head of a snake, a tail, and an ear.

Too difficult to explain why Mother must go hunting after each new doll awoke. Spells were such fickle things and sealing a tricky thing. She must touch them, hold them, speak to them on their funeral-birthday morning. Hear the timbre of their voice. Feel the life beat in their chest. See the ghost behind the glass and the ash of their eyes. And if her spell was cast just so, she would be able to trace the echo of that spirit straight back to the expired form.

Nails for parts.

Nails for pieces.

Nails for daughters.

Nails for family.

* * *

A little over a year now since Cherry-Rose—*has it been that long?* the seamstress wondered.

Seemed like it was only yesterday that she found that gutted doe.

"Hello, you beautiful creature, might I borrow your tail?"

Words flowed from the shadow of a face hidden beneath fangs, snout, two glass eyes, and two mother eyes. Sharp hands reached out from under cape to pull and cut and tear as a hooded shadow whispered secret songs of the dead.

"My dearest, oh, my sweetest sweet, you are perfect, just perfect. I do have a few more spells to weave, but I do believe you will bring us the Blue Fairy."

* * *

A wall of nails. Nails for parts. Nails for pieces. A nail for a tail. Nails for family.

Yes, the seamstress could have sewn each totem inside her dolls, tied the red thread, and set them free to be who they might in their new form, but the forest was such a dangerous place. She could not—for them, she could not. She would not—for all mothers and daughters everywhere, she would not. She couldn't bear the idea of the forest taking from her again. Even more, she couldn't bear the idea of being abandoned.

At times, while recalling Forest-lessons about fathers and mothers and their superfluous nature, if ever a shadow of regret, remorse, or even doubt crept about, she would have to remind Forest, "We are not beasts. I am their maker. I am their mother."

And when Forest listened with its disapproving silence, as only Forest could, the seamstress would continue …

They are mine.

* *Silence*

And we have such a lovely home.

* *Silence*

Such a lovely family.

* *Silence*

Thunder and Butterfly

OUT ON the edge of the world, feeling thrown out into the great wide nowhere, forgotten by all, abandoned by her family, and swallowed by the forest; having been suckled on motherly-murdery shame and groomed to develop a very real almost-brotherly-hate, having inherited only mustache-promises, a little magic, and a life that revolved around making wishes for things to be other than they were, the seamstress found that her cottage seemed always and forever full of never-enough.

The seamstress was left chasing a fatherly ghost whose shape billowed full of never-enough. Who, while in cottage, through trial and error, and error and error, through an obsessive drive for better, for best—for perfection—left her little but a great wall of never-enough. In fact, the only thing that the seamstress felt she had in abundance was this wall of not-enough.

It took a while, but eventually, the seamstress found the lesson her father had left just outside her window. She had told Forest a version of this story a dozen times.

She'd say, "There I was facing the shed, and Mother, and you, Forest, and that mess of a woodpile, and there it was."

She'd say it was then that she finally saw the lesson her father left in the three-, five-, six-hundred-fold wall of shivering almost, almost-brother parts.

This was his last lesson.

What isn't good enough is kindling.

For if any of that wood were good enough, for if any of those almost finished almost-brothers were perfect, they would have been the one. The Blue Fairy would have descended. The wall, the wood, all of the almosts, they were left behind precisely because they were not good enough.

Poor, poor Shy-Blue, thought the seamstress. *Although a mother shouldn't have favorites …* she reminded herself.

Until the seamstress shaped the too too absolutely, undeniably perfect Cherry-Rose, the previous daughter-doll *was* perfect, well, almost … until she wasn't. Until the Blue Fairy made Shy-Blue's imperfections known by wholly ignoring the seamstress' latest offering.

It wasn't Shy-Blue's fault, but alas, Cherry-Rose.

And before Shy-Blue there was Violent-Joy, and before Violent-Joy there was Peaches, and so on until there was Jasmine. Jasmine, the first of the thirteen, who, for a time, was perfect, until she too wasn't. Jasmine was first of these daughter-dolls, but surely now, if each new daughter-doll was an improvement, she was indeed … perfectly lacking. Almost perfect for a time, but clearly not enough.

Never enough. If this story had that orthopteran orator, it might say, "The problem with never enough is that if you believe it has been visited upon your house, you will find it in every cupboard."

The seamstress sat staring out over the wall of wobbling wood, thinking, *Just how is it that daughters cost so much? How do daughter-dolls eat so much? The garden can't keep up. Thirteen is so many mouths. Thirteen is too many wants, too many with too many birthdays, and one month had two, didn't it?*

And … don't the people at market always ask for more, something special, something new, something real, something that won't unwind?

And … isn't that what I have? Too many real dolls, with too many birthdays? Too many, with all their too many wants and all their too many needs.

And … in that month of two birthdays, hadn't I just made the most beautiful daughter of all?

And besides, couldn't I always make more?

The seamstress rocked in her chair and considered the lesson in her father's wall of wood. The never-enough in her garden. The never enough in her cupboards. The too much of thirteen.

Yes, too much. One too much, she thought to herself.

The very next morning, she kissed good mornings onto twelve waiting cheeks and, at the last, before she kissed Jasmine, she held her still and spoke. "Good morning, my darling baby doll, my lovely love, my little owl, my silver-haired beauty, my deadly song of new-moon nights. I would very much love it if you would accompany me to market today."

A collective gasp ran through the cottage as all the daughter-dolls froze; mouths open, but silent; eyes wide, looking like they were trying to blink the world they knew back into focus.

"I … You … You've been such a good girl; I'd like to take you adventuring with me," the seamstress added as if this explanation might keep her daughters' questions at bay. Doubting the intended effect of her words, she turned and began to dust the clocks on the mantel before anyone could speak.

"Mother." Shy-Blue spoke, seemingly wondering sister-hive wonders. "C-can we all come?"

The seamstress cast her eyes over her shoulder in the direction of Shy-Blue's voice and her daughter continued. "If Jasmine can go outside, can't we all?"

"Girls, girls, girls …" The seamstress said, turning back to face her clock—wiping away invisible spots.

A good mother always anticipates her daughters' questions, she told herself.

"Jasmine is the eldest. Her magic is the strongest," the seamstress lied her mother-lies directly into the face of the clock she was dusting. "I am old and only have enough strength to share my magic with one of you. If it must be *one*, shouldn't it be Jasmine? Shouldn't it be the eldest?" she reasoned while scanning the faces reflected in the glass door of the clock. "Let us try this just once, and if all goes well, we could try again."

Defeated, the mannequin-ghost girls gathered on the rug facing the door. No one sang, no one spoke, no one tried to conceal their long, pregnant sighs. They sank down on the floor, laying over one another like a family struck with tragedy, like a family in mourning with one child seated in the middle, smiling as if oblivious to the shared misfortune. All tucked up into each other, laying lifeless with wide, wide, unblinking, playing-dead eyes; they sat and wished their purest wishes … to be like Jasmine.

"Yes, yes my lovelies. This is best. You rest. Let Mother gather her things."

* * *

While the seamstress readied for market, the daughter-dolls all drifted off to other worlds. Some followed dream-memories of lives beneath the night sky; others found the edge of the forest; some imagined themselves dancing free in the clearing. Cherry-Rose found herself rubbing antlers against the bark of a tree; and Violent-Joy, she found herself feeling the dread she felt on many mornings. Dread from a nightmare that came too often.

Violent-Joy thought it silly to fear a dream she couldn't remember, but she did. The feeling … it was horrible, dreadful, pit-of-the-gut twisting.

The dream was loose, too loose, anchored more by smell and flashes of blurred shapes than anything real. The dream didn't make any sense, but it came rushing in, wanting to be understood here and now as she laid on the rug waiting for Jasmine to go to market.

In the dream, Violent-Joy dreamt of a mannequin-sister she never knew anywhere else but in her sleep. The dream flooded Violent-Joy with visions, giving her memories she had never known in her waking hours. A false cottage, a false clearing, false memories of a false never-sister. She remembered that her dream-sister was stuffed on the night of the brightest blue Thunder Moon. Her name was Luna. She knew this because it was she who gave Luna her name.

She recalled how Luna was filled with sweet and heavy honeysuckle blossoms. How her stitches ran through French country fabric, a soft white with small faded freckles of the lightest blue; hair, a golden strawberry-red mane; eyes, green like the bubbled glass in the cottage window. She recalled how, above Luna's left shoulder, about the size of the palm of her hand, was a forest hare drawn in the seamstress's hand.

Sitting there on that rug, Violent-Joy remembered it all, and she began to understand. She began to remember … each full-moon night when she drifted to sleep, Luna visited to sing her this unwinding dream …

A cottage empty of all but Violent-Joy. Dark, save for the moonlight slicing through the rocking chair window. The cottage ticks with grandfather's clocks. The forest door is wide open.

The dream shifts. The edges pull in and twist gray and black. Violent-Joy is in the forest.

The moon is gone. The sky is black. It begins to rain. The runes at the edge of the clearing begin to glow.

Luna is there in the rain, dancing around a fire in the center of the clearing.

The dream shifts.

A candle burns in the shed.

A shadow bows to blow out the candle.

Violent-Joy can feel the thunder in the sky and the electricity in the air.

The shed is like the sky, shadow, gray, and black.

Luna is dancing in the rain, arms outstretched. Spinning.

Violent-Joy is breathing in the honeysuckle. The night is warm, but she is shivering.

Lightning breaks. Thunder claps.

Luna doesn't seem to hear the shed door slam shut.

Violent-Joy is yelling for her to run, but Luna is lost in the fire, the dance, and the rain.

Lightning bursts from the south and briefly throws a long shadow across the clearing.

Violent-Joy yells "run" beneath the rolling thunder.

Again, lightning. Again, thunder.

This time Luna catches the shadow cast across the clearing floor.

"It's beautiful. Isn't it just beautiful?" Luna says to the shadow.

The shadow doesn't speak, but a lightning flash reveals something … something horrible in the shadow.

Luna freezes … just for a second. And then runs straight for the forest.

Lightning flashes.

The thunder speaks, the shadow speaks, and the dream whispers magical words.

Hare, forest, rain, ivy. Lightning strikes near the clearing.

Again thunder, again shadow, again chanting words.

… the huff of Luna's breath.

Then, lightning. Then, thunder.

Then double the rain.

The forest floor awakens and the shadow who blew out the candle, who spooked the hare, who spoke with the thunder, follows slowly through the forest.

Luna is lying on the forest floor.

"Run! Why aren't you running?" Violent-Joy screams, but her words don't make a sound.

The shadow kneels next to Luna.

Luna is writhing. Shivering. Crying. Violent-Joy can see now. Luna is tied up and twisted in the ivy. As the shadow approaches, the ivy pulls—arms and legs outstretched, Luna drawn and displayed like a mannequin-star face down in the wet earth.

Lightning. Thunder. Shadow-whispers.

Luna is crying, "Mma … mma …"

The shadow unties the back of Luna's dress and slides a hand over her middle-seam. It pulls the dress off her shoulder and traces the hare tattoo. It gathers Luna's strawberry mane and pulls the hair gently, just enough to turn Luna's eyes up to the falling sky, to face the shadow, to face the Violent-Joy who is now floating above the trees, to face the Violent-Joy who screams, *run!*

The shadow pushes Luna's head down into the earth, just enough to expose the red stitching on the back of her neck.

One hand full of hair, the other clutching a seam-ripper.

The clouds part and the sky goes silent.

"Mma … mmma … Mommy … Mommy!"

The slow quiet pop of each seam echoes through the trees, and Violent-Joy watches a soft, pale something drift up into the night like a kaleidoscope of butterflies.

* * *

On the rug, waiting for the seamstress to gather her things, waiting for Jasmine to do … *whatever* … laying over Scarlet and Cherry-Rose, legs tangled up with Apple's, Violent-Joy didn't know why she was given the memory of that slippery dream.

In that moment, she didn't care at all. Why that dream came right now, in the middle of *this,* was more nuisance than welcome distraction.

It *was* a distraction from the jealousy, no … the irritation, no … the anger Violent-Joy felt for not being good enough to be chosen. It was a distraction from her growing rage. Rage building at being fooled into believing otherwise, for believing that *she* was special. It was a distraction from everything she wanted to feel. So, while she lay about playing dead in her knot of not-good-enough-mannequin sisters, all the ties that held the memory of that dream were torn, cut, and shredded by a simmering rage. As soon as the dream came, it was forced out and forgotten by the lesson the seamstress had just taught her Violent-Joy.

She absolutely, without a doubt—there was just no other way to look at it—wasn't good enough.

Under a Glass Jar

FROM her knot of sisters, Cherry-Rose watched and waited and pondered Jasmine's fortune. *Jasmine was special indeed, but leaving the cottage?*

Perhaps it was because Cherry-Rose was too new to know any better; perhaps it was because the other daughter-dolls' resolve had been worn thin, worn through, worn out by the sweet, protective, insistent, relentless mother-words. Perhaps it was because Cherry-Rose was still more doe than daughter, more beast than doll, more wild thing than window mannequin. Whatever the case, when the seamstress asked her daughters to entertain each other while she made her market preparation in the shed, Cherry-Rose saw an opportunity.

"Back soon, my darlings." The seamstress blew a kiss as she shut the door.

When the footsteps on the porch faded, Cherry-Rose broke free from her sisters and made for the shed-facing window to trace her mother's movements. She watched the seamstress move across the clearing. She watched her drag her hand over the stalks that grew in the garden. She watched her ignore the reaching hands in the woodpile and enter the shed.

"I have an idea," Cherry-Rose breathed into the window. "Girls, Apple, Fae, Shy," she called to the lifeless gaggle on the rug. "If Jasmine can leave, I bet we can too. There has to be a way. We just need to ..." Cherry-Rose began digging through drawers, rifling under the sink, turning over everything in the girls' closet.

"Found it!"

Cherry-Rose came out of their bedroom all tied and twisted up with a fat, enormously long pink ribbon.

"Shy-Blue," called Cherry-Rose, twirling about with a wicked grin. "Let's try something." She pulled Shy-Blue to her feet and tied the other end of the fat pink ribbon around Shy-Blue's waist.

"Now, whatever you do, do not follow me. Stay perfectly still." Cherry-Rose opened the cottage door, and everyone on the rug sat up straight. No one but the seamstress opened the door, ever. No one even touched the knob.

Cherry-Rose turned to face all the ghost-girls sitting with their perfect posture, mouths agape, and said, "Hasn't anyone ever tried this before?"

Silence. Mouths hanging to match unblinking eyes.

"Hmm, I can't believe no one has tried this."

Eyes to Shy-Blue, Cherry-Rose tugged the pink ribbon. It felt secure. Cherry-Rose gripped the wooden threshold, right leg, right arm tight against the wall. Left hand out into the free air, sliding just beyond the threshold. She wiggled her fingers and looked back at the others, shrugging. "Huh, just like the windows," she thought out loud. Left hand in, joining the right on the living side of the framework. "Okay, okay, now let's see," and she slid her left foot out to the other side. *Wiggle, twist, rotate.* "Huh?" She sighed, turning to the wall of wide-eyed dolls.

"What does it feel like?" Sprinkles jumped up and down behind Scarlet.

"That's just it." Cherry-Rose shrugged. "Nothing. It doesn't feel any different."

"Are you ready?" Cherry-Rose smiled and tugged at the ribbon. "It'll hold, right?"

"Ready? … Hold what?" Shy-Blue's mouth twisted to the side.

Cherry-Rose gave a smile. "Me."

She turned toward the forest, "Don't let go," and walked straight out the door.

There was the sound of chimes and a hint of magic, like cool water running down the seams on the back of her neck, tickling her spine with shivering goosebumps. Then the floor of the clearing rose sharply to meet her face. Cherry-Rose heard muted gasps, voices mumbling as if underwater, a dozen girls jostling about on a wooden floor. There were whispers, birds, and the creak of branches. There was the warmth of the sun, as if she had never felt the sun before; then a soft, cool breeze.

Echoing chimes. Lingering magical goosebumps.

She was dreaming doe dreams. Hooves on moss, sun on fur, velvet on bark.

Cherry-Rose was a playing-dead doll on the other side of the threshold. Her ear pressed into the earth. Eyes wide open, watching a row of ants carry fresh-cut leaves, a butterfly, a sparrow, a circling hawk; ears tuned to the ringing chimes that muted the mumbling underwater sisters. Arms spread in the dirt of the clearing; legs bent awkwardly, unnaturally, on the tiny porch. The underwater bustle building. The sun warming. A forest of life moving out there beyond the veil of trees. A rustle in a bush at the edge of the clearing.

"Shy-Blue, do something! Do something." Scarlet. It was Scarlet's underwater voice.

The ribbon tightened around Cherry-Rose's waist. With a lurch and a pull, pine needles, dirt, and tiny pebbles dug into her trailing, sleeping arms; splinters in her legs. Cherry-Rose was frozen, yet she felt every needle, every pebble, every splinter, and she thought, *This is like the spell that held me still on the funeral-birthday table.*

The pink ribbon dug in hard, harder, like a too tight corset. It tugged. It pulled. It dragged Cherry-Rose across the dirt like she was a lifeless ragdoll. She slid over the dirt and lurched over the tiny lip that marked the tiny porch. Bent in half looking all dead, not even almost alive, until a swarm of hands reached out past the threshold. They grabbed ankle, dress, breast, hair and pulled her back through to the living side.

As Cherry-Rose passed through the threshold, again she heard the hum of chimes and felt the shiver of goosebump magic. She sat up, legs crossed on the cottage floor, and smiled at the surrounding mannequin eyes.

"Cherry-Rose … Are you okay?" Sprinkles pushed her face to Cherry-Rose's face.

Cherry-Rose paused and held a smile for a moment, then let out a laugh as she rolled straight onto her back. "Did you hear that?" Cherry-Rose tried to control her laughter. "Did you hear the chimes? Could you feel the shiver?"

No one spoke.

"It's magic. A spell. It's the play-dead spell. And it kinda tickles," Cherry-Rose said, sitting up to survey her sisters. "Who's next?" The room was silent. "No one?" Cherry-Rose scrunched her almond eyes flat. "Come on. I thought everyone wanted to go outside." Cherry-Rose scanned the room full of avoiding eyes. "Shy-Blue, remember, we are the stuff of mattresses." Cherry-Rose tugged at the ribbon still connecting the sisters. "What have we got to lose? We've already died, haven't we?"

"Right. What do I care? I'm already dead." Shy-Blue laughed with a smile that twisted up one side of her face. Cherry-Rose leapt to her feet and moved to the frame of the door.

Cherry-Rose tugged on the ribbon. "Are you ready?"

Then, with a wink, Shy-Blue walked slowly through the door.

The chimes. The shiver. Her face met the hard wood of the porch.

Quickly, she was pulled back to the living side.

Shy-Blue smiled as she picked and pulled needles out of her fabric. "Worth it."

Apple became the voice of worry. "Girls! Mother. She's never gone too long; we need to get you two cleaned up."

"Apple"— Fae gave a hard stare—"today is market day; we have plenty of time."

"Yeah, goofball." Mojave adopted a mocking tone: "What are you afraid of? We already died."

"Please, this just doesn't feel right," begged Apple, with her wide, pleading Apple eyes. "Please."

"Okay, okay. Just one last go. I like the shiver." Shy-Blue smiled at Cherry-Rose. She sat on the threshold and leaned back to fall over into the forest side. They pulled her back, but before anyone could speak, Shy-Blue held up her hand and said, "Last one, I promise!" She grabbed her knees and rolled sideways out the door.

"Okay, okay. Pull her back. That's it," cried Apple. "Cherry-Rose, please." Apple begged with the side of her face pressed against the wall. "Please." She turned to face the wall entirely. "No more."

"Apple, it's okay." Cherry-Rose tugged at the ribbon. "I've got her."

Just as Shy-Blue was pulled back to the living side, she leapt to her feet and began to laugh and twirl, winding the ribbon up around herself until, like a mannequin top in reverse, she was nose to nose with Cherry-Rose.

"Vi, Peaches, Rey-Rey, Daisy, Mojave, everyone, you have to. You have to!" she said as she kissed Cherry-Rose on her redder-than-red smiling lips.

"No way," said Apple. "No, no, no, no, no, no!" She wagged her finger before setting to unwind the sisters. "We have to get you two cleaned up, or we will all be in trouble." Apple made a concerned face as she untied the knots, dropping the pink ribbon to the floor.

"She's right," agreed Daisy. "Let's not cause any trouble. Maybe we could try again while Mother and Jasmine are at market? They'll be gone most of the day, right? Yes? What do you think, Blue?"

"Yes, of course. You won't tell Mother, will you, Jazz?" Shy-Blue tugged at her dress.

"Never." Jasmine made an X over her chest, squinting at Violent-Joy. *Needles and pins.* "Agreed."

"Sorry for all that, Apple." Shy-Blue blinked rapidly. "There's just something so lovely about passing through the doorway, isn't that right, Cherry-Rose?"

"The chimes are fun, but it's strange."

Cherry-Rose rubbed her chin and tilted her head. "It's like we're inside a magic box or something. Kinda like we're living inside this glass jar and we just can't see its edges. Like, until now, we didn't even know that it was holding us."

Cherry-Rose picked at a pine needle poking out of her fabric. "You know, it's like ... kind of like we're in a cage."

Sprinkles sighed. "It's kinda like we're in a doll's house."

"What does it matter?" Violent-Joy spit into the dying coals. "We aren't real anyway."

"We're more like those stupid wooden soldiers." Daisy pointed to a half a dozen rosy-cheeked figures, dressed with their forever-smiles.

"Toys," added Rey-Rey.

"Dolls," said Siouxsie.

"Zombies." Peaches held up her zombie comic—Eerie #1.

"Almost," Jasmine whispered.

"Do you know what this means?"

Cherry-Rose sat up with a rigid back.

"You do, don't you?"

Cherry-Rose melted backward into the rug.

Cherry-Rose lay unmoving, her eyes closed tight. She drifted far away into a forest-doe-dream. She sniffed the air, hoping to find velvet and moss behind her wet eyes, but all she found was the wolf-chasing-dream, the bowels-on-the-forest-floor dream, the choking-on-blood dream.

"You know, Jasmine ... you're lucky," Cherry-Rose spoke to the ceiling. "I wasn't sure about this before, I was afraid ... afraid of whatever might be out there ... forever is such a long time ..." Cherry-Rose paused, trying to remember the cut of the wind and the warmth of the sun on the other side of the spell. "But now I think ... no, I would ... I would rather take my chances out there in the forest ... than be trapped in a glass jar. I wish I could go with you."

Bye-Bye, Bye-Bye

"I CAN always make more," the seamstress said to acknowledge the scent of her mother that permeated the shed. "Now, where did I put it." She knelt before a row of books; a trailing finger tipped the edge of a familiar spine. Red thread held the page: "*Making Memories—Finding Forgetfulness.*"

The spell came in two parts, combining water and fire.

For the water, a soup seasoned with blood and basil, salt and clove, mugwort, and juniper berries. "And last, to set her free." She pulled the nail that held the dried wing of an owl. She chopped one feather fine and ground its bones with mortar and pestle.

For the fire, a life reimagined; the seamstress found pen and paper and began to write furiously. Something about a forest that had a cottage. Something about a mother who had one less than thirteen mannequin-daughters. Nothing about a Jasmine at all. Twelve. Always twelve. Never more. She placed the words inside a glass jar and touched them with flame. When the fire had done its work, the ash was folded into the soup.

"For forgetting, for far far further away. For family."

* * *

Cherry-Rose was standing before the rug, pointing like a conductor. "Sprinkles, weren't you ... over here? And Daisy, next to Peaches, right? And ..." Cherry-Rose was interrupted by the familiar thud of the door on the shed. Thirteen heads tilted slightly at the sound, and Cherry-Rose ran for the woodpile window. "Never mind. Here she comes," she said, crouched at the base of the window. "Let's just ... just try to be ... normal."

When Cherry-Rose turned to face the rug, she let out a squeak. Violent-Joy was on Jasmine's lap sucking her thumb; Mojave, Sprinkles, and Fae had wrapped their necks with the pink ribbon; Scarlet and Shy-Blue were moaning ghosts with dresses over heads; and the rest were playing dead with eyes rolled, lips pulled, and noses scrunched. Cherry-Rose placed one hand on her hip and swept the other side to side at the mass on the floor. "Perfect. Well done."

The porch creaked; Sprinkles loosed the ribbon and tossed it into the air.

Cherry-Rose smiled and whispered, "Totally normal," and feigned twisting-fainting-doll, collapsing on top of Mojave.

The knob turned. The only sound was the ticking of the clocks. Then the door. Then the sound of a sputter. Three more sputters—one, two, three. Then seven from somewhere, everywhere in the almost-playing-dead-pile. Then the entire mess of mannequin-ghost girls erupted in laughter.

"Haven't moved, I see." The seamstress spoke without a second look. "Just how have you girls been occupying your time?"

Cherry-Rose made shushing lips at her sisters, relieved to see that the seamstress completely dismissed the rumbling horde on the floor and went straight to the pot that sat over the fire.

Jasmine squirmed and coughed and began to lean forward when Cherry-Rose tugged on her dress. She rolled over and fell with her head positioned in Jasmine's lap where she did as Violent-Joy taught. She stuck her tongue out to the side, made an X over her chest, and then stabbed at it with invisible knitting needles.

"We just wanted to spend some quiet time with Jasmine, is all." Cherry-Rose said, still stabbing her chest.

"Yes," added Siouxsie, "We've been getting our snuggles in before she leaves. That's all."

"Beautiful. Lovely. What sweet sweet girls you have all become," the seamstress said without looking up from her pot.

"Jasmine, could you be a dear? The magic is stronger if you help."

Cherry-Rose watched and listened closely, wanting to learn all the secrets that allowed daughter-dolls to move beyond the door. She edged herself as close to the soup-makers as she dared and assumed her funeral-birthday pose strategically on the rug. Through side-cast eyes, Cherry-Rose saw Jasmine lean over the pot, holding her hair as she inhaled deeply. Her face scrunched up instantly.

"Ewww, this stinks."

The seamstress nodded. "Yes, yes, a little. A little more is all we need." She gestured to the bowl of spices on the table with a slight tilt of her head. "Yes, Jasmine, that's it. Three pinches should do. One for the door, two for the forest, and three ... three for your mother. Good magic always needs a bit of spice."

Next, the seamstress moved behind Jasmine, placed her hands on her daughter's forearms, and hung her head on her shoulder. "Now, give it a stir. That's it." Then the seamstress stirred with Jasmine's arms as she blew words into her ear.

Cherry-Rose heard the words in spurts and pieces. Something about memories. Something about happiness ... silly things ... mother things. Something about forgetting all the bad.

* * *

The seamstress sank into her rocking chair, sipped her gin, and stared into the fire. She needed a moment to settle, to shake a faceless father-ghost who had just made a poorly-timed return. "This is all your fault," she told her nothing-face father. His clocks blared their disapproving *tick, tick, ticks*.

Years and years and years and still, the seamstress would often imagine her father near enough to disapprove. He was always somewhere just beyond the hills, beyond the sea, beneath the sea, always somewhere too far to be seen, but not far enough to be entirely forgotten.

Father, always willing to disapprove.

Today, he was there behind the flames.

The chill of the autumn breeze is curling beneath the door and you aren't ready for winter. The cupboards are empty. The garden is thin.

Oh, but Father, you shouldn't worry, she told the flames, *you should be proud, did you not hear the lie I served with that tiny truth? I have learned all your lessons, and because it is so, tomorrow the cupboards will be full.*

Laughter interrupted the vision and shook the father from the fire. A disapproving ghost was replaced by the eyes of a doting daughter laughing with her sisters. Her eyes. Jasmine eyes. Eyes to pierce the sky, ringed hazel eyes that shone like the sun. Eyes of fire, like a twilight flame dancing on the tops of the trees. Eyes of a sun that could have been painted on the backdrop for a play, beaming its perfect golden rays.

"Basil, belladonna, and clove." *I may need something strong tonight,* thought the seamstress as she rocked.

Twelve bowls clanged the empty-bowl clang, bringing the seamstress back to the task at hand.

"Tsk, tsk, tsk," wagged a mother-finger. "Jasmine, my dear, eat up. Eat up. You will need your strength."

Jasmine sighed and made a pouting face as she tilted the bowl. "Finished." She smiled and slammed the bowl to the table. "Is it time?" Jasmine almost bounced out of her chair, unable to hide her excitement.

The seamstress didn't answer.

* * *

"Mother?" Jasmine stretched her neck toward her mother and caught the attention of Cherry-Rose.

"Mother?" Jasmine tried again.

Cherry-Rose watched closely. She felt something stirring her insides, something tugging on the thread that ran back to her wild-forest-echo memory-dreams. Something didn't feel quite right. Cherry-Rose continued to watch Jasmine and tried to piece the something together ... something about chimes and the door. And something about a jar that was a ... what? And why? *Why Jasmine? Why?*

Cherry-Rose scanned the room. She watched Jasmine trail the seamstress and thought, *There is something I am forgetting. Something about bells ... Was it bells or chimes?*

Jasmine brushed past Cherry-Rose and chased away the *something*. At the touch, Cherry-Rose reached out and pulled Jasmine to the back of the room.

"Jazz, when you come back home, I want to hear about everything. All the secrets: forest, beasts, market. Everything. You will tell me everything, won't you?" Cherry-Rose was sure that the slippery *something* was out there beyond the door.

Cherry-Rose moved in to kiss Jasmine on each cheek, to hug her tight, to whisper in her ear, "Everything, Jazz. Everything." She didn't know what it was, but she knew that whatever she had forgotten wanted to be remembered. *Something about the door, or the clearing, or the path, or the forest.*

"Okay, Cherry-Rose. Sure." Jasmine wiggled to break free.

Cherry-Rose, however, refused to let go. She moved her head like a snake to find Jasmine's avoiding eyes. When she did, she stared hard and whispered, "Jazz. Everything. Please." Wide-wide unblinking Cherry-Rose eyes, not letting go of their stare. "Everything!" Cherry-Rose dug her hands into Jasmine's arms as if her life depended on it.

Jasmine didn't speak but gave a slight tilt of her head. Cherry-Rose could see that she was entirely confused. She doubled her grip.

"Okay, my darlings, my sweetest sweets," sang the seamstress over the din of the room, "it's time."

Jasmine tried to break free, but Cherry-Rose ignored the call.

"Cher ..." Jasmine was cut off.

The hands that held Jasmine steady moved to either side of her face. Cherry-Rose paused for a flash and pressed her forehead into Jasmine's fabric.

Cherry-red lips kissed words into Jasmine's defenseless forehead and eyes—one, two, three—

"Evvvv!," *x*, "Ry!," *x*, "Thing!" *x*.

"Everything." Cherry-Rose pushed herself away from Jasmine, holding her tight with her stare.

"Everything," repeated Jasmine. "Sure, sure. And I'll bring you back a treat. I promise." Jasmine kissed her sister's cheek.

"Not a fucking treat, Jazz. Secrets."

"Gosh! Got it. Secrets."

"Secrets."

* * *

Only, there weren't any secrets to tell, because …

… there never was a day when the seamstress made a forgetting spell.

Never a day when she ground bones to dust.

Never a day when Jasmine ate it all up.

Never a mannequin-sister with sunshine eyes and silvery hair.

There couldn't have been, because Jasmine was never there.

* * *

When the seamstress returned from market that night, she dropped her wares on the mannequin-girl side of the door. She hung her wolf-cape at its post and prepared herself, as ever, to be overrun by a flood of smiles and questions and cotton-candied, mannequin-daughter love. Only, she wasn't overrun; in fact, she found herself wholly ignored. When the rush of mannequin-girls never came, she reasoned that the magic of the soup may have been a little too strong.

Yes, yes. That was a strong spell. Everything will be back to normal soon enough.

"Girls, my deary dears," the seamstress tested, "Mother's home." The dolls looked up from where she left them when the sun was still high in the sky. Where she left them at the funeral-birthday breakfast table to prepare for the impending moon. Most feigned loose lifeless smiles and helloes, others waved their mannequin hands unenthusiastically, others seemed to be asleep. All seemed uninterested.

At least I don't have to answer any silly questions. Fairy knows, I shouldn't like to answer any of their silly questions.

They'll be fine.

"Sleep, sleep my lovelies. Have a rest." She lit a match to start the fire that should have been waiting, crackling, warming.

The spell had to be strong and heavy to help them forget strong and heavy things. It had to be heavy to forget a sister.

Just a little hangover. It happens from time to time, especially when using magic like this. The magic had to be very strong, blood strong.

"They'll be fine, right as rain in the morning, right as rain," the seamstress said to the young flames of the fire. "Like too much gin, is all," as she poured her own gin of forgetting. "Yes, yes, right as rain by the morning," she hummed to herself. "All for the best. All for the best." The seamstress rocked and sipped and remembered the day that only she could remember.

Never again, she thought. *Never, never. Never again.*

Never again will I ever sell another daughter-doll.

* * *

Market had been difficult. Jasmine caused a ruckus.

The seamstress could still see those lusting, lunging market-faces. All their grabbing hands. All those pecking birds. All those hungry-eyed wolves, and the hungrier beasts disguised as men who asked how much to borrow the doll, and the market witches who begged to pull Jasmine apart to find the magic sewn beneath her seams, and the bears with hungry hearts who were drooling to pull her apart, but with different intent.

She shuddered, remembering the cold stare of those village Roaches, those empty-eyed idiot boys all dressed up in white T-shirts, denim, leather, and makeup; and those feather-masked girls with their satin and spikes who drooled and spat and laughed with their sick-satin smiles.

It was a trade. A bargain, she reminded herself.

Not just enough cash to make it through winter, no, no, no. Not just to fill the cupboards. It was for ... just in case. Just in case Cherry-Rose isn't the one. Just in case the pixie-dust does what they say it will do.

It was for the pixie-dust. To bring the Blue Fairy. A bargain—Blue Fairy for Jasmine. Who wouldn't make that trade? Didn't Father make that very trade himself? It was a shame about Jasmine's soup though ... needed more time to take proper hold.

The seamstress led Jasmine through the far edge of the market, just beyond the noise of the crowd, beyond the eyes of all those market beasts. Waiting ... The magic of Jasmine's soup had yet to crest when the village Roaches suddenly appeared to encircle the seamstress and her daughter-doll. Five, eight, ten, fifteen Roaches stood posed, all wide-eyed, smiling drooling smiles.

Jasmine doubled the grip on her mother's hand. She began to look as if she believed her mother's stories about the dangers beyond the cottage door. "Mother, who ...?"

The circle closed quickly. Two Roaches grabbed her arms. "She'll be fine," they promised.

Jasmine thrashed about, trying to break free.

"Hush-hush, baby doll." A girl dressed in satin wound around the struggle. She began stroking Jasmine's hair, shushing her like she was a baby who needed to sleep.

"Don't you worry, we'll take good care of her, we're giving her a good home," a boy behind green makeup eyes said as he showed his teeth.

Jasmine thrashed to break free, but the hands were too strong and too many. Despite their hold, she was able to lunge toward her mother like a sail—begging, pleading, crying—bent with the wind. Four Roaches as a mast held her arms locked straight behind her back. Bowed out, opposite her captors, Jasmine petitioned her mother.

"Mama? Mama? ... Mommy ... Mommy, please. I won't ... I ..."

When the holding hands began to pull her away from the seamstress, the sun shook in Jasmine's eyes and poured out rain and screams.

"Mommy!"

At that word, one side of the hold broke, and Jasmine's free hand shot out at the seamstress. Jasmine tore at her mother's arm and wailed sobbing words into her mother's neck.

"No, no, no please no, Mommy, I want to go home.

"I want to …"

Until the remaining Roaches swarmed and Jasmine was lost inside the flock.

* * *

The cottage was quiet, all except for the clocks that ticked their father *tick, tick, ticks.* The forest was quiet, save for the hum of the night and the low drone of the always, ever, under the ivy drone. The seamstress rocked in her chair by the fire and inhaled the perfume of her gin. She wanted to be anywhere but inside the cottage with those mannequin-shaped reminders. But the spell, she had to stand watch just in case the spell went awry—just in case a dream shook someone awake and prodded them to ask about things being different than they were.

She imagined herself out there beneath the night, beneath the ivy, beneath the cool breeze—anywhere but here, waiting for someone to wake with a start.

The girls were still draped all over the table, all over each other. Unmoving. Unremembering. Sleeping. Twitching. Forgetting.

It's good that they are in a daze, she thought as she examined the sparkling vial of pixie-dust she won in trade. *If I had to look any of them in the eye tonight …*

All for the Blue Fairy, she thought as she prepared her gin.

Just a touch. A little pixie-dust for Mother's cup. Before I let you go forever. Bye-bye, Jasmine. Bye-bye.

Beastly Wishes

EVERY night, every morning, every dead moon, every full moon, Cherry-Rose and her sisters made their wishes, but still the Blue Fairy never came. Twilight to night, moon to morning, Cherry-Rose helped her mother make the magical runes to feed the fire.

More and more, Cherry-Rose could feel her mother directing her words at her.

"Wishes, magic, and the Blue Fairy, these are fickle things, my dear."

Full moon. "Have you been a good girl, Cherry-Rose?"

Dead moon. "She will not come for just anyone, Cherry-Rose."

Waxing. "Cherry-Rose, your want, your words, your wishes, must be pure and true if you want *her* to come."

Waning. "You haven't been a bad girl, have you, Cherry-Rose?"

With each phase of the moon, the seamstress would say some version of these words as she lay her runes upon her almost-brother coals.

Full moon. "You would tell your mother if you had … wouldn't you?"

Dead moon. "I need … we need her to come, and if she does … she will make you a real girl. Wouldn't that be lovely, Cherry-Rose? And then we will be a real family. Think of it. You could be real."

The cottage-bound Cherry-Rose didn't quite understand what she was feeling, but the voice from beyond that scratched in the vines of her mind did her best to warn her—told her that something seemed off—told her to keep watch. Forest-lessons flashed to remind her of what happened to some creatures when others felt they didn't quite have enough. *Bad things. Bad bad things.*

* * *

Full into the *never enough*, it was hard to recognize all the wishes that had been answered and even harder to understand the *why* behind the wishes that weren't.

What does it matter anyway, thought the seamstress. *The pixie-dust did what the Blue Fairy wouldn't.*

One pixie-dust gin cocktail and the seamstress was transported back into the warm embrace of time before memory; back into the womb, back into the *before*. Before her mother died, before she ever dared think what her father's face told her: *It was my fault. I killed my mother.* Before her father who hated her with his soft eyes, all full of love, left her to die alone in the cottage at the world's end.

Before pain. Before sadness. Before guilt. Before …

The pixie-dust draped her in a warm summer night, filled her ears with the hum of the moon, her eyes with wide open dark-blue-infinity complete with all its twinkling stars. It brought the *before* she begged for when she wrote her Blue Fairy wishes. It brought the *before* she hoped could stay just a little bit longer. Every time, just a little bit longer. It brought the *before* she needed now more than ever … every day more than ever.

The *before*, however, did not last long and neither did the *never again*.

These days, out here in the cottage, time was not measured by fatherly clocks; it was measured in moon-ritual vials of pixie-dust.

Just a touch. Just a kiss for the gin. "A tiny kiss for Mother," the seamstress sang as her chair rocked. *Daughters? Dolls? I can always make more.*

The months disappeared inside a mug of gin and a touch of pixie-dust; and the seamstress found that the pixie-dust did to Jasmine what time did to her father—just across the clearing, beyond the forest, perhaps under the ivy, no punishing eyes, no crushing smile. In no time at all, she was just another faceless form, free to disapprove from afar.

Once Jasmine was gone, once the pixie-dust was found, the *never again* became not only possible, it became easy. In the space of twenty-three moons, the twelve remaining daughter-dolls became eleven, then seven, then four, and so on, until the only mannequin-ghost girls who remained were the only daughter-dolls she ever really needed.

Shy-Blue and Cherry-Rose, what more could a mother want?

And for a time, Shy-Blue and Cherry-Rose were enough—never less than enough.

Perfect daughters. More than any mother could ask for.

Three, six, nine more moons? Where did the time go? Where did the pixie-dust go? Cherry-Rose and Shy-Blue. A perfect pair ... until two was one too many.

* * *

"Shy. Shy, don't go. Please."

"Come on, Cherry-Rose. No sad eyes. No, no, not the lips. Don't give me the pouty lips."

"But ... what am I going to do alone all day?"

"Cher ..."

"I don't want to be alone."

"You could practice your magic ... or maybe your Connie Francis. Yes, do that. Practice your Connie. And when I get back, you sing and I'll dance."

"Promise?"

"Of course. It's a date. I promise."

It didn't take long for the magic of the soup—stronger and stronger—to do its work.

Soon Cherry-Rose lay on the floor unable to move, the room spinning just enough to ward off sleep. The heavy weight of forgetting had descended upon her. She drifted in and out of time, falling awake, mid-dream a doe, *spinning*, a wolf, *spinning*, a daughter, *spinning*, a witch, spun.

She blinked and the sun was gone and the clocks were unrecognizable and she wondered why the floor was littered with books of spells, feathers, and L-shaped spoons. She had forgotten that she was practicing her magic. She blinked again, shaking her head hard, wondering who was humming that song—wondering why "Who's Sorry Now" was stuck in her head. *There was something ... a promise ... maybe? Yes, a promise, a song, and blue eyes.*

* * *

Only there wasn't a promise, couldn't have been ...

... and those blue eyes, they must have been ... Mother's. Because there never was a sister whose eyes were bluer than the sky. Never a sister who made a promise to dance, who made a cross and hoped to die.

Never, never, never, because there never was a sister who sang with her mother's motherly tone, because if you asked Cherry-Rose, even she would say ... that she was always alone.

* * *

If perfection were measured by wishes answered, Shy-Blue was indeed nearly perfect— just this side of *not*. The satchel the man exchanged for Shy-Blue told the seamstress everything she already believed about her almost-favorite mannequin-doll. Shy-Blue was indeed a work of art. The proof was in the exchange of goods. Her Shy-Blue had given the seamstress enough money to fill the cupboards for months and months, enough that she didn't need to make her own gin, nor even tend the garden in spring; what's more, the exchange gave her enough pixie-dust to practice the frenzy while she waited for each new moon to fill. Yes, Shy-Blue gave her many things, but she never did a thing to bring the Blue Fairy.

If wishes are made just so, if the frenzy is made just right ... and if Cherry-Rose can't do it, some other doll might.

I can always make more.

After Shy-Blue, life in the cottage was a blur. Days were kept in a soupy haze that ran into each phase of the moon—moon upon moon—until twelve moons ran into each other. As ritual dictated, the seamstress timed her blue-gin peak with the changing phases of the moon. New moon ecstasy, waxing crescent high, waxing gibbous dreams, full-moon-orgy. She knew that if she wished just right, just hard enough, just pure enough, that the Blue Fairy herself would come to answer all her wishes. She wouldn't need daughter-dolls to sell at market, she wouldn't need money, nor that damned pixie-dust. *She* would come, and every night would be … *Before.*

"Where are you, Blue Fairy?"

The seamstress made wishes to start over, to find her father, to say all the things she never had a chance to say, to burn that fucking wooden boy to ash, to crawl back inside her mother's bleeding womb, to never have looked into her father's sad eyes, to never know that it was she who killed his true love; to never have experienced her father's sad, wet-eyed smile as he said, "You have your mother's eyes." To have had the courage to scratch out her own eyes when he said it.

"Where are you, Blue Fairy?"

* * *

Moon upon moon upon moon until this very moon where Cherry-Rose did as ever. With the seamstress reciting from her rocking chair, Cherry-Rose scrawled the wish she was taught to wish. That wish, over and over again, in as many ways as the seamstress could imagine; wishes for skin, and wishes for blood and bones, and wishes for that pounding clock that wound inside her mother's chest.

Cherry-Rose hoped, *Maybe, if these wishes come true, if somehow I am made real, maybe my mother won't look at me with those hateful eyes. Maybe things will be different … good … better.*

Cherry-Rose could feel the moon; its light was there like honeysuckle on the breeze, purifying the night. Through the windows. Under the door. Whatever it was, Cherry-Rose thought she felt something different. Perhaps it was the extra ring around tonight's moon, or maybe it was a lingering something behind that "Who's Sorry Now" song; maybe it was the crush of loneliness she felt as she pressed her face against her side of the window. Whatever it was, tonight, while her mother tended the fire and warmed coals for her hookah, Cherry-Rose made different wishes. New wishes.

Mother-taught-wishes were scratched out, wiped out, blacked out.

I wish for ~~skin like mother~~ *claws!*

I wish for ~~a real heart~~ *fur!!*

I want to ~~be a real girl~~ *fangs!!!*

I wish to be ... beast.

As ever, without a word, as Cherry-Rose hovered over her new wishes at the funeral-birthday, wish-making table, the seamstress left to prepare herself for the night's ritual.

Plenty of time, thought Cherry-Rose. She folded her wishes, drew her runes, and tied and sealed them with a kiss. She placed the wishes over her almost-uncle coals and swayed and hummed a quiet "Who's Sorry Now" song to call the moon. Last, she twirled and spat her silent secret wishes into the flames.

Give me claws. Give me fur. Give me fangs. Make me beast.

When the flames took the wishes, Cherry-Rose moved to the window to watch the night under the moon.

The cottage was quiet until the seamstress emerged to mumble her magic over the hearth, ceasing her rant only to pull pale smoke from the hookah arm.

"All the better to find the Blue Fairy," Cherry-Rose heard her say the day she brought the hookah home from market.

Cherry-Rose watched the seamstress exhale clouds of pale-blue, kiss her wishes, both sides, and throw them into the fire. She heard mumbles turn frantic as the blue-dragon-breath-exhale ascended the chimney.

Cherry-Rose kept her post at the window and watched and waited as a pack of roving, glowing eyes made its way across the clearing and behind the woodpile. She knew better than to speak before the seamstress had finished her wish casting.

She found her mother's reflection in the window and waited. When the last ring of smoke tumbled out of mother-nostrils, when the last tendrils swirled and faded before her shaking blue-shot eyes, Cherry-Rose made her moon-time announcement.

"Mother, your guests have arrived."

"Get down, are you *trying* to be seen?" the seamstress snapped, snarling with lips of blue. "They will tear you apart. Is that what you want, Cherry-Rose?" The seamstress reached out with a blue-stained fingernail to shush cherry-red lips. "Quiet, you little ..." she whispered, bringing her finger to her own lips. "Shhhhhh." The seamstress made her eyes small and laughed a horrible laugh. "You *want* them to tear you apart. Don't you? Bad, bad, bad ... Why are daughters so bad?"

Cherry-Rose could feel warmth overcoming her form. She turned away and found her own reflection in the window. Tears welling. Hands holding her belly to keep the warmth from spilling out.

The seamstress headed for the door and threw it open. She dropped her frock and stood there naked for a moment as if taking in the night. Unmoving. Mountain pose. Naked in the moonlight. *Sniff, sniff, snort; sniff, sniff, snort.*

The seamstress spread her fingers wide with a *sniff, sniff, snort; sniff, sniff, snort* and then she spoke.

"Darling," the mother-beast growled. "Mother is ready."

Cherry-Rose moved quickly toward the door, for making the seamstress wait would only invite more stinging words. She took the cape from its post, and with her mother's back to the cottage, Cherry-Rose placed it over her shoulders.

The seamstress turned, and Cherry-Rose tied the cape. "Now, a kiss for Mother."

Cherry-Rose remembered all the wishes she threw in the fire and wished them again— fur, claws, fangs—as she kissed her mother's cheek.

The seamstress turned to face the forest. *Sniff, sniff, snort,* and Cherry-Rose fell lifeless in the rocking chair. Cherry-Rose sat looking at the hooded image in the doorway, seeing nothing but beast; so beastly, Cherry-Rose wondered if the seamstress needed the cape at all. Just then, making her wonder if she spoke her thoughts aloud, four eyes turned to Cherry-Rose.

"Be sure to keep the fire, deary dear. Our wishes must meet the moon tonight. Yes, yes, Mother won't be too long."

The silhouette of a mother-wolf whispered a low wolf-mother growl: "Now, do be a doll and don't you make a sound, Cherry-Rose. Mother is off to bargain with beasts."

Moon-Love Ritual

THE FLAMES from the ritual-fire had settled into a deep orange that threw thick, slippery dream shadows on the otherwise dark cottage. Cherry-Rose was there in her mother's chair, in the almost-dark, positioned to watch the beastly procession cross the clearing and disappear behind the woodpile—wolf, bear, man, stag, doe, woman. She caught her dream shadow-self shivering against the wall and wondered, *Is any of this ... the cottage, this ... life with her ... that out there ... could any of this be real?*

No matter what her mother said, Cherry-Rose wanted someone to see her—to prove that this was real, but they all passed by as if the cottage, as if she, didn't exist at all.

She felt that had any of the passing beasts bothered to look in the cottage window that night, they themselves would have wondered at the sight, for they would have seen not life but poetry of sorts—perfectly tragic, absolutely tragic poetry. A waning fire beneath a mantel of mother-father-clocks and a motionless rocking chair beneath a defeated almost-daughter-doll—*because she won't let me forget that I'm not quite a real girl*—positioned like Leda awaiting her Swan. One leg over the armrest, arms open wide to the night. Unblinking eyes full of the moon, waiting, wishing, hoping for someone to fulfill her mother's promise of some sort of beautiful violence.

From her playing-dead poetry pose, Cherry-Rose watched her mother slink behind the woodpile and she felt something entirely new—

Rage.

While the beasts of the forest took in the night beneath the moon somewhere beyond the woodpile, Cherry-Rose gathered every word she dared never speak, nor dared even wish, and let them fill her up.

New-moon rage. Waxing rage. Gibbous rage. Full-moon mannequin-ghost-girl rage.

She cursed the wishes she was taught to wish.

All those wasted moons. All those perfectly wasted runes. *Hundreds of wasted wishes*, she thought as she moved to the funeral-birthday table to gather her wishing paper.

Pen in hand, "To be a real girl." Cherry-Rose laughed a bitter laugh. "I wish to be a real girl," still laughing.

"No." She shook her head.

"No, no." She pounded her fist into the table. Her eyes began to wet the pages stacked high with dozens of invisible waiting wishes.

The pen moved furiously, but there weren't any words. She felt too much for words. She began to scratch and scrawl and stab a black ink explosion of pure emotion on paper. Over and over, *stab, scrawl, scratch* … fire.

"Fuck … you." She hesitated using the words that were only for mothers.

Then the words came, printed in bold black: "FUCK YOU."

Cherry-Rose bit and chewed the paper and spit it into the fire.

"Fuck you."

She spat at the flames and kicked and cried at the hearth and mantel. "Fuck you, fucking, fuck you," she spat.

* New paper …

I hate you mother

She threw the words into the fire.

"Paper. More paper. I need more paper."

She turned over everything on the table, knocking over the pitcher of gin.

She shook open and threw the useless books that should have been holding scraps of paper and tossed them aside. The books soaked up the gin that dripped to the floor.

Cherry-Rose flew to the bureau drawers built into the back of the cottage. She left them hanging open like chewing mouths who drooled and spat ribbon, thread, scissors, and fabric.

Nothing.

To the table by the rocking chair.

Yes!

Cherry-Rose pulled the drawer open with such force that paper and pens fell to the floor. Hands. Knees. Belly. She lay on the hearth and grabbed pen and the paper. She began to write and cuss and burn each paper as if possessed by the frenzy beyond the woodpile.

I hate you *into the fire. *I hate you* *into the fire. *I hate you* *into the fire. *I hate this cage* *into the fire. *I hate this doll house this cottage this clearing I hate this life I hate your magic I hate your face your lies your wishes* *into the fire.

I hate your voice it makes me want to puke until there is no more of me I wish I were never made I wish you never found me on the forest floor I would be eaten by wolves all over again if only to never have been reborn here to be kept in this dolls house no wonder your father wanted a son no wonder your father left IhateyouIhateyouIhateyou

Exhausted, Cherry-Rose collapsed over those last words. She couldn't quite throw them into the fire. *Perhaps tomorrow. Yes, perhaps tomorrow,* as barks and howls called Cherry-Rose to the window. Nothing to see outside the window but shadows and shivering almost-uncles. Nothing but more shivering, more barks, and more howls. With the beasts serenading the moon, Cherry-Rose moved to her room. Resigned to the night, she settled into bed beneath her bedside window to watch the smoke of her words, her tears, and her rage climb into the sky. Beneath her covers, she imagined the words eclipsing the moon, blotting out the night, choking the … serenade … that … sang her … to … sleep.

As she slept, the forest came alive in her mind. The trees shook. Patches of snow fell through the branches with a terrible crash. The trees hummed a low hum as they crept into the clearing with their violent lurches, their voices echoing like limbs snapping and a million dry leaves breaking. The ivy too flooded the clearing to bring its children, its snakes, and its rats, and all the tiny black beasts that crawled beneath.

The night swarmed with dozens and dozens of beastly eyes lurching out from the veil. They were all there, every one of the beastly full-moon-ritual woodshed-visitors. All there to make the frenzy. A lusting woman with glowing eyes beneath a feathered mask, a wolf, man as wolf, woman as wolf, a horse who was also woman, a bear, a bear as woman who was man; and all the eyes of the forest ghosts who haunted the soulless limbs of the woodpile. Above it all, the giant ghosts of Nephilim that planted the trees of this forest so many once-upon-a-times ago, and somewhere behind that veil of trees, a flock of mannequin-ghost girls whispering names. Too many all at once. Speaking in tongues.

Visions swam and spun, dream upon dream. A dream within a dream. A dream of days and days, dusks and dawns over and over. The hum of the trees built to a scream to hold the night, to chase away the closest star, to call the moon, to call those spirits from beyond the night. And they came. The great winged beasts and the great fornicators of lusting poetry whose books filled her shelves—their faces—each visage filled the sky, each a constellation—the manticore, Bathory, Caligula, Eurydice; de Sade, the Swan, Nin, Eros and Psyche.

From their perch, the constellations of the mad-starry sky watched the smoke that rose from the cottage as if to a nest of bees: to call, to awaken, to drive out the queen from the moon, so that she might give audience …

The smoke shook the moon and all its rings. It quaked above the cottage like some hovering, twitching lover pulling invisible strings attached to the arms and legs in the woodpile; like it was pulling at the vines and the void inside the dreaming Cherry-Rose. The hum of the forest, the rattle of the wooden limbs, the beat of the pinecone heart buried in a mannequin-doll's chest, it all became the voice of the moon, so full that even in the softest whisper, it shook the whole of the night.

I am coming.

At these words, the smoke from the night fire—the smoke of tears, wishes, and rage, the smoke that rose to meet the moon—became umbilical to the earth. The pale-blue light, the shining promise of the great witch of the sky, Ur-lover, whore of the night—the Blue Fairy— pulsed with the beat of the night as she herself dripped from the moon to fill the plume.

The night beyond the dream went silent with such force that it woke Cherry-Rose. She sat upright, startled. Something was wrong. The moon should have been just outside her window, but it and the howls were gone. Clocks were there, everywhere, but they too were silent. Cherry-Rose slid out of bed and peered through her open door. Nothing. Nothing but the shadow of a cape hung by the door.

Cherry-Rose moved to examine the cape that looked wholly different from the one she had come to know. It was pale blue-gray, like the moon. Edged in soft fur. Cherry-Rose's hand followed the fur down to a small tail and then up to the hood capped with two tiny antlers.

Just as Cherry-Rose touched the antlers, the clocks came alive and struck three. The cottage and the forest and all its beasts were reborn: tick, tick, ticking, the crackle of the fire, the barks, the howls, the wails of the full-moon ritual.

And the moon lover in the sky, the pulse of the umbilical smoke, spoke again.

I am coming.

As if in a trance, Cherry-Rose approached the dying fire. Her hands moved over her body to the pulsing hum of the forest, to the pulse of the umbilical smoke that tied the earth to the sky. She pulled her nightgown over her head and placed it on the coals. Its black smoke fed the cord and the hum grew louder and louder and the words came closer still.

I am coming.

The voice blew open the cottage door, and a forest howl of panting, tangled beasts rushed into the cottage, chasing the moon that spilled at Cherry-Rose's feet.

I am coming.

She moved to the door and took the cape. As she pulled on its hood, Cherry-Rose could feel the mother-magic that bound her to this place breaking. The heavy spells of forgetting, all the half-truths, all the twisted lies, the lies upon lies that made up the story of her life, began to unwind. Shadowed memories came crashing in to give her the life she had forgotten. It gave her a life lived with twelve mannequin-sisters. Faces and names came in flashes: Violent-Joy, Sprinkles, Scarlet, Jasmine, Rey-Rey, Mojave, Daisy, Siouxsie, Apple, Fae, Peaches, and Shy-Blue.

"Shy-Blue, you promised," Cherry-Rose heard herself whisper.

Cherry-Rose crossed the threshold and heard the chimes. She felt the tickle run down her seams, and she became part of the forest, she became daughter of the night, she became beast. She snuffed and snorted beneath her hood and the words came again.

I am coming.

Cherry-Rose followed the pulsing smoke past the shivering woodpile, toward the shed just visible from her bedroom window. Through the frenzy—the bears, the wolves, the women, the horses, the men, and the mother too tangled in howls to take notice of the Cherry-Rose—to a giant table positioned just between the woodpile and the shed. She had never seen this table before as it lay hidden from view of the cottage, but standing here now, she knew its secrets. This was *her* ritual bed. This was where *she* bargained with beasts, this was where the howls were made that shook the cottage clocks and its wooden soldiers. This was where the growls were made that huffed and puffed the birds from the trees, this was where she gave a bit of herself to take a bit from the beast—because that was how one made the deepest magic.

Cherry-Rose's hand followed the pulsing, tumbling, pale-blue smoke that moved over the moon-love, ritual table and she did as it instructed. She crawled upon the altar. All fours like beast until she turned to face the calling moon.

The pale smoke swirled and moved over her body. It showed her how to open herself to the night. As she lay there, all beast with gnashing teeth, two eyes for this plane, two antlers for another, faded-green lustered breasts and knees pointing to the night, the umbilical smoke that rose to meet the moon began to take form. It was titan, then bear, then wolf, then doe. Last, its true form, the most beautiful, and horrifying, and wonderful being whose eyes were the moon, whose lips were the shining rings of the moon, whose breasts were the stars, whose sex, the night between the stars.

The Blue Fairy touched the earth and the forest orgy froze. All time stopped but that which fell under her gaze.

If Cherry-Rose could have seen anything beyond the light of the Blue Fairy, she would have seen grass and leaves held tight by the silent grip of the frigid breeze; birds immobile, held in mid-flight, decorating the air of the night sky; beasts frozen mid-snarl, mid-bite, mid-kiss, mid-fuck.

Cherry-Rose waited like a quaking lover; feet squared, knees high, torso propped up by shivering arms beneath an antlered hood, slack-jawed cherry-red lips facing the approaching Blue Fairy. The pale-blue form moved like mist over Cherry-Rose, who settled back slowly and melted into the altar. She tilted her head to the side, ready, waiting, hoping to be split in two, to have her belly spilled on the floor, to have her liver devoured, her neck torn open.

She was ready for change, for something ... anything real; for the end, an ending, for a new beginning, a different ending, for death, even life ... even Forever.

The Blue Fairy as moon-fairy lover, blue-whore of the night, the mother-slut of the wet dripping sky, hovered over Cherry-Rose. Moon-ringed eyes to Jupiter eyes. Cherry-red lips to stardust breasts. Knees bent and open. Feet planted and gripping. Waiting. And the place that was the night between the stars, the Blue Fairy's womb-flower, became cock, full and hard.

The Blue Fairy whispered without words in a voice made for moon-lovers, a voice that was the night. *You are the wet of the earth.* Pale-blue slid over and into the belly without womb. *I am the seed of the moon.* Moving with the hum of the night. Pale-blue over the chest with the pinecone heart. *I will fill you up* ... Moonlight lips draining breasts of earth and clay and vines and fur and feathers ... *with the milk and honey of the moon.* Whispered lips on lips. *Only you* ... Pale-blue, moon-ringed eyes bore into Jupiter eyes. ... *can make yourself whole.* Lips on stars, stars on lips. Moon-lit lips over inked heart.

Cherry-Rose ascends into frenzy. Blue Fairy dissolves into night.

Nails

CHERRY-ROSE woke with a start, feeling lighter than ever. Feeling like a flood swept over her, through her, dragging with it all her broken bits—all her shattered glass memories—leaving her feeling hollowed and cleaned out. Drained and torn open by the night, Cherry-Rose wondered, *Was it all a dream?* In the haze of a morning all full of wild morning dreams, anything could be real: a funeral-birthday for a fawn, a cottage on the edge of nowhere, a seamstress mother, a Blue Fairy lover. She crawled out of bed, aching from a night of not enough sleep, wondering what could have happened to her nightgown, and then it all came back to her. The dream. *Was it a dream? The Blue Fairy, did she ...*

I have ... I have sisters. It wasn't a dream at all, was it? Mother? She ...

Cherry-Rose clung to her duvet and moved slowly toward her bedroom door. She peeked out from her room, just enough to see the seamstress lying on the hearth, dead to the world.

Cherry-Rose crept just beyond her door, looking for signs of life. Still breathing. Breathing in heaves and spurts like a beast riddled with sickness on the precipice of death. Beside her, a bottle. In her hand, a note. On that note, the words that Cherry-Rose wrote for tomorrow's fire, no, today's fire, this morning's fire. Words of piss and hate and fury; words of rage. She felt a pang of guilt and a rush of fear for leaving them laying on the floor, for not having burned them like all the others.

What was I thinking? Tomorrow's fire?!

Over the fire, Cherry-Rose could see a pot filled with a simmering soup. On the table, root vegetables, and bottles, and spices, and a small brown and white tail.

The Blue Fairy gave her the memories. Cherry-Rose saw all the lies that became her life turn to ash to fortify all those soups of forgetting. Cherry-Rose knew there wasn't much time. Abandoning the duvet, she crawled on hands and knees to the table. Slowly. Quietly. *Shhhhh.* She peeked under the table and spied the seamstress still playing dead. Then she crouched with eyes at table level; her hand slid out slowly between bottles and over papers until it felt the touch of fur.

Behind the table, mouth to the sky, Cherry-Rose swallowed her tail.

Down

   dOwn

      doWn

         dowN

            down

Cherry-Rose began to quake under the spell of change. Chimes shook in her head like she was caged inside a clock. Chimes rang sharp, like cold, hard knives cutting away the fog of spells, cutting the strings that were once held by a mad mother.

There was motion on the hearth. Cherry-Rose couldn't wait any longer. She crawled under the bed to find her funeral-birthday box. She would need her birthday clothes.

Cherry-Rose threw on her black dress and her black slip-on shoes. She placed a crown of dried marigold on her head. She grabbed three books and her journal—satchel over shoulder, *no pieces left behind. Leave nothing for Mother's magic.* She heard a laugh, sad and low, creep out from the hearth, and she quietly edged her way to the frame of the door.

In the low light cast by the dying fire, she could just make out a crooked face bent by the night, bent by hate, creased and etched by stone and grout.

Closer. Testing. Closer. Creeping. Quietly.

Just close enough to have one last look at her face in the fire light.

Sleeping? Is she sleeping?

Closer.

Cherry-Rose bent down and leaned in to find eyes closed but running as if in dream. She stared, marveling at the way the pale-blue colored the seamstress.

Closer.

Tiny blue spiderweb veins covered her eyelids.

Closer.

Her cheeks, decorated in a pale-blue rosacea.

Closer—hovering. *Too close?*

Seamstress lips edged in shimmering moonlight turned up into a smile. "Yes, do give Mother a kiss."

Cherry-Rose fell back, tumbling toward the forest door.

"Bad, bad, bad."

Sliding backward, arms and legs moving too fast for her body, Cherry-Rose kicked away the floor and pushed away the rug until she uncovered her grandmother's stain, until she hit the furthest wall.

"Why are daughters so bad, Cherry-Rose?" The seamstress lurched to prop herself up—elbows then palms pressed against the stone of the hearth. "I can always make ..." Her words went unfinished when her arms slid out from under her shaking form.

Cherry-Rose ran as fast as she could out the door. Three paces beyond the porch, however, she stopped, feeling entirely lost on the other side of the door.

The shed. Supplies. I will need supplies.

She ran past the wooden wall of twitching forms, past the ritual table, and straight into the shed. There was so much, too much to see. It was a museum of bits and pieces that smelled of marigold, juniper, and earth.

Fabric of all shades and in dozens of patterns, jars with buttons, bowls with buckles, wooden blocks with wigs, small cages, baskets with latches, bundles of flowers, dried marigold hanging from every post, and a wall of thirteen nails and thirteen names—her name and the twelve she had once forgotten. Twelve names for the mannequin-ghost girls of her dream.

Cherry-Rose spoke the names scrawled into the wood over the empty nails, and memories of faces flooded in. Next to the nails and the names, she counted seven other nails tied with seven red threads. Seven tiny perfect red bows choking seven cold gray nails. Seven tiny bows, beneath seven unfamiliar, never-sister names: Lilith, Lucy, Lee, Letty, Lilly, Lucia, Luna. "Luna?" Cherry-Rose said aloud. She scratched her head, wondering where she had heard that name before.

A memory came like all the others, like a dream. Cherry-Rose could see Violent-Joy frantically rummaging through the cottage. She was looking for something, but she didn't know what. Violent-Joy said it was a feeling, an idea, a dream, like the lyric of a song she had always known, but at this very moment, for the life of her, she couldn't remember. She said it was right there. She could feel it. Like a worm digging behind her eyes, pushing against her fabric, wanting to get out.

Violent-Joy threw open the armoire to sift through the hanging dresses. "Nothing." A basket of ribbons: "no, no, no."

"Vi, what are you looking for?" asked Apple.

"I'm not sure," Violent-Joy replied without looking up. "White. Blue. No, white with tiny flecks of blue. No. Small, faded blue shapes on white. No, no, no, yes. Yes!" She held out a small patch of fabric. "I knew it!"

Her sisters looked on, confused.

"Vi, what's going on?" said Peaches.

Violent-Joy dashed to the curtains beneath the sink. "Help me find them."

"What?" asked Sprinkles. "What are you looking for?"

Violent-Joy dumped the first container of market trinkets out on the cottage floor: buckles, buttons, a thimble, small spools of thread, round pieces of glass.

"Not here. Help me find them. The sun. Two eyes like the sun with two rings, little crowns." Violent-Joy dumped out container after container, everything, and everyone onto the floor to help sift through the mess until Betty asked, "These? Are we looking for these?"

Betty held out two glass pearls, centers glowing like the sun.

Cherry-Rose remembered something about Violent-Joy's dream. Violent-Joy told her something about a Luna, something about the scent of honeysuckle, the butterfly wings, the wolf-cape, *her* cape, the red thread, the seam-ripper. Something about a doll that lived, if only for a moment, beyond the threshold. But before they had time to fully comprehend Violent-Joy's story, before they could remember that they all had a version of that dream buried somewhere within their stitches, the soup of forgetting did its job.

Nails. Dreams. Memories.

Spinning from the weight of flooding names and rushing memories, Cherry-Rose was unsure why she entered the shed at all. She turned to run out of the shed and saw thread, and scissors, and the seam-ripper—into her satchel—and there on the back of the door, the antlered cape from her dream. Fur, antlers; everything she dreamed, minus the tail. Cherry-Rose didn't hesitate. She tied the cape around her neck and pulled its hood over her head. In a flash, all the nails and all the dreams that were memories, and memories that weren't dreams, cut deeper still.

Cherry-Rose staggered and stumbled out the door, settling herself at the edge of the moon-love-ritual-table, holding herself up just long enough to swoon under the memory of last night's kiss. A scream from inside the cottage tore through that memory and helped her find her feet.

"My tail. Where is the tail, Cherry-Rose?!"

The seamstress screamed over the sound of glass breaking from somewhere inside the cottage. Then came silence. Then came song.

"Where are you, Cherry-Rose?" the seamstress sang in a haunting mother-voice.

"Mother found your note, Cherry-Rose. Come out come out wherever you are."

Not waiting any longer, Cherry-Rose ran past the cottage, through the clearing, toward the narrow path leading into the wide-wide forest, and for the first time since wolves tore through an antlered doe, she felt very much like something other than a sad, lonely, miserable and useless mannequin-ghost girl.

II

Eat, Fuck, Die ...

The Ivy-Night

CHERRY-ROSE paused for just a moment at the edge of the clearing. She steadied herself, resting her hand upon a stump etched with Blue Fairy runes as wave after wave of ghost-sister memories flooded in. The latest flood gave her memories of mannequin-sisters marking her flesh. She could feel Violent-Joy straddling her chest to give her the heart she always wanted. *Anything other than that rattling pinecone.* "A heart of flowers and fire ... so you won't need to waste your wishes," said Violent-Joy. Her right thigh, Scarlet's tiger; *climbing, clawing, tearing, ready to pounce.* Her left, Shy-Blue's lotus; "Oh, to be a lotus-eater," they'd laugh. Only now after the Blue Fairy did Cherry-Rose realize the irony of that wish.

She knew she didn't have much time, but she needed a moment to adjust her eyes. She looked hard into the forest that she had only known through visions from another life—from books, magazines, comics; from her perch beneath the cottage window. She always marveled at how the view from the window differed from her forest dreams. The bubbled glass made the forest look like an underwater, two-dimensional wall of green. Whereas the visions that shook her awake at night reduced the forest to a twisting tunnel of green. But here on the edge looking in, the forest was more like the sea she found in poetry; it looked frightfully deep, endlessly wide, and unsettlingly alive.

Cherry-Rose stood on the edge of the clearing to consider the tiny path that led to those other-side-of-the-wall worlds. From the hoed edge of the clearing, she stood on her tippy toes, attempting to peer through the trees, to find the furthest edge of the path that led her sisters to market. There was nothing to see, or rather, too much to see. It was only a moment, but with the seamstress inside doing Fairy-knew-what, it already felt too long. Feeling the danger of lingering, realizing there was nothing to gain from standing on the edge of the clearing, Cherry-Rose took the seam-ripper from the satchel and addressed her new host. "Hello, Forest, remember me? I'm Cherry-Rose. I believe I died not far from here."

To her surprise, Forest answered in the vines, twigs, and feathers of her mind.

Hello, Fawn-girl. How could we forget?

We never forget.

For a moment, Cherry-Rose imagined that it was she who filled in the answers to her forest-dialog, that she gave Forest its words. However, when Forest spoke again, she knew she was wrong.

Where are you going, Fawn-girl? ... Stay with us, rest. Yes ... yes, this is where you died. Would you like to see your bones?

And just ahead of Cherry-Rose, a small clearing opened between a group of tall trees crawling with slithering ivy.

There is no need to go any farther. Come and lay with your bones.

Cherry-Rose wondered, *Was that clearing always there? Did I imagine it?* She walked a little faster, skirting its edge while looking for her old bones, looking back toward the cottage clearing as she did. She was ready to turn her walk into a run, half expecting to see the seamstress behind her dripping with rage. She saw nothing but Forest and the faint outline of the cottage barely visible through the trees.

As she slowed to take a longer look back at the cottage, she saw that the trees and their branches began to lean away from the path, to create a clear view to the cottage's front door. Ahead, the trees leaned further in. Long limbs bent down, stretching, closer, closer to obscure the path.

Cherry-Rose sensed what Forest was trying to do. In a flash, she turned away from the cottage and broke into a run, keeping pace just ahead of the closing trees—deeper and deeper into the forest. On and on, she ran as fast as she could, away from the rush of nightmare trees, away from the cottage, into the unknown. Now with each step, the trees seemed to close tighter behind as if pushed by a cottage tide. On and on they leaned, stretched, reached, and grabbed, and closed in on Cherry-Rose, but she pushed, tore, ripped, jumped, and ran on, deeper and deeper still.

Stay. Won't you stay with us.

Deeper still she ran, and Forest called Ivy to cover the winding seamstress-worn path.

Fawn-girl!

Cherry-Rose ran straight on, weaving beneath and between, over and under the reaching Forest, only knowing for certain that she was running away from the cottage.

The forest floor slid and shifted. Ivy took the thin market path; gone, no earth, only dark-green winding leathery leaves and vine. As she ran, she felt the chill of her first-memory visions —visions of something on her heels. Claws and fangs. They were there. Cherry-Rose could feel arms reaching out, swiping at the air just behind her back. She glanced back to meet the claws that would tear her open, but there was nothing—nothing but green and a darkening world of waving ivy arms. No cottage. No path. Gone. Everything gone. Just green. The forest behind Cherry-Rose had become a wall of branches, covered in climbing ivy, cresting, rolling, reaching toward her like a nightmare wave.

Faster. Faster! screamed the Cherry-Rose who watched from beyond her dreams, and Cherry-Rose ran all the faster.

Why do you run, Fawn-girl? Listen to the birds sing. Listen to the cicada call. It is time to be still. Wouldn't you like a rest? Yes, yes, stay with us a little while and rest.

Cherry-Rose could feel the tingle of seamstress magic behind Forest-words. It *was* the forest: birds singing, cicada chirping, branches tugging, ivy slinking, but somehow it was also *her*. It was *she* who gave the birds their song, and it was *she* who begged the cicada to call, *she* who asked the trees to do what they might, *she* who enticed the ivy.

The birds did their worst and wept a soft lullaby of a sleeping song for Cherry-Rose. While the birds sang their hypnotizing lullaby, the cicada petitioned the trees to quicken the night ahead of the cutting, slashing Cherry-Rose. She could hear them speak: *spread your branches and stifle the sun, dear friends. So that we might sleep, so that she might join us beneath Ivy.* The trees answered and spread their branches wider still across the forest ceiling, and when the trees had no more to give, Ivy shot to the sky to fill in the patches of blue between the branches. Ivy stretched on bare limbs, across and over to meet itself on the other side, mirror branches, mirror trees to fill in all the spaces, to bring the dark, to quiet the sun; *let us bring you the night so that you might sleep.*

The noon sun disappeared entirely—a false ivy-night had fallen.

Cherry-Rose ran on, lost beneath the forest sea of night. Dark ivy waves rode the canopy above her, and ruthless slithering ivy currents dragged and pushed her below. The path was… there was no path.

Forest voices closed in beneath the wave, holding out its branches like knotted arms, as if asking, pleading, begging. *Stay, Fawn-girl, stay. Yes, yes, we are so soft and warm. Time to sleep. Time to sleep. So soft.*

Cherry-Rose could feel the weight of the warm ivy night behind her eyes pressing softly, inviting her to sleep.

Darling, darling, lay your head down on our leaves of green. Let us hold you. Let us cover you for the night, 'til the morrow, 'til the morrow …

Cherry-Rose had been running for so long. So fast. So tired. She felt Forest worm its want inside her stitches. It spoke through her pinecone heart: *please, please, rest my child, just for a moment.* She could feel it—she wanted nothing more than to give Forest what it needed. She was so tired. With each step, it grew more and more difficult to break the ivy hold as it reached for her ankles. More and more difficult to cut the stubborn vines. More and more difficult to run.

Sisters. I have to find my sisters, she reminded her disparate parts. *I have to find my sisters*, as the dark ivy sky began to close in on her slowing feet. *I have to find my sisters*, over and over until a faint light appeared just above the pulsing edge of the heaving forest. Until the birds somewhere beyond the reaching trees could be heard chirping. Until cicada warmed by the sun somewhere beyond the leathery green began to call. Until Cherry-Rose felt her seams tingle, until she heard the chimes, until she burst through the furthest edge of her mother's chasing magic, until she breached the last tree on her mother's side of the forest and threw herself on the ground near a row of stumps.

Dangerous Wanting, Secrets for Thread

PANTING, coughing, wheezing, struggling to settle her pinecone heart, Cherry-Rose positioned herself with her back against a sapling on the thinnest edge of the forest to pull the twigs and leaves from her hair.

A small knoll pecked with stumps marked the furthest edge of a curtain of trees. Grass and withered stumps this side, forest, that. And far below the sloping grass, at the nexus of several worn paths branching out to places unknown, the market. It had to be the market, for her mother told her it was the only thing to be found on the other side of the path.

When she finally settled herself, she looked like a long-discarded ragdoll. All doll, worn and aged—dragged over dirt and tossed aside—legs spread, arms lifeless on either side, palms up, head tilted and bent down slightly, eyes wide open and angled toward the market but staring through—out into the far, far, farther away. She sat facing the market that swallowed her sisters, chest heaving, Forest-chase-mantra running: "I have to … find my … sisters." Cherry-Rose breathed and mumbled her mantra; and, when she was able, her eyes focused.

Below, she saw the market moving like the cottage clearing on moon-ritual nights. Her mother's stories filled in the scene—an orgy of chattering beasts grinding about beneath the wide-open sky. Beasts bargaining with beasts for beasts … for toys, for trinkets. She closed her eyes and imagined her sisters on the wrong side of the aisles, led on leads, caged, penned, sold. … Eyes still closed, still wading in the far far farther away, she found the market song. All of those other-side-of-the-aisle beasts, the birds in cages, the cows on leads, the dogs and pigs in pens, all were singing their somber counterpoint to the overriding melody of the bargaining beastly chatter. Cherry-Rose heard their song pouring out from the valley. She breathed and added her own lines to the market melody. *This is where the lesser of us are sold, bagged, split open, or eaten. This is where my sisters were taken, broken, lost, and forgotten.*

Far, far, farther away …

Cherry-Rose remembered seamstress warnings about that which lay beyond the cottage, beyond the clearing, beyond the forest. *Deeper, deeper, darker, deadly.* On cottage nights when she laid awake and imagined a market full of wanting faces full of teeth and fangs, hungry lusting faces, Cherry-Rose could picture the seamstress shaking her Norma mug at the mannequin-girls. "Out there, beyond these walls, beyond that clearing, every step further away from this door is danger. Each step further away is even more dangerous. Teeth that bite, claws that tear, hands that want, and they all take, take, take, take, take."

It seems that sometimes even wicked mothers tell the truth, thought Cherry-Rose. *Even if only to shade a lie,* she corrected. *It seems that is the magic of truth—it often works best when paired with a lie.*

Upon returning from the far, far, farther away, Cherry-Rose found that the sun had crossed the sky quickly, and it seemed as if the doubling of a stump's shadow caused the song of the market to wane. With her back against the tree, just there on that knoll, Cherry-Rose felt, considering all things, that she was as safe as she had a right to feel. It seemed that the seamstress's forest spell had no hold here; and Forest too seemed leery of the market. It was as if the trees had turned away from the bustle, the beasts, and the stumps.

Stumps … too ghastly to look, she reasoned for Forest.

The ivy, however, seemed less sentimental. It may have been slowed out on the furthest edges of the forest floor, but if all those days staring out the cottage window taught her anything, it was that the ivy was relentless. *Slowed, yes. Stopped, never,* thought Cherry-Rose. *Ivy never stops being Ivy.*

Cherry-Rose knew it had no fear reaching beyond the edge of the forest. How many times had she watched the seamstress chop at the ivy with her hoe, burning whatever crept into the clearing?

Mother-work taught Forest-lessons—*Ivy is relentless.*

Forest behind, market ahead—danger danger.

An itch running up Cherry-Rose's seams told her that if she wasn't vigilant, the unrelenting ivy would drag her back to meet her bones, or worse, to find her mother somewhere in the middle of the forest. But everything she knew about the market told her that it too was full of danger. She tightened her grip on the seam-ripper, repositioned herself against a tree, and decided to wait for the cover of night before she tested market aisles.

Waiting, watching, the market ebbed and memory-dreams flowed in like a rushing tide behind heavy eyes.

* * *

In bed with Shy-Blue. Only Shy-Blue. There wasn't anyone else. The seamstress must have been off hoeing ivy, or making gin. All arms and legs tangled up in each other. Noses pressed between necks.

It tickles when she breathes.

"Keys and locks."

"What?"

"Keys and locks. That is what we are doing today."

"Locks? Hmmm …"

"I sketched them out last night. See …"

"Me first."

"Key left forearm. Lock right. Same for you, so when we dance your key faces my lock, and mine yours."

"I hope she doesn't come back soon."

"I hope she doesn't come back at all."

"Maybe the ivy will get her."

"Shhhhh, keep it down, come on, you know how she hates it when we laugh."

* * *

Cherry-Rose stirred as the seam-ripper slid from her hand and landed on her lap. Her one open eye told her that the pink of the sky was fading quickly.

* * *

"Violent-Joy. Apple. Sing us some June Christy. Sing 'How High the Moon.'"

"Shy, they sing. We dance. Come on. Come on. Shy ... get up, lazy bones."

"Fawn-girl!"

"Sure, okay, Cherry-Rose, we'll sing, but you're next. You and Peaches."

"Fawn-girl? Hello there ... Fawn-girl."

"Vi? Apple?"

"Fawn-girl? You should really wake up now."

Apple broke into song and Violent-Joy screamed.

"Fawn-girl ... Fawn—"

Cherry-Rose kicked and flailed. The seam-ripper tore at the air and her legs went wild. Both ivy and crows went flying, filling the air with green leaves, caws, and a murder of crows.

"What ... How long was I ...?"

The very last edge of the day's color was dropping beneath the horizon. The market was empty ... gone.

The seam-ripper did its job. The pieces of ivy that tried to crawl up her leg were left cut and ripped to bleed down her fabric.

"Bad Ivy! Give me back my shoe," Cherry-Rose yelled as she cut and yanked at a brave ivy arm.

Cherry-Rose leapt to her feet and chased down the wounded, thieving ivy. "Mine," she snarled as she swiped her shoe from its winding tendrils.

"Dangerous creature, that weed," said a voice on the stump-side of the forest.

Cherry-Rose stood motionless, seam-ripper and shoe ready to strike.

"Always wanting," said another.

Her head lowered slowly, then turned sharply over her left shoulder.

"Dangerous wanting," said another.

Her eyes slid to the right.

"Who's there? If you come any closer, I'll cut out your eyes."

"All of our eyes?"

"But we are so many."

"Who are you? Where are you? I'll scream."

"Hmm. I wouldn't do that," said the voice beyond the trees.

"You shouldn't want to call the wolves, Fawn-girl," said another.

"Nor the bears," said another.

"Nor the men," said another.

"Yes. Particularly the men. Those beasts really fancied the other dolls the seamstress made. Didn't they?"

"Dangerous wanting," said a voice full of sympathy. "Just like Ivy, dangerous, that lot."

"Yes, dangerous," said another.

"Other dolls? You've seen them? Where are my sisters? Do you know where my sisters are?" asked Cherry-Rose suspiciously.

"Come. Sit, girl. Find a stump," said a voice.

"Market is gone," said another.

"Those beasts are gone," said another.

"Other beasts soon waking," said another.

Cherry-Rose peered out from behind the last tree on her side of the forest to see who belonged to the teasing voices. The hillside was all grass full of stumps and peppered with black birds. Leaning out further still, she saw the berry-blue of night chasing away its cobalt, azure, sky-blue edges. And nothing belonging to those voices. An empty square far below. Empty winding paths. Grass, only grass ... and stumps ... and black, hopping birds.

"Come on, no more games. Who's there?" Cherry-Rose limped out of the forest, brandishing both the seam-ripper and a shoe.

"Just we," said a voice to the right.

"And stumps," said a voice to the left.

"And stumps," said the crow hopping at the feet of the one-shoed mannequin-girl.

"We. Crow. And stumps."

"Nothing to fear, Fawn-girl, we don't eat glass eyes. Come sit, rest, trade with us."

"Are you not here to trade?"

"The seamstress always came at dusk."

"So much thread."

"Lovely thread for our nests."

"Have you any thread?"

"Secrets for thread."

"Secrets for thread," kraa'd seven stirring crows, their words echoing into the sky.

"I … I do. I think. I think I have some thread." Cherry-Rose sat atop the stump closest to the forest and dug through the satchel slung across her body. Her fingers dove past her journal, worn copies of *Howl*, *Wuthering Heights*, and *The Sorrows of Young Werther* to find fabric, scissors, pincushion, pins, hip flask of gin … patches, hair, a ball of green thread, and a ball of red thread. "I do have thread," she said, holding out both the red and green. "Secrets for thread?" Cherry-Rose repeated, turning the phrase into a question.

"Secrets for thread," said a hopping crow.

"Cut us each a piece, Fawn-girl, and you may ask a question," said another.

"Red."

"Red, Fawn-girl."

"The red thread, please."

Seated at the stump, she positioned her feet out wide with her knees knocking together to make a table. She cut the red thread and began to toss the pieces on the grass. Seven pieces, one by one; and one by one, seven crows flew in, each to take their share. They flew and fluttered and caw'd and kraa'd, red thread in claw; then seven crows settled, calm and quiet. They surrounded Cherry-Rose as if they were awaiting a sermon from the stump.

Being new to this arrangement, entirely unsure of the protocol, Cherry-Rose sat, impatiently waiting for secrets to fly, wondering when they might speak.

Seven black-feathered birds stood perfectly still, staring back at Cherry-Rose.

When it seemed they might never speak again, she sighed and asked, "Secrets for thread?" sounding a little defeated.

"Secrets for thread," repeated the crow nearest her feet.

"Okay, sure. Tell me, crow, where are my sisters?" Cherry-Rose glared at the lone white eye that stared up from her feet.

"Fawn-girl."

"Cherry-Rose," she interrupted.

"Fawn-girl," ignored the crow. "They were here."

"I'd prefer if you could tell me where they are now," said Cherry-Rose, her voice giving away her growing impatience.

"Fawn-girl. Do you carry our thread to our perch? Do you build our nests? No. You do not. You give us pieces. You give us what you have. You give us thread. And we give you what we have. We give you pieces."

"Yes, yes. Fine. Fine. I see. Pieces. Please give me your pieces."

"They were all here. One by one," said a voice to the left.

"Tears. So many tears," said another.

"They all gave so many tears," said another.

"Yes, but where did they go? Who took them? Please. Please," begged Cherry-Rose.

"Gone. Gone. Gone. Gone," caw'd seven swirling crows.

"Gone," said the lone crow standing at her feet.

"But where?" Cherry-Rose dabbed at her welling eyes.

"We do not know for certain."

"There were men, women, witches, beasts."

"And children."

"We don't know all, but we do know where children go," said the crow.

"They go to school."

"Just over the hill."

"Down the middle road."

"They go to school?" echoed Cherry-Rose.

"Yes, they go to school," said the nearest crow, leaping to take flight.

"Go to school," kraa'd six black shapes following the first.

"Go to school." They caw'd as they swarmed and swooped, disappearing somewhere over Forest.

Pixie-Dust & Bye-Bye Eyes

DOWN the middle road. Off to school.

The sign reads *William Hale Academy for Children of All Sorts.*

First day jitters.

First day journal entry.

Sisters, remember how at bedtime we'd list all the things we'd do if we were able to live beyond the door? No matter all the crazy things we whispered to each other, we all said we wanted to go to school like Betty and Veronica. Well, all I can say is that this is not Riverdale. Those comics got it all wrong.

Cherry-Rose saw the market reflected on campus. Same fangs, same claws, same snouts and snarls, beaks and feathers—masks over teeth—bear, wolf; man and woman, mannequin-doll; children of all sorts. It was a throbbing mass of life. Everything, everyone under the sun scrambling like insects exposed beneath an overturned log.

The similarities, Cherry-Rose learned, did not end there. Early school observations were much like those of the stump-side market view. One must move when asked, told, prodded, directed, demanded. Lesser things went in pens. Everyone herded from class to class at the sound of a bell. To the dorm room at the bell. Lights out at the bell. Wake up at the bell. Pencils down, pencils up at the sound of a bell. Cherry-Rose didn't want school, bells, pencils, and cages. She didn't want a glass jar with a new lid. She wanted her sisters, and it didn't take long to realize that they weren't here.

As any true forest creature might, Cherry-Rose was leery of Forest's treeless, stump-side counterpart. It was at the end of her first day on this side that she envisioned her last.

She told her journal, *I'll give it 'til dead-moon night. I'll see what I can see. Lay low, look around. If they are here, even one of them … If they aren't, I'll see if I can gather some clues, and then I'm gone.*

"William Hale Academy for Children of All Sorts." Cherry-Rose read the neon-blinking words aloud. She was annoyed at the sign that was seemingly positioned to shine through her dorm-room window to simultaneously prevent sleep and to blot out the stars. From her bottom bunk, she watched not the stars but the bed above hers push perfect cushioned squares through the bed's underwiring and springs. The springs whined as they stretched and stretched, bouncing closer to Cherry-Rose's face as the bear-who-was-girl did her roll and stretch wake-up routine.

Cherry-Rose caught her reflection in the window between pink flashes of neon. William, **Blink,* Hale, **Blink* … and watched her breath fog and bend the light as she quietly read along. "All Sorts."

All sorts? I am definitely in the right place.

~ ~ ~

Same window. Same reflection. Same morning-motivation ritual.

"Okay, Cherry-Rose. You can do this." Her finger made a heart on the breath-stained glass. "One more day 'til dead-moon night."

Dead-moon night. Just one more day and bye-bye, thought Cherry-Rose. *There is a bed, there is food, and there is no sign of the seamstress. I can do one more day.*

"All sorts," Cherry-Rose repeated, looking around the girls' dorm. She sighed. *This … school, it is just too much like the cottage,* she told her journal, feeling all its promising promises held together with invisible things. *Magic and Lies*, she titled the top of the page.

All sorts. School had its walls, teachers had their rules, and beneath it all, like the vermin that crawled beneath forest ivy, school even had its Roaches. Here, they were much like the true keepers of the forest, the lowest earthbound overlords, underneath over-watchers, ivy over-runners. It was they who broke every beast down—no matter how big and horned and fanged—to their smallest bits. In the forest, they served Ivy, the lord of rot, decay, descent, and death. They were a swarm, a blight, a blessing to the leathery green-leafed beast that worked to reclaim all forest-bound forms. But these Roaches, of the Children of All Sorts variety, crawled about in the light of day without proper shame. Here at the William Hale Academy for Children of All Sorts, they were everywhere under the wide-open sky and all the more dangerous.

Roach, wolf, bear, man, woman, teacher; Cherry-Rose learned that school in its entirety could be reduced to an awkward forest-like social ranking exercise. Surely, considering the Roaches, there were bigger, stronger, more ferocious creatures on campus—teachers with their pop quizzes, wolves with their fangs, men and women with their claws. Each of them might have even thought it was they who ruled the school, but in reality, it was the Roaches. Like in the forest, it was they who truly sat atop the food chain, and here at school, it was much the same.

This stump-side of the world too, had that seamstress sickness. Pixie-dust was everywhere. It was in the classrooms. In the dorms. Students had it. Teachers had it. It was inescapable. The school failed at many things, but it succeeded in teaching Cherry-Rose the finer points of the pixie-dust frenzy. It seemed that if one were more beast than not, one vial and tongues would wag and drip blue drool, eyes would shine wide, all mad and unblinking; claws, fingers, teeth, fangs seemed to lengthen as if ready to tear at books, papers, straps and fur; jeans and leather jackets. And if one were more … not-beast-at-all than actual beast … the pixie-dust was sure to add one more beast to its number.

The teachers, they taught class with their slow blinking blue-shot eyes, desks aglow with pixie-dust hookah. "Stay after, would you, deary," they'd hiss, breathing their pale-blue. "I'd love to find out just who you are."

The students were worse.

The boys-who-would-be-beasts, grinding teeth, thumping chests, howling in the halls. "Hey, doll, dontcha wanna meet the Blue Fairy?" The blue-shot boys roaming the quad, all flexed and ready to pounce. "Hey baby-doll, come sit with us, we don't bite," they'd laugh while snapping their teeth, arms reaching to pull at invisible strings.

The ladybirds and bears made their own ritual nights in the dorm. "Too good for us, are you, Cherry-Rose? Loosen up. You don't have to be such a bitch."

While the pixie-dust colored the nails of many at the William Hale Academy for Children of All Sorts, it also colored many dream-vision memories for Cherry-Rose.

* * *

"Sprinkles. Don't. She'll know. She always knows. Put it down. She'll be right back. Please put it down." Shy-Blue leaned on Sprinkles' arm as she pleaded.

Sprinkles pulled away, shielding their mother's favorite mug. "Shy, she is scaring me. This stuff makes her crazy. She is scary. This is wrong. All wrong."

"I don't know. We can't. Please don't do it, Sprinx. Please tell her, Cherry-Rose. Please. Not now, okay?"

Cherry-Rose took the mug from Sprinkles, considered it for a moment, and handed it back to her. "Come on, Shy, don't be scared. What's the worst thing that could happen?"

"I know, I know. We are already blah-blah-blah, but this is different. It feels ... I don't know ... bad. Worse than death bad. Come on, Cherry-Rose, you know. You've said it yourself. There are things worse than death."

"Shy, I know, I know, but I'm with Sprinx. Something has to be done. Do it, Sprinx. Just do it ... or give it to me ... Hurry. She'll be back soon."

When soon came, it was, "Girls. Sprinkles. Norma? Have you seen her? Shy-Blue, Cherry-Rose, have you seen Norma? Sprinkles? Look at me.

Girls … hello? Girls … GIRLS! Where the fuck is Norma? Where. The fuck. Is Norma?"

"In … the …" Sprinkles stuttered.

"In the what? Out with it, girl."

"In …"

"What?! Say it. Where is she?"

"In the …" Her hand finished the sentence, gesturing to the fire.

And we just sat there and ate the soup. All three of us. And I let her cut my hair while I ate. And we just sat there smiling while she used my hair to tie Sprinkles' hands.

"Hold out your hands, darling. That's a good girl."

Cherry-Rose was given the memory like a dream. She watched from beyond as three oblivious smiles beamed from three oddly posed mannequin-ghost girls seated at the funeral-birthday breakfast table. Three sets of wide-smiling teeth exposed beneath those gone-gone, bye-bye eyes, looking through everything, directly at absolutely nothing at all. Until Sprinkles was ushered out the door … until three smiles became two.

* * *

In school, Cherry-Rose learned that beasts, like the seamstress, were everywhere. Like the seamstress, they all needed the pixie-dust because they too were sad and lonely, or maybe it was because they had just forgotten who they were, or maybe they just gave up on who they could have been. *Did everyone's father live under the sea?* Whatever one was, beast or no, it seemed that the whole of the William Hale Academy for Children of All Sorts was intent on teaching Cherry-Rose a lesson that she didn't want to learn—that life on this stump-side of the forest was no different than life in the forest. Life here, just like there, was all about survival, the frenzied orgy of beast on beast, the fur, the claws—fangs of beast on doe.

Everywhere. Everything. It was all screaming, neon flashing to blot out the stars—

EAT … FUCK … DIE

Just John, Brother ...

FIFTH period. Ten minutes to the lunch bell.

Ten minutes, I should get out of this place. Just go. Leave today. They aren't here. They were never here.

What am I doing here?

From her desk angled just so, the room-length window at the back of the classroom gave Cherry-Rose cottage-window visions. Out there on the other side of the graffiti-etched glass, a clearing of sorts. The quad. It sat out there as if it were quietly waiting for its lunch-time ritual, its high-noon student orgy. A small amphitheater, spread beneath the sky, a nowhere, a nothing until the noon bell transformed the space into a swirling vortex of fury edged in wide concrete steps and red brick, all capped at one end with a row of classrooms.

A few days back, somewhere in her journal, Cherry-Rose wrote: *The lunch bell is like the sun setting on a full-moon night. Everyone is just waiting for a sign, for permission to go wild.*

Today seemed no different.

Eight minutes before the bell ... Cherry-Rose let her cottage visions run. She recalled wild eyes looking into the clearing, into the cottage, from behind a curtain of trees, waiting for the sun to set. The sun firing orange, red, and pink over the tops of the trees, spreading long, haunting shadows, the ivy moving with the dying sun as if a river of vermin and insects were growing beneath.

Cherry-Rose could see them now as if she were looking in from the trees. There stood a lust of mannequin-girls gathered at the window, each staining the glass with breath, nose, and hands, each one wishing the wish she wished in that moment on the mannequin-side of the glass. Each of them wishing to gain access to the other side of that glass.

Feeling all lost and sick about choosing *this* inside-the-glass life, the wrong side of the glass life at the Academy, Cherry-Rose stared longingly out her window. She spent much of her time writing, piecing together shattered dream-memories, and when the dreams no longer made any sense, she made new dreams and made new wishes. Today was for new dreams, for dead-moon wishes. Dead-moon-night wishes on a dead-moon day.

Cherry-Rose could almost hear the seamstress musing as she rocked and sipped from Norma. *Strong magic on a dead-moon night.*

Heavy magic, thought Cherry-Rose as she wrote out a few lines; wishes for her sisters and something new—wishes for a homeroom classmate.

If she stretched just a bit in her seat, Cherry-Rose could see him sitting just on the other side of the quad. Every day, ten minutes before the bell, he was there sitting with the guy everyone called Brother John.

His face in his book, probably still reading Jude the Obscure; *that's what it was, right? Jude? Jude.*

The words in Cherry-Rose's journal began:

Dear Blue Fairy,

He's got the Ju Ju Hand on my pinecone heart.

Ugh, he is so beautiful. Of course, we sit on opposite sides of the room. AND, of course, he doesn't even know I exist at all.

~ Homeroom strangers! ~

I wish that Gideon ... knew that I was alive.

I wish that Gideon would ... anything, before I leave, before it's too late.

One minute before the bell, Cherry-Rose could hear the classroom take a collective breath. Desks that once creaked and scratched at the floor fell silent; the second hand that flowed smoothly on its descent struggled on its climb. It froze every four seconds and made a sad, lurching ascent. As if timed with that staggered ascent, the teacher inhaled. "If anyone would like to, you know, work on their project during lunch, I'd be happy to assist. My door is always …" the teacher exhaled pale-blue words, "open."

Four seconds of lurching silence and her knowing smile crested with the ringing of the bell.

"Dismissed."

The bell triggered Pavlovian beast-drool, the lengthening of claws, the beating of hooves, the gnashing of teeth, the thumping of breasts, snouts to the sky. In a flash, desks dragged and moaned as chairs slid across the floor. Children of all sorts burst through the doors that penned them in, eager to find each other newly transformed under the naked sky of the quad.

* * *

The sound of the lunchtime rush gathered and echoed throughout the quad amphitheater. Brother John stood patiently and let it wash over him, seemingly unmoved and disinterested.

John Dashwood, a pair of forest-green eyes framed in black makeup—a thin bar of a mask. Hair, jet black, styled in a pompadour. Lips painted with a glittering something beneath that makeup mask. A small scar running up from the left corner of his mouth, extending his perfectly imperfect smile. On the scar side of his face, below his ear, a small black and gray tattoo: snake-eating-tail. His T-shirt, white. His leather, black. Sleeves pushed up tight. His jeans, worn and blue, folded at the bottom to reveal heavy black boots. Pockets full of tiny plastic vials. Vials full of pale-blue. Pixie-dust pale-blue in vials weighed out and labeled—little, more, and most—*Shoot Me, Snort Me, Fuck Me.*

Brother John stood poised atop the edge of a brick staircase, one foot up flat against the wall, leaning back into the cool shadow of a tall brick planter. Not hiding, but preferring the shadows. He watched the horde descend the steps to the center of this concrete nowhere, looking for *a nail that needs a hammer*, as his old man used to say. He stared out blankly into the chaos, looking lost in a dream behind his mask; looking out through and beyond the noise of swirling bodies, through and far, a thousand miles far, to take in the whole of the herd; to watch for the lame, the sick, or the stray, and then ...

Brother John spoke without violating his pose. "Jude the Oblique, the Oversight, the Obtuse. No, no. Jude the Obsolete. You ever gonna finish that book, Gid?" His eyes still looking through the last push of bodies pouring in from a distant hallway.

Gideon didn't answer.

John didn't expect him to.

For almost two years, it was the same thing every day.

Brother John leaned, watched, and breathed deeply through his scar-stretched and glittered smile, twisting it up all immaculately crooked and sickly gorgeous. Three deep breaths, and then on the third, to complete his lunchtime ritual, he exhaled and bowed over Gideon, who sat reading some antiquated something on the steps below, to deliver his daily quip.

"Gid, ol' boy," Brother John, sniffed at the air, "I have a good feeling about today."

Gideon didn't answer.

John didn't expect him to.

The same thing every day, ever since *this John* became the latest *Brother John*.

* * *

"You earned it, brother," said the outgoing Brother John. He coughed and managed a smile. His smile, a mouth full of white teeth, spilling red drool. His head tilted on Just John's shoulder. "Take ... care of him, Gid," as both Johns did a syncopated dark-alley slow dance. "Take ... care of him," between spits and spurts of red.

Ever since that day, it was the same permanent hall pass, the same red bricks, the same gang; the same three long, deep breaths finished with a bow. The same thing every day, ever since Gideon watched Just John slide and twist a switchblade up and under a surprised—no one sees the second switchblade—but deserving Brother John's bottom rib.

The same thing every day, ever since a gang of chirping Roaches swayed and pulsed with bloodlust. Ever since Just John's goodbye-embrace ended with a long, slow dip into a dirty pot-holed puddle.

Ever since Soon-to-be Dead John's red poured out to fill that puddle— to complete the transition, to make Just John the new Brother John.

Brother John lowered Almost-Dead-John's head into the growing mess of the alley floor.

Ever since Brother John genuflected in the filth and kissed Just-Dying-John's forehead. Ever since he spoke the last words Just-Dying-John ever heard. "It is a hard road, brother. But you knew the rules. What does the old man say? 'If you want to rule the school ... it's no pixie-dust for you.'"

* * *

Lunch time. As children of all sorts made their way to the picnic tables below, an off-set eye of a lunchtime storm formed with Brother John at its center. A dozen plus six Roaches had gathered to settle in for their daily round of prayer and parables. Brother John touched Gideon's shoulder. Gideon closed his book and took his place along the brick wall.

* * *

Gideon.

His name wasn't Gideon.

No one knew his real name. The school believed it was Gideon Dash-wood. It wasn't.

Just John knew his name once, although he never spoke it. One day, a long long time ago, Just John found a boy eating out of a trash can behind the Los Angeles Zoo. He was all long hair, backpack and plastic bag, torn jeans and tennis shoes. The boy looked about fifteen; he was thirteen.

"You alright, kid?" Just John asked.

The kid didn't look up. He didn't seem alright.

"Okay, not alright. Not from around here, huh?"

The kid stared hard as he pulled an orange drink out of his plastic bag and took a swig.

"Hey, kid, you like soft serve?" asked Just John sliding a board that revealed a secret entrance to the zoo.

One ice cream on a bench in front of the monkey exhibit and Just John got the story.

The kid was from somewhere in the Hollywood Hills. Had a sister. Mom died. His dad changed; he got worse once the stepmother came along. Things got weird and they eventually just ditched the kid.

"Dads are the worst," Just John said beneath the crunch of his sugar cone. "So, like, where's your sister?"

The boy shrugged. "Dunno."

"Like, gone? Or what?"

The boy nodded, seeming more interested in his melting ice cream.

"Hey, whatchu got in there?" Just John worked his thumb toward the backpack.

The boy kicked the backpack in Just John's direction. "Your dad ..."— Just John began to work the zipper on the backpack— "had to be one of those goddamn tweakers; they make real shitty parents."

Just John rifled through the backpack, grunted, turned it over, then emptied its contents out on the bench. "Books? That's all you've got? Fucking books? And this one, what the fuck are you doing with this? Gideon's Bible?"

"Motel." The boy wiped the back of his hand across his mouth.

"Sure, sure. Alright, *Gideon*," Just John teased, having already forgotten the boy's real name, "we won't be needing this." Just John tossed the book in the direction of the cage.

"Hey, Gid, you know *Rebel Without a Cause*?" Just John didn't wait for an answer. "I've got some work to do up at Griffith Park. Stick with me, kid Gid. I've got the hook up."

Cherry-Sad, Cherry-Stray, Cherry-Pop

As was determined in that alley so many moons ago, ever since that blood-in-the-puddle day, Brother John had been top Roach on campus. When he leaned, they swayed. When he spoke in his low, slow, sweet tones, they settled into silence. When he moved, they swept and dove and chirped, like a flock of carnivorous birds. And on this day, when Brother John saw Cherry-Rose skirt the edge of the quad and all its chaos, her head down, distracted and alone, dangerously alone and beautifully ripe, looking all stray and sad about it, perfectly, perfectly ripe, he smiled; they smiled.

Sad strays, *a true delicacy*. John pictured her on her knees, her face squared against the bulk of his blue jeans, and his smile widened, sending ripples through the flock.

"Gid, something timid this way comes. A beautiful patchwork stray, six o'clock."

"New girl. Homeroom. Cherry something."

"Cherry something? Hmmm, Cherry-Sad, Cherry-Stray, Cherry-Pop."

The flock of Roaches sensed a shift in the air, and they flowed to take up the wake of Brother John's gaze. All eyes became Brother John's eyes. Brother John's smile became their smile. Brother John's lust, their lust. Brother John moved out of the shadows and turned to better his spotlight gaze. The Roaches scattered, drifted apart, and then came together like a flock of birds floating in behind Brother John to make up a loose impending V. The V shaped a trailing cape of laughing, taunting, twisted humanity as John inched toward this fumbling doe on the edge of the herd.

Brother John slinked in slowly and smoothly, unnaturally so, like he was floating, like it was a lazy day on the boardwalk and he had nowhere to be. He moved, they moved, all gliding around the outer edge of the quad. Just behind. Gaining.

* * *

Cherry-Rose paused, flustered and distracted. She pulled at her satchel.

Brother John, closer.

"Where is it?" Cherry-Rose slowed as her hand dove into her satchel. She rifled through her bag, desperately seeking evidence that she hadn't left her journal behind in class.

* * *

Brother John approached with Roaches in tow, carving an effortless path through the meandering student body. Closer, closer—almost floating as if riding the morning mist, pulling his Roaches along with the lure of his thousand-yard smile. Closer, closer—just far enough behind Cherry-Rose not to be noticed, but close enough to pounce.

"Come on, don't tell me ... No, no, no." Cherry-Rose turned to run back to the classroom as images flashed—*chaos at the bell, journal in bag. No. Journal sliding past bag. Journal hitting the floor.*

One turn, one step and she ran directly into Brother John. She froze and his wake flooded in. The slow swarm of Roaches settled and inched and wove all around, forming a living circle, a wall of panting, heaving shapes. They were tugging, pulling, falling over each other on the edge of a tiny bubble made just for two.

I, I ... I'm so sorry." Cherry-Rose looked up to see Brother John's beautifully crooked smile beaming down. Taking a step back, Cherry-Rose finally saw that she was surrounded by a horde of Roaches—chirping, clicking, laughing.

Brother John raised his hand and their *clicks* turned to smiles.

"It's alright, baby doll. Where's the fire?" He lowered his hand, and those smiles began singing a soft round of "Frère Jacques."

Cherry-Rose scanned the Roach wall and saw the horde as a singular beast—all wide-smiled, all teeth with shining sparkling lips, all sick-painted eyes—moving as one, throbbing and pulsing to the beat of the song.

"Come back, baby doll, come back," said Brother John. "That's right, here I am."

Cherry-Rose looked back to find Brother John positioned behind a pale-blue bump of pixie-dust that was laid out on the back of his hand. It shimmered just between his forefinger and thumb.

"And there you are."

His hand lifted toward Cherry-Rose, toward those full, still fumbling, cherry-red lips.

"Hey, beautiful, first one's free."

In her few weeks at the William Hale Academy for Children of All Sorts, it was evident that Cherry-Rose was of a different sort. So much so, that it was rare that the other students spoke to her. It was not so rare that when they did, the words were heavy with rocks and sticks. It seemed that even among the other-normaled, the drooling beasts, and those electrified pixie-dust dreamers, Cherry-Rose was an outcast, feeling all forest freak, mannequin-nothing, all unwelcome ghost in an ugly shell. So, when the words came, whatever they were, and they did not come with sticks and stones, the pinecone beneath her stitches began to warm.

As his words sank in, Cherry-Rose understood their intent: flattery offered for complicity, or compliance, or some such thing. However, he could never know that she was armed against such snares and traps. Before the Blue Fairy had loosed Cherry-Rose upon the world, long, long nights in the cottage alone with the seamstress had prepared her for this Somewhere World. The seamstress, all high on her Blue Fairy gin, rocked in her chair and ranted her nightly rants to the clocks on the mantel, to the fire, to Cherry-Rose.

"Everything seems a bargain until it isn't," the seamstress warned. "They will show you something beautiful, and it will be. It will be the most beautiful thing you've ever seen. It will be beyond beautiful. Beyond anything you could have wished, likely something you didn't even know existed until this very moment. And darling-darling Cherry-Rose, they will want you to touch it. To stroke it. Smell it. Maybe even taste it. Yes, yes, just hold it for a moment with your eyes, with your fingers, between those cherry-red lips. Then they'll say, 'Darling, darling, darling … the first one's free.' They will beg and pout with soft, soft, soft, almost sad eyes. 'Nothing to lose, darling.' How can you say no?" The seamstress smiled a blue-lingering smile and said these words. "But, baby doll, they are takers, and they will do what takers do. They will take and take. And take, take, take until there is nothing left of you, and what's more, sweetie, they will have you paying for it the whole time. Beware, beware the bargain that comes sniffing for you."

The pixie-dust was indeed beautiful. It was reminiscent of the Blue Fairy herself. Pale-blue and shimmering, not unlike that pulsing umbilical smoke she sent to the moon not so long ago. Cherry-Rose knew this dust was false, just a pale-blue echo, but Brother John composed the scene so artfully. Without closing the gap between them, his forefinger managed to pierce the painted heart on her chest. Their connection shivered with invisible strings—the painted heart, the strings, the pale-blue shimmer set off against the white of his skin, all framed exquisitely in a black leather sleeve and spot-lit by a perfect smile. Cherry-Rose could feel it tingling with artistic intent.

"Dormez vous? Hey, baby, you in there?" Brother John squinted a little. Still holding his pose, perfectly still, beautifully still, not throwing stones, not throwing sticks. Cherry-Rose knew what Brother John seemed to know … he had her. She was there, doe frozen by the oncoming boy of the pale-blue light. Her false tattooed heart pounding, trying to leap off her chest, not because she was scared, but because she too was preparing to pounce.

Cherry-Rose wanted him to pull those invisible strings. To feel his hand upon her painted heart. To let the ivy surge of his ivy eyes wash over her so she might find *Her* again. Yes, to find *Her* again, she'd let the ivy wash over her body. Nothing else mattered—a last lover's embrace under the ivy green of his eyes, beneath that smile. *Yes, just once more, to remember that night on the altar.* Cherry-Rose was so lonely. *Just one little ... that's all I need.*

It was there waiting for her, and it shone like the moon of a million years ago, brighter, larger, closer, so close that its pull moved her insides hard against her chest like a surging tide. So close, its waves broke upon her pinecone heart like the sea crashing against the rocks on some forgotten shore, in some poem that Cherry-Rose might have memorized.

Roll on, Thou deep dark blue ocean ... roll!

She felt lost and dizzy beneath the waves of "Dormez-Vous." The pale-blue ebbed again, pulling at the sea in her chest, begging her to lean in. Just then, in that moment, Cherry-Rose might have remembered the words the seamstress gave her as she rocked herself into madness, but she didn't. She might have said that it was of her own free will that she denied her first taste of blue, but that wasn't so. Cherry-Rose swirled with the sleeping song that wove through the twigs, the vine, and the vermin in her mind, and she was pulled—deeper, deeper—in with the pale light of the pixie-dust.

Dormez-vous rang and she reeled.

She edged in toward Brother John's leading hand, she gathered her hair and pulled it to one side. Leaning in, further, further still—deeper, deeper—poised to give herself away entirely, to melt into the pale-blue, the leather, the smile. But just before she slid up Brother John's hand, from beyond the wall of Roaches, over and through the wall, a grinning, giggling wolf-girl appeared and tossed a small green notebook to a denim-clad boy hidden in Brother John's shadow. Gideon. *Has Gideon been standing there this whole time?*

Gideon with those deep brown eyes, those impossibly brown eyes. Whose black paint dripped from his eyes like soft tears. Whose skin was tan like a hide burned by the sun. Whose hair was jet black like a crow feather. Whose quiet pose, set against the madness of the moment, reminded Cherry-Rose what she had written in her journal that very morning.

Homeroom boy. Gideon in the corner. Jude-the-Obscure *boy. Let me be the pages. Read me. Speak your words over me. Mark me with your pen. Move your fingers over me. Trace my lines, my seams, my dreams.*

It was there in Gideon's hands, spine broken, book bent in half in belt-high hands, head bowed, Wolf-girl climbing over his back, pointing at a page. Laughing. In tears. Cherry-Rose could feel the stab of his eyes over her words. All her tragically romantic, horribly hokey, Jude the Obscurian homeroom-boy fantasies.

Mine. My journal. My poetry. My runes. My wishes. My never-supposed-to-be-seen ...

Her mouth fell open as if to scream. Brother John finally broke his pose. He looked over his shoulder, and Gideon shrugged at him.

Brother John turned back to face Cherry-Rose. "Last chance, baby doll."

But the spell was broken. Her gaze never left Gideon. Cherry-Rose watched as hands slid over her words. She followed them to the bottom of the page, down, down, down, each line appearing behind her eyes to turn her insides to jelly.

He paused for a moment, looked up through a crest of fallen hair. Hazel-rimmed brown eyes found hers. He closed the journal, tucked it beneath his arm, and mouthed the word ... "Run."

With that word, something inside Cherry-Rose snapped. In a flash, she became all wild and forest and doe. And she did run ... she ran as hard and fast as she could straight at the wall of Roaches.

* * *

Brother John held steady, entirely unshaken. He stood watching, the smile never leaving his face as Cherry-Rose crashed through the singing Roaches. Unmoved, he watched her fade into the distance as two Roaches in satin took his pause for permission. Within seconds, two feather-masked girls flew into frame to bury their faces in Brother John's hand. The moment was gone. Cherry-Rose was gone.

Snort. Sniff. Grind. Huff.

"Tut tut, baby birds, tut tut," Brother John said, smiling over the two bodies writhing before him.

Huff, grind, sniff.

Snort, kiss, tongue ... all beneath the gentle touch of Brother John's stroking hand; all to a chirping serenade of *"Dormez-Vous."*

* * *

When the feathered dance ended, Brother John turned to face the boy with the journal, and the horde of Roaches went quiet.

Brother John wasn't angry. He knew who Gideon was. They all did.

When the entire flock of Roaches followed Brother John with an imitation of style and mannerism that bordered on obsessive, Gideon alone stood apart. At first, Brother John felt this was so because Gideon had a healthy aversion to the greatest form of flattery. It didn't take long, however, for Brother John to change his perspective. Gideon didn't just act different; he was different. From the heart tattoo on his neck, to his painted fingernails, to the poetry scrawled on the denim of his jacket, he was the poet Roach. The quiet one who always seemed to prefer the darkest corner of the house of Roaches, who had no interest in pixie-dust games and feather-girl fantasies. And Brother John preferred him this way. All poetry in the face of filth, reminding him of a time before anyone called him Brother John. Gideon was poetry itself, hard to understand, but somehow all the more beautiful for his complications.

* * *

Brother John stood motionless in the center of the hushed circle of waiting Roaches—his crooked smile grew.

"Sooo ... juuuust ..."—he began to wipe his hand on his jeans to the beat of his words—"what the hell ... was that ... all about?"

His smile betrayed his tone. He laughed. They laughed.

Gideon blushed and bowed his head slightly, lifting it just as Brother John reached out and mussed his hair. "We lose more meat that way, don't we, Gid?"

It's a Blue World

IF ONE were to ask Cherry-Rose why she ran, she wouldn't be able to say. She'd say something like it felt like a million bees came alive behind her eyes, or maybe she'd say she was on the edge of something, on the edge of a moment where something inside was winding her up like a toy. One more turn and she might pop.

Standing there in the quad, Cherry-Rose felt all on edge, pressure building as she stood there watching Gideon read her journal. Oh, how the pressure built and built. "Dormez Vous" fed the stinging frenzy; and the buzz and the sting of those crooked smiles and that satin-wolf-hyena laugh filled her with poison. So Cherry-Rose, all seams on fire, all threads electric, all pinecone heart aflutter—all instinct, all survival—ran like a frightened doe.

Cherry-Rose ran and the world tumbled and crashed in and around her as she tore through campus.

On her funeral-birthday, Cherry-Rose was given many gifts, not the least of which was life after death. It was one of those memories that even the strongest spell couldn't shake. It was one of those memories that no magic could take. She had died. She had. And, having lived and died, if she was ever sure of anything as she ran from the quad, it was that she was in fact dying now.

This *was* dying. This was the end of things. Again. At the base of her gut, she could feel all those laughing Roach eyes, like claws to the abdomen, tearing her apart, spilling her insides for all to … for Gideon to see.

Her world was tumbling … school for forest, laughing eyes for death, Roaches for wolves; the world became a new funeral-birthday death-dream with Roach eyes that tore like fangs, pierced like claws, and howled like stalking wolves.

The kaleidoscope that was the rush of death fell in again … Cherry-Rose stumbled as she ran.

Shift.

… with Roach eyes that stalked like fangs, tore like claws, and pierced like wolves.

Cherry-Rose, faster, faster. She ran and limped and stumbled down the hallway that became forest. She couldn't bring herself to look, but she knew they were there.

Shift.

… with Roach eyes that pierced like fangs, stalked like claws, and tore like wolves.

It was fangs in liver. It was the long forever-kiss creeping up over her spine, over her shoulder, around her neck. A lover's kiss just beneath the ear and jaw, just there, shredding the meat of the fabric. No, it was Brother John, satin jacket-neck-scarf-wolf-girl, Gideon, and a dirge of "Dormez-Vous" Roaches, and all those sick lips with their sickening sick sick smiles and those cursed eyes; those chasing eyes who would take what they might and leave her for the ivy.

Again—again. All over again. This *was* dying.

Dying down the forest of the hallway, dying up the forest of the stairs, dying in the forest of the dorm; crying as she filled her satchel, crying as she tied her cape. Running, dodging, pushing, panting, stumbling until the din of the school became the din of the market and the din of the market became the familiar hum of the forest and the hum of the forest was drowned out by funeral-birthday visions. Cherry-Rose ran and ran until she fell at the base of a juniper tree. All fours, gut heaving, neck stretching, eyes watering. Her stomach turned inside out to spill pure adrenaline bile, to feed juniper roots.

When there was nothing left, no Roaches with their hungry biting eyes, no fear telling her to run, no bile left to spill, she threw herself onto the ground, not caring if the seamstress could sense her return. Hoping that she could. *Do it. Cover me with ivy*, thought Cherry-Rose, wanting nothing but the brief rest she felt on that first death-day, wanting nothing but the dark, empty space between fangs and her funeral-birthday.

She waited and listened to the breeze, but the trees did not stretch to obscure the sun, and the chimes did not chime, and the ivy did not chase. Still heaving on all fours, Cherry-Rose pulled and tore at the lazy ivy that lay around her doing nothing at all. She spat at it and cursed it for giving up so easily. Still, it would not cover her.

Maybe the seamstress was right. Maybe the world is too full of fangs and claws. Maybe I should have stayed in the cottage. Maybe I should go back.

She stretched herself out beneath a tree and pulled at the tall grass and clutched at the earth. She watched the clouds move. She watched the crows fly. "Hey, birds. Secrets for thread? Thanks for nothing." Cherry-Rose sniffled and wiped full, fat tears. "Thanks for nothing." She crossed her arms and lay her head down. She closed her eyes and breathed into the soft earth, "Thanks for ..." where she drifted off to sleep in the shadow of her juniper tree.

* * *

Cherry-Rose fell into a memory-dream, looking through the cottage.

"Thanks for nothing." Shy-Blue looked up from under a mess of Cherry-Rose hair—splayed out on the rug beneath the dreamer. "Who taught you ... to ... dance ... like that?" Shy-Blue's words came out in spurts, paced between laughter and tears.

"You did, you jerk! Thanks for nothing, yourself." The dreamer kissed Shy-Blue's lips to quiet her taunts.

"Okay, okay," Rey-Rey said as she pushed at the Cherry-Blue pile.

The dreamer tumbled over, erupting into her own bout of laughter and tears. "Next," the dreamer said with her palms pressed into her eyes. "Next song." The dreamer stood with Mojave's help and caught her breath. "Next song. Daisy's turn. Daisy, Daisy! Tonight is a blue moon; could you sing 'It's a Blue World'?"

"Frank, Ella, or Tony?" asked Daisy, standing in front of the hearth to a backdrop of crackling wood and clicking clocks. The seamstress, stage right beneath the window, played stagehand, sewing her bits and pieces, making performance dress alterations and matching accessories. "Here you go, my lovely," she said, handing Daisy a sash.

"Julie! Please, please, do Julie London." Cherry-Rose bounced on her toes.

"No way, Julie's your thing. Today ..." Daisy turned her back to her sisters and faced the roaring fire. "Pardon me while I get into character," Daisy said, glancing back over her shoulder. "Today." Daisy wiggled her fingers at the flames. "Today." She rolled her shoulders, snorted, and spit at the flames. "... Today ..." Daisy held one hand high and touched her chin to the opposite shoulder— "you dolls can call me Frank."

The dreamer saw herself standing there holding hands with Mojave and Sprinkles; Violent-Joy and Shy-Blue were leaning in from behind, trying to squeeze their way into the front row. Mannequin-daughter dolls, all on tippy-toes, swaying like swallows in flight, waiting for Daisy to sing. When she did, the gaggle of ghost-girls swooned at the sight.

* * *

The crows were wild at sunset, cawing like a cottage full of mannequin-dolls under a Frank Sinatra spell. They became part of the waking dream. They were between worlds. Cawing into the dream as Daisy sang. Cawing at the sun as it dipped to paint the sky pink. Cawing at Cherry-Rose who still slept in a forest, forgetting that mothers aren't the only beasts.

* * *

Cherry-Rose woke to a black-dotted screaming sky of birds that went silent as she sat up against the juniper tree. In a flash, the birds were gone. The only motion bled in soft and pink from the western sky. Coloring each cloud, raining down to fill all the spaces between the trees, painting the hazy twilight world in such a way that it became backdrop for her waking memory-dream. Out there in the twilight, still rubbing the sleep from her eyes, Cherry-Rose watched the cottage scene fade out just above the trees—Daisy's song still echoing through the pink haze.

"It is a blue world, isn't it?" Cherry-Rose said to no one at all. "No sisters. No clues. Nowhere to go. No one to …" Cherry-Rose sighed, thinking of the boy who told her to run. "It *is* a blue world."

Cherry-Rose stretched out against the juniper tree, wondering at whatever it was she was feeling. *Is this love?* It was hard to be sure. Love seemed much more complicated in the cottage. Whatever it was, Cherry-Rose knew that this felt different from doll-house love.

Eyes closed to the clouds that rushed past the crowded canopy, Cherry-Rose asked again, *Is this love?* and thought it couldn't be, it wasn't, it was, and began to sing "It's a Blue World."

* * *

The forest was full of beasts. Beasts that walked on four legs and two, beasts that swam, beasts that flew; beasts that crawled, slithered, and slid; beasts that bargained, begged, bullied, betrayed; and beasts that clawed, fanged, and fucked. But one beast, the likes of which she had never seen before, not from her cloudy, bubbled side of cottage glass, not from the halls, the quad, nor her desk at the William Hale School for Children of All Sorts, sat legs crossed, his back against a redwood. A beast whose nap was disturbed by the presence of another, who was entirely unlike any other.

The beast sat up at the echo of a song bleeding pure twilight melancholy. His eyes were still closed, but he could smell the pink hue of pain carried by the dawn. He was wholly intrigued, no … better … worse? He was enthralled by the disturbance.

The breeze carried the song, the song carried the essence: *Someone fragile. Someone sad. Someone, perhaps, in need of help; or maybe it is just my dinner,* he smiled to himself. *Either way,* he thought, *the sweet timbre that tells this creature's story is delightful. Lost, abandoned, lonely. Hurt, gushing … the song, like a chest wound bleeding badly. This song. This voice. This is a wounded creature in need of her mother … or her maker.*

This beast was indeed all beast, but he was also more than most. He was a bear of advanced intellect and need, who preferred the finer things: caviar over salmon; wine over water; and gold over dirt, dung, straw, and feathers. He was refined and sophisticated, but as he was starting to notice, he was also very hungry.

"Now, now, Salvatóre, we mustn't blindly serve our baser drives." He rubbed his belly and chuckled. "A voice like that does not wander through the forest every day. However," he reasoned, "if I can't be Mother, perhaps I *will* have to help this creature find her maker."

Salvatóre scratched the underside of his muzzle as he drank in the melancholic song. He smiled wide beneath the tree, showing the forest all his teeth. He let the song wash over him as he compiled a list of his favorite things: *Caviar, gold, wine!, and that voice above all others.*

"She's dancing." Salvatóre could feel her soft steps ripple through the earth. *Left, right, left;* he could hear the words warble and roll. *Oh, my dear, I could eat you up.* He could feel the loss, the hurt, the want trill out as Cherry-Rose moved beneath the boughs. *She's swaying;* he moved with her against his tree, smiling as the bark scratched his back. *Now she is twirling.* Salvatóre could taste the pain and the longing that sprang from the earth as she swept side to side. He heard her heart rattle with a fear that dovetailed into sadness; *She is lost. Like a lost, wounded creature.* Her song was a beacon of lonely light, of bright splintering heart wounds. Salvatóre knew this dance well; it was the beginning of the end of the chase. The moment the prey realized they couldn't run another step. It was the spiral that spun the desired to present their soft underside. A surrender announcing that they were ready to meet snout and fang, swinging paw, pad and claw. Because, whatever, however, somehow for those found in this dire state (Salvatóre didn't really understand it as much as he knew it to be true), running even just one more step seemed far far worse than facing his toothy grin.

Swaying, he smiled. *She's alone. So alone. Too too alone. This is indeed meat on the edge of surrender.*

He turned and stretched to find view of the voice that sent him that echo. Just behind, just over, and around, there she was, as strange as she was beautiful, dancing in a dirndl, white on black, a silvery cape tied over her shoulders, crow-feather hair flowing, the lightest pale green skin swaying, and those blood-red lips singing, humming, calling.

This one, she is like a bell. Her song ringing out to all those wolves and bears and forest jackals, all those other beasts with their baser needs, their less-refined wants, who would be quick to fill their mouths with her meat, or her mouth with theirs. Beasts! Salvatóre shuddered at the thought. "Darling darling darling, I will have to save you," he whispered from the shadows. "Yes, yes, yes, I will have to save you."

A plan came quickly. "Oh, green-forest fairy, you've made this one too easy." Salvatóre drooled as he scratched his belly. *One shouldn't spook such a creature,* he thought as he inched one tree, two trees closer. Quietly, silently, slyly, with clever-clever intent, he took a seat at the base of a tree in full view of the unknowing Cherry-Rose, as if he'd been there all along. Softly, sweetly, almost inaudibly, he began to hum with Cherry-Rose, smiling, thinking that it was indeed a blue world after all: *cobaltly, azurely, indigoly, sultrily, skyly, sorrowfully, sadly, and wonderfully.*

Wonderfully, wonderfully wonderful if one knew what to do about lost, wounded, lonely, green-fairy children.

* * *

Cherry-Rose heard a low hum accompanying her song. It was like a voice that might visit in dreams, but she knew it wasn't hers. Her dance wavered with doubt for a moment, but she continued to sing, peeking over bushes and around trees as she danced, never seeing the bear sitting like a forest pilgrim, cross-legged in perfect posture, in full view not twenty feet from her. When she had exhausted all of the less-obvious hiding places, she turned and found herself inches from a bear. Green-fabric nose to black snout.

"Hullo," said the bear.

* * *

Cherry-Rose had seen a bear smile up close once before.

Kerack!

With a crash, a wild golden bear stumbled through the cottage door—drink in hand, throwing each daughter-doll against the floor, the mantel, the bureau, the wall. He staggered, as if blind, onto the living room dance floor and balanced himself awkwardly against the wall. He slid forward, his free paw and claws dragging in support, etching a trail into the wall—leaving permanent evidence of his circuitous path. His slide was becoming a fall until he ran into an overstuffed bookshelf. His drink spilled on impact. His paw searched frantically for purchase, fumbling across the top shelf, scattering books upon scattered sister-dolls, but his balance was restored.

He was wild-eyed like those other-side-of-the-glass, full-moon-frenzy woodpile beasts. He smelled of sulfur, and blood, and meat, and smoke. His neck was stained a rusty red. His eyes were ablaze and fur on edge, looking all high on drink and murder.

The bear leaned against the bookshelf and examined the room while rubbing his eyes. "Mary, Mary, my Marybelle." The bear slurred, "My kingdom for a drink." He hiccupped as he wiped the back of his paw across his muzzle. "My kingdom," he said, laughing as if he remembered a joke.

The seamstress stammered as she picked up the books the bear had sent flying upon his entrance. "Uh-uh …" she coughed. "Just a moment, my dear." She scanned the room of scattered mannequin-girls and gave wide, frightened eyes, mouthing *play dead* to every corner of the room.

Shy-Blue couldn't hold her pose—the forgotten, wall-and-floor-seated ragdoll—slipping. Slipped. Her upper body slumped to join her legs at the floor. The bear spun about the room to locate the origin of the disturbance but seemed too impaired to identify its source. With renewed focus, however, he took notice of forms that had previously escaped his vision. The bear bent to make blinking eyes at a clump of unblinking mannequin-girls. Apple, Scarlet, and Mojave did their best to play dead.

"You are losing it, baby." He took turns locking eyes with Violent-Joy, Peaches, and Betty before he bumped the side of his head with his paw. "Losing it." The bear wobbled into the center of the room, then steadied himself. "Come on, baby, you just need a little *blue*. My kingdom for some pixie-dust."

He reached into the purse slung over his shoulder and pulled out a paw full of pale-blue. He moved paw to snout as if he were drinking from the moon herself, and he huffed and puffed and he snorted, letting the excess run down his chest to line his fur. Then he chomped at the air with beastly snorts, bouncing as if to shake the blue from his fur. Cherry-Rose watched the pixie-dust float to the floor—*so beautiful*—like a million falling stars. He stomped and stamped and grinned and howled and began circling the room, looking ready to pounce on whatever might need pouncing.

Playing dead isn't as easy as it sounds, thought Cherry-Rose. *It never is.*

Time slowed. It seemed like hours since the bear had broken in, but the record player told the time. Song two, side B of "At Budokan" told Cherry-Rose that it had been three minutes and forty-five seconds. She knew exactly how long it took to get to her favorite song on this album.

thousands of incoherent screams

"This next one ... is the first song on our new album."

From across the room, the bear's blue-shot, hazel eyes found Cherry-Rose against the wall.

"Yes, please and thank you," said the bear, pumping his right leg into the floor.

He sniffed and snorted at the air. He began to flex and his grin grew and grew. The smile was like none Cherry-Rose had ever seen before; it grew so large she thought it might split his face wide open.

"Surrender, baby doll, surrender," the bear's twisting smile began to sing as he danced his way toward Cherry-Rose.

There was nothing to be done but nothing, so Cherry-Rose doubled her playing-dead efforts. She made sure not to violate her pose, holding her head perfectly still, tilted just so, in the I-am-definitely-not-a-real-girl pose.

"What do we have here, honey?" said the bear as he swayed with the music in the direction of Cherry-Rose. "Have you been sewing companions for your Papa Bear?"

He turned to ask Mother—Marybelle?— and found that somewhere in the chaos, she had removed her apron and her dress and pulled on her ritual cape. She stood before the bear all wolf-breast woman, growling a low growl.

"Well, well." The bear bent his gaze toward soft-petalled pink. "You better watch out, honey, I'm gonna put some salt on your tail." His drunken sway steadied beneath his face-splitting grin.

Mary, Marybelle, mother …

The seamstress stood naked and motionless, growling at the bear, her arms extended as if to block her bedroom entrance. The bear huffed in return and dropped to all fours, and in a flash, he bound across the cottage. He swept the seamstress from off the floor and threw her onto the bed. The seamstress bowed to the headboard and growled and pawed at the sheets. The bear dug in behind.

Claws tore into the feather-bed and they rained down over the frenzy.

When the growls subsided, when the feathers had settled, when the lesson was over, the seamstress emerged from her room, tied the front of her cape, and moved to prepare water for tea. Without a word, the bear bound out the door on all fours, bringing all the playing-dead back to life. The sister-dolls dusted themselves off as their mother, who the bear had named Marybelle, apologized for the intrusion.

"I'm so sorry, girls. Don't be scared. He was just a little silly, is all. Just a silly silly bear. So much excitement. Let's get you girls off to bed, shall we?" Apple approached their mother with her head down. "Everything will be better in the morning," Marybelle said while drying Apple's tears. "The forest," a queue began to form, "it is worse than I imagined." Fae was next. "It is so dangerous out there and it is only getting worse." Marybelle held the corner of her handkerchief for Scarlet, Mojave, and Peaches. "It is so strange for one to come into the clearing on a moonless night." Shy-Blue and Betty joined the queue. "Even stranger that he should wander indoors." Daisy, Jasmine, Rey-Rey, Sprinkles. "That pixie-dust makes … animals forget their ways." Violent-Joy and Cherry-Rose.

"Now, now, my children, I am sure that you have many questions." Marybelle pulled at the sheets that held Betty and Scarlet. "So many questions." She fluffed a pillow and placed it beneath Peaches. "But, if you love your mother," she tugged at a duvet, "please save your questions for morning. Mother needs her rest. And Mother knows her daughters need their rest. All your questions will be answered in the morning."

"But …" Mojave began to sit up. Marybelle quickly extended a finger to Mojave's lips.

"Not tonight, Mojave." Marybelle made the shushing sound. "Get your rest, my darling."

And she shut the door.

When morning came, it was, "Now, now, my children, save your questions until we have broken our fast," but after breakfast there wasn't anything to speak of at all because there wasn't anything to remember because there never was a night of feathers flying, never a record that skipped to daughter-dolls crying. There never was a bear that knew their mother's name. No, there couldn't have been, because a bear never came.

* * *

Marybelle's smiling bear was dangerous, but this black bear with his auburn patch sitting before Cherry-Rose didn't seem dangerous at all. He was calm and still and smiling … sweetly? He seemed an entirely different sort of bear, and indeed he was. He wore a hat decorated with a single feather, tilted to the side, anchored by the one ear it covered. His visible ear was pierced with a row of small golden hoops. His chest hung heavy with gold chains, the largest with a pendant that spelled *Salvatóre* framed in gold like this—SalvatórE. Tight against his chest hung a large bota bag upon which his claws tapped out the "It's a Blue World" beat. He looked kind and refined. Approachable, even.

Cherry-Rose was cautiously wary, although this bear bore none of the marks of the wild beast that once shook the cottage. He seemed more like the always-walking-upright sort of bear. A dandy-bear with clear, bear-hazel eyes. No trace of hunger, no trace of moon-lust, no trace of pixie-dust.

There in the forest, beneath a juniper tree of bile and berries, before this very dandy-bear, Cherry-Rose realized it was much too late to play dead. Cherry-red lips to black snout, visions of feathers descending behind her eyes, she had to decide what to do about this humming, tapping bear. And before the "O" died in Salvatóre's "Hullo," Cherry-Rose had already consented to whatever the fates had in store. She took one step back, straightened her dress, and replied, "Hello, Mr. Bear."

Before she was able to wonder at the growing grin that became a laugh, the bear tapped the earth with paw and said, "Please sit and sing with me, green-fairy girl. Sing with me, 'It's a Blue World.'" He smiled, and without waiting for a sign that she might comply, he began to sing. His voice slow-burned low and warm like those voices on the 45's that she and Violent-Joy spun at the cottage—Nat King Cole, Frank, Bing, Dean.

She sat facing the bear, facing the tree, forgetting school, but not forgetting the boy with the heart on his neck, and she became someone else. She was not a lost and lonely doe, nor the scared, made-up, sewn together, mannequin-ghost girl who ran away from school ... She filled herself up with that voice, that bear, facing that tree, in that forest, and for just a moment, everything felt ... magically transformed. She sang "It's a Blue World," and she felt perfectly at ease.

When the song was finished, the bear said, "Hello, my dear, I am Silvio Salvatóre, and my Green-Fairy Girl, you have a voice that was made by sweet honey bees. So sweet. So sweet."

Cherry-Rose smiled. "But sir … Mr. Bear …"

"Silvio Salvatóre," the bear interrupted. "Call me Salvatóre." He pointed to the pendant that framed his name and gave a wink.

"Salvatóre, I am no fairy-girl. I am a …" She paused, realizing it wasn't often that she got to explain whatever she was to … anyone. "I'm a … doll. No, mannequin. No. I am a doll-girl."

"A doll-girl? Of the forest-seamstress?"

Cherry-Rose gave a slight nod.

"I've heard that she has her father's gift. Yes, it seems to be so." Salvatóre tilted his head to better examine her form. "Yes, yes … and did the seamstress give this green-fairy, doll-girl, mannequin-something a name?"

"I am Cherry-Rose."

"Yes. Yes, indeed. I should have guessed. You are indeed a Cherry-Rose."

Gold and Honey

Lost beneath a mountain, obscured by a curtain of trees dripping with ivy, sat a fountain. The fountain in the middle of a clearing became stream, stream became river, and the river wound its way through the forest. Mountain side, the fountain marked the path that flowed into a system of caves. The first and largest cave, seeming impossibly wide and impossibly deep, was Salvatóre's pride: Fontainebleau. He had transformed the cave, complete with spot-lit fountain, into the preeminent this-side-of-the-forest night club. Deeper still, smaller rooms that became dressing rooms, prop rooms, and offices made up the whole of Salvatóre's operation.

Tonight in Fontainebleau, a soft hazy red light revealed a great room dressed in red velvet, lined with belly-up tables, and red leather booths. Booths and belly-ups gave way to a hardwood dance floor that pulsed with bodies and bodies on bodies everywhere, beast upon beast grinding their Fontainebleau moon-ritual dance as the band warmed them up for the night's show.

Beneath the chatter of beasts of every kind, glasses clinked like muffled bells. They called and clanged and rang as if to announce seamstress magic. They rang with glasses full of gin, all ripe with fat olives that dripped their juniper and salt. They clanged with glasses full of whisky that swam with sweet blood-black cherries and the skin of a fruit. And they called clinking, ringing, singing—more, more, and more—begging to be filled. The bodies growled and the dancers grumbled and the beasts howled their growls and grumbles until their glasses were filled and filled again. And when they were, the replenished jerked and twitched and pitched all about the dance floor, impatiently waiting for those cherry-red lips to do what they did.

* * *

Cherry-Rose stood shaking behind the shadow-side of the curtain.

Cherry-Rose could feel the ivy chasing in her mind. She had to find a way out of her latest forest vision. Head down, fingers intertwined, she tried to conjure a happy memory. She focused on the tattoos on her forearms. She held Shy-Blue's lock and key in her mind for fear of losing control entirely.

Bile was building.

How long can this go on? she wondered.

Like claws in her abdomen.

How did I get here?

Warm in her mouth, like the long goodnight, forever kiss.

"Why, why, why do I do this to myself?" Cherry-Rose said aloud, wondering when her stage fright might begin to fade.

"Oh, my, my, my Cherry-Rose," said Salvatóre, gliding in silently behind—breathing soft words into her ear. "Oh, my green-fairy girl, why do you torture yourself so? Breathe. Just breathe. Like I taught you. It'll be over before you know it."

* * *

It had been a month. A month of nights like this. A month of this not-so-soft-side of the velvet uneasiness, a month of this shadowed side. A month of feeling Salvatóre's presence edge in behind, feeling his forever-grin carving the darkness backstage. A month of "just breathe" whispered out from the shadowed side.

A month, and still her parts and pieces got all twisted up at the thought of singing for anyone other than her sisters. Cherry-Rose closed her eyes and let the memory-dreams float in.

All of her sisters danced and swayed as Cherry-Rose conjured The Shirelles, snapping her fingers, shaking and dipping her shoulder with the ebb and flow of the "Will You Love Me Tomorrow" beat, belting that pure sweet honey. Even now, behind the curtain, she could hear them filling in their ghost-sister backing vocals. She could hear them howl their *ahhs* and *ohhhs* as they laughed and twirled around Cherry-Rose.

That is who we were. Cherry-Rose held on to the memory, trying to forget the seamstress, trying to forget magic, the soup, the spells, the hurt.

This is who I am.

It was hard to hold onto *those* memories. Pre-show jitters reminded Cherry-Rose of different cottage performances, when the cottage-audience began to fade into half-remembered nightmare dreams. And if Cherry-Rose let the bile have its way, its warmth would conjure those *other* memories. Those soup-dream, magic-vision, witch-mother performances where on the hearth she performed to an ever-shrinking sister audience.

Mother, do I have to? I'm so tired.

Magic dreams where twelve dancing and swaying sisters were culled one by one, leaving behind an eerie audience of five mannequin-somethings drained and twisted by layered spells of forgetting.

"Oh, deary dear, my Cherry-Rose, the show must go on."

Mojave, Daisy, Violent-Joy, Sprinkles, and Shy-Blue stood like sleepwalking zombies swaying in place to match Cherry-Rose's voice, all sleepy and melancholy.

Half-dead, half-sick, all-sad living-dead-girl dances. Feet grounded, arms hanging, heads lowered, bobbing slightly. Their shoulders moved slowly, perfectly out of sync with that beautiful, but dragging, slurring Cherry-Rose voice.

Five, four, three, two, none.

The performances wound on, even after Cherry-Rose performed to none but the woman with the blue-shot eyes.

* * *

The shadows on this side of the curtain liked to play tricks. If she let the shadows have their way, she'd see the hood of the wolf-cape bobbing in time with the rock of *her* chair and that chair rocking in time with Salvatóre's band. And at the base of her red stitches, she'd feel the click-click-click ... *CLICK-click-click* ... of blue-edged fingernails tapping out the beat on that blue-stained mug—counting in time with the click-click-clicking heels and hooves on the dance floor. Then she'd hear herself pleading ...

"Mother? ... Do I have to? Pleeease ..." drawing out her "ease" to the tune of frustrated surrender—bowed head and closed eyes; the quiet tap of the foot in sync with clenched fists that pumped a single pump at the floor.

And she'd hear the pixie-dust answer.

"Just one more for Mother, darling. Just one more, then you may sleep."

If the shadows had their way, the bile would build and ...

* * *

It had been a month since she met Silvio Salvatóre under that juniper tree. A month since he laughed and spoke the words, "Well, what do you do for money, honey?"

A month since Cherry-Rose answered with silence.

A month since, "No money, huh? Well, as luck would have it ... I have a business, a club. Fontainebleau, perhaps you've heard of it?"

A month since Cherry-Rose replied, "I haven't," and then she apologized when she saw Salvatóre's smile fade. "It's just that I haven't gotten out much. I went straight from the cottage to school. So, I really don't know much at all."

A month since Salvatóre recovered sufficiently to say, "No home? No school? No money? That is a hard road, but if you come with me to Fontainebleau, I could make you a star. If you visit my club, you will see that not only am I a clever interior designer, but I am also the forest's leading entrepreneur." He held his paw in the air as if counting claws. He ticked off his achievements.

"Designer, entrepreneur, an unrivaled talent-scout, and manager for only the best forest-born talent." The bear grumbled. "There used to be a fifth something. Well, never mind."

A month since Cherry-Rose replied, "Thank you ... thank you for the offer, but I'm looking for my sisters."

"Looking for someone? Are they lost? Or is it you?" He chuckled a month ago. "Either way, my dear, you *must* come back with me. Hundreds come through my club each night. You know what they say—if one is lost and would like to be found, one must stand one's ground. Come with me, Cherry-Rose. Come and be found at Fontainebleau."

A month since the erudite interior designer forgot to mention the "fifth something," that he was also a well-practiced and clever negotiator. "Yes, yes, lost or looking, being famous is the best way to be found. With that voice! If they are out there, they will come to you."

"A star? Famous?"

* * *

The red haze disappeared. The cave went black, and then a single spotlight hit the curtain to break up the shadows on the Cherry-Rose side of the velvet.

The bustle building in the black beyond the edges of the spotlight shook the floor. The beastly crowd was wild. Cherry-Rose felt as though the entire forest were here at Salvatóre's club tonight. She peeked through the red of the curtain and looked beyond the black of the cave to find the giant fountain glowing its faux Blue Fairy light at the club's entrance. Hoping as she did four nights a week, twice each night, to see the silhouette of some lost sister who might be called cave-side.

Nothing, always nothing. Always no one.

A light flashed from the pit and trumpets belted out their first notes.

Cherry-Rose swam in the empty nothing behind the long, thin slit in the middle of the red curtain.

She could hear Salvatóre's voice ringing in her head all the way from his side-stage seat: *Hold. Hold. Wait, baby doll. Wait. Wait for your cue. Let the bustle build. Let the beasts howl. Let the music from the pit tell the crowd when to settle.*

And she did.

She stood ready to pierce the veil. Like a breech birth painted mannequin-doll, she pushed one naked leg through the red slit and let it hang motionless on the spotlight side. Whistles turned to chorus howls, as if the band, the fountain, the dead-moon had shapeshifted the room into werebeasts. The pit light flashed again and the heel of the hanging leg touched down. Slowly, one hand, one arm … the other, then Cherry-Rose.

Let the bustle build and boil.

Every night, every time, for almost a month now, all the beasts hidden in the hot smokey black stomped and clapped and howled mad howls as she pushed her body through the crush of the red velvet curtain.

Her dress—black sequin, strapless, heart-shape over her chest, slit running high, high, higher to show that faded-green tattooed thigh that she teased through the curtain. The trumpets built their frenzy in sympathy with the crowd of beasts and then faded to cue the crowd to settle, to make room for the singer. Just then, two black sequin gloves hung, spread wide like a crow on a breeze, hands limp, all faux marionette; head tilted slightly to the side, eyes open wide, unblinking, lost out there on the blue-fountain horizon, teasing, waiting, holding …

Hands fell, head fell, gloves inched up the mic stand while cherry-rose-colored lips breathed the first words of the night: "I've Got the World on a String."

Her lips teased the mic. Her words poured out slow and full, hanging just above the smoke, all full of sex and scent, like sweet orange-blossom honey; hanging to drip its essence into hungry wanting, waiting ears.

For a little over one hour, Cherry-Rose shook the crowd. She held everything with a heart on the edge of ecstasy, filling those lusting eyes, teasing those drooling snouts, feeding those hungry ears pure, exquisitely, painfully slow and warm, all suffocatingly sultry Cherry-Rose.

To signal the close of the show, trumpets blasted as the curtain fell. The spotlight dilated and disappeared into the soft red. The floor shook, glasses chimed, beasts cried, and Cherry-Rose waited in the black to let it build. Again, to let *them* call her forth; as Salvatóre would say, "The waiting, it pulls them closer to the edge of madness. You'll know. You. Will. Know." He rolled one paw over the other. "Let the madness build."

Tonight, like every night, from the soft black back side of the curtain, she could still hear Salvatóre laughing as they ran through the set during their very first rehearsal, almost choking on his words as he laughed. "Gold and honey, Cherry-Rose, honey and gold."

The crowd began to chant her name—*Cherry-Rose, Cherry-Rose, Cherry-Rose*—and she could feel it—it was time. Out of the black, appearing as if out of nowhere, in the flood of a single spotlight, Cherry-Rose stood motionless at the mic, waiting for silence. Howls grew with barks and wild applause at the sight. In return, Cherry-Rose played near-mint, back-in-box, starlet with mic and accessories, waiting for the magic word that would allow her to speak again. She stared blankly through the crowd, beyond them, to the fountain ... beyond, to the slippery darkness that made up the forest night ... beyond, as if she weren't alive at all.

Cherry-Rose wasn't aware that she had let seamstress-lessons slip so easily into her performance, but alas, this was pure Marybelle. *The best way to bargain with a beast is to let them have their way for a while, and then ... when they think it's all over ... you have yours.*

Beyond, until the beasts grew tired of stomping and howling and having their way ... beyond, until she was sure that she had them.

Cherry-Rose spoke just above a whisper. "Thank you ... thank you for coming, I love you all ... You've been amazing."

Wait.

"Okay, Fontainebleau, this is it, my last song for the night," ... *wait ... breathe ...* "'Why Don't You Do Right?'"

The horns rang out, and in an instant, the crowd in the cave at Fontainebleau filled the dance floor, swinging as Cherry-Rose dipped and shook her shoulder to emphasize the "Why Don't You Do Right" plea. Then, on the last note of this last song, Cherry-Rose revisited her opening pose. Arms outstretched, eyes wide and unblinking, affecting a lost, lonely gaze that sent sad eyes far far away, somewhere out there, far, far, beyond the fountain. The trumpets squealed with her last breath and the air rushed out of the room as the curtain fell.

A collective sigh crushed in hard as the red haze of the house lights tore through the darkness to tell the crowd it was time to go home. When the sighs became grumbles and the grumbles turned to growls and the growls became howls, Salvatóre again became prophet. A wild emphatic applause was followed by the slow drip, the almost silent fall of wadded paper; then came the chime, the clang, the rain of coins. Paper and coins over and over until it sounded like a hailstorm trying to fill the void that Cherry-Rose left on stage.

Salvatóre was always first to greet her backstage. Always sure to remind her that he was always right about this sort of thing.

"Gold and honey, Cherry-Rose. Honey and gold."

Always You

CHERRY-ROSE was performing pure magical musical alchemy, just as Silvio Salvatóre had envisioned. *Lead to gold? Bah, buffoons,* he'd say, teasing the alchemically-inclined. *We make gold from honey. Honey from ragdoll.* Even more than magical musical alchemy, Salvatóre saw Cherry-Rose as alchemy herself: neglected, misused, a lower element of discarded parts and pieces. *She said it herself that day in the forest, no? A doll, a mannequin,* thought Salvatóre, feeling proud of his role as catalyst, no, as critical element for this transmutation.

An average shade of fabric, an unwanted spool of thread, the wasted garbage of the forest floor made into something wonderful, into the desirable, the valuable, the coveted, the rare and exquisite. Initially when he saved Cherry-Rose, Salvatóre felt like a thief who stumbled upon a lost treasure. *Mine all mine, with all rights and privileges, and so on and so forth.* But in their short time together, he had come to feel like a father to Cherry-Rose. If pressed, he might even say that he treasured her like a daughter, or rather, after a few bottles of wine, that he daughtered her like a treasure. Whatever the case, wine or no, Salvatóre trusted his bond with Cherry-Rose.

Despite his undeniable bond with Cherry-Rose, there was nothing that Salvatóre trusted more than his business acumen. Over the years at Fontainebleau, he developed theories anchored in the addictive rush of applause, earning potential, and the pull of fame. He found that the three, when operating in harmony, produced an unmatched spiritual experience. From his seat as Guru of Fontainebleau, he believed that Cherry-Rose had ascended to heights hitherto unachieved. There was just no arguing with the pure economics of their situation. Because this was so, Salvatóre tried hard not to break character—concerned father, guru, loveable bear— when Cherry-Rose announced that first thing tomorrow morning, she'd be leaving the cave for a few days.

Relax, Salvatóre. Relax, he told himself. Reminding himself, *There is just no arguing with what we have here, and besides, she has had a taste of fame. No one walks away from that!*

"I'll be back in plenty of time."

Salvatóre could hear the warbling in her words.

"Maybe even tomorrow. I just need to ..."

It's her stage fright all over again. Salvatóre could smell the warmth climbing out from her belly.

"I just need to check in. Who knows? If one of my sisters has returned, maybe I stay an extra day ... two days ... maybe three, no more than three. I will definitely be back before Thursday morning rehearsals. Definitely ... I would love for them to see me sing at Fontainebleau."

Salvatóre stroked his muzzle while he considered all the ways that he could mishandle this situation.

Fear, rage, the whip, a cage. No, no, Salvatóre. We are better than that.

He knew, most often, yes ... he *was* better than that. Besides, he had come to adore Cherry-Rose.

Salvatóre cast out the demons who stoked his wicked thoughts by silently reciting a mantra he had built from hard learned lessons—*Birds sing so much sweeter without a cage.*

Salvatóre measured his response. "Thursday, you say? Yes ... yes, of course my child.

"By Thursday, definitely ..." Cherry-Rose nodded and clasped her hands together at her waist. "Oh, I almost forgot, I have a new set I want to try.

The band has the music. They'll need a couple of days to dial it in anyway. Copies are on your desk."

See, she is making plans. Nothing to worry about at all.

"Of course, my dear. As you wish, my Cherry-Rose. Thursday, you say?" Cherry-Rose bounced in place. "Oh, Salvatóre. I was ever so … well, just a little nervous."

"Whatever for, my child?"

"Nothing. Oh, nothing." Cherry-Rose raced around Salvatóre's desk, wrapped her arms around his neck, and spoke without break.

"I'll be back Thursday to run through everything before the show. Don't worry, I know these songs inside and out. I know you'll worry. You're making that face. Don't make that face." She scrunched up her face to mirror his. "Don't make that face and don't worry. I just need to see if there is any news about my sisters. A clue. A sign. Something. Anything. I've been here a month and nothing. We're selling out every show and no word. I've been thinking, maybe they went to look for me at the cottage. News does not reach the cottage fast, or at all, you know? Maybe they're there and they just don't know where to look. Or maybe they are trapped like I was. I don't know. I just have to check. For peace of mind. You understand, don't you?"

Salvatóre, ever the entrepreneur, nodded along with every word and thought, *Well, even if she finds only one … no mother, no money, no strings … pure gold.* He rubbed his muzzle. "Yes, of course, my sweet, I hope you find them," said the loveable bear. "And if you do, bring them home to Fontainebleau," said the guru. "We have plenty of room in our cave. Don't we, dear?" said the father.

"Yes. Of course. Of course."

Salvatóre rested a paw on Cherry-Rose's head. "Cherry-Rose, dear, would you consider an …"

She was already shaking her head *no* beneath his paw before he laughed and finished, "an escort. Okay, okay, I thought you'd decline. At least let me give you a ride to the other side of market," he said. "Straight through the forest is so slow. I could drop you near where I found you on our 'It's a Blue World' day."

"Well, it is a long way." Cherry-Rose smiled and nodded beneath his paw.

"Yes, Salvatóre, yes. I would love an escort to our 'It's a Blue World' place."

* * *

Was it leaving Fontainebleau, the return to the 'It's a Blue World' place, or the looming return to the cottage? Whatever it was, it got Cherry-Rose thinking. *The world is a hard enough place, even harder when you are in the wrong place.*

Cherry-Rose knew plenty about being in the wrong place, and she saw the irony in her willful return to the wrongest of places. However, she wasn't returning to the cottage a broken mannequin-ghost girl looking to be absolved by her mother. That version of herself no longer existed. She felt entirely reborn since that day she died under the gaze of the Roaches, entirely remade since the day she emptied her gut at the base of that tree, entirely rejuvenated at Fontainebleau. She was going back, yes; but she wasn't *returning* at all.

Remade, or reborn, a casual-mannequin-visitor, or ghost-girl-liberator; whatever she was, as the carriage slowed, Cherry-Rose began to question the version of herself that thought this trip was a good idea. There was a small voice that wished Salvatóre had fought harder, or at all, for her to cancel the trip to the cottage. Though if he had, she still would have gone. Only, if he fought too hard, she couldn't be sure that she would have returned.

Cherry-Rose wanted to be strong, she wanted to be right about who she thought she was, she wanted to be the one to decide her own fate. So, when Salvatóre, who remained silent the entire trip, finally cleared his throat to say, "You know, if you'd rather, we could stroll about the market. Have some breakfast perhaps, and who knows," she somehow felt a little relieved that he attempted a small distraction, whose intent, Cherry-Rose believed, was surely to, with subtle yet clever design, distract her from leaving entirely. The nudge was just enough to propel her forward toward the cottage, and also soft enough that she looked forward to her return to Fontainebleau.

Cherry-Rose left Salvatóre's offer unanswered. She stood and kissed the top of his snout and said, "Oh, Salvatóre … Thank you for the ride. I'll be back soon."

"Promise?"

"Never," she said with a smile.

Cherry-Rose waved as Salvatóre drove off down the hill and through the market square. When he was out of sight, she walked the forest's edge until she came upon the stumpy knoll where the cottage path began and ended. She sat for a moment on the secrets-for-thread-stump, glaring at a murder of crows as they hopped and picked through the wet grass. "Hello, remember me?" Cherry-Rose dragged her feet in the grass as she addressed the birds, "I don't mean to sound ungrateful, but if I'm being honest, I can't help but feel … misled."

The nearest crow paused, *hop, hopped*. Head … *click-clicking*. Its closest eye *darting*, stump, satchel, antlers, lips, seeming as if it might respond to Cherry-Rose. It didn't.

"I see, we aren't …"

The crow didn't wait for her to finish her thought. It took flight and dragged the murder directly over Cherry-Rose in the direction of the cottage.

"… speaking," Cherry-Rose said to the empty grass as she pulled her seam-ripper from her satchel. "Sure, I did meet Gideon at school. As embarrassing as it was … I guess I should thank you for that." She lazily scanned the trees that lined the cottage-path while blindly stabbing the seam-ripper into the stump. Cherry-Rose stabbed and stalled and wished for the crows to come back; she wasn't quite sure she was ready to start her journey.

She turned to face the forest, still thinking of Gideon, wondering, *Whatever became of him*? She thought of homeroom, Jude, and the poems scrawled on his jacket.

To delay her trip, Cherry-Rose sat in the grass at the base of a stump, dug her seam-ripper into the soft soil, and began to carve a heart. She traced heart-grooves deeper and deeper while she remade Gideon's denim poems in her head for her own use. "Sonnet 53." Thinking, *My substance is flotsam.* "Love Sonnet XI." *I Crave Your Mouth, Your Voice, Your Hair.* Feeling, *I crave your neck, that tiny black heart on your neck.* "Music, When Soft Voices Die." Wishing, *I want to sing softly for you.* "I Carry Your Heart with Me." Dreaming, *After I find them, I'll find you.*

When the poems faded, Cherry-Rose carved 'cr' inside the heart, made a plus sign, then looked up into the forest to consider the path that led to the cottage. From her stump, she could see that the path through the forest was all but swallowed by grass, leaving the thinnest river of earth as a trail. It looked like it had been quite some time since anyone had come or gone down the path that led to the cottage. None since she, Cherry-Rose guessed, but she hoped that she was wrong. The forest did have a way of closing in quickly. *I really could be wrong,* she reasoned while thinking she wasn't.

Perhaps someone found another way, at least one of the twelve. Anyone. Perhaps there are other paths that lead home, thought Cherry-Rose, believing there weren't.

Cherry-Rose struggled to find the strength to leave her stump.

Into the soil, inside the heart, just below the plus sign, she dug a deep-grooved capital "G." When she finished, Cherry-Rose let out a long sigh and stood to admire her work. "First things first," she said and turned to face the forest.

"I don't know why I am so worried," she said, straightening her dress. "There is no reason to worry any longer. Things are different now. There is nothing to fear."

Left foot.

"I know how her magic works."

Right foot.

"She has no power over me."

Left foot.

Cherry-Rose carefully stepped onto the cottage path. One step in and she paused to listen for threshold chimes. Nothing, only the rustle of branches. "Perhaps she is sleeping," she said, continuing deeper down the path. There were no chimes, there was no trace of magic, yet the forest appeared to be aware of her presence. With each step, it seemed more alive. With each step, its branches inched further into the clear spaces that once held sky. With each step, the moaning trees shook the tall grass and roused the ivy.

Cherry-Rose held still to measure the warning. There seemed to be no intent to chase, no desire to wash her beneath the ivy. No sign of *her* magic. She addressed the trees.

"Pardon me, please, Forest. I will do no harm. This was my home. I am … I am coming home." Cherry-Rose spoke with an eye on the ivy.

Forest paused, Ivy paused, leaving the echo of its rumble running through her mannequin-frame.

"Don't you remember me?" asked Cherry-Rose, pulling on her antlered hood. "My bones are here. It's me, Cherry-Rose. Fawn-girl," she said, feeling a little silly for thinking the hood might help.

Forest stood silent. No wind. No rustling leaves. No motion on the forest floor.

"Fawn-girl, yes. We remember."

With the echo of the forest still ringing in her head, the boughs moved to release the sun and the wind blew and parted the grass to show the ivy lining the edge of the earthen path.

"Welcome home, Fawn-girl."

Cherry-Rose gave a slight bow and considered the word *home* as she walked on.

Home? What do I know of home? What is home, anyway? Can it be home when it is the wrongest of places?

Wondering, *Why did I even say that? Home? The cottage wasn't a home. It was a lie at best, and at its worst, it was a cage, a trap, a strange sort of purgatory she made to keep me from leaving. Do I even have a home? Maybe it is here beneath these trees. It was. Maybe this is where I am supposed to be—with my bones. Maybe I was never supposed to leave. No, no, I was. Everything dies, and when it does, it leaves. But I was never supposed to come back. At least not now. Definitely not like this.*

By the time Cherry-Rose considered all the ways that home was the wrongest of words for the wrongest of places, she had reached the edge of the cottage clearing. She hid her frame behind the last tree that edged the clearing, that faced the cottage. "Careful. Danger, danger," she whispered into the bark of the tree.

It only took one eye to see that Forest had been hard at work while she was gone. It leaned further into the clearing to claim the sky. Ivy too. Ivy who, until recently, had never gone long unchallenged, unpunished, un-hoed, crossed into the clearing and climbed up and over the cottage. From where Cherry-Rose stood on the edge of this shrinking clearing, she knew Ivy's intent. This was Forest's promise—cottage as gutted doe.

Looking on at the ivy-shell of the cottage, Cherry-Rose thought, *This isn't my home. This isn't anyone's home. It's just … bones.*

No signs of life, Cherry-Rose moved out from behind the tree and crossed the clearing.

Could she still be alive? Couldn't be. She'd never let the ivy take her if she were alive.

Cherry-Rose found a long, wide, splitting crack in the wood of the ivy-covered door. Without actually knocking, she whispered through the crack, as an uneasy visitor might, "Knock, knock." When no one answered, "Hello?" She waited, listening for movement. Nothing. She pulled at the ivy and found a hole of a knot in the door. "Marybelle?" she said over the hole.

Marybelle? thought Cherry-Rose. The name sounded wrong, all wrong. Having never uttered her mother's name before, it crawled out of her throat timidly, unnaturally—so wrong it sounded like it was spoken with a voice that was not her own. But, as she reminded herself before she spoke again, Marybelle would have to do, for she would never again call *her* Mother.

"Anyone home?" Cherry-Rose slowly pushed the door open, breaking Ivy's hold.

The room that was home to a dozen ticking clocks and countless clicking records, that was often stage and dance floor, was silent and cold. Cold and silent and it shrank beneath a cloud of smoke that hung from the ceiling. The cottage reeked with the smell of earth and stank with a hint of sulfur. There were signs of struggle. A struggle, or madness. Broken glass, books torn to shreds lying next to a smashed father-grandfather clock, all its parts and pieces scattered on the hearth. The surviving clocks were left unwound and silent, faces frozen in horror from witnessing whatever they witnessed. On the funeral-birthday table, dust, marigold, a roll of familiar faded-green fabric, a jar of glass eyes, another with black buttons, and some loose thread wound halfway up the leg of an almost-finished form.

From where she stood, Cherry-Rose could see that Marybelle's bedroom door was open. A giant pouch hung on the nearest bed post. She had seen it before—the night-bear, the stumbling bear, the feathers in the air, mother-naming-bear. Marybelle's huffing snorting blue-shot hazel-eyed-bear. That was his pouch. His pixie-dust. Beyond the post, in the corner, hidden on the nightstand, a faint blue flame came to life … blue, bluer over orange glowing coals. An umbilical hookah arm reached into the darkness beneath a wolf snout, reaching into a form shrinking beneath a wolf-cape shell.

Marybelle? Cherry-Rose tiptoed closer.

It was Marybelle, but it wasn't. Like the seamstress who was Mother, but wasn't. She wasn't any of these any longer, if she ever was at all.

Not Mother. Never Mother. Marybelle? No, not Marybelle, not anymore.

Whatever she was, she was something altogether new beneath her cape and hood, breathing and heaving like a sick woodland beast.

Cherry-Rose stood stunned for a moment, unsure how to address her maker.

"Hello" was all she could think to say.

Eyes widened beneath the hood, and the form gave the slightest twist of a smile.

Cherry-Rose crept closer still to the smile beneath the hood.

No. Not my mother, not anyone's mother at all.

Cherry-Rose watched the snout inhale blue and fire; coughing, spitting blue-gray smoke and phlegm. She was all animal now, sounding all sick and riddled with disease.

Cherry-Rose moved closer. Too close. Close enough to see that the hooded eyes shone all gray-blue-cataract haze.

The shape made gravelly whispers from under snout. "Come closer … closer still," she coughed and wheezed, the words sounding as if they scratched and crawled up from bile and bowel. "Come closer. Come. Come." Coughs ripped and tore as a reaching hand raked at the air. Its long nails and pale-white skin, sick and veined with blue.

Cherry-Rose didn't know why, but she did move closer. From the furthest bedpost, she found her way to the side of the bed and stood looking down at a sick shadowed smile framed in Shy-Blue's long, blonde hair.

"You don't know how lucky you are."

Milking the hookah. Exhaling blue-gray.

"Born …" Drooling hatred and piss. "… Without a heart."

Cough … wheeze … the back of her hand trailed, leaving a smile of blue-edge teeth.

"Lucky, lucky, lucky."

The shape laughed through the phlegm, her wolf snout shaking through the convulsions.

"Dolls don't need wishes, do they?"

"Marybelle? … Marybelle?" Cherry-Rose struggled with the word. "Marybelle," she repeated, half to hear the sound again, "I need to know … where are my sisters?"

The wolf snout bobbed as the face beneath the hood snickered at the request.

"Who … is … Marybelle?" said the shadowed figure as it choked out each word.

"I … am Mother."

"My sis …" Cherry-Rose paused, realizing that Marybelle would be more likely to help if it were for her benefit. "Your daughters … are …

lost. I would like to help you find them. Can I ... help you? Please ... please let me help you find them."

"Gone," said Marybelle with a gravelly voice. She lifted and shook a shivering hand as if she were shooing a pest out an invisible door. "Gone. All gone."

"But ... who ..." Cherry-Rose was interrupted by that shooing hand.

"Boys and bears," she coughed.

"Women and wolves," she smiled.

"Witches and thieves," she laughed.

Disbelieving the cold delivery of each line, Cherry-Rose stared hard into the hazy blue-gray cataract eyes, hoping to find a sign of the person she used to know.

There is nothing there, thought Cherry-Rose. *Nothing resembling a mother.*

Marybelle spoke again, as if to drive home the point. "They all loved your sisters so."

Cherry-Rose thought she could detect a disgusting sort of satisfaction in Marybelle's voice and wanted to reason it away. "But, but ... aren't you ... sad at all? I ... I ... I thought—"

Marybelle interrupted Cherry-Rose with a mocking tone. "But, but, but ... you, you, you. Always you," wheezing as she spoke. "Ungrateful. You heartless little ... doll. You think you are best, don't you? You think you are better, don't you?" Marybelle gasped and drew in a few shallow breaths. "I ... I made you." She growled as she choked through a cough. "And *She* ... *She* came to you?" Marybelle beat the hookah arm against the nightstand. "You took ... *She* was mine. Thief ... You little thief.

Such a dirty thief.

Father warned me; the forest is full of takers."

Before Cherry-Rose had knocked on the cottage door, before she crossed the forest, before she even left Fontainebleau, she had resolved not to feel anything for her maker. She had resolved not to give in to emotions that might let the seamstress manipulate her. She promised herself that there would be no tears, no sorry, no sadness, no anything, no nothing. But promises were hard to keep in the cottage and at the edge of Marybelle's bed, beneath the crush of her maker's words, there *was* sadness and there *was* sorry and there *was* too much to name.

When Cherry-Rose sighed at giving into her feelings, when she lifted her hand to dab her eye, Marybelle sat up straight and shot a thin, pale hand out from beneath the cape to snatch Cherry-Rose's arm. It dug and pulled; Cherry-Rose tumbled until she found herself seated on the bed, staring straight into Marybelle's blind, blue-gray cataract eyes.

Cherry-Rose pulled against the grip, but she found herself unable to break free.

Marybelle shivered and spoke. "Mother … *She* …" Blind eyes began searching the room as if to protect a secret. "Mother … she told me that … you'd … betray me." She wheezed and breathed her hate like syncopated poetry.

"Long ago … Mother came in a dream … I should have … listened. Mother said … I'd be betrayed by the one I loved most. I stitched you up … I gave you life … You were mine.

"I … I made you … I loved you. You are mine. And you … Always you."

The pale hands with their mother-claws dug deeper into Cherry-Rose's arm. Cherry-Rose felt the words cutting; and the tears that she swore to keep locked away began to well again.

"Always you."

The words drove into Cherry-Rose and spilled a single tear onto Marybelle's gripping hand. At the touch, her claws released and Marybelle settled back against the headboard. Cherry-Rose looked up to find the hood of wolf settling over a smile on Marybelle's face. Fur, and snout, and fang hung over blue-gray cataract eyes. Marybelle relaxed, soft and heavy. Forever.

Ceremony

Everything dies.

Cherry-Rose sat unmoving at the edge of the bed, trying not to let the moment run away with her. Trying to remind herself *everything dies. Everything is supposed to die.* Thinking, *This is the forest and this was Mary-belle's DIE in the eat, fuck, die of it all.*

Because this was so, because this was the way of things, and because the blue-cataract beast was no longer capable of expressing otherwise, Cherry-Rose sat staring into the void beneath the hood, trying not to slip into the madness of the moment, trying to find a way to hold onto herself. "Everything dies." She ended the phrase with a soft, surrendering *hmm* at the irony of her own existence.

As Cherry-Rose spoke the words, a flash of pale-blue, the slightest sparkle, began to drift from the bed to the floor to the door. She rose and followed the butterfly-light as it flew toward the marigold on the funeral-birthday table and disappeared.

"No ... no ... no." The words came out slowly with each trailing step. Then, "No-no-no-no-no" all at once as Cherry-Rose began to realize what was happening. "No. Please. How?"

As soon as she asked "how," she knew. She flashed to the shape laying on the funeral-birthday table ... and it ... It moved. The almost-finished-mannequin-something, all sewn up with no eyes, no nose, no mouth, no face. It began to quake and shudder and slither on the table. Its rattling arms steadied. They pressed to arch the back of the legless beast; its face stretched toward the ceiling. The flat faceless form scanned the room like a blind snake who could feel the heat of one who wandered too near its nest.

There were no eyes to see, no nose to smell, nor a tongue to taste, but there was motion beneath the fabric. It seemed to swarm with life, like a million beetles were crawling beneath its skin.

Cherry-Rose, hands to mouth.

The vermin beneath the fabric moved furiously and pushed out against the void to give it shape. Face—eyes, nose, mouth—Marybelle? Searching blindly with fabric eyes. Seeming to mouth silent curses with sealed, muted lips.

A gasp escaped Cherry-Rose, and the Marybelle-shaped-something whipped its head to find the source of the vibrating sound. Still blind, still silent, still searching. Arching, bending, writhing. Then …

The beast lay its head on the table with shivers lurching and rattling through its form. Almost as soon as they began, the shivers settled until the beast shook with one final quake. In seconds, the room swung from madness to silence.

Cherry-Rose crouched down to sift through the litter that covered the floor. She picked up a broken piece of glass and held it over her head, ready to strike. With her free hand, she guided herself along the wall and angled to move in from behind the form. She inched toward the back of the table. Closer. Closer still. Her leading, empty hand guiding along the table's edge. Just touching the …

The form lurched to life, knocking the glass from Cherry-Rose's hand. It thrashed for a moment and then crashed back down onto the table where the beast began to shake and writhe, beating its head against the wood, over and over and over. The flat, expressionless face pounded into the table with a horrible thud and the crunch of a thousand broken things. It thumped and thrashed and beat itself wildly until its seams split and it spilled its putrid, rotting contents—feathers and fur, beetle and roach, maggot and almost-uncle meat, paper and ribbon—until a pale-blue butterfly-light escaped to fly through the cottage haze, to the hearth, and then out the chimney.

The feathers flew and mixed with clouds of dust that rose to meet the hazy smoke bound up in the rafters. Cherry-Rose crumpled onto the floor. One eye to rafter clouds. Feathers falling like snow to decorate her body. Cheek, eye, hand; arm, leg, lips, feathers.

Somewhere in the rafters, Cherry-Rose saw Marybelle's last days unfold.

Death approaching. Needle, fabric, thread. A sick, sick, and sicker hand shaking as it cursed the eye of a needle. She knew time was running out. The end was coming fast. Too fast. Not enough magic. Not enough time. Her last mannequin-shell was shaped too late. Cherry-Rose turned her head toward the hearth, and there on the stone, she could see the book resting on top of her funeral-birthday quilt. She crawled to it and found feathers splitting pages titled "Leviathan" and "Levitate." Cherry-Rose traced the spell that called the ivy—*Leviathan.*

It wouldn't take much magic, reasoned Cherry-Rose, *to ask Ivy to do what it has always wanted to do.*

And the quilt. It can't be a coincidence. Did she use the quilt to call me? She did … She tried to … She was trying to trap me here with her beneath the ivy.

Cherry-Rose closed the book, stood, and returned it to its shelf. "Nothing left behind," she said as she kicked at her quilt, realizing she would never truly know if she came of her own free will.

It was too much for Cherry-Rose to believe. She began to swoon her funeral-birthday dance all over again. It seemed the seamstress, even in death, was still spinning her about the center of the room. Spinning. Wanting to unbelieve it all. Spinning to bring the fallen feathers back to life. Spinning. Her legs followed her eyes as they swirled around the room, piecing together this crooked story—to the book, to the mannequin shell on the table, to the bones on the bed, to the ivy on the window, the window, the window, to the floor, to the door, to the chimney.

She called the ivy, to seal me inside. She ... they ... they were waiting for me. She was holding on ... for this ... to suffocate me under the ivy.

Cherry-Rose saw the almost-spell of an Ivy death as a waking dream.

The cottage was adrift on a forest sea. Ivy as Leviathan reaching out, up, beyond, bursting through the surface-edge of the clearing. Fat tendril-arms breaching, swarming, reaching ... up, over, across. Covering, holding, winding, winding, winding to break the cottage-hull of this rudderless forest-ship.

As the waking-dream unfurled, as if to complement the scene, the cottage moaned, and creaked, and bowed beneath the weight of the ivy, snapping Cherry-Rose from the daze of her dream.

Cherry-Rose glared at the mess on the floor and sat on the rug to let the moment settle along with the feathers.

Surely, this could have been much worse. The mannequin form wasn't finished. The cottage was still standing. Quilt or no, she must not have had the strength to complete the Leviathan spell. Called or no, thought Cherry-Rose, *it didn't matter. If Marybelle had any magic left, she would have ... but she didn't ... she couldn't. And now, she is gone forever.*

Cherry-Rose lay on the rug, content to become part of the mess until she could decide what to do next. She considered the ivy covering the windows and the long reaching beams of soft light that managed to find their way between its leaves, and thought, *The sun is going down.* She spoke to the ceiling. "There isn't much time. There is work to be done."

Cherry-Rose leapt into action and collected her three mother-shells—the mannequin-shape, the hooded cape, and the mother-bones. She wound them in a bedsheet and dragged them to the woodpile.

To the shed for tools.

Before a wall of shivering, clicking, Marybelle almost-mourners, Cherry-Rose dug a shallow grave.

If there was a way ... If Marybelle's cataracts had cleared, if the eyes of the hood could shine with life, if the mother-doll had eyes at all, if the knot of the winding sheet had given way—if there were a way—those eyes would have seen Cherry-Rose on her knees hovering over their hole. They would have seen her poised to push a pile of earth behind two hands shaped in a wide V. They would have seen her stop and tilt her head thoughtfully. They would have heard her say, "I can't believe it, I almost forgot," and they would have seen her disappear from view.

Moments later, they would have seen her return against the backdrop of the twilight sky. They would have seen her stand over the grave, priest, shaman, thief, daughter, holding a book as if she were about to deliver a eulogy, a soliloquy, or spell. However, she spoke no words.

Cherry-Rose opened the book titled *Graveyard Diary of Not-Mother Names* to its middle page, the one split by Shy-Blue's pencil, and she read silently from the left: *Stevie, Carol, Eddie, Connie, Joanie, and Jean*. Cherry-Rose flipped through the book and scanned hundreds of names. Each page four columns of tiny, tiny, Shy-Blue print, each page, dozens upon dozens of not-mother names, of mothers who were never there, of mothers who perhaps ... would have mothered differently.

Cherry-Rose took the pencil that split the book, and on the page's blank, yet-to-be-filled side, she wrote the name *Marybelle*. She closed the book, bent down, and placed it atop the winding-sheet. There were no tears, there was no sad, there was no pain, no emotion at all, not even joy. Knees in earth, hands in a V, Cherry-Rose filled in the grave.

When the hole was filled, Cherry-Rose rested at its edge with side-swept legs. She patted the mound of fresh earth, and thought, *perhaps ...*

Into the soft earth, Cherry-Rose wrote the name *Marybelle*. She considered it for a moment and then wiped it away. She then wrote *daughter* and considered it for as long as it took for her to complete the word. That too she wiped away. At that, she stood and straightened her dress, dusted herself off, and spoke to the mound. "Your mother was right; you *were* betrayed by the one you loved most—your father."

Cherry-Cordial

IT WOULD have been easy to walk away, to leave the cottage in this state. But Cherry-Rose had sisters to consider.

They could be out there, and if they are, they'd come home, wouldn't they? They'd have to. There is nothing else; the forest, the clearing, the cottage, this is where they'd come because there just isn't anywhere else to go.

Windows torn open, freed from Ivy. Door pried open with a rock. Time for fire. Time to burn. Time to clear Marybelle's death scent from the cottage. There was plenty to burn, so much to burn.

First, Cherry-Rose filled the fire pit in the middle of the clearing. Fabric, anger, thread, and hate; glass eyes, rage, and buttons and lies and lies and lies; the parts and pieces of a broken clock, envy, and a pixie-dust pouch; and wishes, and dreams, and too many seamstress memories.

Next, she prepared her space. She pulled the rocking chair to the porch and lay her funeral-birthday quilt over its back. She angled the chair just so, standing behind it for a moment to ensure that the arms framed the fire pit.

Last, Cherry-Rose crouched over the fire pit and set the kindling alight. When the flames began to spread, she took her seat in the rocking chair and watched the flames devour the waste. She needed to see it all.

She needed to see the fire rage on into the moonless sky. To make sure that the fire took what it could.

The fire grew little by little until it roared with a fury, hate to heat, fuel to ash, spilling the last of the seamstress into the sky. Much like Marybelle's mute-mannequin shell, the fire spent its fuel quickly, flames futilely beating hard against the night. In no time, the flames surrendered to ash and flickering coals. It was in those coals that Cherry-Rose lost herself. She watched waves of heat rise from the coals that warmed the white bed of ash. Somewhere in that pit, beneath the white ash and the black of night, beneath her quilt, Cherry-Rose found sleep, full of dream.

No sun. No moon. No dark. Just blue, sky-blue. But there. Over there. Way out on the edges. Over the trees. Pushing up from the mountain horizon. Something was stirring.

As soon as the dreamer registered the something, it began moving in from the edges. A cold, gray-black darkness began to take shape on the edge of the dream and push into the blue from both horizons. At the center, between the dark horizons, a forest, and at its center, a clearing that sat beneath sky-blue void, an empty spotlight of blue firing straight up into nothing, blueing up and through to pierce oblivion.

Beneath the blue, at the center of the great void of the blue oblivion, the cottage lay fallow. No. It was gone. As soon as it was there, it wasn't. Below, not the cottage, but Cherry-Rose. Only Cherry-Rose.

Was there ever a cottage?

Cherry-Rose. Always Cherry-Rose.

Cherry-Rose just there, rocking her chair over Marybelle's grave.

From nowhere. From above. From beyond the blue sky. From sleep. The Cherry-Rose beyond looked down through the blue of the dream to find herself dead to the world save for the soft tilt of her left foot that kept the rocking chair in motion. The dreamer watched the mannequin-Rose girl below, full of ash and earth, all red lips against the screaming blue of the sky, rocking her chair into the soft earth. Cutting deep, deep, deeper grooves into her mother's grave.

The sleep swam in sadness. A sadness that sank into and through the dreamer. It was as if everything Cherry-Rose burned that night, everything that became fire and fury, that became the ash and ember ascending into the night, every word that Marybelle spat while Cherry-Rose sat at the edge of her bed, cut a gaping wound into Cherry-Rose's chest. It was as if her pinecone heart were anchor for the crushing blue sky and the chasing black, the weight of her anchor driving her deeper and deeper into the soil.

The Cherry-Rose from beyond the dream tried to speak—wanted to speak—couldn't speak. She gave the dreamer flashing images. Gideon mouthing *run*; Roach faces taunting, *dormez-vous*; Satin-wolf-girl laughing; forest-wolves chasing ... *Why won't you run?*

The Cherry-Rose below, who swallowed the sad, sad sky to pull in the black, just sat and rocked in her chair. Mouth open. Eyes open. Chest open. Her hands gripping the arms of the chair as if the chair itself was keeping her from folding into the void of her own chest. Meanwhile, the dreamer beyond the sky felt sick at knowing what was to come. Sick at knowing that the Cherry-Rose below was still sinking. Sick at knowing that the beasts she buried were trying to add one more to the grave.

From above, she watched the dark edges of the dream become clouds of ivy that swam with a swarm of knotted shadows. Shadowed somethings. Bodies. Hard, black-green tendrils churning the dead, turning piles of warm rot. On the leading edge of the dark horizon, in the wash of the ivy-sea, fat ivy fingers pushed up inside twelve mannequin-ghost-girl shells to play puppeteer. They were writhing, reaching, crawling, hanging sisters, all wide empty-eyed, mouthing a silent warning ...

The Cherry-Rose beyond the sky cried for the Cherry-Rose below. She felt helpless out there in the beyond, but there was nothing to be done. The dream was set. This was happening. The ivy edge of the dream had reached the chair.

Cherry-Rose was no longer above and below. There was no longer a dreamer and a dream. There was only Cherry-Rose in that chair, the grave, and the ivy. She could feel the dream shake as the ivy pulled and snapped the wood of her chair. She could feel the ivy winding up her arms and legs, pulling, dragging, digging, making her marionette, twisting her form and her face to greet her hanging sisters. The ivy pulled hard at Cherry-Rose's black mane, forcing her head back, her eyes open, splitting her cherry-red lips, wider and wider to swallow the last blue of the sky.

The ivy wound tighter. It began to burrow, to dig, to root into the earth of her form until it spat buds that bloomed full cherry-red blooms; beautiful cherry-red corpse flower blooms that reeked their death musk, stinking their rot to call the dead.

Blue sky swallowed. Gone. Above, nothing but dark skies, churning ivy clouds. Below, the rocking chair shattered entirely. Gone. Cherry-Rose falling apart. Limbs bound by ivy, she lay over her mother's grave, becoming part of the soil. Ivy weaving through, down, deeper still. Cherry-red death blooms now bursting from her open chest, splitting her breast, spilling her parts and pieces, reeking her death-scent to call her maker. And she came. Wolf, doll, rotting mother reaching up through the earth to meet the dreamer's descent. Ivy, claws, hands digging into form and fabric, pulling down, down, down. Hands driving up Cherry-Rose's torso, over bloom, breast, neck until they covered the red of those lips, until cold cataract eyes held the dreamer's Jupiter eyes, until the corpse-mother whispered, "Oh, baby, you should have run."

Birdsong

CHERRY-ROSE woke slowly, sensing that something had changed, but remembering nothing but the fire. She opened one eye and was surprised to find herself still on the porch, in the rocking chair, beneath the quilt. In a breath, she found that her memory placed her just where she sat. She held perfectly still and scanned the clearing. A low fog slid languidly between the porch and forest. The chill of the pre-dawn mist was heavy and laced with dew; and despite the odd feeling she had running up her seams, she found nothing out of place.

Cherry-Rose dragged both the chair and the quilt back into the cottage. She repositioned the chair over its grooved spot by the hearth, folded the quilt, then tucked it beneath an end table. It was then that she saw a small silvery something on the floor.

"What's this …" Cherry-Rose bent to retrieve an L-shaped spoon hidden along the edge of a piece of almost-uncle firewood. "So many …" Cherry-Rose settled onto both knees before the small pile of wood to find a litter of L-shaped spoons hidden in the corner. Their image shot her full of moon-market memories. They told Cherry-Rose that Shy-Blue was exchanged for … who cares, whatever, and a box of chocolates.

"Look, darling, look. They're just like you," the seamstress offered, biting through a chocolate something to reveal an oozing red center. "It's a cherry-cordial, baby. You're a cherry-cordial." The seamstress threw the other half of the treat somewhere within the shadow of her hood and said, "I could just eat you up."

The memory had the dream in tow and it rushed in to take her breath. Cherry-Rose fell back, climbed a chair, and stumbled into the funeral-birthday breakfast-table—reaching, flailing, spilling paper and pencil onto the floor. Cherry-Rose followed with a thud. Knees to hardwood floor, back arched, hair hanging to surround the edge of her paper where she wrote out her dream with a furious hand. A dream of blue and sadness, of marionette sisters and Ivy. A cherry-cordial dream in which she was the center. A dream in which her mother tried to eat her all up.

When she finished, she folded up the paper, wrote runes on both sides, and tied it with red thread. "These are words for tonight's fire."

Cherry-Rose tucked the paper beneath the quiet clock in the center of the mantel, setting its pendulum in motion and disrupting its perfect dust outline. She ran her finger through the dust and said, "This morning is for cleaning, clues, and The Cramps. Let's see what we can see while we set this mess in order. First things first." She pulled a stack of records from the shelf. "Some Poison Ivy for the ivy dream. *Smell of Female*." She managed an uneasy laugh, still trying to shake the image of her body bursting with cherry-red death blooms. She lowered the needle and Poison Ivy twanged her guitar. Lux howled out "Thee Most Exalted Potentate of Love," and Cherry-Rose imagined Gideon calling her Turtle Dove.

Cherry-Rose began by winding the clocks. Each running at its own time, beginning anew from wherever they left off. "I just like the tick-ing," Cherry-Rose shrugged to the room. Next, Cherry-Rose dusted the records and shelves that lined the walls. The record player was spinning *Smell of Female*, Side B, when she noticed an empty space in a shelf that should be holding books. In a flash, she ran to the shed, emerging with a box of books that she dropped beside the funeral-birthday table. Cherry-Rose made two more trips and set out two more boxes as the record player pulsed its runout-groove beat—*thump, tha thump, tha thump.*

Cherry-Rose spilled the books onto the table, dozens of books of all sizes. Books like *Dream Walking, The Many Hidden Things, Full Moon Magic, Dead Moon Magic*, and *Clockwork Spells & Sewing Secrets*, but these books were too tall, too fat, too many—they were not the books missing from the shelf. No, they couldn't have been—*tha thump, tha thump, tha thump*. In the last box, the box buried beneath the others, and tucked into the furthest corner of the shed, Cherry-Rose found what was missing from the shelf—a stack of notebooks written in familiar mannequin-sister script.

For as long as Cherry-Rose could remember, all the sisters wrote. If they weren't dancing and singing, and playing games between the phases of the moon, they were writing. On any given day, half a dozen mannequin-ghost girls could be found bent over their notebooks. Apple sketching her dresses, Scarlet scratching out her poems, Daisy and her songs, Rey-Rey and her recipes, and Sprinkles and her histories. And at the end of the day, one by one, each daughter-doll returned their book to the shelf, until one by one, like her sisters, they too disappeared from view and memory.

Cherry-Rose remembered, not long after her funeral-birthday, Sprinkles interviewed her so she might write *her* story—*thump, tha thump, tha thump*. "Now, don't be shy, Cherry-Rose. This won't hurt a bit," said Sprinkles, holding a pen over paper—waiting for Cherry-Rose to settle into the idea of having her wolf-bleating dream set in a more tangible form. "I always start with Mother's version, you know, after her *Knowing* spell, and then an interview, and then I dream to fill in all the empty spaces."

In time, Cherry-Rose did give Sprinkles the story—snout in soil, fur on bark, a sweet patch of wild strawberries that diverted her attention ... blinking at the twilight sky before she felt the weight of hungry eyes.

Sprinkles told her how rare it was that she could recall so much detail. "Many stories," Sprinkles said, "were harder to recall. About half needed a dead-moon séance intervention. But Fae, Peaches, Violent-Joy ... they seem to have dream-memories like yours where the past hasn't faded in the slightest. Vi especially."

Cherry-Rose turned the notebook now to find Violent-Joy's scrub-jay story, remembering that she had such a different feeling about her change—almost as if she didn't mind at all. As if it were a game. As if it were welcome—*thump, tha thump, tha thump.*

Strawberry Moon. Happy birthday, Violent-Joy.

Cherry-Rose read the first line and recalled the cottage birthday ritual. It was the game they played for each mannequin-ghost girl, reenacting their origin story as written by Sprinkles, as told by the dead now living on their funeral-birthday. Cherry-Rose read the words aloud, and Violent-Joy's birthday ritual came to life on the cottage floor—*tha thump, tha thump, tha thump.*

Violent-Joy stood in the center of the rug wearing an off-white, knee-high nightgown and a feather mask. She turned slowly, finger over lips, under beak, eyeing twelve sisters and one mother who stood in a circle holding hands while facing the mannequin birthday. When Violent-Joy completed a full turn, she spoke.

"The Brightest Light"

"The sun was warm on my wings—behind, falling slightly toward the top of the trees. When I turned to climb toward the sun, I saw a sky bluer than Shy-Blue's eyes."

Violent-Joy smiled a wicked smile, for Mother always said that nothing was bluer than Shy-Blue's eyes. She held the smile for a moment, then gave a nod, and the room came to life. The room swayed with a flock of mannequin-daughter-dolls in scrub-jay masks. Twelve masks of feather, glue, and string fitted to twelve spinning, swarming, squawking sister-dolls. Climbing over furniture, over each other, arms out as if in flight. Each sister rose and dove and swirled around Violent-Joy in funeral-birthday tribute.

"I was following a grasshopper."

The seamstress *hop-hopped,* and the girls screamed and chased and the seamstress laughed and cried and shrieked. Violent-Joy stood upon her toes and raised her voice to be heard over the din of the room.

"It dove into the tall grass of the clearing"—everyone in mask froze—"when I saw a swarm of bees."

The mother who was grasshopper became buzzing bee.

"The bees moved like a cloud, just where Mother plants her garden."

Violent-Joy whispered each word with a peculiar rhythm, and the seamstress swayed and buzzed and twirled to make herself a swarm.

"I did—I do love bees so. I surrendered the grasshopper and dove for the bees."

Twelve girls in mask kaa'd and crowed and laughed and made arms like beaks and mouths like beaks and ate the bee who was laughing Mother.

"But bees, they are so small, and they were so many. More and more I chased and laughed and filled my belly."

The mother who was swarm danced between the chomping mouths of her twelve masked daughters.

"Three more bees and the sun caught my eye."

The seamstress threw herself against the door as if she were chained. Her face writhed in horror as she pulled a tiny mirror out of her dress and shined its reflected light on the narrator. Violent-Joy began to whisper, shading her eyes against the flashing light.

"The grasshopper was there waiting for me against this very cottage window"—Violent-Joy pointed to the window beyond her mother's rocking chair—"teasing me with his bright shining light. So, I surrendered the bees and consented to play his game. I turned and climbed and climbed into the fat belly of the sun, higher and higher"—the girls in mask began to move in a slow circle around the whispering voice—"higher and higher"—walking faster around the slow counter-spinning narrator. Faster and faster, running with the rise in Violent-Joy's voice. "Faster and farther until the sun, he stole my breath."

The girls stopped and turned and glared at the seamstress who was taunting-grasshopper-with-shining-mirror. "Then." The girls in mask all took one sneaky step toward the shining light, "I," and another. "Then I," and another. "DOVE!"

Violent-Joy bent toward her mother and threw back her arms as if in flight. The room kaa'd and crowed and screamed as those in mask charged the shining light. The face behind the light shrieked and yelped and began to laugh as each feathered girl smothered the mother-light. All thirteen daughter-dolls fell down, down, down, dying thirteen scrub-jay deaths in a pile at the foot of a mother who was grasshopper.

—*thump, tha thump, tha thump.*

The day was lost to the pages, one funeral-birthday ritual running into the next, until Cherry-Rose began to wonder a new wonder.

These stories, these endings, did they really occur by chance?

Cherry-Rose eyed the other books spread out before her on the table with their leather covers and their strange words and read Shy-Blue's title again.

"Silly Sad Fox, Big Bad Eagle"

Shy-Blue had taken a bow and explained, "Silly because foxes should know better than to come out into the open—shouldn't they, Mother?"

Cherry-Rose recalled Marybelle's smile and gentle nod and knew that nothing in the cottage ever happened by chance.

She turned the page, and the title of her own story cast out the image of Shy-Blue as fox being tickled to death by twelve dive-bombing-sisters as golden eagle.

"Twilight Fawn"

Her eyes itched and burned and welled from the strain of so many stories. Cherry-Rose ran her fingers over the page, tracing the tiny antlers Sprinkles had drawn sprouting from the furthest edges of the "T" and the "N." She paused there and looked out the window to find the pink of the sky spilling over the edge of the trees and her twilight-memories began to swirl. *Snout in soil. Velvet on bark. Hoof on moss.*

—*tha thump, tha thump, tha thump.*

Cherry-Rose closed the notebook and said, "We have done enough today, haven't we? I do believe it is time for our fire."

Cherry-Rose gathered all the notebooks and returned them to their proper place on the shelf, pocketed the dream she left under clock—*tha thump, tha thump, tha thump,* and … "Oh my … I completely forgot about you," she said, just realizing that the record player had been spinning and thumping all afternoon. She silenced the record player, put a matchstick behind her ear, and set out for the clearing to lay uncle-limbs in the pit. "Not yet. Almost," said Cherry-Rose, sitting cross-legged in the patchy grass surrounding the pit—waiting for night to take hold.

Above the clearing, moments before the violet sky swallowed the last of the pink, the first stars began to shimmer. Cherry-Rose leaned forward, and with a scratch upon the stone of the pit, she set the wood alight. The flames took hold and quickly pumped their fury into the sky. She pulled at the red-threaded bow that held her dream. Thread in fire, she opened the folds of her paper and held out a corner to feed the flame. The fire bit slowly—testing, then faster faster until Cherry-Rose was sure it would take it all. The flames chased her words, and she threw the dream into the pit— watching the paper becoming a floating twisting mass of orange-edged words that quickly ran black. Equal parts seemed to settle into the pit as others flew into the night. The words were gone. The night took them as per their agreement—she to paper, paper to flame, flame to ash, ash to night.

Constellations slid above the void of trees that the clearing made while Cherry-Rose watched the flames become coals, and when the coals had no more heat to give, she covered them with earth and dusted herself off, ready for sleep. So, to the door, across the floor, and under the covers, Cherry-Rose tucked herself up for a night's sleep.

In her bed beneath the window that framed both the stars and the thinnest chalice-moon, in the cottage that still echoed with the dream she sent into the fire, Cherry-Rose tried to prepare herself for a night of different dreams. She imagined her words floating off to some fictitious place, where the Blue Fairy slept, where Marybelle words didn't cut so deep, where mothers weren't made of bitter bones, where Gideon was Lux … and she, Turtle Dove. Where … she wasn't … alone.

In sleep, dream eyes search a bedroom window for the moon and it was there, now fat and full, shining with blue feathered rings.

"A storm," said the dreamer, "I feel a storm is coming."

Her words called to the night and shook the rings from the moon. They tumbled to the earth—titan, bear, wolf, doe, lover, light—more falling feather of light than drop of rain, more ash on the breeze than shooting star. Closer, closer, closer still, straight toward the cottage, straight on for the bedroom window. Until Cherry-Rose found herself face-to-face with a tiny electric-blue hummingbird floating just there on the other side of the window's bubbled glass. But as soon as it was there, it was gone.

The Cherry-Rose beyond the dream could see the bird hovering over the firepit, beating its wings furiously, whipping the wind, conjuring a storm. Clouds swept in full of thunder and rain; and the wings beat a frenzied wind, stirring leaf and ash—lightning, tearing the ivy—thunder, shaking the earth, faster and faster until the clearing itself was on the edge of a tornado.

The cottage rattled and shook and the dreamer who watched from her window dove beneath her covers, pulling them higher, winding them tighter against the violent storm.

Louder, stronger, faster the cottage moaned a horrible moan, and the roof of the cottage was torn from its frame. Walls exposed … wind ripping, clawing, tearing. Clocks flew, banging their chimes and bells straight on into the Never. Records spinning, crashing, scattering out into the Nothing. Books, toys, and pieces of wooden boys splitting, thrown out into the Void. Nothing remained but the chimney, a few walls split, broken, cracked, and culled to half their height, and the dreamer unscathed, hiding in her bed somewhere beneath her covers.

When the cottage was swept clean of all but the dreamer, the humming-bird turned to the sky. Again, her wings beat a wild wind and blew the rain and clouds from the dream. The Cherry-Rose beyond saw a diorama in decay. A small fire beneath a crumbling chimney, a bed, and a frightened something quiet beneath the covers. The only motion, the electric-blue hummingbird who turned and dove toward the chimney. It hovered there just above its smoke, darting an inch left, then an inch right, and back again until it hung there perfectly still as if riding the gray clouds between a blind blur. Hovering until it turned its beak to the night and then dove again into the chimney.

Wings and flames and smoke flashed upon the hearth where the electric-blue hummingbird appeared, like ash, like a feather, to become the Blue Fairy gliding in step toward the dreamer. Bedside, the Blue Fairy pulled back the covers to find Cherry-Rose curled up in a ball, knees touching elbows, hands over ears, eyes closed tightly, sheets stained with tears. The Blue Fairy slid into the bed, hummingbird, goddess, lover, dream, and held Cherry-Rose. They lay tucked up into each other, shining full-moon arms wrapped around a pale-green waist, and pale-green hands wrapped over full-moon arms.

Breathing. Shivering. Holding. The Blue Fairy hummed a strange milk and honey song —and the dreamer answered.

> *There will be pain*
> *I am not afraid of pain.*
> *There will be more pain*
> *I am not afraid of pain.*
> *... Much more pain?*
> *There will be death*
> *But I've already died.*
> *There will be death*
> *I am not afraid of death.*
> *There will be a wide sea*
> *My grandfather sailed a sea.*
> *There will be a whale*
> *My uncle knew a whale.*
> *There will be blood*
> *I am not afraid.*
> *There will be blood*
> *I have no blood.*

Cherry-Rose awoke from the dream and was surprised to find that she was alone. Her moon-light lover was as real as she wasn't, as everything in this almost-life seemed to be.

It was as real as Her first visit, thought Cherry-Rose. *As real as any mannequin-doll dreaming Blue Fairy dreams. Is anything real at all?*

Cherry-Rose peeked over the edge of her bed, searching for echoes of the dream. Ceiling and walls intact, she glanced out her window, searching for an electric-blue anything. There was nothing but the sun's faint glow just bending through the trees. She noted that there'd still be some time before it burned through the wispy fog that hung in the clearing. Still feeling the echo of the dream, she climbed out of bed to see if the clocks and the books and the toys and the records managed to remain in this world. From her post at the frame of her bedroom door, she could see that they had. With a sigh, Cherry-Rose quit her watch for the strange and out of place and turned to climb into bed ... and there on her pillow, perfectly centered in all its electric-blue, a tiny feather. Cherry-Rose pressed the feather in her hand, folded her arms over her chest, and fell back to sleep.

When Cherry-Rose woke again, the sun had already swept halfway across the tops of the trees. She followed the light that slid in through the window and found the seam-ripper on the funeral-birthday table. With it, she worked the seam that edged one side of her inked heart and tucked the feather inside. "I shouldn't want to lose this," she said as she sewed herself up.

When the feather was tucked away, fluttering in place over her pinecone heart, she sat at the funeral-birthday table and wrote out her dream.

... something about a hummingbird and a storm ... Ivy and ash. Something about death and pain—something about blood and feathers—a feather.

Penny for Your Thoughts

CHERRY-ROSE could sense a change. Nothing overt announced in the shift. It was subtle, but it was there all the same. The feeling, it was much like the bird-song dream. As if something blew through the forest, the clearing, the cottage, and purged the hate from the soil and sky and left it somehow precisely, exactly the same, but somehow altogether new. The shift, whatever it was, also swept through Cherry-Rose, telling her she had to stay one more day.

She couldn't leave the cottage covered in ivy. The seamstress may have hastened Ivy's arrival and fueled its assault, but with or without the seamstress, the ivy was still Ivy. There was no way it would retreat on its own. So, it was decided. She'd have the cottage in good standing before she left *… for whoever might come.*

Cherry-Rose headed out to the shed to find the hoe and the shears. With tools in hand, she spent the day reclaiming the cottage and the clearing. She began tracing the edges of the clearing and she snipped the fat vines that fed Ivy's overreaching arms. She pulled at the leaves and the knotted limbs that covered the cottage. Then she raked the waste into piles wherever they fell—one, three, five, seven piles. As the sun began to sink, she stuffed each pile with uncle-arms and legs, dried weeds, and grass.

Decorated each pile with a dried flower edge. Topped each with a woven crown of daisies and waited for the sky to swallow the sun.

Cherry-Rose sat upon the stoop of the porch and watched the night move in from the eastern horizon. When the last of the light was chased from the clearing, she wound one, three, five, seven bouquets of marigold with twine. Next, she pulled three black hairs from her head and tied them around the dream she had folded up inside her pocket.

When the night was ready, Cherry-Rose stuffed her dream inside the nearest pile of waste, touched match to a bouquet of marigold, and then placed the torch upon the tower. Again and again, one, three, five, seven twirls as seven torches lit seven piles of waste. Cherry-Rose watched from the porch as the fires quickly spent their fuel on towering flames. In no time at all, the flames were reduced to seven smoldering black moons burned into the ground of the clearing.

Cherry-Rose saw herself reflected in those black moons and that smoldering ash. All smoke, no fire. Nothing left to give. She was thankful that the flames too, were ready to turn in for the night. So, she shoveled dirt to quit the ash, to seal this cleansing, so that the cottage, the clearing, so that she might be free from the sickness that marked this place.

Cleansing complete, Cherry-Rose made for the cottage door. She dropped the shovel at the foot of the porch—she was ash; and she kicked the rock from the front of the door—expired. Feeling all hollowed out mannequin-ghost shell, Cherry-Rose dragged herself to her room. She settled beneath her covers and pulled her funeral-birthday quilt over her head, like dirt over ash, so that the night might let her rest.

Sleep came quickly, as did dream.

Cherry-Rose appeared in the middle of a wide dark sea, beneath a wide dark sky.

Nothing to see but black, nothing to do but swim ... or sink.

Treading water. Entirely Lost. No light, no hope, Cherry-Rose was feeling wet and blind in the womb of the Never until out there on the furthest edge of the dream, the black everything of the sea and sky was split by a faint light. The horizon was drawn by the crown of the rising moon.

The dreamer swam for the moon.

The moon was full and fat on the belly of the sea. Its light echoed out over the swells churning moon-mirage on top of moon-mirage until mirage was made whole. Until mirage became a shore, an island, a beach, a something.

The dreamer swam for the something.

On and on she swam, and just as she was about to reach the shore, the tide pulled her further away. Over and over again, each time, the tide pulled her further away.

Still, on and on she swam until her arms and legs grew heavy, too heavy to swim much longer. The swells built and rolled and waves crashed and Cherry-Rose was no longer swimming at all. She was sinking. Arms flailing, legs kicking, just enough to take one last breath.

Legs slowing—arms giving out—the vines of her mind running visions of a lonely life on the bottom of the sea.

One last ...

She begged for land as she spat. She pleaded for land as she choked. She wished for land as she sank.

Cherry-Rose felt a surging tide pull her under. Salt in throat, nose, and eyes. Swallowing the sea.

Down.

dOwn.

doWn.

dowN.

down.

Until ...

The surge of the sea threw her into the sky and then broke her upon the horizon. Cherry-Rose was shat upon the moonlit shore. She lay there wet, naked, and dripping like the stinking afterbirth of the sea. Thrown from her host, useless and spent.

The island seemed to be a sloping dune of a beach that ran straight up against the horizon. It was all sand, black sky, and moon. It was empty of all but sand and the scent of marigold. Cherry-Rose lay where she was thrown. Her gut returning the sea to the shore. Panting, puking, coughing up the black Forever-brine. Breathing hard into the wet sand of the shore. Breath after choking breath, exhaling the sea, inhaling nothing but the scent of marigold. Not a flower to be seen and yet the island was sick with the scent.

The scent of the flower told Cherry-Rose where the dream had taken her. This was the in-between place. This was dying, or the moment just after. This tiny barren mound of sand in-between the sky and the sea was the funeral-birthday place, the place where the marigold called. And if you found this shore it meant ...

She began to piece the dream together.

Before?

Forever?

When doe became pale-blue butterfly, when butterfly became mannequin-ghost girl.

The Cherry-Rose beyond the dream warned dreamer. It begged her to remember ... "After the musk, there was a spell, a prick, a promise."

The dreamer didn't care. She wanted sleep. Body parallel to sea, face to pale moonlight, Cherry-Rose lay tucked up into the sand as if to sleep with the moon. She began to settle into the sand and saw movement on the horizon. The smallest edge of a shadow, a small stain, was eclipsing the base of the moon. The shadow grew and grew, a thin vertical line, rolling over the edge of the sandy horizon. It split the moon down the middle until shadow tumbled over the shore straight for Cherry-Rose—titan, bear, wolf, lover ... Brother John, all cool with his hands pushed deep into jean pockets.

The dreamer didn't care. Brother John was there confirming all her beneath-the-waves Forever-worries. This was the Blue Fairy Island of Dreams for All Sorts. This was the lesson. This was doe on sandy forest floor. This was ivy as sea. This was what happened when you were made by magical means. She knew that the tide would come for her. She knew that she belonged to the black at the bottom of the dream, to the Forever, and she knew that Brother John had come to take her there.

Cherry-Rose prepared to surrender and he spoke.

"Hi, baby, penny for your thoughts?" His voice hummed all sweet and deep like Johnny Cash, all smooth and full of Sunday mornings.

The words. The tone. The Sunday morning something. The *Forever*. It didn't matter. Worry dripped away as the sweet honey of his voice poured over her shell. She felt his eyes reach into her eyes. She felt the snake on his neck winding up her spine. She felt the scar of his smile pulling at her rat's nest of a womb. She saw his hand reach out slowly, as if to ask. He dropped to one knee. He *was* asking.

To be asked ... never had she ever wanted anything more. Whatever he was asking, the answer was *yes*.

"Remember me?" His hand lay outstretched ... still waiting.

Tears welled as gentle waves tested and pulled at the sand that lay beneath her form. She reached up and took his hand. Her eyes found *his*, forest green. She held the hand for a moment, then released it to roll over onto her back. Her back now wet from the encroaching sea. Brother John found her eyes again ... as if to ask. Whatever he was asking, the answer was still *yes*. Brother John over Cherry-Rose. Water beneath. He kissed the red of her lips, the soft of her neck, the heart over heart on her chest ... Down, dOwn, doWn, dowN ... down.

* * *

Cherry-Rose awoke feeling broken by the sea and Brother John. Tears flowed, but not for the sea, nor the moon, nor the funeral-birthday musk, but because she was alone ... and because it was Brother John. Because it wasn't Gideon.

She was lonely. She wanted to be held, touched, loved. She wanted Peaches, Daisy, Apple. She wanted Shy-Blue. She wanted everyone—

everyone? She wanted Gideon. She was sure she wanted Gideon. She lay in bed half-awake, cursing her need and the dream that gave her Brother John. So, with her eyes closed and the covers pulled high against the cool morning, she stayed in bed and searched behind her eyes for the heart-shaped tattoo that stirred her awake on all of those *other* mornings. When she found Gideon, she held him there just long enough, wishing he could stay a little while longer and for a time, she made it so.

When Cherry-Rose had enough of bed, she got up and wrote her dream and made a wish. Not the wish she wanted to make. Not a wish that would make all the loneliness disappear. She made the wish that she *had* to make, even if she didn't quite understand what it meant. She made the wish she knew the Blue Fairy would answer, for it couldn't be any other way ...

... something about being ready for other shores.

When the wish was written, she placed it inside a glass jar and touched it with a match. She watched her wish roll and shrink under the flames, and when ash settled in the bottom of the jar, she set about to gather her things, to return to Fontainebleau.

"Okay, I'm leaving," Cherry-Rose announced to the cottage. "I don't know if I'll be back, but perhaps someday. Who knows ... Oh, I almost forgot." Cherry-Rose took pen to paper and scribbled a quick note, "Fontainebleau, xoxo, cr," and placed it under the jar on the funeral-birthday table.

* * *

Cherry-Rose stood with her hand on the knob that led to the forest, and she lost herself for just a moment. She turned to face the cottage one last time and thought about how much it had changed over the last three days. Standing there facing the clocks, the books, the records, and the toy soldiers, she had the strangest thought. For just a moment, maybe even less, yes, less than a moment, she felt that no matter what happened out there on the other side of this door, even if her sisters never returned, perhaps ... one day, this could be her home.

Like a Bad Penny

CHERRY-ROSE crossed the clearing and stopped before a wall of trees edged by a moat of freshly hoed ivy. Hood on, eyes down, black hair framing black shoes touching the tips of green leathery leaves, she was frozen by the realization that in returning to the cottage, she did not do what she set out to do. For all she had done, for the fires, the burial, the dreams; for the library of sister-notebooks, there were still no sisters to be found. She still felt a complete failure. Tears she no longer had a reason to hide rose and flowed and stained her dusty shoes. Sobs following tears ... tears upon tears. When the tears made her dusty shoes new again, when they shone as they did on her funeral-birthday, she stepped over the thin line that separated the uncanny of the cottage from the wild of Forest and made a new wish. "One. Just one. Please. Let me find at least one."

Cherry-Rose smiled as she entered the market. She had come to appreciate its existence, feeling a sort of kinship with the market itself. Were they not both made up of bits and pieces, the useful and the useless, the horrible and the exquisite, the beautiful and the beautifully unnecessary, all sewn together here, all held together seemingly by sheer chance and desire? She saw carts and tables and boxes full of fabric, rugs, and records; and boxes of buttons and bows, shelves of books. There were candles and comics and jewelry; and animals in pens, meat hanging from hooks, skin hanging from hooks, chickens waiting for the block. Disparate elements being thrown together … to make something else live and breathe; that she understood.

It didn't take Cherry-Rose long to notice; the market teemed with satin, denim, and leather-clad Roaches scurrying about between the stalls. They wove in and out of view, appearing to take no notice of Cherry-Rose. They'd approach then drift away, they'd pass by and then turn, seeming to be interested in someone's wares until they weren't.

Are they circling?

Cherry-Rose watched and named them as they passed: Anchor, Dagger, Dice; Rose, Eagle, Skull—too many to remember. No matter, Cherry-Rose only had eyes for Snake and Heart. Wanting to see Gideon, but not now, not under these circumstances, not after that dream, not after that morning. Not wanting to see Brother John because … because of that dream. Thankfully, both were nowhere to be seen.

In an attempt to remain unseen by a trio of approaching Roaches, Cherry-Rose quickly turned to face the nearest booth where chickens were stacked in cages five-by-three high. They were all so quiet. Cherry-Rose shuddered, thinking of mannequin-sisters in cages and porcelain dolls under bell jars. *This could have been me, a life of caged quiet; then into a burlap sack, and onto a chopping block.*

"What? Sorry, pardon me. Oh, yes, good afternoon," replied Cherry-Rose to the attendant, only now realizing that the someone who had been standing between her and the cages had been attempting to greet her. "What's that? No, no. Nothing for me. I'm just admiring your chickens. They're so calm."

"They are, aren't they? Funny thing about these chickens," said the attendant, opening three of the wired doors.

"Give them food and water for a time, and then after a while, they'll forget they ever wanted out."

Run, run, why don't you run. Cherry-Rose flashed to the unheeded warnings she heard in the cherry-cordial dream.

"For this sort of animal, life in a cage sure beats life out there in a forest all full of bears, wolves, and weirdos," the attendant said with a laugh.

Cherry-Rose tried to return a polite laugh but couldn't. She threw on her hood and turned, determined to walk straight through the market until she reached Salvatóre's side of the forest.

Roaches were swarming again;

*Swallow ... Ship ... Anchor ... Lips ... Snake and Heart ... *Fuck.*

Not now, please not now.

She pulled at the edge of her hood to hide in its shadow, hoping they didn't see her. Hoping harder that even if they had, they too would walk by. She turned sharply toward a woman peddling glass shaped into tiny, colorful forest creatures and pretended to be interested. A tiny glass bear, a wolf ... *I don't have time for distractions* ... a snake.

Cherry-Rose thought of the glass jar she left atop the funeral-birthday table. The jar with the wish and the wish on fire and that shore somewhere out there in that dream. And the boy from her dream. *No, no;* she shook that thought away. She pushed it out with thoughts of the homeroom boy she didn't really know at all, and yet who she felt she knew best.

... a doe. A snake and a doe. A snake ...

A voice reached out over the din of the market. "Of all the people." It ran sweet and deep, all full of Sunday mornings. Creeping up like a whisper.

Instinctively, she pulled at the edge of her hood and darkened her eyes. *Calm. Slow.*

Shaking.

Breathe.

The eyes beneath the hood turned slowly to find two Roaches, Snake and Heart, both smiling their smiles behind new eyes. Brother John's mask was red and thin, Gideon's a thin white line, not over his eyes like the others, just under.

"Hello again," said Brother John. With a slight bow, he continued. "I believe you know Gideon, yes? Proper introductions all around. We shan't suffer informality, shall we, Gid?"

"I am John," he said, extending his hand, "Brother John."

Cherry-Rose tilted her head.

"No, no. Not his brother, rather, not *just* his brother. I am their brother." Brother John used the hand she did not shake to motion behind Cherry-Rose. She turned to find a gang of satin, denim, and leather had somehow woven in behind her. "Everyone's brother. I could be your brother too if you'd like." He rubbed his chin and lifted his brow. "Or anything else you like, for that matter."

Cherry-Rose stood motionless with her dream racing through her head, remembering the sea, the shore, the boy who wasn't Gideon, his words, his hands, and that slow morning following the dream. "Hello, I'm … I'm Cherry-Rose," she said with her redder than roses lips peeking out beneath the shadow of her hood.

"Oh, we know. You are quite famous these days … Gid, where are your manners?"

"Hello again." Gideon spoke from beneath the fallen crown of hair that hung all devilock between his eyes. He picked up Brother John's cue and affected proper formality as he extended his hand. "Gideon. Pleased to officially meet you. We had homeroom together, remember? Mr. Clift?"

"Hello. Pleased to meet you." Cherry-Rose took his hand, thankful there was no mention of her journal. "Homeroom?" She tilted her head, pretending she had to think about it for a moment. "Yes, that's right. Homeroom."

"Apologies all around for not introducing myself properly on our first meeting. Sorry for spooking you on the quad." Brother John began to walk a full circle around Cherry-Rose. "It's just a little performance I put on for new customers. I'm sure you understand. I should have guessed you were too refined for such an approach. A plague upon me, my dear, for an ill-mannered Roach." Brother John bowed, wasting his best George Bailey impersonation.

"Oh, that? The quad? I had already forgotten."

"Yes. I am sure you had … Since it seems we are starting over, silly performances aside, just how are you set for pixie-dust, baby doll?"

"Pixie-dust?" Cherry-Rose laughed. "No thanks, John, I'm good. And you can call me Cherry-Rose."

"Yes. I am sure you are, Cherry-Rose, and it's Brother John. Please, call me Brother John."

"Hmm, John will have to do," Cherry-Rose replied, imitating his tone. "I am not sure that our two chance meetings bridge the connection that would necessitate such a prefix."

"As you wish, Cherry-Rose. As you wish. Let me know if I … no, no, if we, *we*"—gesturing to the ring of Roaches with his palm to the sky—"can help you with anything. Anything at all."

"*We*," Cherry-Rose playfully twisted his tone, "appreciate the offer, but no, nothing that I can think of at the moment. It was lovely to meet you both, I … I really must be going," she said, testing the situation, half-worried the Roaches had other plans for her.

"And just where," inquired Brother John, "might you be heading, Cherry-Rose?"

"Uh … Fontainebleau."

Brother John feigned surprise. "D'ya hear that, Gid?" He slapped Gideon's shoulder. "Fontainebleau."

"Yes, Fontainebleau," replied Cherry-Rose. "I have a show tonight."

"Ya know, as luck would have it, we have tickets for a show tonight at Fontainebleau … If I believed in coincidences." Brother John leaned into Gideon. "Do you believe in coincidences, Cherry-Rose?"

"I … uh …" Cherry-Rose stammered. "I'd say I don't."

"Kindred spirits," said Brother John. "I've found that coincidence is what you call it when you aren't ready to acknowledge that all your choices led you to this moment. And here we are …" Brother John's voice trailed off as Cherry-Rose stole glances at his brooding brother.

"Well, it seems we are headed in the same direction. Wouldst thou allow some company?" Brother John asked.

Cherry-Rose searched Gideon's face. His lips did not mouth a warning. They were posed in perfect pouting posture. His eyes were wide. Wide and blank. No warnings. Calm. Beautiful. Nothing. No sign of danger. No sign that he once read a journal filled with secrets, wishes, dreams, and future lovers. Nothing. Nothing but those still chestnut eyes and that tiny black heart on his neck.

"An escort?" Cherry-Rose replied again with an appropriate nod to Brother John's affected tone. "I decline, but thank you kind … uh … John. I must be on my way."

"As you wish. Although, Gid here will be disappointed. He tires of me so easily, don't ya, Gid?"

Gideon gave Brother John a sideways look, then turned to face Cherry-Rose. "See you tonight, Cherry-Rose. I am really looking forward to seeing the show. We have heard such great things." His voice was soft and lovely, full of sincerity, none of the pregnant Brother John innuendo, none of the smile with the wink.

"Yes, great things indeed …" said Brother John with a slight nod.

As his words trailed, Brother John put his arm around Gideon and ushered him past Cherry-Rose. "See you tonight, Cherry-Rose."

Gideon looked back for a moment, giving her just the edge of a smile before they parted and then pulled the wake of Roaches in tow. Cherry-Rose watched them fade into the crowd, and as they turned down the next aisle, just when they were out of sight, she could hear Brother John shout, "Hey, baby doll, almost forgot. Break a leg."

Fuck.

Dagger, Eagle, Praying Hands

"THERE'S my Gold and Honey," said Salvatóre with his booming, fatherly, loveable-bear laugh. "There's my Honey and Gold." His words echoed throughout the cave. "My dear, my sweet sweet Cherry-Rose, are we alone? Where are the others? Will others be joining us?"

"Hello, Salvatóre," said Cherry-Rose, still lost in her market Roach encounter. "We are alone."

With those words, she headed straight for her dressing room. For Salvatóre, it was like she had never left at all. He didn't bat a bear lash. "That's a good girl. Getting right to it." For, as he understood the world, this *all business, back to work, back to the dressing room, get ready for the show*, that was just what one did. That was what one should do and it was … as it should be. *Back to the hustle.*

* * *

In the dressing room, Cherry-Rose exchanged her cape and dirndl for her robe and sofa. She hoped to find Gideon behind her eyes for just a moment, but all she found was her forest motto glaring all neon and blinking: *EAT*, all hot— *FUCK*, scratching— *DIE*. *This is really it*, she thought. *There is no avoiding it. Marybelle, the forest, even for the Roaches, it's the same.*

CHERRY-ROSE: BLOOD & WISHES

Humph.

Considering Forest's motto, she thought, *There sure isn't much room for the small things in life when the world is busy trying to take you … or take you apart one way or another. If this is life, this sure isn't enough.*

But this, Fontainebleau, singing here … it has been great. Salvatóre has been great, but I have forgotten myself. Haven't I? Or did I find myself? But my sisters. I never intended on staying this long. Yes. And the dream—the dreams. They were telling me something. Like they want me to leave. Like the dreams are telling me I have to go. Like leaving is how I find my sisters. If I'm sure of anything, I am sure of that. They won't come here for me. Maybe they can't. All the more reason to leave. If they're out there, I have to try. Don't I? If I were lost, I would want to be found …

I will play out this week and then I will find them. Salvatóre will understand. Right? Yes. Of course, he will. It is Salvatóre, after all. He knew I was looking for them when we met. It isn't his fault. He was just wrong—fame, staying in one place. It just didn't work.

"Cherry-Rose, Cherry-Rose … Ten minutes. You are on in ten," a voice called from behind the door.

"Ten minutes," Cherry-Rose repeated. "Got it."

She decided. *Four more days, eight more shows, and I'm out.*

* * *

Salvatóre was indeed confident in his worldview; however, despite his confidence, he watched Cherry-Rose closely just to be sure. *One can never be too sure about how an investment might pan out in the face of new stimuli.* His doubts, however, were quickly put to rest. For when Cherry-Rose returned, ready to work, she confirmed everything Salvatóre believed about the world. It was all about the gold and honey, the honey and gold.

Sisters? Bah! Who could walk away from fame and money? So much money? So much fame? Salvatóre thought as Cherry-Rose approached the curtain.

She returned just as he knew she would. Not only did she return, but she seemed more put together than before. She seemed settled, calm, calmer;

more centered, unflappable in the face of the madness that was pre-show rehearsal; quiet in the backstage-storm that was all-out chaos just moments before the music cut in to obliterate the bedlam.

* * *

Cherry-Rose held onto the curtain's center seam and peered out at the crowd. She thought of Brother John and Gideon somewhere out there, hidden in the darkness, just beyond the frame of the searching lights. She stood there staring into the black, feeling all the cocoons that the seamstress shoved inside her seams becoming butterflies all at once—with every flutter, the bile built. And just when she felt she might burst, Salvatóre's opening number roared in to chase away the butterflies.

"Of course, change the set as you like, but for me, for this old bear, for *them*, for *them*," Salvatóre implored, gesturing to an empty venue behind stone walls, "Is it not what *they* want? We must preserve the opener. It is so perfect, too perfect. And you, my dear, you play it to perfection. The crowd loves it, no? It just ties everything together so neatly, because you know … You aren't what you are."

Cherry-Rose consented, for she knew it was true. She wasn't what she was. Not only did the crowd love that song, they needed it. They needed it and her homage to the strings that should have been, that might have been, that could have been. Yes, in tribute to the strings that should be pulling and jerking at the joints of a mannequin-doll. It was too perfect to abandon.

"The rest of the set's yours," said Salvatóre. "And I want you to know, I love the new set. Truly. There is nothing more Cherry-Rose than this." He waved a stack of sheet music. "Nothing more beautiful and melancholic, nothing more Cherry-Rose. Pure Cherry-Rose. And you should know, nothing makes a crowd drink quite like sadness. Love, bah! Two drinks and they're off looking for a room. But cast a line into the hearts of fools who may have been stupid enough to believe in true love, and they will stay all night and drink until they can't see straight or they've run out of money. Hopefully both. Singing, crying, washing their tears away with drink after drink. Perfection. That is all I have to say. Perfection." He paused to swallow a bottle of wine. "I knew it, Cherry-Rose, this business is in your blood! Gold and honey, Cherry-Rose." Salvatóre paused for effect and to grab another bottle of wine.

Cherry-Rose waited, thinking, *He never, never doesn't say it twice.*

"Yes! Honey and gold."

So, tonight, Cherry-Rose bit into beastly hearts with the songs that kept her alive inside the too small cottage walls, with the songs that made her dream of other lives somewhere out there beyond the forest. With the songs that made her dream of someone out there, all parts and pieces like her, sewn up and held together by tiny threads and tiny knots. With the songs she sang all alone in the fog of her mother's soups and spells of forgetting. So, after Cherry-Rose and the trumpets built the crowd up with "I've Got the World on a String," they broke them down, down, down, and further down with the new set.

Cherry-Rose crooned the pure melancholy of Connie Francis. Down with "Breakin' in a Brand-New Broken Heart." Further with "Everybody is Somebody's Fool." Further still with "I'm Sorry I Made You Cry." And when they thought they couldn't go lower, Cherry-Rose crushed them with Patsy Cline's "Have You Ever Been Lonely (Have You Ever Been Blue)," and last, she tore them apart with a song written for a life she had never known, but somehow felt was written for her alone: "I Fall to Pieces."

A chorus of applause, howls, grunts, and huffs rained down on the curtain as the crowd begged for more. An encore was never a certainty with Cherry-Rose; Salvatóre taught her to tease the crowd. "Sometimes do … sometimes do not do. It will drive them mad. Mad for more." Tonight, she felt their need swirling with images of snakes and hearts and relented. She parted the red curtain and stood motionless at the mic, waiting for the applause to die.

Just like story time in the cottage, she thought.

"All quiet now, everyone, quiet before Mother tells her story." The ghost-girls knew the seamstress wouldn't utter a word until they all stopped rustling about.

Like the seamstress, she waited and waited, a painted picture, a perfect doll, a mannequin-ghost dream until the pandemonium became frenzy and the frenzy became a commotion and the commotion became silence. She stood for one beat and imagined having a life where she might know what it meant to live the words that she sang tonight, the words she felt with every fiber of her fabric being. A second beat, feeling that these songs were her true wishes. A third beat; she whispered to the crowd, "'Who's Sorry Now?'"

* * *

If asked, Cherry-Rose would have told you that when she sang this song, she didn't move an inch … just as she rehearsed. She would say that she remained perfectly still to provide contrast to the melody. An artistic choice to illustrate the power of the song. To allow the melody to drive the feeling and the meaning into the crowd, but it wasn't so. She was gone, lost entirely. She was the melody. She was the song. Eyes closed, hips swaying the slightest sultry sway, shoulders rocking ever-so …

And the crowd went wild.

* * *

It was indeed as Salvatóre predicted; she was a natural, a star. Salvatóre couldn't believe that he had ever worried about her returning to Fontaine-bleau. *No one with a gift like this could walk away.* Salvatóre was pleased with himself for taking his own advice; *they do sing so much sweeter without chains.*

* * *

"You wanted to see me?" Cherry-Rose leaned against the doorway leading to Salvatóre's office.

"Yes, yes, please. There are a few men here to see you," said Salvatóre from behind his desk.

Cherry-Rose saw the heads of three familiar men turn in her direction: Dagger, Eagle, and Praying Hands. Eagle smiled, Praying Hands gave a slight nod, and Dagger stared. They were part of that swirling hissing hoard that spilled in around Brother John and Gideon at the market. Cherry-Rose searched the corners of the room for others, but there were none. No Snake, nor Heart.

"They are here to … what was it?" Salvatóre seemingly asked himself. "To … to buy your contract, they said," rubbing his muzzle. "You'd be going with them, they said. I didn't have a choice, they said." Salvatóre laughed his bear laugh, patted the top of his desk, then wiped his eyes with the back of his paw. "I apologize, my darling Cherry-Rose. Please, please come. Sit.

"Gentlemen, please give us a moment." Salvatóre motioned for Cherry-Rose to sit in the highbacked chair angled in the furthest corner behind his desk. "I would hate for Cherry-Rose to think that I made decisions about her fate unilaterally." He winked to the three.

Praying Hands returned a tight-lipped, nodding smile. Dagger and Eagle didn't blink.

Cherry-Rose sat in the chair, hemmed in by large, hanging rugs. Salvatóre took a seat on the floor facing Cherry-Rose and began to whisper. "Now, Cherry-Rose, these men want to take you from me."

Cherry-Rose went cold at his words, sinking as they wrenched at her gut. Salvatóre seemed to register the change in her demeanor and closed in to comfort Cherry-Rose. Salvatóre patted her hand, stood, and walked behind the chair, facing the Roaches. "Don't be scared, my Green-Fairy Girl," he whispered, resting his snout on her head, "Don't you worry. No one could take you from me."

Little did Salvatóre know, Cherry-Rose wasn't scared. She was angry.

I let it happen again. Take you from me? she thought, the words ringing loud behind her screaming eyes.

Only now did Cherry-Rose see that she had let it happen. It was just the way of things, and Salvatóre was proving it so. It was the cottage all over again. Worse, it didn't just happen. She chose this. His words were seamstress words, mother words, clever beastly words, words for binding and keeping and taking.

I don't belong to anyone, Cherry-Rose told herself, feeling Salvatóre's breath drip over her crown.

"The buyout is fair," interrupted Eagle.

Praying Hands nodded in agreement, still smiling that smile.

Dagger, still … nothing.

Is that Dagger guy even alive?

"Please, please, I'll be right with you," said Salvatóre calmly, like a perfect host. "Just give us a moment, dear sir, all I ask. Just a moment."

Salvatóre lowered his voice and made very quiet words: "Don't you worry, Cherry-Rose. I'll be right back."

"You really ought to take the deal," said Eagle through lips that didn't seem to move.

"One moment, my darling," Salvatóre said to Cherry-Rose as he made his way to the Roach side of his desk.

"Gentlemen, I don't mean to appear impolite, but this sort of offer requires a moment of consideration." The bear paused with one paw in the air. "Please. I implore you." He leaned back on his desk as he continued. "Could you just give us a moment without interruption, my good gentlemen? Perhaps you three could wait in the hallway?" His paws rested as if in prayer over his chest. "A few minutes to discuss things with Cherry-Rose is all I ask."

Praying Hands stood and said, "Look, Salvatóre, no hard feelings, but you don't really have a choi— "

With one paw still in prayer, Salvatóre whipped the other sideways through Praying Hands' throat.

Praying Hands stood with one hand on his neck while the other leaned on Salvatóre's shoulder. His eyes found Cherry-Rose just as all of his red … ran down … the white of his shirt, just before he hit the floor, just as the bear spoke to Dagger and Eagle. "Now take your friend and get out before I …"

Eagle to straight razor.

Dagger to switchblade.

Dagger smiled behind a mask of splattered blood. "Funny enough, bear, had you taken the offer, not taken the offer," carving the air slowly with his blade, "this was how tonight was going to end." He smiled and pulled his forefinger down from the corner of his eye, dragging with it the Praying Hands blood that decorated his face. "We were just hoping that your little girl wasn't going to be around for this part of the show."

Eagle cracked a smile to say, "But que será será."

Cherry-Rose pulled her legs up onto the chair and hugged her knees. From the deepest corner of the chair, from behind her knees and unruly hair, she watched the Roaches move to divide Salvatóre's attention, but he was fast. Too fast. His paw slid up the front of Eagle and spilled his bowels on the floor.

Dagger turned to run.

Two steps and Salvatóre dropped him to the floor. He pounced and crawled up Dagger's back, one paw to head, one claw to kidney. Then it was claw through spleen—mouth to liver.

"Liver," said Salvatóre to the mess on the floor. "It has been a while since I've had human liver. Yes, liver and tongue. Tongue and liver." Salvatóre laughed. "And wine. We must have wine to celebrate." The bloodstained bear stood facing his wall of bottles. "The benefits of home. Always cellar temperature." Salvatóre pulled a bottle and sabered it with his claw.

Cherry-Rose sat motionless in the chair and watched Salvatóre devour the Dagger tongue and three bottles of wine.

"Pardon me for a moment, dear." He moved to hover over Eagle. "Ah yes," Salvatóre laughed through the blood and wet flesh of Eagle organs, and three more bottles of red, and then to Praying Hands' liver and tongue. "I'll be right with you," Salvatóre hiccupped, holding up his paw in his soft "just a moment, gentlemen" gesture.

One. Two. Three more bottles of wine.

Cherry-Rose scanned the carnage on the floor and saw herself in her funeral-birthday dream, a bleating deer torn open and gutted, motionless on the forest floor, her sweet bits savored and swallowed. *But this. This is different*, she thought. She knew why beasts killed in the forest, but this ... *This? They were fighting over who gets to own me?*

"Now, deary dear. My dearest Cherry-Rose," Salvatóre slurred, "lips redder than wine, redder than rose, redder than blood, red red redder than wine. Didn't I just say that? I did, didn't I? Well, I do love wine. Redder than ... redder than ... all the red things I love," said the bear as he staggered. "The world is such a dangerous place." He moved toward Cherry-Rose, downing another bottle, but Cherry-Rose couldn't hear him any longer, or rather, she heard, but she no longer understood, for she was no longer Cherry-Rose, she was doe ready to run and he was a bear. Her pinecone heart raced, and her hind legs shook, and her wide-wide eyes quaked at the sight of the looming bear. She saw Forest. Path. Trees. She smelled the metal of blood and the soil of earth, and with it, she knew what she had to do. Finally, she was ready to heed her own pleading nightmare warnings, but just in case she wasn't sure, the Cherry-Rose behind those pure animal eyes screamed it again. *RUN!*

Cherry-Rose leapt out of the chair and burst into stride as fast as a deer with a racing heart, shaking legs, and quaking eyes could run.

But how could a wild animal, or even a Cherry-Rose, know that fresh blood was a trap? Animals weren't made with eyes to see such clever things; beasts, yes, but animals, no. There was a bright flash and a sharp knife of pain as she slid, soft head into hard desk. Soft doll onto hard floor. Forest ghost-girl into night night dream. And just before she lost the world to the vines behind her eyes, from somewhere in the haze of her dream, she heard Salvatóre pacing, soliloquizing to the mayhem.

"No choice, you say? I am a bear. *Thee* bear."

Cherry-Rose heard Salvatóre's words blink in and out with consciousness. Words and phrases sputtered in, spaced with void.

"I am ... Salvatóre. I decide. I ... Just who do you think ... my place? You want to tell me ... my roof? Trying to ... my ... Rose from ...? Is that it?"

Salvatóre kicked at a lifeless shape. The wet thud of the Praying Hands-flavored rusted brown connected all the vines behind Cherry-Rose's eye. She rubbed her head and watched Salvatóre rage. "Filthy Roaches. Look at them." He downed another bottle of wine. "They thought they were going to take you from me." Salvatóre hiccupped, then laughed in Cherry-Rose's direction. "Never. Never, never. You are mine. All mine, mine, mine."

Cherry-Rose's voice emerged soft and weak as she struggled to sit up. "No, Salvatóre, I don't belong to anyone."

"Oh, but you do. Eight shows a week for twelve months and a day; you signed the contract yourself," he grumbled. "Try to break that contract and you will wish you hadn't." The words tore at Cherry-Rose, hurting far worse than the throbbing pain in her head. Her face fell to her lap.

Salvatóre must have understood that he had gone too far. He began to back away from his blood rage. "I am sorry, honey. So sorry. They just made me so angry. They wanted to take you from me. They wanted to split us up. … You understand, don't you?"

Cherry-Rose looked up to see Salvatóre approaching, paws out—shoulders hunched slightly,—his eyes attempting to hold her eyes.

With each Salvatóre step, Cherry-Rose slid backward across the floor, dragging blood and gown until she was backed into the corner. "Honey, where are you going? There is nowhere to go."

Pinned, her arms and legs still worked against the floor as if they might help her climb the wall.

Salvatóre squatted with paws on knees and spoke softly as one might to a scared and injured animal. "Shhh … Shhh. Settle. Settle. Shhh … It's going to be okay. I promise. Everything is going to be okay."

Cherry-Rose's eyes still shook, but her arms and legs did begin to settle.

"That's it. That's better. We just need to calm down. We are safe here. You are safe here. But, yes, you are right to be worried. Those Roaches, they are everywhere. Tonight, the club was full of them. You see, don't you? It just isn't safe out there. You will have to stay with me. Only I can protect you."

Cherry-Rose wanted to run, but blood, a bear, three bodies and all of their various pieces were blocking the door.

Breathe, Cherry-Rose told herself. *Breathe and be clever.*

With a deep breath, Cherry-Rose straightened her dress and spoke—calmly—evenly—slowly. "Salvatóre, thank you for protecting me. I ... I really appreciate it. I really do. What would I do without you? But, you do know that I can't stay here forever. I do have to find my sisters."

As soon as the words left her mouth, Cherry-Rose knew her mistake. *Now is not the time to reason with a beast.*

Salvatóre's smile faded and he blinked hard. He paused, nodded, dusted his knees, and stood up straight. Her words seemed a sobering tonic. "Hmmm," said Salvatóre with a slight tilt of his head. He reached out with his paw as if words might follow; his snout moved as if they might, but he only *Hmmmed* again. If Salvatóre did speak thereafter, Cherry-Rose couldn't say. The *Hmmm* was the last thing she heard before a blinding blur that was paw crashed into her head to turn the room black.

Ding, Dang, Dong

STEEL and straw. Blind hands reaching out to feel cold steel, grasping at loose straw. On all sides, steel and straw.

Ding ... Dang ... Dong ...

Caged.

Not sort of caged; not with a lifetime supply of books and records, cottage-caged. Not even the I've-chosen-to-live-in-this-cave-of-a-club, earning fame and fortune, Fontainebleau sort of a cage. But rather the literally in a square cell walled with steel bars six inches apart, floor lined with wood and straw, sort of caged. *Caged.*

The room was swaying. Singing.

Is the room singing? wondered Cherry-Rose.

It seemed like it was singing, all smooth and wired straight into her fibers: *Ding, Dang, Dong.* The room was warm. Wet and warm. Face pressed into the floor; loose, damp straw matted to her face. Eyes tight and heavy.

Yes, the room is singing.

Ding, Dang, Dong ... Ding, Dang, Dong, are you sleeping, are you sleeping, Cherry-Rose, Cherry-Rose? Sonnez les matines, sonnez les matines ...

Ding ... Dang ...

A star fell toward a mountain, at the base of a fountain, spun into a cave, backstage, into an office, into a cage behind a wall-hung rug, into the thumping screaming vines behind two whirling eyes.

And that song. What is that song doing here?

Hands on steel bars.

Ding.

There was a bear ...

Dang.

Where is Salvatóre?

Dong.

Where am I?

Cherry-Rose was neither alive nor dead, neither awake nor asleep. If she were awake, she couldn't speak. If she were alive ...

Am I dreaming?

Trapped. Confused. Scared.

The bright migraine-lights of pain flashing behind her eyes made it difficult for her to open them at all. Bright flashing light, even when her eyes were closed.

The singing voice paused. "Gid. Is she alive?"

Gid, who's Gid? It's that "first one's free" voice. Brother something. Brother Snake? ... And Heart?

The light filled her up from the base of her empty nest of a womb to the twigs and feathers in her chest; it gave her the night like a shattered mirror. Shimmering hot reflections of the night tore behind her eyes. It was all there ... hurting, cutting, bleeding as the pieces flashed—shards, knives, blades, and blood.

The pain struck like lightning, blinding everything for a moment. It gave Cherry-Rose fleeting words, riddles, and blurred quicksilver memories. *Black.* A wall. A mirror. A window. A room behind a desk. *Black.* A cage in that room. A cage behind that mirror that was a window. *Black.* On the furthest wall, nails held posters of a dancing bear. *Black.* "Silvio Salvatóre, the Dandy Dancing Bear." *Black.* Loose straw. Cold bars. Chains. *Black.*

On the wall, nails for holding parts and pieces. *Black.* For keeping and binding. *Black.* A chain, a large studded collar, a leather whip, a leather crop.

Black. A wine-drunk bear sprawled out on his chair staring lifelessly at the scene he had composed. The dead boys artfully arranged all over his floor, walls, and sofa.

Black. The office was all Jackson Pollock *Number 1,* all hate and lust tangled up in a knot.

Black. It was Ushio Shinohara with love hate love jabs dripping black guts and red blood all over the walls.

Black. It was Picasso's *Three Musicians* made under *Guernica* skies.

Black.

She didn't know if she was sleeping and dreaming or awake and wishing she were sleeping and dreaming. The haze was too heavy, it was too much, all too much at once. The cage and the straw and the steel and the murder; Dagger, Eagle, and Praying Hands; and now, the *Black.* A black heart, *Black.* A pale hand with black nails stroking her hand with that sweet, soft voice that was more dream than real.

Is it Sunday morning already?

Black.

"Cherry-Rose, wake up. Wake up. We have to go."

Black. A snake eating his tail. *Black.* Thick ivy swarming behind heavy eyes. *Black.*

The walls crawled with Roaches. The heart. The snake eating his tail. It was pure under-the-ivy madness. Visions of Snake and Heart spilling over the bear, hugging him from behind until his neck smiled purple, red, dirty brown down his coat.

Black. The room was alive with satin, denim, and leather.

Black. Gone. Everything gone.

Dagger, gone.

Eagle, gone.

Praying Hands, gone.

The bear who smiled from his neck, gone.

All gone. All bear-bear bye-bye eyes …

Black. Everything gone. Satin, denim, leather. Blood. Gone. Everything gone. Everything but the pale hand holding hers and that singing voice behind that song. *Black.*

Cherry-Rose opened her eyes to find Gideon holding her hand and Brother John leaning against a wall of collar, whip, and chain; smiling that scarred smile, jingling a ring of keys to the tune of that song.

Black. A snake eating his tail singing, "Dormez-Vous, Dormez-Vous."

III

Pleasure Island

Running From the Dawn

WHEN Cherry-Rose hit the Oldsmobile's vinyl backseat, the world came to her colored in brand-new strobe-light violence. She heard it all again: Eagle's guts hitting the floor. *Wet. Slap.* Brother John *click-clicked* the car and something under the hood roared to life with a cry that whined and stabbed deep inside Cherry-Rose's ears, all shrill screams and horror, all Dagger under Salvatóre. The car jumped forward and twisted a fishtail, spitting dirt and rubber into the pre-dawn mist; Cherry-Rose flashed to Praying Hands' carotid painting the walls and the ceiling.

Cherry-Rose wanted to ask, *Am I being saved or stolen?* The words, however, refused to come. She didn't have the strength for words. She barely had the strength to hold on to the back of the bench seat, to keep an eye on Brother John and Gideon. Arms locked tight, she watched the hood swallow the road—liver, tongue, Salvatóre. She concentrated on slow, deliberate breaths to help weigh the question she couldn't manage to ask.

Dull rusted-brown knuckles gripped the wheel. Brother John's knuckles. Salvatóre's dull-rusted brown. A tiny mirror over the front window said that Brother John's eyes were still wild from the kill, still high from staining Salvatóre's breast with his own color.

Avoid the mirror.

Bile built and was swallowed. Cherry-Rose turned her gaze to the passenger's seat where a small yellow light threw shadows over a thin book split open with a blood-rust thumb. Gideon's thumb. He was lost in poem. He didn't have any eyes for the mirror. Just sighs. Long, deep sighs.

The answer to her question built slowly. *They ... they saved me. They saved me from Salvatóre.*

Gideon's finger dragged over the page. Blood over "animal, soup, and time." He closed the book, then leaned forward to switch on the radio in time to hear someone barking and howling, someone named Jack. Jack said that this next golden oldie was Sugar Pie DeSanto's "Going Back to Where I Belong."

Farther. Further. South and west. Running from the approaching dawn. Cherry-Rose could feel it; they were speeding toward the impending edge of the *ivy* dream, the *pulling down* dream, the *cherry-cordial* dream. Everything here measured for murder. She could feel the sun waiting just below the horizon, ready to sprint forth to murder the morning star. She could feel the sun itching to slit the throat of the waxing crescent moon who, like her, was barely hanging on. She could feel the sun twitching at the seam of the eastern sky, drooling in anticipation of dining on crescent moon tongue and liver. She could feel the soft light bleeding into her birdsong dream, reminding Cherry-Rose of when those words were kissed into her ear. *There will be pain, there will be blood, there will be death.*

What else did she say? There was *something else.*

Tired, drained, scared, Cherry-Rose couldn't think clearly.

Wishes, yes, wishes, she thought. *I don't need memories; I can still make wishes. I wish for everything to be as it was. Funeral-birthday mornings forever. Everything as it was forever. Twelve sisters forever. Those cool cottage mornings. The cottage on full-moon nights. My Blue Fairy. My books. Just my books. And the records. Maybe the seamstress was right. She was right. I only want to dance and sing.*

Too much? Is that too much? Just tell me. Yes? Okay. Okay then, even further back. Just a day. To my death day. Even just after ... you decide. I just don't want to feel their fangs again. But yes, just after that. Leave me on the forest floor. The dirt. The ivy. Even the ivy.

Cherry-Rose let go and sank deep into the back seat imagining she was sinking into the ivy.

"Cherry-Rose. Cherry-Rose. Cher—" said the homeroom, *Jude the Obscure* voice. Gideon gently patted her hand until Cherry-Rose blinked back into the moment. "There you are. You nodded off there for a bit. We have to walk into town from here. Can you hand me your bag? Oh, and I hope you don't mind, I borrowed your book. I found it when we packed for you."

Gideon offered his hand.

Cherry-Rose reached up through the dream ivy with a bag and then placed her hand in his. "Th ... Thank you," said Cherry-Rose, climbing out of the car, yawning behind the back of her hand.

"Can you smell that?" Gideon asked as he eased her out of the car. "We haven't far to go now. I love the smell of the ocean. Have you ever seen the ocean before? It really is something. You're gonna love Santa Cruz."

There will be a wide sea.

Cherry-Rose stumbled at the too much of everything; too much headache, too much blood, too much ivy sleep behind her eyes to walk without faltering. Gideon caught Cherry-Rose by the waist. "I've got you. Hang on," he said ushering her away from the car. "We can rest here for a sec. Brother John's gonna throw a few branches over the back of the car. We'd prefer it not be seen from the road, at least not right away."

Brother John patted the trunk of the car. "It may surprise you, ma' lady, but this baby ain't ours."

"Take this, you'll need it, we have a ways to go." Gideon, handed Cherry-Rose his jacket and threw her bag across his shoulder.

Cherry-Rose thought to say thank you. She didn't. Nod.

"All right, homeroom honeymooners ... we gotta cut."

At those words, Brother John's face changed. He held up one finger to get everyone's attention, then he brought the finger to his lips and paused for a moment. The finger fell from his lips to point straight at Cherry-Rose. When her eyes met his, the finger pointed at the white line on the oncoming side of the road. Cherry-Rose followed the finger. Once in place, Brother John moved to the line just in front of Cherry-Rose; Gideon slid in place behind.

The eerie silence of the foggy pre-dawn, single-file, white-line procession made Cherry-Rose feel like she was in the haze of a waking dream, sleepwalking with Roaches. And the Cherry-Rose walking this white line, in this dream that wasn't a dream at all, wondered more unspoken wonders.

What are we doing? What am I doing ... so far from Fontainebleau, so far from the cottage, so far from the forest?

She walked and walked for what seemed like hours and watched what was left of the forest give way to a world she had only read about. Where dirt became asphalt, where the black of the asphalt shoulder gave way to concrete and a row of hazy, blinking streetlights and soon, others who blinked—red, yellow, green. Where the trees and ivy from those other worlds spread out thin to make room for buildings, cars, and blinking signs.

Just when Cherry-Rose was about to turn her wonder into words, Brother John turned and began walking backward. "Hey, Cherry-Rose," he said, breaking the silence. "You a Moons Over My Hammy girl?" Brother John hitched his thumb over his shoulder at a building full of people.

"What? Where are we? This place? No, no. Please, no. You can't be serious. I've never ... I haven't ever ... I can't ..." Cherry-Rose held out the edges of her dress and pulled at her cape as she pleaded with Brother John. "It's just ... I am not really dressed for this sort of place. And besides, I thought we were trying to avoid attention."

"Oh, my dear, it is six a.m. at the fuckin' Denny's in Santa Cruz. Trust me, you are far from the strangest thing they've seen this morning." Brother John turned and swung the door open.

Eat.

(Fuck [die]).

* * *

"Somethin' to drink?"

"Yeah, hi. Coffee." Brother John turned to Gideon.

Gideon held up one finger. "Two, please."

Brother John pointed his finger like a gun at Cherry-Rose who sat perfectly still in the middle of her bench looking very alone.

"And a … ah …" Brother John prompted.

Her mouth was open, but nothing was coming out. … *nothing, two, three …*

Brother John held the gun pose and said, "A vanilla shake and … a"—he held his middle finger to his temple like he was reading her mind—"A Moons Over My Hammy for the lady."

A wide sea and …

The phrase fell out of the sky when the server turned away from the table. Cherry-Rose could smell eggs, bacon, and salt on the air. The ocean. It was the ocean.

A wide sea and a … what?

And …

All thought was interrupted by the delivery of drink and food.

Once the table was set, Brother John tipped his coffee in Cherry-Rose's direction. "Cheers."

"Cheers," said Gideon and Cherry-Rose, both repeating the gesture.

After a moment of silence, Cherry-Rose spoke without looking up from her straw. "Would this be a good time to inquire …"—she paused to run her straw through her shake—"where might we …"—*sipping*—"be headed?"

Gideon slid her a thick, off-white business card.

Centered gold cursive, two words. "Pleasure Island."

Cherry-Rose peered over her straw, still sipping, and reached out with her free hand to examine the card. On its back side, a phrase printed above a phone number: *Fay çe que vouldras!*

"I don't understand," said Cherry-Rose. "What does all of this mean?"

Gideon turned the card back over to the Pleasure Island side. "It means, this is where we're headed. Pleasure Island. It's a sort of burlesque speakeasy."

"Imagine an old monastery, you know the kind … all boredom and hellfire, properly converted into a place of fun and hellfire." Brother John slapped the table at his joke.

Gideon continued while Brother John smiled into his coffee. "And the back of the card. That means, 'Do what thou wilt …' or do as you might wish, a slogan borrowed from Rabelais."

"I am afraid I've never heard of him," said Cherry-Rose, exchanging her straw for a spoon.

"Right, right, no one has … except for this nut." Brother John motioned a hitchhiking thumb at Gideon. "But burlesque-style speakeasy, that you do know. Essentially the same gig you had at Fontainebleau."

"Same gig?"

"Yeah, you know, singing. Same gig you had with Salvatóre. Speaking of Salvatóre," said Brother John without a pause, "Sorry 'bout all that back there at Fontainebleau … wish you didn't have to see all that. We didn't know you had a front row seat in Salvatóre's … guest room, or whatever that was. Anyway, by the time we arrived, it looked like the negotiations had broken down. He was wild. Truly wild. Isn't that right, Gid?"

"Yeah, there definitely was no reasoning with that bear."

"I guess it doesn't matter. Salvatóre …" Cherry-Rose didn't finish the thought. "I … I was leaving Fontainebleau anyway," said Cherry-Rose to her spoon as it scraped the bottom of her fluted fountain glass.

"Wait, wait." Brother John looked over the edge of his coffee cup. "You were leaving anyway? What?"

Cherry-Rose nodded with mouth on straw, searching the bottom of her glass.

"And just where were you headed?"

Eyes, lips, straw. Cherry-Rose tapped Gideon's Pleasure Island card in the center of the table. "Here. It seems I was coming here all along."

John made wide eyes at Gideon; Gideon made eyes back.

"Funny. We were sent to see if Salvatóre could be persuaded to part with you. And now we find out that you were heading to Pleasure Island all along?" Brother John turned his words up into a question. "If that don't beat all." Brother John slapped the table and broke into a laugh. "I guess we didn't need to persuade the bear so hard … We did it again, didn't we, Gid?" Brother John, elbowed his bench mate. "Whale sure is gonna have a laugh about this one."

And a whale?

Brine, Pine, Piss ... and Puke

"MA' LADY," said Brother John as he held open the back door that led into the Denny's parking lot. Cherry-Rose approached the exit, tying her cape, chewing on the maraschino cherry she saved for her last bite. Gideon in tow, denim over his shoulder. Brother John acting as if they were exiting a limo. Red carpet unfurled.

"No pictures. No pictures, please." He swept his hand from the floor to the sky as if to offer *all of this* to the disinterested duo.

The lot was wet with drizzle and heavy with the scent of brine and bacon and piss and pine. Brother John offered an asphalt kingdom made up of a flickering light post, a pickup truck with a rusted hood, two sedans, one with a sheet of black plastic taped where a window should have been, and an overturned trash can that called to a gaggle of seagulls. Cherry-Rose threw on her hood against the morning mist and marveled at the work of the dawn. The encroaching morning light transformed her surroundings from forest-in-fog to a foul collection of broken things.

This definitely is not the forest, thought Cherry-Rose.

"Hey, Cherry-Rose," said Gideon, motioning to the curb. "You and I, we gotta hang here for a bit."

Cherry-Rose moved to the curb and sat curled up against the morning chill, arms around knees, still chewing on her cherry stem. Gideon stood with his hands in pockets, close, but not too close. He cocked his head, looking oddly serious for the moment, considering their seriously odd breakfast. It was as if all of a sudden he was contemplating life itself. He just stood there staring at the parking lot, lightly tapping his boot against the curb.

"We've got a car stashed in a garage down the road," said Gideon without violating his pose.

"You two relax, take in the scenery." Brother John nodded to the parking lot. "I'm going to see if I can get in and out without spooking the neighbors."

"They haven't seen us in a while," Gideon said while still staring out across the parking lot. "You know? … School."

"Finals were a bitch," added Brother John.

Cherry-Rose looked at Gideon and began to wonder if the change in his demeanor was set off by the idea of being alone with her.

Brother John patted Gideon on the shoulder, winked, and set off down the street.

Gideon tapped the curb again.

Cherry-Rose caught Gideon watching Brother John out of the corner of his eye.

Tap … sigh … tap, tap, tap …

With Brother John well on his way, Gideon turned to face the street.

Cherry-Rose leaned back with her arms braced on the sidewalk to watch Gideon from beneath her hood. He sat arms crossed over knees, face framed, chin in arms, eyes out there with the asphalt and fog. Cherry-Rose wanted to say something. To say *thank you,* for … for what? She didn't know how to thank him for whatever happened on the quad. She knew she should, but she didn't know how to do it without bringing attention to her journal. And the journal … reminding him of that was the last thing she wanted.

For as much as Cherry-Rose thought she should say something about the quad, she couldn't believe that *he* hadn't. And the blood and the cage. There was just too much to say and seemingly no way to say it.

The quad, the pixie-dust, Salvatóre, walking in the dark to Denny's; it was like all of this was normal. No need to talk about it because, somehow, this is *normal. And he is just sitting there ... thinking ... what? What could he possibly be thinking?*

Cherry-Rose could see Brother John walking into the mist at the end of the street, and just as he was about to slip from view, he paused and turned. He leaned back into a wide smile, hands tucked in leather. Walking backward, he shot one hand into the air to give a wave. Then he spoke in a voice that pretended to be a whisper, but wasn't at all. "Hey, kids, don't do anything I wouldn't do. You got ten minutes, tops."

Brother John's teasing line was all Cherry-Rose needed to break the unspoken unspeaking arrangement. "Brother John ... is he ..."

"Always like that?" said Gideon, finishing the question without breaking his stare. "Never not."

Cherry-Rose spied Gideon from the shadow of her hood; pose still fixed—asphalt and fog. She saw a little color in his cheek and decided to let him be for the moment. But, like all moments spent in awkward silence, they moved too slowly. Cherry-Rose was anxious. Gideon was unchanged. He seemed full into a deep, red-cheeked meditation. She wondered if he would say anything at all before Brother John returned.

When she was certain that he wouldn't speak, she said the only thing she could think of that wasn't about her journal, or pixie-dust, or murder.

"Does this place always ... smell like ...?"

Cherry-Rose sniffed at the air for effect, and let the open question hang. She was hoping Gideon would fill in the spaces. He did not. She sniffed the air again, but this time, not for him. The smell was as unique as it was repulsive. Beneath the warmth of the sun, the morning was ringing full with the bouquet of Denny's meets sea, meets forest, meets trash and stagnant gutter water.

"Like ... *this*?" Cherry-Rose finished, thinking perhaps she shouldn't have inhaled so deeply.

"What? This place? The curb by the dumpster in the Denny's parking lot? Yeah, just like that guy." Gideon nodded down the street that took Brother John. "Also, never not."

Gideon was smiling. Cherry-Rose didn't want to lose momentum, so she followed with the only other line of questioning she could think of.

"Do you live here? How do you ... I mean ... school ... How do you do it?"

Gideon ran his hand through his hair, each word emerged slowly. "No ... Well ... Sorta ..."

"Sort of?" Cherry-Rose refused to abandon the chase.

"You know? ... weekends ... holidays ... summer break. During school, we stay in the village near the market. When we are here, we stay at Pleasure Island ... not too far from this place."

Cherry-Rose scrunched up her face, finding even more questions in Gideon's response. "And does this sort of thing happen often?"

"This? ... Often? No. Well ..." Gideon's words drifted again.

When it seemed he wasn't going to finish his thought, Cherry-Rose turned to face Gideon. Her eyes narrowed. "I don't understand ... I don't understand what's going on with you? Are you mad at me?"

Cherry-Rose wanted to stop herself. She had strayed far from her very small list of safe-to-discuss topics, but it was too late. "I can't believe you are even making me ask ... after ... after everything ..." She looked to the sky to keep tears from spilling over.

"I'm sorry. I ... uh ... mad. No. Never. I just ... I know this is all crazy. I can see how for ... other people, *any of this* is a lot. I just don't know what to say about all of this. I don't know what I'm *allowed* to say."

Gideon looked down between his boots; the crown of his hair fell between his eyes. "But I am really sorry. We couldn't have guessed how things were going to go with Salvatóre. That wasn't what we wanted ... We didn't know," the words trailed for a moment, "we'd have to ... steal a car."

"That's what surprised you?" Cherry-Rose leapt up at the sight of a long black car that seemed angled for their edge of the curb, "The car?"

"And when things like that happen," Gideon continued, sounding a little defensive while completely ignoring her question, "this is just how it's done." He finished and stood next to Cherry-Rose.

"Hey, Cherry-Rose." Gideon placed his arm on her shoulder.

Cherry-Rose turned to face him, and when their eyes met, he lowered her hood. "I am really sorry."

All it took was the slight quake in his welling eyes for her to see that she was right about him. He was sorry. This was the Gideon the Obscure, the boy she had written about in homeroom. This was the boy she saw in her early morning waking dreams.

Gideon continued. "I'm sorry about the silent treatment back there. It's weird. There are rules. We ... I can't really talk about this stuff. I could get in a lot of trouble. But you'll see. He'll tell you. Whale. Whale will tell you everything you need to know. And if something doesn't seem right, you just let me know, and we'll figure it out. Okay?"

Cherry-Rose nodded with wide, unblinking eyes and felt herself leaning in as if she might kiss Gideon.

Just as it seemed that Gideon too might be leaning in, Brother John's hand reached out the open window and banged the top of the car—*clang, clang, clang.* "You lovebirds ready?"

"Aaaand, sorry about that guy." Gideon shook his head, opened the door, and folded the seat down. "After you."

Cherry-Rose slid past Gideon and climbed in. Gideon pushed the seat back, hopped in, and hung his arm out the window.

Brother John adjusted to find Cherry-Rose in the rearview mirror. "You ready, kid?"

Cherry-Rose shrugged, and he revved the engine as if to purposely agitate the parking lot's horde of seagulls.

"We sure are glad you decided to come with us," said Brother John through dark sunglasses that made bug eyes in the mirror.

Cherry-Rose didn't speak.

Glad I came? thought Cherry-Rose, staring at her dual reflection in the black of Brother John's glasses. Still wondering if she actually had a choice.

The rumbling black smoke machine rolled on with the motion of the sea. Windows down, elbows out, pulling in the wet of the morning mist.

The car tore down the road but was unable to outrun the parking lot's morning musk. Cherry-Rose breathed wave after wave of exhaust, piss, and pine. Everything all at once churning in concert with her Moons Over My Hammy and vanilla shake.

"Hey, no, no. Not in here," said Brother John with his rearview bug eyes. "Cherry-Rose. Don't you ... Do not puke in the car. Do not."

"You gotta sit up straight," added Gideon. "Keep your eyes on the road and it will pass."

Cherry-Rose repositioned herself, feet planted firmly, spread behind the driver and passenger seats, arms gripping the back of the front row vinyl, eyes wide, asphalt focused. Cherry-Rose felt as if she were drowning in dream. Swallowing the too much of whatever added its pure heat to the churning storm in her gut. She could feel it building from the base of her empty womb, up her seams, warm, warmer, warmer, until she lunged forward over Gideon's right shoulder to hang her head out the window. Until she spilled hot bile down the side of the black-smoke machine.

Something Borrowed,
Something Broken, Something ...

HIS OFFICE was dark. Beneath the trees dark. Beneath the ivy dark. Beneath the waves of a black-sea, black-sky-dream dark.

Dark.

Darker.

Darker.

Cherry-Rose stood awkwardly near the doorway beside Gideon and Brother John.

His office reminded Cherry-Rose of Marybelle's shed. The walls seemed to be dripping with latent magic. Parts and pieces. Spent shells on nails. Nails in walls. Nails hanging with forest totem. Mounted beasts, each waiting for their wishes to be answered, waiting for their Blue Fairy to drop out of the sky. There hung a bear, a wolf, a rabbit, a fox, and a deer. Inside a display case, an owl, a scrub jay on a perch, on another a hawk, a magpie, a woodpecker. Floating lifeless in clear liquid, a snake, a scorpion, a spider. Bookcases and their cache were framed in mounted vermin: a squirrel, a rat, an opossum, a raccoon. Behind a desk, a young girl painted in oil.

"Cherry-Rose, pleased to meet you." He crossed the room and offered his hand. "It truly is a pleasure. I've heard so much about you. I'm William."

William. He was an unassuming but well-built man wearing jeans, loafers, no socks, and a button-up shirt. At first glance, he looked too young to own much of anything, let alone Pleasure Island. However, his salt and pepper hair revealed that he was at least twice the age of Brother John. He rolled up his sleeves to three-quarter length and black ink peeked out. A tail belonging to something on the underside of one arm, tentacles belonging to something else on the other.

His name is William. William, said the Cherry-Rose beyond the dreams. *William Hale.*

W… Hale.

W.H.A.L.E.

Run. Swim. Something. Get out.

"Thank you," Cherry-Rose said in a whisper as she shook his hand.

"Cherry-Rose, please," said William, motioning to a pair of leather chairs positioned before his desk. "Please, sit anywhere you like."

Swim. Run. Something

Perhaps it was the time they spent on the drive and the walk, or just sitting at breakfast, or maybe it was that they freed her from Salvatóre; whatever it was, Cherry-Rose looked up at Gideon and Brother John for permission to ignore her chirping inner-voice. Gideon smiled and Brother John winked—permission granted.

The voice beyond was persistent, but the Cherry-Rose standing within the gates of Pleasure Island knew that everything else—Mother, Forest, Blue Fairy—Brother John and Gideon—wanted her to stay. With a slight nod, she took a seat as William slid into the chair behind his desk.

"Boys, a job well done. Thank you," said William. "You will find that you have been well-compensated."

Cherry-Rose turned to see Brother John and Gideon offer a small silent bow.

"Johnboy, do be a dear and get the door, Cherry-Rose and I have a few things to discuss. Perhaps you two could go and check in on our ... little problem. I hear that we are making progress. I imagine that recent events may swing things in our favor."

William's eyes followed the swing of the door. When it clicked shut, he beamed out from behind his desk with soft blue-gray eyes and a sweet, easy smile. Eyes that could have been made in the cottage fire. Eyes that told a story much different from the story his office seamed to project. Cherry-Rose found that the eyes, that smile, they transformed the dark, ominous, forest-shed-feeling into something actually inviting.

When the smile was held, just this side of long enough for it to be too long, William sighed a long, soft sigh that slid into a soft honey tone. "My daughter Emily," he said, motioning to the painting behind his desk. "Beautiful, isn't she? Wasn't she?" he corrected. "She would have been a beautiful young lady by now. Maybe like you, but alas, she drowned a few years back."

Cherry-Rose tried to calm the urge to fidget under his steady gaze. She could see the seamstress mouthing her warning: *play dead, my sweet, my darling, play dead.* Cherry-Rose observed the seated mannequin-ghost-girl pose, the almost-living, definitely probably not alive, almost-girl; the mannequin-as-poetry pose: feet set squarely beneath knees, hands on the lap, one atop the other, back straight, head straight—*as if a string were tied to one's crown tugging gently from the sky. Eyes ... they don't blink. Lips, they don't breathe.*

William continued. "It may surprise you to learn, I know your mother quite well. She is quite the entrepreneur."

Cherry-Rose squirmed in her seat.

"Perhaps I exaggerate our connection. I should say, I knew her. I grew up in the village. Saw her at market every now and then. I trust she is doing well?"

"She's ..." Cherry-Rose looked to the floor. "Dead."

"Oh, I am so sorry, Cherry-Rose. That must be hard. I can only imagine how difficult it must have been for you ... I know what it is to lose a loved one. Losing a mother is no small thing."

Cherry-Rose kept her gaze on the floor, not quite knowing what to say. "How rude of me, I've rambled on. Can I get you something to drink?" He motioned to the bar behind his desk.

"You must be parched. When the boys called in, they told me that Salvatóre had you locked up. Full circle, I guess. The caged became the keeper. Such a shame that he couldn't break that cruel cycle. I'm not really sure that he began your partnership with a suitable end in mind. You've really had some tough luck, haven't you?" William pushed his chair away from his desk.

"Was that a 'yes' to the drink?" William asked "You had such a long journey."

Cherry-Rose nodded.

William turned to his bar. "Just one second," said William, drawing out the "one" until something poured over ice. "Here ya go." William handed Cherry-Rose a Tom Collins glass, all ice and bubbles edged with a wedge of lime.

"Thank you," whispered Cherry-Rose. "So … the school …" Cherry-Rose started to say, taking the glass.

"Yes. That. Well, it seems that if you donate enough money, they'll name a school just about anything," said William, returning to his desk. "Local boy makes it big in the city and all." William laughed and said, "I can imagine that you have a few more questions, but I'm sure you're hungry and tired. Let's start here. I know that you have been through a lot, uprooted, a new town far from home, without a mother. I wonder, would you consider staying here as my guest? I know that everything— this place, me—all of this is new to you, but you do know Brother John and Gideon. Schoolmates, yes?" He nodded. "They'll be here all summer. We could set you up for a week, a month or two. Longer. Shorter. Whatever you like. Think about it. No rush at all."

"You said you knew her?" asked Cherry-Rose, ignoring his offer. "Have you seen others like me? Did she … did you … buy from her?" She stumbled through the question, unable to hide the shake in her voice.

"I grew up in the village. Everyone who had ever been to the market knew about the doll-maker who lived in the forest."

William leaned in and spoke a little softer. "Did I buy from her? No. But there is something I was hesitant to mention earlier as its news may have derailed our meeting. There is someone here I think you know. She has been living ... working here at Pleasure Island."

"And you're just telling me this now?" Cherry-Rose sprang to her feet. "Who is it? Where is she?"

"Perhaps if you hold your questions ... it's probably best I show you."

William pulled his jacket over his shoulder and opened the office door. "You should know ... something strange happened to her this last weekend."

* * *

Hallway. Door. William.

Whale.

On the other side of the door, tears. Sobs and tears. *I know those tears,* thought Cherry-Rose.

William opened the door and made way for Cherry-Rose.

All of Cherry-Rose's dream worries, all of her wonder about the nails, the parts and pieces, the beasts hanging from walls; all of her wonder about the dark, dark, under the sea office; all of the desire to *run,* to remember, even recall the Blue Fairy birdsong warnings—they were gone because ... Shy-Blue.

There. Right there. Shy-Blue wrapped up in Brother John's arms. Crying into his chest. Brother John doing his best "shhhh, shhh, there, there" two-step.

Gideon was standing just inside the door. He took Cherry-Rose's arm and silently ushered her further into the apartment. Shy-Blue was in the middle of a fit. Wailing. Crying. Hands beating the leather on John's shoulders.

Moments earlier, just before William opened the door, William tried to prepare Cherry-Rose for what she'd find. "You should know, she's been a wreck since Monday night. A total mess. It came on all of a sudden. Like something inside her broke," William said. "She's been dancing here for a few months now. Top bill. Sunday's matinee performance went well, great, better than great, but she didn't show to rehearsal on Monday. I sent Johnboy to check in on her. He said she was just sitting on the floor as if in a trance, staring at the wall with tears streaming down her face."

Cherry-Rose already knew what they couldn't know. On the day that Marybelle died, all of her memory spells were broken.

Shy-Blue's hidden memory life, her sometimes dream and sometimes nightmare life that only visited in the small waking hours of the morning, too hazy and strange to be anything but dream, but wasn't at all, came crashing down and spilled over her … all at once.

That day, without the soft and necessary buffer of the haze. Straight, uncut, memory-hammer revealing a life she didn't even know was hers. Everything that was hidden deep inside, the good memories, the bad memories, the memories that were so good one wonders why they had to go bad at all; the memories that were so bad, one wonders if the good were worth it at all; right there, all at once.

"Shy. Shy … Shy-Blue. It's me. Cherry-Rose. Ch—"

Shy-Blue slowly turned at the sound of her voice. She paused, reached out as if to test the air, and leapt to tackle Cherry-Rose. Shy-Blue pinned her to the floor and the fit started anew. Sobs and sighs built up until they were both crying uncontrollably. Brother John moved to pat Shy-Blue on the back. She lurched away from his touch and locked her knees tight around Cherry-Rose, her arms under her head, her hands full of black mane.

"Shy. Shy. I can't. I can't breathe." Cherry-Rose gasped half waiting for Violent-Joy to jump out and yell, "Buried alive" before she piled on.

"Shy-Blue. It's okay. I'm here now. Shhh, shhh, shhh." Cherry-Rose tucked Shy-Blue's hair behind her ear, and she made the shushing sound until she felt the knees that gripped her torso relax. "I found you. I can't believe it. I found you."

"Don't …" was all Shy-Blue seemed able to say. "Don't …"

"Shy. Never. Never, never. I won't leave you. I won't ever leave you."

* * *

Cherry-Rose woke on the floor beneath Shy-Blue. Shy-Blue was asleep, breathing long and slow deep breaths into Cherry-Rose's neck.

How long have we ... Cherry-Rose wondered at the ceiling.

The room was dark. The floor was cold. They were alone.

... and the Cherry-Rose that begged her to run, that scratched behind the vines in her mind, said, "You found what you came for. Now take Shy-Blue and get out before it's too late."

Rules for Roaches

CHERRY-ROSE promised William that she'd take a few days to consider his offer. However, she didn't really believe that there was much to think about. After all, there were eleven lost sisters to be found. So, a small courtesy … just a few days to appear to give William's offer careful consideration. Cherry-Rose felt it was the least she could do. *William has been so generous, so kind and thoughtful,* she told herself. She didn't yet have the heart to tell him that at the end of the week, not only was she leaving, but she was taking Shy-Blue with her.

With each passing day, Shy-Blue looked more uneasy. Unsure, avoidant, pained. Never enough time to talk about what they should talk about. Her. Marybelle. Her. The Blue Fairy. Them. Their other sisters. This. This place. Cherry-Rose recognized every look … every distant stare, the gentle look away just as she entered a room, the look of discomfort and deep thought that settled upon her countenance if they happened to occupy the same room for too long. Were these not the same tactics that she employed to keep William at bay? *But why?* It took seeing Shy-Blue dance at Pleasure Island's nightclub to understand why she seemed eager to avoid any sort of discussion of the subject. Up there on that stage, with those lights, and all those beasts out there in the audience panting and howling for her, Shy-Blue was electric, beautiful, happy.

Cherry-Rose knew what Shy-Blue seemed unable to say. Shy-Blue was shaken by her awakening, but she was never going to leave.

"But if you could have seen the shed," said Cherry-Rose. "If you had seen those nails and those bows and those names … if only you could have seen Peaches and Scarlet, and Rey-Rey and Jasmine, everyone twisted and tortured in my dream."

Cherry-Rose felt Shy-Blue's lack of understanding from behind her blank stare. Her words began to unwind as she continued arguing her case.

"You don't understand …" Her words seeming so far away … "My dreams …" *Farther.* "They aren't just dreams …" *Further.*

Unwound.

Shy-Blue interrupted and placed her hands on Cherry-Rose's shoulders. Cherry-Rose leaned into her hands and let her arms hang lifeless, her face making the *head-slightly-tilted, eyes-wide, mouth-open, playing-dead* face. Normally, this routine would have Shy-Blue returning the stare before they both erupted into laughter, but today, Shy-Blue blinked hard at Cherry-Rose and spoke.

"Our sisters are scattered all over Fairy-knows-where. They could literally be anywhere. And everywhere else I've been, well … nothing comes close to this place. And look … no, no, no. I see you … I know what you're thinking. There is no way I am going back to the cottage. And besides, this place … It's beautiful. And you sing! You could sing here. It could be me and you on that stage. And, honestly, they've been so good to me … ever since Brother John found me …"

Cherry-Rose betrayed her pose. Her eyes got even bigger and her lips mouthed, "Whaaaa …"

Shy-Blue shook Cherry-Rose. "No, no, don't try to change the subject, not now. See, that's why I didn't bring any of that up."

"But, Shy-Blue, I …" Cherry-Rose tried to speak but was overrun again.

"No, no. Not now. We aren't talking about that now. Stay … say you will stay and we will have plenty of time to talk about all of that stuff.

But this, this is important. The point is ... you know where we came from ... this place is great. And Brother John, he ... William, he took me in."

"But Peaches and Vi and ..." Cherry-Rose managed to say.

"William has connections. He knows people. I'm sure he'll help us find them. I know he will. I just never knew to ask. But, either way, we can't just wander around aimlessly. And you know what, it has been a long time. We should probably just face the facts: our sisters, they're probably either dead or happy."

Dead. Or happy? There was something to this, thought Cherry-Rose. *That's why no one else came to the cottage. They either couldn't—dead. Or didn't want to—happy. Why else? Dead or happy.*

Wondering if she was capable of, no, deserving of, being happy.

"Sure. Sure. Dead or happy. Either way, I think I would prefer to know," said Cherry-Rose.

"This is a lot to give up," whispered Shy-Blue as she settled her arms around Cherry-Rose's waist, "just to know."

In that embrace, Cherry-Rose found, in silent, irritated, and definitely annoyed reflection, that Shy-Blue was not wrong.

This place is beautiful. It is indeed a lot to give up. And I can sing.

And maybe the desire to run is tied to guilt for wanting to be happy. Thanks a lot, Marybelle.

Cherry-Rose knew that only mother-magic could weave that spell.

Whatever the case, it seemed impossible to convince Shy-Blue that blindly searching for the others was the answer.

* * *

Cherry-Rose stood naked, playing dead in front of her no-room studio mirror, and considered all the whys and all the maybes and all the motherly-magic that had her insides churning and twisting. When they were all considered, Cherry-Rose told the mirror, "Pleasure Island isn't the forest, and William isn't Marybelle. There. That's it. This isn't the forest and he isn't her. It is decided." With that decision, for the first time since finding Shy-Blue, the voice beyond her dreams went silent.

It was upon her return to William's office the next day that Cherry-Rose began to believe that the voice beyond her dreams might be capable of more than internal dialog. The voice was silent, but now it pushed its dream images into the waking world. A scan of the room told her that all the animals on all the plaques, held by all those nails, and all those birds on all those perches, and all the vermin holding up all those books, were now posed in oddly twisted ways, with oddly twisted features. The birds were frozen in motion with wings stretched at various angles, heads tilted, beaks open, shrieking silent warnings. The bear smiled with all his teeth, the rat snarled like a wolf, the wolf like the fox, the fox like the opossum, the raccoon smiled like the bear, and the rabbit and the deer hung with eyes too wide, brows too high. *Were they always like this?* Cherry-Rose asked herself when she knew that they were not.

She sat across from William, next to Shy-Blue, and reminded herself, *This isn't the forest. He is not her.*

In my dream ... after the sea, Cherry-Rose reasoned, wanting very badly to see the good in something, *there was Brother John asking ... and after Brother John ... didn't I find Gideon behind the dream? And didn't they take me to Shy-Blue? Shy-Blue. How can that ... how can any of this be bad? How could being happy be bad?* She wanted the dream voice, in all its silent protest, to be wrong about something—for once. She wanted it to be wrong for Shy-Blue ... but also for herself.

She is right here. Shy-Blue is right here.

* * *

The sisters sat mirror-matched in chairs perfectly angled to suggest the focal point of the room. At the apex of the chair's invisible lines, a desk, and behind that desk, hidden behind a single sheet of paper, William. The room was quiet; *before a storm quiet,* thought Cherry-Rose. For all the quiet, the knot of things that twisted her gut began twisting anew. The feeling reminded Cherry-Rose of cottage nights when her insides would rumble right before lightning would strike.

She could hear *her* voice: "Girls, girls, my sweetest sweets, you must … away from the window. Lightning will take a daughter at a window as soon as it would a tree in the forest."

The knot and the nerves that made the rumble twisted and grew. They gave her sight and showed Cherry-Rose what she would see on the other side of William's paper.

The paper that was mask hid an ever-widening smile of perfect teeth, a jaw that split wider and wider until those perfect teeth were pushed free from bone to make way for obscenely pointed fangs. Behind the smile, the teeth and the fangs were joined by widening wolf eyes, two becoming four to see right through the paper, to see behind her eyes.

Just when Cherry-Rose felt she was about to scream, a hand on hers chased the dream away. Cherry-Rose could hear herself breathing—too hard, too fast. She turned to find Shy-Blue posing as Marybelle on lightning-storm nights—smiling with finger over lips, making her *hush-hush-darling* face while silently tapping her finger over pursed lips.

Dream shattered, the paper-mask became paper, not mask; and the beast became William, not wolf; and Shy-Blue became Shy-Blue, not Marybelle. Cherry-Rose steadied her breath and reminded herself that the rumble that gave her a knot, whispers, and a waking dream didn't mean a thing. Because the wolf who was a mother was gone and the sister who needed to be found, was. Shy-Blue was right there; and the man who sat behind the paper was just a man.

Cherry-Rose squeezed Shy-Blue's hand to test her waking-dream theories. She *was* there, and the worry began to fade. When her eyes were able to focus, she found a soft smile on a face that seemed like it might have been staring at her for hours.

William pushed the paper to the edge of his desk, angled just so to silently direct Shy-Blue to bridge the distance.

"Do be a doll."

Shy-Blue took the paper.

"What do you think?" asked William.

"That's it," said Shy-Blue, "same performance contract as mine. Are you ready to have some fun?" Shy-Blue handed the paper to Cherry-Rose.

Cherry-Rose knew she was supposed to be reading the contract, but she couldn't. She sat staring blankly at the words on the paper, not reading, but imagining it as mask, wondering what she was becoming for everyone else while she was hidden behind the page.

"Take your time, Cherry-Rose. Sign it, don't sign it. Take it back to your place and read it over. Do whatever feels right." William slid a pen out to the edge of his desk.

"But our sisters, we—"

William jumped in before Cherry-Rose could finish. "I know how much they mean to you. I do. As I mentioned to Shy-Blue, I have a few leads. With you here … now that Shy-Blue too has her memories, nothing would bring me greater joy than to reunite all of you. Regardless of your decision, we will find them … In the meantime, either way, as a performer or as a guest, any friend … any sister of Shy's is welcome here. Sign, don't sign. Either way, if you will have it, the apartment is yours for the summer."

Cherry-Rose took the contract and scanned the lines. *Pleasure Island Performance Contract, blah, blah, blah …*

Money which means freedom and stability comes with staying. Shy-Blue comes with staying. The man with the soft eyes, who was once a father, who seems to look upon Shy-Blue as a daughter, who might see me … who promised to help us find the others, he comes with staying; and the boy with the heart tattoo … he …

"I wouldn't really worry about it," said Shy-Blue, leaning in to speak behind the back of her hand. "I never read mine and everything has been fine. Please say yes, please say you'll stay and do the show."

"Shy …" Cherry-Rose paused, pretending to read the last lines of the contract. "Of course, I'll stay. I'd love to do the show with you." Cherry-Rose took the pen in hand. "It'll be fun, right?" She handed the paper to William.

William smiled and signed just below her name. "We are so glad to have you, Cherry-Rose."

"You won't regret this," said Shy-Blue, dabbing the corners of her eyes.

"Now, you and Shy-Blue take some time and get some rest. You've both been through a lot. Cherry-Rose, let's get you acclimated. Shy-Blue, when Cherry-Rose is ready, let's see if we can update that Fontainebleau set. I've got the perfect tagline: *one dances, one sings, no hearts, no strings.* People will go wild for this stuff."

Cherry-Rose wasn't used to sympathy. Anything even poorly disguised as understanding almost felt like much more than she deserved. *Get acclimated? Rest? As soon as I could walk, Marybelle was twirling me about on the cottage floor. For her, I was never more than a toy, but here with William … maybe I could be something else.*

She felt the warm feeling of belonging rush over her, and it made her too dab the corners of her eyes.

* * *

The cicada in her stuffing, the doe who was Spirit, and the Cherry-Rose beyond the dreams reasoned for the mannequin-ghost girl.

The cicada: *It is hard to see the patterns when it has never been any other way.*

The Beyond: *When one imagines that dreams are just dreams and our beyond-the-dream-voice perpetually skipping—run, run, run.*

The doe: *When memories of pain somehow cling tighter than those of joy, wanting to see a way around the pain becomes survival.*

The cicada: *When she doesn't want to run any longer because she has always been running … even before this life.*

The Beyond: *Since before there ever was a Cherry-Rose.*

The doe: *Running. And just how did that work out?*

The cicada: *Ask the wolf.*

The Beyond: *Ask the Ivy.*

The doe: *Ask the mother.*

* * *

After her session with William and Shy-Blue, Cherry-Rose decided that any worry she was feeling was the product of her upbringing. That this, the awkwardness permeating this life shift, was solely attributable to the discomfort of unaccustomed joy. After all, if the seamstress taught her anything, it was that it was entirely very hard to be happy. And wasn't that the best revenge? Settling into the quiet stillness of the moment that accompanies the realization … I *am* happy. As Cherry-Rose settled into her new apartment, she decided that this was so.

Her apartment was modest. A small single room with a single window, a sink, and a toilet. A copy of *Howl* on her pillow, antler cape hung on the back of the door, a rod holding a funeral-birthday dress and a few hand-made treasures. Simple and modest and just down the hall from Shy-Blue. Everything she could ever need.

Day one of rest. Page one of diary. Cherry-Rose wrote,

Hello Virginia,

We did it. I got my room.

New home. New diary. New start?

She finished the page with a squiggle that ran wide and wild to the bottom.

Next page.

Sisters,

This place is almost perfect. No, it is. It is perfect … almost. As close to perfect as it is, if I am being honest, it is hard not to feel guilty, sad, and lonely without you—even with Shy-Blue.

Dead or happy. Can it really be that simple?

Pleasure Island and William. There is a lot to take in. Perhaps my guilt is creating doubt. Shy-Blue is here and she is happy. I will try. I am trying. Trying to remember that this isn't the forest and he isn't the seamstress. This is where I found Shy-Blue. This is Gideon's home. This is my home—for now.

Day two of rest. Day two of diary.

Sisters,

I know that I have no right to complain, but this room ... it is a little quiet without you. I could use a record player ... AND some records. At least a few more books. I could use some new books. And some room to dance. Do I really need this bed in here? The bed is a little big for one. Just how did Shy-Blue ever get used to sleeping alone?

Still getting used to being one. I'd rather not get used to it.

I will find you—all of you.

Day three of rest. Day three of diary.

This place is so quiet. Too quiet? Maybe I am claustrophobic? I am sure I am. I blame Her. If it wasn't for Shy-Blue living down the hall, I'd have gone stir-crazy by now.

By day four, moments after waking, Cherry-Rose was feeling the frustrating itch of too much rest, behind too many walls, without enough stimulation.

* * *

By day four, Brother John too was frustrated, because since day one, Cherry-Rose had breakfast with Shy-Blue, lunch with Shy-Blue, rehearsal ... dinner with Shy-Blue ... walk with Shy-Blue ... visit with Shy-Blue ... talk all night with Shy-Blue.

Brother John decided he needed a diversion.

* * *

"Hey Gid, could you do me a favor?"

A favor? Gideon lifted his brow.

"Could you do something about Cherry-Rose for me?" Brother John asked as he followed Gideon into his apartment.

Gideon turned to face Brother John, leaning back against the kitchen counter. He squinted against the question.

"Nothing crazy, I just need you to give her something to do for an hour or two. The show is coming up, and you know how they are, always changing things last minute. Shy-Blue asked if I could ..." Gideon watched as Brother John stumbled over what he knew was a lie. "Help her out with ... a few things."

Help her out with a few things? Gideon knew just how he was *helping her out.* He was breaking the very rules that Whale expected Brother John to enforce. The very rules that transformed him from Just John to Brother John.

First rule: You don't fuck the talent.

Blue-Sunday. After Shy-Blue came, it had been five shows a week for the last few months with two on Sunday. Over the last few months, Sunday matinees were their thing. While Whale was off doing whatever Whale did on Sundays, between shows, Brother John would sneak off to Shy-Blue's place. First, it was just Sundays; then, it became whenever they thought Whale was "out at sea" (Brother John's code for Whale had left Pleasure Island).

Second rule: You don't fuck with the pixie-dust.

Blue-Monday. "Monday was too much," said Brother John. "You weren't there, man, she fucking lost it. She was going to leave. She was going to run away. She was screaming, yelling at me that her whole life was a lie." Brother John ran his hands through his hair. "I had to do something. It was all I could think of. Just a little to calm her down. It's no big deal. Everyone does it. Couldn't hurt ... and it didn't. It totally didn't. You've seen her, man, she's fine. It saved her. Kept her from running. You know what he'd do if she ran. Just a little in her tea and she dropped that crying act and she was back on top of me, just like her old self. Made her forget all that bullshit."

"You know this is trouble, right?" Gideon said, standing with his hands shoved deep into his pockets.

"Come on, man. I've got this. We've got this. You gotta relax. Maybe you should try some blue. You should. Like seriously. I've got you ... I'd be right there with you. It's me and you, man. Always me and you ever since

I found you dumpster diving for corndogs. Think about it, man. Me and you forever."

"Seriously? No fucking way. You're losing it. I *am* thinking about it, and I know what's going to happen. *You* know what's going to happen. Things have been getting a little too crazy around here. We should cut. Get out of here. Bring her, don't … I don't care, but either way, you gotta drop the blue. You know it's going to show, right? You know how it works. You have about a week, maybe two, and then it'll show up in your eyes … you can't hide it with sunglasses forever. In another week, it'll be your skin and nails. After that, man, you're gone, not dead, but you'll wish you were. Have you already forgotten?"

Brother John dropped his head and leaned back against the wall.

"Did you forget what Whale did to Mikey? Do you remember what he made us do? What we did for *him*? In case you forgot, he's out there under the lemon tree." Gideon pleaded, "Come on, man … let's drop this, leave everything, and just go."

"It isn't that easy, Gid. He'll find us. They'll find us. Remember, we're part of the people who find people. There's nowhere to go … Come on, don't look at me like that. Fine. Fine. FINE. I'll think about it. I promise. But for now, I just need some space. We … Shy-Blue and I …" Brother John slid his sunglasses back and pushed the heels of his hands into his eyes. "We just need some space. We've got to get our heads right. Get back to where we were before she broke. That's all I need. Just a little time to make it like it was before. I just need a little help from you. That's all I'm asking. Just a little help. Maybe you could find Cherry-Rose and show her around? Like the boardwalk, or a bookstore—you guys like books, right? Or a … I don't know, man, like just take a long walk in the garden, something, anything. I just need some time with her … This one thing. Do this one thing and I'll think about it. I will. I'll … come up with a plan to get us out of here."

Gideon was silent. Head down. Feeling like the sun was pouring all its light into the front of his skull. Feeling like if he put the tip of his boot through a wall, it might release the pressure.

"Come on, man … I promise." Brother John groveled like a sad leather-clad clown, eyes wide, wet, and shaking.

The sight of Brother John crumbling before him, the Brother John who never blinked, never cracked, who never broke, who was now broken down and crumbling, did the job of the boot. It exploded the star that was flashing its pain behind Gideon's eyes.

Gideon saw those lips smiling that warm Brother John smile through dripping eyes. His hands pushing the words out from the center of his torso that seemed to be holding all his invisible pain. They reached out, and Brother John wrapped his arms around Gideon and hung his head on his shoulder.

"Fuck … Okay … Fine. I'll do it. You got it, man. One diversion before dinner."

Circling the Lemon Tree

"THEY hate me. They ... really hate me. That was awful." It wasn't the band, the arrangement, or even William. It wasn't that rehearsal went poorly, because it hadn't. In fact, it went perfectly. Cherry-Rose was amazing. It was Fontainebleau all over again—an almost empty theater, and still the howls from the band filled the room and chased the midday moon. It went too well; too well for the half a dozen other girls who Shy-Blue promised "would just love her." It went too well for those who had been working that very stage long before they had even heard of a Cherry-Rose, who didn't care that there was a Cherry-Rose, who, upon the next full moon, would wish that there never was a Cherry-Rose at all; who, upon William stopping Cherry-Rose halfway through "I Fall in Love Too Easily" to inform everyone that Cherry-Rose would be headlining, muttered something about a certain someone always being eager to take on a new pet.

"Come on, it wasn't all that bad," said Shy-Blue, pulling Cherry-Rose toward their monastery apartments. "They just need a little time to warm up to you is all."

"Hmmm, I'm not too sure about that. Not one of them ... not one of them said a word to me. Did you see the way they were looking at me? Dagger eyes. Pure dagger eyes."

"I'm pretty sure they just didn't know what to say. I know you didn't get out much when you were at Fontainebleau, but you were kind of a big deal. I imagine they were just a little … intimidated. They'll come around. Trust me. Don't give it a second thought."

"Trust you … Not a second thought," repeated Cherry-Rose, pausing at her door to make a scowling face.

* * *

Gideon heard Shy-Blue's footsteps fading down the hall, then he came out of hiding. He positioned himself near Cherry-Rose's door and leaned against the wall. Water ran. A drawer opened. A drawer closed. She was singing. Humming something. He held his breath. Waited for just the right …

Knock. Knock. "Hey, Cherry-Rose. It's me, Gideon."

The humming stopped.

"Wondering if …" He continued to speak to the suddenly silent room. "If, uh … If you've got nothing else to do … I thought you might like someone to show you around."

"Why, hello sir," said Cherry-Rose as she opened door.

"Sir, huh?" Gideon laughed. "Why hello, my good lady."

"And where have you been these last few days? I was beginning to worry."

"I, uh … Whale, he uh … I dunno. I've just been laying low," said Gideon, attempting, then abandoning, the lie. "I was wondering," Gideon interjected, hoping to change the subject, "could I possibly interest you in a tour of our lovely estate?"

"I'd love to, but I think Shy-Blue and I have—"

"Funny thing," interrupted Gideon. "I just saw her. Something came up, I guess, so I thought … uh … here I am."

"I see. Sent to my rescue, were you?"

"Not at all. I just thought … you haven't been here long. I thought you might like a tour of Pleasure Island … since I, uh, heard Shy-Blue was gonna be busy."

"Hmm, suspicious," teased Cherry-Rose. "Suspicious indeed," she said with a smile, "but also intriguing. I accept."

* * *

It was a short walk down the hallway to exit courtyard side. Gideon held the door, then offered his arm to Cherry-Rose. She took it and spoke as if reciting from a Pleasure Island tour guide pamphlet.

"Pleasure Island. It is a large, sprawling property." Cherry-Rose released Gideon's arm and ran ahead. She turned to face Gideon as she skipped backward, laughing as she continued. "An old monastery converted into apartments and offices. At the far end of the property"—her arm pointed somewhere—"an old church converted into a night club. Beneath the Stars and the Deep Blue Sea. A true delight. And right in the middle of it all," she stopped her backward skip to sweep her arms wide, "a huge central courtyard surrounded by an array of apartments and offices."

"Ah. I see. Of course, you've had the tour," said Gideon behind a blushing smile.

"Well, I have been here for a few days. Perhaps you could tell me about the courtyard flora?"

Cherry-Rose loved the courtyard. It was decorated with scattered citrus trees, and a wild assortment of unruly shrubs, bushes, and blooms that all threatened a network of winding paths. She ran her hand over the foxgloves while drinking in the pained look on Gideon's face.

"Hmmm. I can't say that I know too much about that stuff." Gideon rubbed the back of his neck. "I'm sorry. This is … silly, right?" Gideon lowered his head.

"No, no," said Cherry-Rose. "Pretend I don't know anything. Please. I'm enjoying this. Really … please, pretty please." She hopped in place.

"I'm sure you are. Okay, you asked for it. Here we go." Gideon straightened his denim jacket and snapped his collar up. "Best tour ever coming up."

Gideon shoved his hands deep in his pockets, and Cherry-Rose took his arm. With his free elbow, Gideon gestured with a useless, half-hearted poke at the air. "Over there," the elbow shook toward the far end of the sprawling property, "as you know," he said, casting a squinting sideways eye toward Cherry-Rose in protest to this superfluous dialogue, "Beneath the Stars and the Deep Blue Sea."

"Ohhhhh. Ahhh. Yes. Beneath the Stars." Cherry-Rose repeated the phrase as if it was the first time she heard it. She held her hand to her brow to shield her eyes, pretending to strain to see across the courtyard.

Gideon's elbow shot backward. "Back there," he said, ushering Cherry-Rose around the edge of the garden, "that's the, uh … monastery."

Cherry-Rose rubbed her chin thoughtfully. "Hmmm. The monást–ery. I do believe I've heard it pronounced differently," she joked.

"Come on." Gideon pleaded with a sad sort of laugh that sounded more like he was on the verge of surrender.

Cherry-Rose started to laugh. "Okay, okay, this *is* silly. But I've got an idea. If it is indeed *my* tour, I'd prefer a different sort. How about," Cherry-Rose paused with her finger to her temple, "you tell me all about yourself? Yes, that's it. I'd like one Gideon tour, please."

"Uh, yeah, I don't know. Are we looking to make silly worse? Because if we are … my story is just the thing. It … maybe silly isn't the word. Whatever it is, I'm not sure I've ever told it … I'm not sure if I can."

"Awww, come on, all the more reason to tell it. You can't say that and not tell the story."

"I don't know, Cherry-Rose. It's weird. I don't really like to talk about that stuff."

Cherry-Rose pouted and released his arm. "Hmmpf. I see, on the clock. Can't get too personal, I suppose."

* * *

If Brother John broke through Gideon's resolve earlier today, Cherry-Rose burned it to ash. He didn't know why, but there was no one else in the world that he would rather tell his life story to than Cherry-Rose. This was why, she was why, ever since her arrival, the *Rules for Roaches* voice chirped so loudly in the morning … in the night, in the shower, in the garden. And the desire to tell her, to let her in, if only just a little, to share what Gideon felt only she could understand began to grow out from that ash.

Gideon sighed. "Okay, sure, what do you want to know?"

Cherry-Rose smiled, took his arm, and squeezed it tight. "Everything. Tell me everything. Start at the beginning."

"Everything? Hmm … I'll do my best. Damn. Okay. The beginning. I'm from LA—Hollywood Hills I guess.

My parents … our parents. I had … I … I have a sister. Things were hard for us. Our parents. I'm not sure they wanted to be parents. That's not true, my mom did, but she wasn't around long … not long enough. Our dad started to change and then one day, she was just gone. Like, one day she was there … I remember her … and the next, she was gone. Then … then someone else was there. And then after that … we …"

"Wait … What?! Did you ever ask your dad about …?"

"No way." Gideon interrupted. "It's hard to explain … Speaking up was a good way to get some bad attention. I guess I just assumed she wanted out like we did. Maybe she had to get out the only way she could. That had to be it."

Gideon wanted to stop talking, knew he should. It could have been the impending twilight or the daylight moon just visible above the bell tower; it could have been that the weight of carrying his story doubled at the precise moment he discovered someone worthy of hearing his secrets. He carried all of it for so long, so long that none of it seemed real any longer. Maybe it was because he knew only Cherry-Rose could understand; maybe it had nothing to do with any of that, maybe it was just Cherry-Rose. Whatever it was, he couldn't stop.

He told her about his parents, the father who only spoke softly after he laid lashes with his belt, with his *I-wish-you-didn't-make-me-do-this* voice; the stepmother who made eyes and spoke with her *you-better-not-tell-your-father-about-this* voice. He told her about his sister who shouldn't have had to deal with their shit at all.

"One day I stole some money from my dad so we could run away. They caught us about a mile down the road. My dad told me if we ever did it again, I'd be sorry. And of course, we did it again because what did I care about sorry? Staying there was worse than ..." Gideon paused. "I figured, what could they do to me that they hadn't already done? But you know what? ... I was sorry. When they found us ... she grabbed my sister. My dad took his belt. They made me watch. My stepmother held my head, she kept yelling, 'Look ... look you little prick, look what you made us do.' They were right. That hurt worse than any beating I ever had."

Gideon slowed his pace as the church bell rang. "A few days later, they said they were sorry ... that they wanted to start over ... they said they had a trip planned for us. In the morning, they drove us out to the beach. I'm not sure what I was thinking, but after we pulled up, I ran into the water ... must have gotten pulled under. Riptide or something. Woke up on the beach spitting water, wondering how the sun was already setting. It was weird ... the beach was empty, everyone, my dad, his wife, my sister, were gone."

"They just left you?"

"I guess so. Either I lost them, or they lost me. It's strange, but it's like I left everything out there under the water. Everything that came before the beach—my mom, my sister, my dad and his wife—it's all like a strange dream. Sometimes I wish I could remember everything. Most of the time I don't."

"I'm so sorry," said Cherry-Rose. "I know what it is to live with hazy memories. I know what it is to be lost." She gripped his arm tighter.

"Gideon, I'm so sorry. I ... I don't know what to say. I ..."

Gideon stopped. "Right? What can anyone say? I was lost in LA, like everyone else. Maybe ... maybe more like abandoned ... I don't know. I guess it feels like being lost when you can't go home no matter how horrible it was. It doesn't matter anyway. Brother John found me and the rest ... you know the rest."

Gideon pulled at the leaves of a lemon tree. "I ... I don't know. I don't know why I'm telling you all of this. I'm sorry for gushing. It's a lot. It's hard to talk about … harder when I'm still trying to figure things out. Maybe we try to finish this story some other time?"

"Of course," said Cherry-Rose. "Best tour ever." She shook Gideon's arm. "It was perfect. Thank you. Really. Thank you."

Gideon looked away. "Okay, time to get you back, I suppose."

Just as Gideon turned to head back, Cherry-Rose pulled at his elbow and led him to a tree whose branches bowed, fat and full with lemons.

Cherry-Rose twisted a lemon from the tree. "Would you like to stop over at my place for some tea?"

And so Faintly ...

CHERRY-ROSE couldn't say with any certainty when life became defined by a feeling of lack, but she knew the feeling had been creeping in for some time. First, there was the emptiness in the sisterless cottage; next, loneliness even amongst her peers at the William Hale Academy for Children of All Sorts; then isolation at Fontainebleau. While it was easy to believe that the lack was somehow attributable to her mother's soups and her missing sisters, there seemed to be more to it, for here at Pleasure Island, even with Shy-Blue filling in much of the empty spaces, life still seemed best decorated by the wishes, dreams, and desires that filled her journal. As Gideon trailed, Cherry-Rose heard the words she had written that very morning.

Someone to read to, someone to find—beneath the covers, someone to make like the Blue Fairy on a harvest-moon night, someone to paw and tear and taste my tongue, someone to ...

"Make yourself at home," said Cherry-Rose, waving to Gideon who stood inside the frame of the open door looking more guard than guest. "I promise I don't bite."

"Uh ..." Gideon shifted, looking all timid. Slow blinks were followed by a hand massaging the back of his neck, and Cherry-Rose saw her studio new again through the gaze of her visitor. A bed, a pillow, *Howl* on that pillow: lame. Duvet, kitchen, bathroom: boring. More books, a chair, a table: void.

"I'm sorry … there aren't really a lot of options, but you can sit anywhere you like." Cherry-Rose pulled at Gideon's elbow until he was squarely inside the frame. "Please, come in. Sit, sit … anywhere. Let me get this tea started and then I'll tell you all about *my* … family," said Cherry-Rose as she edged toward the kitchen.

"But," Gideon protested. "But we don't have a lot of …"

"So, the tea," interrupted Cherry-Rose from behind the kitchen counter and her awkwardly low-hanging cupboards. "I make my own. Sage and lemon from right here on the grounds," she said, ducking to find Gideon standing, looking confused. "Sit. Sit," urged Cherry-Rose.

Cherry-Rose filled the kettle and peeked again beneath the cupboards to find that Gideon had gotten it all wrong.

Come on! The chair in the corner? … Howl is right there on the bed … And he left the door wide open …

Cherry-Rose imagined that the door was left open because he was a gentleman, because he knew he couldn't trust himself if it were closed. In that brief moment, she lived a Santa Cruz apartment wooing scene. She saw herself standing on her bed, a balconied Juliet to Gideon as Romeo below. "Your eyes. Your beautiful eyes. Those lips, those cherry-red lips," he'd say from his bended knee.

* * *

Just audible, but growing, and seeming to pulse through the wall, came something like the syncopated beat of an old dryer running on its last leg—*thump … tha-thump … thump-thump*—until the electric rush of the kettle bubbled violently to obscure the rhythm.

Cherry-Rose never could have known that while she dreamt of Shakespeare lovers on Santa Cruz shores, Gideon was busy considering breaking one of the cardinal rules for Roaches … the rule that he was sure, if she listened very carefully, she would have heard Brother John breaking down the hall—*thump ... tha-thump ... thump-thump.*

* * *

"Careful, it's a little hot." Cherry-Rose set two tea cups on the tiny wall-set table.

Gideon blew over his mug as Cherry-Rose took a seat on the edge of the bed. She told him all about her family, her twelve sisters, how they'd all laugh and dance and sing, how there were so many happy times; how those times were too brief.

Cherry-Rose paused to sip her tea and to shift the tone of the tale.

She told Gideon about her not-so-perfect family. The cottage trap, the spells, the soup, the thirteen that became one, her escape, her return, and just as she was telling Gideon about her time at Fontainebleau the pace of her story began to slow with the onset of a lovely but almost unsettling realization.

How rare, thought Cherry-Rose. *He is just ... he is just listening. He isn't making big eyes. No grunts or scowls of surprise and judgement. He is just ... listening.*

Cherry-Rose leaned in and said, "It's strange ..." Her words trailed off for a moment as she paused to watch Gideon sip his tea. She loved how his eyes still held hers as he took a sip—red makeup line, thick lashes, brown eyes spilling over the edge of his cup. "For a while there, I was beginning to ... to believe that Salvatóre saved me, but it was you all along. You saved me from *him*." Cherry-Rose placed her cup on the table and swept her legs up onto her bed.

At this, Gideon lowered his eyes, seemingly lost in the cup he held between his legs.

"I just can't," Cherry-Rose continued, "I can't imagine what would have happened if ..."

Gideon jumped in abruptly. "Cherry-Rose, I, ah ... Thank you for the tea. It's really ... uh ... lovely. But it's getting late. I gotta cut. You've got a full day of rehearsal tomorrow and I have strict orders to make sure you get your rest."

Cherry-Rose furrowed her brow. "Strict orders? Are you sure about that?"

Gideon smiled. "Well, perhaps it was more of a strongly-worded suggestion."

"As you wish. Will I see you tomorrow?"

Gideon placed his mug on the small end table and stood awkwardly. "Of course. And if you like, I'll be here bright and early tomorrow. We could go for a walk before breakfast. I promise not to point out any landmarks … There's a cool bookstore in town … we could hit that after it opens. Like ten o'clock, I think. Shall we?"

"That sounds lovely. A walk, then the bookstore," echoed Cherry-Rose.

Waiting near the edge of her bed, Cherry-Rose felt her ghost-sisters at work. The studio came alive; its walls echoed the faintest of heartbeats— *tha-thump … thump-thump … tha-thump.* She tugged at a button on her dress—*tha-thump*—and waited for Gideon to lean in—*tha-thump … thump-thump*—and nothing.

Determined not to let the moment pass, Cherry-Rose moved toward Gideon. She pressed her hand over his heart to feel the heartbeat she was sure brought the room to life. She reached up to kiss him on the cheek. "Thank you for a lovely time," she whispered without pulling away. "It really was … lovely."

"Uhhhh … thank you."

Again Cherry-Rose waited. She stood motionless with her hand still pressed into his chest. She followed Gideon's avoiding eyes; down, down, down to his searching hand. She watched his hand slide up her arm until it covered her hand that was still pressing into his chest. She could feel his heart rattling, shaking, bursting beneath their joined hands. Her eyes were locked on his downcast gaze, waiting for him to look up, knowing what would happen if he did. She felt a gentle squeeze and their hands began to fall. Her eyes followed their hands as they fell to rest between their bodies. She sank into the moment, feeling a rush at the bridge they made. His hip, his hand, touching her hand, her hip.

Cherry-Rose could see the blood pumping behind his painted heart. Faster. Harder. His chest rising and falling. Breath soft and shallow. She could feel the beneath-the-covers-warmth running up through her seams.

Her floor-set eyes found the edge of the door. It leaked in that damned yellow hallway light. It pushed through to break up the darkness she needed to complete the scene. Despite its intrusion, she knew that the shadows had parted such that the soft yellow would point straight to the copy of *Howl* resting on her pillow, *someone to read to, someone to ...*

The door. It was right there waiting to be closed and all she had to do was ...

She felt him stir. Sway. Hold tighter for just a moment ... their bridge began to strain as he leaned toward the shadowed side of the door.

Yes. Close it. Close it.

In that flash of a moment, Cherry-Rose was busy composing a poem called *Push the Light Beyond the Door*. It was composed of darkness and bodies and beastly growls.

As he reached for the door, their bridge tumbled entirely. Her fingers slipped from his hand and he ... he slipped from the room. Eyes downcast, but smiling, face full of blush, he made quick toward the garden.

Alone again, Cherry-Rose found herself in the shadowed solitary of the too much of her apartment. Dangerous *Howl* needing, waiting pillow wanting, begging bed hoping, silent Cherry-Rose ... deflated.

Morning Raven –
When Tomorrow Came

THE NEXT morning, Cherry-Rose lay awake, unsure if she had slept at all. She was waiting. Waiting for the door that separated the garden, the hallway, and hers to rattle with the rush of air. Waiting for the scent of the garden to push in beneath her door—lemon, lilac, lavender, Gideon. Waiting … quietly whispering a morning poem. Shelley's words for the morning's ghost-sister memories: "*I love all waste—And solitary places.*" Until …

First came the lilac and lavender.

"*Where we taste / The Pleasure of believing what we see*"—still whispering.

She slid her book underneath her pillow and quietly moved to place her ear against the door. Lemon came with the sound of Gideon's back sliding down the dividing wall. Her whispers became the voice that only she could hear …

Is boundless, as we wish our souls to be …

A *tap, tap, tap* came softly from the hallway.

Her hands shook, waiting to be steadied by his; her eyes, bright and full, were ready to close in his embrace; her lips, smiling their wide morning smile, ready to find Gideon on the right side of the door. Cherry-Rose wound up like a clock, like a snake, like a wolf ready to pounce and burst through the door all eyes, lips, hands, ready to tie this moment to the one that was cut too short the day before.

Cherry-Rose opened the door—slowly, quietly—so as not to spook that which was prone to run.

"Hello! Good morning."

Gideon looked up from the floor, book quivering on his lap, eyes floating full and beautiful above a thin line of red. He smiled, soft and lovely.

Cherry-Rose half-hoped that when she opened the door, the immense wave created by the tide of their energy would push Gideon into her arms, crashing the pair into her bed; however, she would have settled for Gideon scrambling to his feet to deliver a shy morning kiss on the cheek. She got neither.

"I mean," said Cherry-Rose, quickly changing tack. "Won't you please come in?" She stood in perfect posture and straightened her nightshirt. "Perhaps some tea while I dress; I shan't be long."

"Good morning, Cherry-Rose. I'm good. I've got company." Gideon held up a copy of Plath's *Ariel*. "I'll just wait here 'til you're ready."

* * *

"As promised, one tour. No landmarks." Gideon stood at the door leading to the garden and ushered Cherry-Rose through. Lemon, lilac, lavender, Gideon. Bees diving, hummingbirds teasing, bushes shaking with a forest of tiny fluttering somethings. The garden was alive and Cherry-Rose had questions.

"Please remind me, why are we out here walking in the chill of the morning when we could be inside having tea?"

Gideon looked pained. "Cold? Whatever do you mean?" He laughed as his breath became cloud.

"It's just that yesterday we had tea, and this morning, you seemed ... a little ... I don't know ... Distant. Did I say too much yesterday?"

"No. Not at all. It's just that ..."

"What?!" She slapped his arm. "Say it."

"Truth?"

"Yes. Absolutely. Always. Truth."

"It's just that there are rules. We just … can't."

"Rules? For me and you?"

"No. Yes. For us. For Roaches. I think Whale prefers us working without distractions."

"Are you sure? What about Shy-Blue and Brother John? They seem to be spending a lot of time together."

"Brother John and Shy-Blue … they are … rehearsing. Working on the show." Gideon stumbled through his words. "Like her routine or something. The set, maybe. I don't know what they do exactly. We shouldn't even be talking about it." Gideon lowered his voice. "We could get them in a lot of trouble. If Whale even hears that they are … and we are," Gideon paused, seemingly distracted by a morphing cloud, "maybe…"

"Maybe what, having tea?"

"Spending too much time together. We could be in a lot of trouble."

"But William, he seems so …"

"Seriously. I've seen it. I've been there when it's happened. We don't want that. You don't want that."

"Come on." Cherry-Rose stretched out the *on* emphatically. "Couldn't *we* rehearse? You know, like Shy-Blue and Brother John? It'd be fun. I'll make tea and sing. I could try new songs for the set. You could listen, read, give pointers, whatever—you can just do whatever Brother John is doing. Rehearsal, yes?" Cherry-Rose hopped backwards in front of Gideon like she was leading him toward a secret surprise.

Gideon squinted, lips tight, hands pushed into pockets. "I … we …"

"Come. On! Tea. Tea at least."

"I don't know," he said as if he were actually considering the offer.

"Just tea. Just come over. Look, you don't even have to come in." Cherry-Rose bargained, fully imagining that there'd be no way he wouldn't.

"Sure. Okay. Tea. Just tea. Me and you and we leave the door open and then we hit the bookstore."

"It's a deal; we leave the door open at the bookstore." She laughed, still hopping backwards.

* * *

When tomorrow came …

Call: *Tap, tap, tap.*

Response: *Tap, tap, tap.* "Who goes there?"

Call: "Good morning … Darkness, and nothing more."

Response: "Good morning, my dear raven, would you like to wait inside?"

Call: Silence

Response: "You do know the poem, right? Last I read it, the raven eventually goes inside."

Call: There are rules for Roaches and although I'd prefer to make the dryer run with you, I'll wait out here and read poetry, because if he found out … I'd end up buried half-alive under the lemon tree.

Call: "No thank you. I mean, Nevermore," corrected Gideon. "I've got Elizabeth Browning today." Gideon lowered his head and raised the book.

Response: "As you wish."

* * *

And so, for a few weeks it went something like this—lilac, lavender, lemon. Tea—bookstore, tea—record store, always hallway.

* * *

When tomorrow came … *Evermore,* every morning, this morning, Cherry-Rose, opening-night morning, Gideon was Roach as Raven announcing the day: *tap, tap, tap … Evermore.*

Evermore, every morning; this morning-ritual required an ear to the wall to ensure that he did not disturb too early.

Evermore, and moreso each day, this morning ritual brought ripe images of Cherry-Rose in the midst of long morning stretches accompanied with soft morning sighs. On this morning, he who was oft the image of calm, centered, and silent, was howling inside.

"Fffuuuu …." That too-loud voice that beamed hot-neon pornography against the wall of his skull told Gideon that he should be in there, magician, shaman, priest over flesh, over fabric, over body, conjuring those criminal animal-morning sighs.

There are rules, he thought as his thumb pressed into the seam of *Antony and Cleopatra*.

"Where was I? Act IV, Scene XV…" *rules for Roaches, rules for tragedies.*

* * *

Cherry-Rose knew he was there; *lilac, lavender, lemon … Gideon.* She learned to make him wait. She loved to make him wait. She could feel it working. *It was working, it is working …* and this, this torture was the price exacted for inciting those sad, sad solitary, *completely unnecessary,* she reasoned, lonely Cherry-Rose, waking-dream mornings.

She heard his back slide down the wall as he sat, she could hear him breathe through that wall, and today she heard his frustrated sigh.

Would he … almost, she thought, *just a little longer. Maybe I should …*

A soft stir … the bed made more noise than she. An almost-lover, an almost-romance, an almost-boyfriend, for an almost-girl …

The scent of Gideon, the thought of Gideon, his morning-wall whispers ran up her stitches, conjuring images—a body, his … supine on that forest-ritual table. Cherry-Rose descending from the sky; titan, bear, wolf, doe, Ur-lover to take Gideon as the Blue Fairy took her. Cherry-Rose weaved her other-side-of-the-wall magic to make the blood behind Gideon's tattoo race, to make his heart rattle and shake, to make the book that she was sure he was holding quiver … like she was quivering.

Call: *tap, tap, tap.*

The call sent Cherry-Rose into the throes of her Blue Fairy descending fantasy, reigniting the solitary morning-revenge ritual. Moan … stretch … sigh … repeat. Hoping that each was quiet enough not to be too obvious, but loud enough to be heard if he wished to hear, just loud enough that he might try the door.

It's unlocked, she imagined saying full of her morning sultry. But in the moment, she had no words. So, the door never rattled and the hallway was too quiet.

Torture and torment were tricky business, but alas, the seamstress taught Cherry-Rose all she'd ever need to know about that pair. The trick, as she unconsciously observed, was in the reprieve. Without reprieve, the subject becomes numb. Conditioned to the torture, numb to the torment.

When it was time, Cherry-Rose wondered, *Is he still there? He better be. Shhh. Quiet.*

Quietly, she lit the flame beneath the kettle and then inched toward the door. She cracked it just so, hoping to catch a glimpse of Gideon visibly pained, or better yet, about to reach for the door, but neither was so. Not pained. Not reaching for the door, but also not gone. He wasn't gone, but he was … he was lost in his book.

She knew she waited too long, or perhaps teased too much.

Not fully understanding or ready to believe Gideon's preoccupation with the Roaches odd commingling rule, she thought, *Perhaps this situation calls for a more direct approach.* Cherry-Rose readied herself for a morning reveal that was poised to remove any doubt about what "let's have some tea" really meant. She silently opened the door and stood in the frame, legs wide, torso split by the threshold. Her head full of warm, before the dawn, beneath-the-covers thoughts; breath still quick, eyes still fire, lips still pouting cherry-red. She was dressed for revenge: eyes, lips—nightshirt barely reaching the middle of her thigh.

Still, he was still gone, but not gone, mumbling lines with his eyes closed.

Cherry-Rose stood glaring her morning sultry pose over the unknowing Gideon. He sat legs crossed, book in hand, hand nestled between legs; head hung over book, her book—*Antony and Cleopatra*—thumb in the crease. Cherry-Rose watched as his mouth moved silently to the rhythm of the words, like he was memorizing each stanza. Cherry-Rose tried to find consolation and meaning in the fact that he seemed so lost in the book that she had recommended.

"An allegory. Bad things happen when you mess with true love," she recalled telling Gideon just yesterday as she handed him a worn copy of the play. "Sorry about all the scribbles. Please pay no attention to my notes. I write all over my books."

Breath still racing, eyes still burning. Cherry-Rose waited for his eyes to shift from the tragedy in his hands to the one standing before him. But they didn't.

Nothing. Seriously! Just how long ...?

Ready to be noticed, Cherry-Rose issued her response to his too-long-ignored morning announcement—reprieve: *tap, tap, tap ...* Cherry-Rose clicked her fingers hard on the threshold.

Gideon looked up with his slow, sweet, every-morning smile.

Annoyed, she waited for him to speak.

"Good morning. Thank you. I love it." Gideon held the book with praying hands.

Cherry-Rose melted. She could feel the poetry in his smile—in their connection; his eyes, her eyes ... his lips, her lips ... his hands all over that book, thumb pressed deep into its crease.

Cherry-Rose watched him cradle the book, his manner fully devoid of any evidence of the suffering she had hoped to imbue.

Just quiet enough to be ignored, not so loud as to be heard at all, she thought, cursing her too-subtle torture.

"Good morning." Cherry-Rose sighed, still wanting to be annoyed, but finding that in the face of that smile, she was unable. She returned the smile. "*Antony and Cleopatra,* I am glad you like it." She flashed the rhythm of the very words that she had committed to memory—*My heart was to thy rudder tied ... And thou shouldst ...*

The kettle screamed to shatter the moment, and she burst from the scene muttering something about a morning full of tragedies.

* * *

This was their morning frenzy. Days upon days of call and response. Each day a soft "Good morning." Each day the lure of the calling kettle. Each day to tempt with an open door; and each day, she'd chase the tea kettle and return to find Gideon on the floor of the hallway. He'd sit just on the edge of the threshold defining the rules that divided their worlds. Hallway and bed—safety and sex—books and tea—danger—danger. Cherry-Rose knew where she'd find him and why.

On this morning, as ever, he was there. The door was left wide open with excruciating design. Cherry-Rose tested and tempted, purposely sliding in and out of view in various states of dress until she settled, ready for the day, on the edge of her bed. Legs crossed, tea in lap. Cherry-Rose watched Gideon sitting at the edge of the threshold in mirrored pose—legs crisscrossed, book between, tea on book—danger—danger—finding it hard to hide her glowing, morning-stretch smile behind a sip of tea.

"What?" He smiled back, laughing a little. "What's up?"

"Nothing. The usual. You know …" She knew he did. Every day over the course of these last few weeks, he inched a little closer. She knew that if things kept going this way, when tomorrow came, she might find Gideon on the right side of the threshold.

"The usual. Yeah … Are you nervous for the show tonight?" Gideon asked, breathing into his tea.

Cherry-Rose took note of the change in subject.

"Always. Every show … Always nervous."

Cherry-Rose was waiting for Gideon to follow up. He didn't. He seemed very concerned with the bottom of his tea cup.

"How are you enjoying *Antony and Cleopatra*?" she asked, hoping to spark the proper sort of conversation.

"Good … you know? Like super good. I love it."

"Uh huh." She nodded, waiting for more, but nothing came.

Cherry-Rose reasoned that his lacking follow up was all the evidence she needed to know that where she saw passion and missed opportunity in *Antony and Cleopatra*, he saw tragedy. *Clearly, he doesn't want to talk about it. There are rules, for blah, blah, blah …*

"Yeah, super good." Cherry-Rose held her teacup against her breast, imagining teacup as asp filling her shell with its warm venom. "Do you have a favorite scene or line perhaps?" Wanting him to speak one of the many she underlined, *perchance to read his eyes.*

"Umm, what was it? 'By the pricking of my thumbs,' something like that." The words came hidden behind his teacup—his eyes peeking just over the edge, hiding a wide smile behind wafts of steam.

Macbeth! *Clearly, he does not want to discuss* Antony and Cleopatra.

Cherry-Rose felt tragedy overflowing, pouring from his eyes to teacup to floor.

"Ah yes … To be, or not to be," she said with a laugh.

"Precisely … it's as if you recite from the page." Gideon smiled. "If you like, I'll read you a few of my favorite lines after your show tonight."

"Tonight?" Cherry-Rose protested, turning her smile into a pout with eyes as full as her lips. "Now, please." She patted the bed. "Come. Sit."

Gideon countered, "We don't really have a lot of time this morning. Brother John mentioned that you and Shy-Blue have a morning walk-through or something … opening night and all."

Cherry-Rose scrunched up her face and squinted, letting out a disapproving, "Hmphhh."

"Seriously, come on, Cherry-Rose, finish yer tea, we gotta cut."

A Dream of a Dance

BENEATH the Stars and the Deep Blue Sea. It was mad whisky eyes in
dinner suits and floor-length dresses, faces with wagging tongues bit
between pearly fangs, others with clenched teeth framed within twisted
sativa smiles, and wide, wide, wider blue-shot eyes that hovered above
cherry-red cigarette-lamps. Painted claws and wide crushing paws danced
the smoke around the room until they were ushered to their seats by a voice
that boomed through the P.A.

"One dances, one sings. No hearts, no strings."

Shy-Blue was pure magic.

During rehearsals, Cherry-Rose unwittingly channeled Salvatóre. "Shy,
this is the trick. Tempt and tease, but never give it all away. You know?
Make them suffer a little … maybe a lot," Cherry-Rose added with a smile.
"The suffering, it's what makes them come back."

And she did. Shy-Blue took everyone to the edge. She lined them up
with a burlesque showcase that built a collective hope throughout the
audience. Hope that everything Shy-Blue put them through, everything
that they had been through together, had been sealed by an unspoken
promise. The promise that the last of her Seven Veils would indeed fall.

Oh, how the crowd suffered. Blood built and boiled, teeth snapped and
snapped, fangs dripped-dripped their drool, and a chaos of whistles, caws,

and howls seemed to inspire Shy-Blue to consent. One last veil. Hands over veil. Eyes on hands. The whole of Pleasure Island— eyes on hands. No one saw the curtain falling. Veil in hand. Eyes on hand. Chaos settled into simmer, the simmer to a drum roll, the drum roll to silence. The whole of Pleasure Island—silent. Shy-Blue released the last veil. Eyes on …

The veil did hit the floor, but oh, how the crowd suffered. The falling curtain outpaced the veil and the room fell into madness.

Wait. Let them suffer.

When the curtain rose again, Cherry-Rose stood where the veil had fallen. She was all sleeves, collar, slit unwavering in a sparkling mannequin pose. Arms straight, wrists turned up, head askew, eyes out there, over, beyond. Holding until … Cymbals crashed, then trumpets blared to cut all of Cherry-Rose's invisible strings. Her hands fell, then her arms, then her head dropped low, low, lower, as if a line were being released in spurts, and when her head lifted to find the audience standing in silent awe, her voice cut them down.

"Don't change a thing," said William at her first rehearsal. "It is perfect." Whispering to Brother John, "Only great suffering could have shaped a voice like that. What a beautiful, beautiful mess."

It was the Fontainebleau murder set all over again. Yes, Cherry-Rose sang and crooned her melancholic, blood-stained set all over again. For all her suffering, she made them suffer. For all her wants, she made them want. For all her dreams, she gave Pleasure Island new dreams. The set rolled until the last, until Cherry-Rose, accompanied by a cacophony of drums, cymbals, and horns tied the end of her set to the beginning. Again, she hung all crucified, invisibly tied in her mannequin encore pose.

All of Pleasure Island was under her spell. She could feel the room coursing with magic; *Her* magic. She could feel it in the wild applause that shook her core. She could feel it in the heat of the spotlight. She was becoming … something. If she had the words, she might recall her moon-love, ritual night. She might say that this was it—the feeling of the frenzy right before *She* disappeared, leaving her quivering in the night. Yes, right there in that moment, she was becoming a crooning Blue Fairy priestess, bridging the moon-ritual ecstasy for all those applauding, howling beasts, for all of Pleasure Island.

… make them wait, make them wait before you slide your hand up that mic stand.

And when she did, Cherry-Rose could hear Salvatóre's voice … *Honey and gold, gold and honey.*

* * *

The monastery's post-show party room was fashioned like a small club, fit with bar, turntable, and record collection. The room ran with hot-wired electricity that spilled over from the show. Connie Francis was playing, whisky was flowing, and in the center of the room, Whale was winding around Shy-Blue, asking Brother John not to go far with that bottle.

"A toast, a toast. Everyone. Yeah, you." Whale held his glass toward Gideon. It seemed that he too noticed that Gideon was trying to slip away, having drifted toward the furthest corner chair.

"Everyone. Gideon, come on. Johnboy." He held out his glass for a refill.

"Girls, girls, everyone, a toast." Whale smiled, waving everyone closer. His glass made small calling circles over his head until he was satisfied that everyone was squarely on the rug. "Amazing. Just amazing." He clinked every glass and made eyes until they all threw back their drinks. "Johnboy, another round. Another round."

Brother John poured.

"Again. To Shy-Blue and Cherry-Rose." He drank. Paused. "Everyone, please," motioning with his glass.

Again, Brother John poured.

As the glasses were filled, he continued. "Where was I? Yes, to Shy-Blue and Cherry-Rose. One dances. One sings. No heart. No strings. It was perfection." He winked at Cherry-Rose, who appeared to be feeling the whisky's magic. "And you." He pulled Shy-Blue closer. "You were perfect."

* * *

As Brother John left the circle to flip the record, Cherry-Rose turned to clink glasses with Gideon, but he had slipped from view. She found him already sitting in the corner, book in hand. His book-cast brow furrowed as if the pages were troubling him.

Cherry-Rose faded back to lean against the wall, to watch Gideon for a moment, to see if he too might look for her and he did. Cherry-Rose found his smile, but his gaze suddenly turned to the couple who stood between them in the center of the rug. His brow made the worried book-furrow. Cherry-Rose's eyes followed and found Whale whispering private toasts into Shy-Blue's ear. He was mouthing words with a smile that sank into the deep of Shy-Blue's neck, and with each word, his lingering hug wound its way tighter around her hip.

Cherry-Rose could see that Brother John, now seated on a sofa, was also interested in the spotlight slow dance. His eyes dark beneath his mask, leg all cool over the arm of the sofa, scarred smile beaming as if he knew something that no one else could possibly know. Gideon returned to his book.

I see, thought Cherry-Rose, *pretending to be more interested in what Shakespeare might say about love and sex than what anyone here might do about it.*

Leaning hard into the shelf, Cherry-Rose was spinning. She found her smile and stumbled over to see if she might be able to draw Gideon out from the corner, thinking, *I'd like some breath on my neck.*

"Nevermore?" Cherry-Rose asked as she held up her glass. "Oh sonnets, changing it up, I see. Which is tonight's favorite?"

"Nevermore," answered Gideon, smiling up from his book. "You know, traveling light." He flashed the cover of his tiny book of pocket sonnets. "Tonight, it is 53. You know, *What is your substance?*"

"Whatever do you mean, dear Raven," said Cherry-Rose, who stalled between sips of whisky in the hopes of recalling anything about 53.

A trill of laughter tore out behind Cherry-Rose, demanding Gideon's attention. Cherry-Rose followed his eyes to the pair dancing on the island rug.

Whale had wrapped entirely around Shy-Blue. Nose. *Mouth? Teeth?* On neck.

"Be careful, Cherry-Rose, " whispered Gideon.

"Of ...?" asked Cherry-Rose as she watched Shy-Blue slow dance with Whale. Whale holding her at the waist, Shy-Blue locked in the rhythm. Whale humming "Who's Sorry Now." Brother John looked over at Cherry-Rose and gave a smile as he lifted his shoulders in an *eh, whatever* gesture.

"Wait, are you ...?" slurred Cherry-Rose. "Don't be jealous."

"What? No ... of what?!" Gideon exclaimed through a whisper. His head dropped to his book. He sighed, and when he looked up at Cherry-Rose, she thought she saw his eyes begin to glisten. "You know what?" Gideon continued. "Never mind."

Gideon closed his book and drew a long, slow sigh. "I'm sorry. I'm an idiot. A total idiot. And maybe a jerk. Maybe. What I should have said was, you were really amazing tonight. Like out of this world."

Cherry-Rose leaned in and pressed her hand onto the book covering Gideon's lap. "Yes. Yes. All true and more." She rubbed her chin, feigning deep thought, and said, "And since you seem enthusiastic about righting your wrongs, perhaps a bird might finally find its way through my window tonight?"

"Cherry-Rose, come on, you know the rules ... He's watching us, you. He is always watching. Someone is always watching. It's not safe here. I've told you before, he isn't who you think he is. He is not a good guy." Cherry-Rose stood up straight. Gideon leaned in and continued. "Look, I've said too much. It just isn't safe. You should go to your room and get some rest. Can I walk you to your room? We should get outta here before it gets weird. Let's get outta here. Please?"

Feeling the effects of the whatever-was-in-her-glass, Cherry-Rose whispered a little too loud, "Walk me to my room?" Pretending to be offended. "No, no, no, no, no you don't." She waved her drink. "Don't you know the rules? Sir, that would never do!" She pressed her free hand into the heart that Violent-Joy gave her.

CHERRY-ROSE: BLOOD & WISHES

"Fuck. Thanks a lot," said Gideon. "What are you trying to … Fine. Fine, you don't want to leave. Cool. You think I'm jealous, whatever. I'll leave you to … whatever. Look, I gotta cut. I'll see you tomorrow, okay? … I'll … I'll just see you tomorrow."

* * *

Cherry-Rose slouched into the vacant corner chair and watched Whale and Shy-Blue dance in the middle of the room. As they swayed, she felt all of the growing sad and lonely that was crouched and waiting to pounce upon her when she went home to her one-bedroom void. "Someone to sing to," she mumbled to the floor. "Someone to dance with …" Her finger traced invisible hearts and Blue Fairy runes into the leather. "Someone to …" until Shy-Blue's slow twirl laugh brought her back to the dance, and with it, a horde of swirling ghost-girl cottage memories.

She found Whale leading the dance as seamstress, as mother-father, … *no, no. Something about his smile, his hands, the teeth behind the grin,* thought Cherry-Rose. *More like the grinning bear hanging in his office—* the room continued to spin against the dance—and the dance, beneath an imaginary sky of falling snow. No, it wasn't snow. It was feathers. A falling sky of feathers.

Cherry-Rose slid to the floor and watched the dancers and tried to steady herself between long, hazy blinks. Eyes—*blink*—snow-feathers—kiss; smile—*blink*—feathers—whisper; hands *blink*—feathers—squeeze; teeth—*blink*—feathers—bite. The effect made Shy-Blue a jewelry-box ballerina who was just beyond the veil, twirling in the dark until illuminated by long-blink, hazy lightning strikes of consciousness. Cherry-Rose was surprised to hear Shy-Blue laugh as if she didn't notice the room spinning in the dark, as if she didn't see the feathers, as if she didn't feel the bite at all.

"One, two, three." Whale sent Shy-Blue on a crash course for Cherry-Rose.

Cherry-Rose eyes, ceiling bound, feather bound, moon bound, blinking the are-you-really-real? blink at Shy-Blue, at an upside-down smile hidden behind a mess of blonde hair.

The record had long gone untended. It clicked softly in its runout groove as a hand reached out to pull the wobbly Cherry-Rose to her feet.

"Sing me a song, Cherry-Rose."

After a few uncertain steps, Cherry-Rose too became box-wound-clockwork ballerina. The twist of the dance within the haze of the night ushered in a new rush of cottage memories. She remembered her first dance, the funeral-birthday seamstress dance, and the following wolf-bleating dream—dying, living, dancing—all in one day. Heavy legs spinning, loose limbs flailing, she wasn't dancing with the seamstress as much as she was holding on, and this dance with Shy-Blue was no different. Cherry-Rose anchored her head atop Shy-Blue's shoulder and she held on lest she'd crumble into a quivering doe in the middle of the floor, poised to heave up the bile of the night's falling feathers dream.

"Come on, Cherry-Rose, sing to me," begged Shy-Blue as they staggered-swayed and spun in the center of the room. Each spin flickering Whale and Brother John in and out of view ... a quivering wall of almost-somethings.

Someone to sing to ...

Cherry-Rose breathed softly into Shy-Blue's neck, "I love you, Shy. I really ... I just love you," and she picked up the song where Whale left off. She sang softly, sweetly into Shy-Blue's ear, "Who's Sorry Now," slow dancing until the words became a hum, until the hum became silence, and silence, slow warm breath on Shy-Blue's neck—their host still blinking in and out of view behind those cottage-memory feathers—those eyes, that grin, those perfect teeth.

How many nights had Cherry-Rose slow danced with Shy-Blue to entertain the seamstress? How many nights did they sing and dance all high on magical soups of forgetting, the world feeling heavy and edged in hazy full-moon rings? How many nights did they fail to see the danger behind those watching eyes?

Slow spinning with Shy-Blue, she could feel that she was wrapped in the haunt of the haze, but the voice beyond the dream was still silent, thinking but not saying, *all too often, what is felt is little understood.*

Spinning, Cherry-Rose wondered at what kept her spinning. *Is it the drink or the rush of the applause? Is it the dance, Shy-Blue's neck, those eyes watching from the couch? Is it Gideon? All of it? None of it? Something else?*

Whatever it was, all those hazy cottage nights were coming down to color this moment. Something was there, wanting to be seen, heard, noticed; like the fleeting edge of a dream in the fog of waking, like a voice beyond the sea of that black-sea dream, behind the haze, beyond the moon, begging to be understood.

Cherry-Rose held on to Shy-Blue like they were a pair struggling in a marathon dance, like they were acting out their last dance swaying under their mother's spell. *Haven't we done this before?*—wanting to give up— wanting to lay right there on the floor—wanting to crawl beneath the covers with Shy-Blue, but somehow still dancing. She needed to ... to finish, to start then finish, to piece together this itching something before she let go of Shy-Blue, before the end of the night shattered the spell and called the warbling voice that waited in silent protest somewhere above this dream of a dance.

Almost.

Ear, lips.

Lips just above collarbone, lips on ear.

It was gone.

Goodbye Forever, For Now

BROTHER John watched the night's dancers with much interest. He knew Whale's performance was as much for him as it was for Shy-Blue.

Staking his claim in true Whale fashion, thought Brother John, *practically planting his cock flag right here on the goddamned rug.*

Brother John tried not to be offended; after all, he knew what he was doing during Whale's out-to-sea hours.

Motherfucker can sense when a girl has got eyes for someone else. Ain't that right, Mikey?

Still, Brother John found it hard not to be offended, and every day, it became a little harder. Brother John knew what was going on in that office— in-between all their in-betweens and their rehearsals. Same as ever. Same as always.

Shy-Blue wouldn't say, but then again, what could she say? Doesn't matter. Whale said it all in his dance on the rug. Said exactly what he wanted to say. Hands off. Mine.

Brother John never cared much about what Whale did before, but then again, Brother John had never broken the rules before. Never had to.

"I'm afraid we're losing her," Shy-Blue announced to the room, swaying more than dancing with Cherry-Rose. "This one needs to get to bed."

CHERRY-ROSE: BLOOD & WISHES

"Probably for the best," replied Whale. "It's been a long day."

Shy-Blue lifted Cherry-Rose's arm and used it to wave to Whale and Brother John. "Good night. Night, night, everyone," said Shy-Blue.

Cherry-Rose lifted her head. "Hey, look at me, I'm a puppet." She laughed in Brother John's direction.

"Hey, Johnboy," said Whale, getting to his feet. "It is getting late. I should follow suit. It is very likely that Mrs. Hale will have waited up for me. Do me a favor and see to it that they get to their rooms safely. We have to do this all over again tomorrow."

"I'm on it," Brother John replied, quickly leaping to his feet.

"Hey, Johnboy ..."

Brother John paused at Whale's call, already imagining his pocket full of quarters ready to feed the imaginary fuck-machine that Gideon said ran too often during his tea time.

"Never mind. Nothing. It's nothing ..." Whale paused as if considering something. "Forget it. I'll see you tomorrow."

* * *

Beneath the silent gray sky sat a lemon tree; beneath the lemon tree, Gideon; beneath Gideon, Mikey, or what was left of him. The cold bite of bones, the sting of the night, the relentless sound of the ocean breaking just beyond, the unfortunate awkward exchange with Cherry-Rose; it all made Gideon uniquely aware of his position in the universe. Like Whale to Mikey, the gods were shoveling their wet, ashen sky upon he who had misstepped.

It is time for a choice, thought Gideon. Follow Brother John's path and end up breathing soil next to Mikey, or cut.

Laughter and light burst out at the far end of the compound, hammering the misty gray, but as quick as it came, it was gone. The door slammed shut and left only laughter. Three distant shapes edged in the soft gray of the night stumbled home; arm-in-arm, lurching and laughing toward the entrance to the monastery.

278

It hurt to hear the laughter. It brought regret. He reflected on his missed opportunities. He knew he was wasting his mornings with Cherry-Rose. Worse, he felt it was wrong to waste what he was feeling when he was with her. He had never felt such a connection, and to have it stifled by this place, he knew he was wasting his life here at Pleasure Island. The situation made him aware that he was losing what he liked most about himself, perhaps what she liked best about him, in the worry and stress of simultaneously trying to be near Cherry-Rose while also trying not to get too close.

He thought about the rules for Roaches and Cherry-Rose and that gray crushing sky. He thought about the lemon tree and Mikey, who lay beneath. He thought about hands and zip-ties; wide, scared eyes and loose shoveled earth. He thought about this morning, *yesterday morning? It was this morning,* and Cherry-Rose standing over him in that T-shirt that barely covered her ... He thought about Brother John and that goddamn out-to-sea fuck-dryer that would surely be running tonight. He thought about leaving, he thought about having to leave, he thought about how none of it mattered anyway because no one ever really got away.

Gideon could hear Cherry-Rose's fading laugh as the door to the complex slowly banged shut. He sat for a moment in the darkness and thought, *You know what? ... Fuck it.*

* * *

In the yellow fluttering light of the hallway, Gideon stood with his back against Cherry-Rose's wall thinking, *today. Everything changes today.*

Tap, tap, tap ... Thinking, *forevermore.*

Tap, tap, tap ... Thinking, *what the hell have I been waiting for?*

Tap, tap, tap ... tap. Thinking, *I should've said it this morning. I need to say it today. Today, I'll just say it. Cherry-Rose, I love you. Let's get out of this place. Me and you. We can run. We can start over anywhere.*

Tap, tap, tap ... Is she already asleep, wondered Gideon as he slowly slid down the wall. As he hit the floor, he heard *it.* "Great, just great," said Gideon, full of regret at the noise that came clanging down the hall. Brother John's goddamned dryer … it was knocking and banging like someone threw a shoe in there.

"Like a machine, Brother John. Well done," said Gideon to the empty hallway. "The Whale is out to sea," he sighed, promising himself that he would not stay here long listening to that racket.

Tap, tap, just five more minutes … tap …

The cold hard floor was made more so by the pre-dawn chill. The chill blew its way into the hallway, beneath the door, and stirred Gideon from an uneasy dreamless slumber, so uneasy he wondered if he had slept at all. The drool on his denim-jacket pillow, however, told him that he had been out for some time.

Tap, tap, tap … There seemed to be nothing in Cherry-Rose's apartment, nothing but … *tap, tap, tap* … silence.

Night after a big show, the whole place was dead quiet: Pleasure Island, the courtyard, under the lemon tree, the hallway … *tap, tap, tap.* In the perfect quiet of morning, a morning that seemed more between worlds than of this world, Gideon could hear someone fumbling with a door down the hallway. He quickly scrambled to his feet and slid around the corner, just out of view.

Gideon settled with his back against the wall. *How would that look … Sleeping at Cherry-Rose's doorstep?*

From the edge of the hallway under jaundice lighting, Gideon peeked around the corner to discover the name of the shape who disturbed his slumber. The form at the end of the hallway didn't make any sense. Barefoot, dark hair—a mess. Shoes in hand. Someone … not Shy-Blue, bent over trying to coax Shy-Blue's door closed without making a sound but failing miserably. He sat against his hidden wall and sighed. Gideon saw all the morning's out-to-sea events play out on the wall like a stop-action orgy.

* * *

Cherry-Rose, five a.m., crash face first into bed. Shoes in hand. Shoes drop to the floor. Dress unzipped. One strap holding it in place. The other not. Sleep was instant.

Cherry-Rose woke to a dream of an emptiness filled with a quiet calm that was so quiet, a "just before the first breath on the funeral-birthday table" sort of quiet. So quiet, if she had the strength, she would have screamed, but she found that even keeping her eyes open was too much trouble. The quiet hung about like a foggy morning, only it wasn't morning any longer. The sun was far too high. Her throat was far too dry. Her legs felt far too shaky and weak. Her memory of the evening far too … nothing. With one eye open, wishing the sun away, it came. Slowly, in shreds, tattered bits frayed, blinking … blinking … blinking. Pieces sewing themselves together despite Cherry-Rose's desire to return to the emptiness of sleep. Loose fragments. No heart. No strings. Hands on a mic stand. A standing ovation. A few drinks.

Arms. Faces. Fangs.

Legs. Teeth. Tongues.

Cock. Breast. Fox. Snake. "Gideon? Gideon!"

"*Ffffuuu …*" Cherry-Rose scrambled to her door. There in the hallway, Cherry-Rose found the *empty* of her midday wakeup-wish.

Wait … Against the wall, half-crumbled, Cherry-Rose found a line written on a scrap of paper: "On the morrow he will leave me, as my Hopes have flown before. Then the bird said, '*Nevermore.*'"

Lunch time. If they were awake, Shy-Blue and Brother John would be waiting for Cherry-Rose in the cafeteria. No one ever waited for Gideon. For as long as Cherry-Rose could tell, Gideon had always taken his lunch in the garden. Brother John would say, "Gid likes to sit under the fruit trees to ponder original sin origin stories."

Noon sky. The world beyond Cherry-Rose's apartment seemed full of noise and clatter. The sun blaring, birds screaming, beasts milling about, Roaches chattering, head throbbing full of its bits and pieces: arms and legs and Shy-Blue and Brother John. And Brother John. And John. A world entirely empty of the brief nothing that Cherry-Rose wished for in her waking, between-world haze. Cherry-Rose wanted nothing more than the void of sleep, to pull the covers over her head, to hide away to try to make sense of the night, but she had to find Gideon. Cherry-Rose knew where she'd find him. He'd be sitting in the garden under the fruit she used for her tea, under the tree where he buried his friend, *under the tree where he ponders original sin.*

* * *

"You know, it's strange … on this morn', I heard no rapping on my chamber door."

Gideon didn't look up from his book.

"May I." Cherry-Rose gestured to the grass in front of Gideon. Gideon nodded. "I missed my Raven this morning." Gideon didn't speak. Cherry-Rose crossed her legs and waited.

Gideon sat staring at his book … "I missed you too."

Cherry-Rose reached out to place her hand on his knee and waited for words, a clue, a soft smile, a scream. Anything. She could sense a change, but *there was no way he could know. Could he?*

"Hey, Cherry-Rose … I, uh … I gotta. I have to get out of this place."

"What? No! Is it about this morning? Because I can …"

"No. No, it isn't. And you don't need to explain anything."

"Please, why are you—"

"Please let me finish. This is hard … I can't … please. I've been thinking about this for a long time, even before you came along. In fact, I think I might have already left if you hadn't come along. Things have been getting out of control here. Brother John, he's been … he's walking a dangerous path, and I'm afraid that if I stay, I'll end up under this tree with him. Whale is always watching, and … there's no forgiveness here. There are no second chances. Whale, this place … they just swallow people whole. And besides, you've inspired me; I think maybe I left some things behind that I need to find. I'm trusting you with this. If they knew why I left …"

"I would never …" Cherry-Rose whispered through a quaking voice.

"They'd find me … they would, and … but if anyone does manage to find me, I hope that it's you. But not like this … here. I just can't be here anymore."

"But when …" Cherry-Rose was unable to finish.

"Tonight, during your set."

They both sat in silence for a moment while Gideon pulled at the grass.

Cherry-Rose searched for Gideon's eyes, but they were far away, looking like they were searching for something on the other side of the sky.

He sat quietly for a moment and said, "I … I was trying not to … I didn't want to say anything, but I just need you to understand that I tried, and although it seems it wasn't meant to be right now, I want you to know that we are okay. Truth, right?"

"Always … of course." Cherry-Rose tried to smile to show him that everything would be okay.

"The thing about this morning … I tried. I *was* there."

"I know, I saw your note … and I am so sorry."

"No, you don't understand. I was there … all night."

Cherry-Rose was confused.

"After the party, after I left, I came out to the garden to do some thinking. Saw you three go inside. Anyway, a few minutes later, I followed." He paused. "You know, to fly into your room. Only you weren't there."

Cherry-Rose felt like she was punched in the gut.

"At first, I thought you might have been in the shower or something, so I waited for a bit. Ended up falling asleep in the hallway. Saw you walking back this morning."

"I … I … I've just been so—" Cherry-Rose felt the hard weight of shame push into her throat. Her face fell. Her mouth was open, but she couldn't speak.

"It's fine. I mean, I was the one who said there were rules. And really … Really, it doesn't matter. None of it matters. None of *this* matters." Gideon held his hand out in a faint gesture to the Pleasure Island compound.

"I know what I have to do. I'm done with this place, this life. Whale. Brother John. The Roaches. Pleasure Island. Do whatever you need to do, Cherry-Rose, do … whatever you want. But be careful. Break the rules, and he will get you."

"Please, please stay. He doesn't mean anything to me, not John, not William …"

"William? Who the fuck is William? Unbelievable. Are you fucking Whale too?"

All of her insides were out. Cherry-Rose folded to sob into her hands.

"I'm sorry, don't … I didn't mean to … look … he's dangerous. Just be careful; he's not who he seems. Here on that stage, in his office, in his fucking bed, over his desk, you're just one of his possessions … everyone here, we're just playthings." Gideon took a deep breath. "Damn it. I'm sorry, Cherry-Rose, this is not how I wanted this conversation to go. I just want you to know that no matter what, I … I see you. I do. I really do. I see you. And what we have is different. We are … could have been … different."

"Gideon, please."

"I can't. I … can't."

Gideon pulled an envelope out of his book. "I wrote this for you. Don't read it now. Later. Maybe after your show tonight. Maybe tomorrow. I just want you to know that I really enjoyed our time together. I want you to know that I think … you are amazing. And I really do hope that you get everything you wish for."

For the first time since Cherry-Rose sat, she found his eyes.

"When you find time … read the letter … promise?"

Cherry-Rose couldn't speak for her tears, but her eyes never left his. She nodded slowly with wide eyes as tears pooled and fell. She watched Gideon wipe his eyes and flashed to all their mornings—all their threshold moments where he sat patiently just beyond, just out of reach; all their *Nevermores*, all their regrettable almosts, all the unanswered dark-side-of-the-door wishes, that might have, could have been answered on this very morning.

Would he be leaving now if they had been answered?

Gideon stood.

Cherry-Rose reached out desperately, her hand reaching for Gideon, begging for purchase. Cherry-Rose found his hand hanging. Lifeless. She gipped it tightly and pressed it against her cheek. Begging, "Please, Gideon. Please." Cherry-Rose looked up to find the heart tattoo, to find his eyes, and as she did, she could feel his hand slipping away.

"Goodbye, Cherry-Rose."

Cherry-Rose closed her eyes against this very wrong ending; when they opened, she found her journal at the base of Gideon's tree.

Crashing High

THERE was a time when Cherry-Rose wondered, *If, as doe, if I had only died somewhere else, out of reach of the seamstress and her magic, would I be there with Her now? Would I be with my Blue Fairy?* And there was a time when Cherry-Rose wondered, *If I had a mother who wasn't Marybelle, a magical seamstress, a witch, a wolf, would I be here now at Pleasure Island?* And there was a time when Cherry-Rose wondered, *What would it be like to know the boy with the heart on his neck? He was so sweet, so beautiful, so thoughtful.* She'd often think, *I would like to know him better.* And there was a time when Cherry-Rose wondered, *Where are my sisters? What could have happened to them?* But Cherry-Rose hadn't wondered any of those wonders for quite some time now.

She had Shy-Blue, but the other sister-wonders were far, far away. Lost. Gone. Dead or happy. And the boy with the heart on his neck ... *mornings are so quiet ... too quiet.* She preferred not to think about him; and Pleasure Island, *Have I not become what I was meant to be? What Marybelle always wanted ... A Blue Fairy priestess in sequin dress,* she might have thought if she bothered to think such thoughts at all. But she didn't, because nothing, nevermore, none of it mattered anymore.

Cherry-Rose took comfort in the predictability of Brother John's tiny, blue-swirling vials—Take Me, Make Me, Break Me. *So few things in this world do as promised.* The pixie-dust, however, was indeed moon-love ritual in vial, nose, and tea. It beautifully hid all those unwanted memories behind other things, beneath the fingernails that she painted black; behind the blue-stained edges of her redder than rose, double-cherry lips. Everything clouded in pale-blue flickering haze, pushed down deeper, deeper, darkly, darkly behind her thin, black Roach mask; everything buried so deep behind her eyes that swirled their blue-shot storms that she didn't have to wonder all her worrisome wonders. Best of all, Cherry-Rose would say, if anyone bothered to ask, she didn't have to remember that once upon a time, her mornings were not so lonely.

Time stopped at Pleasure Island. A month? Three? Six? A month that felt like three or six … whatever it was, it was a blur. Pleasure Island, the Whale's Island, it swallowed her whole.

Whatever it was, it was day six of a three-day binge. It's funny how all the wonders faded away.

Cherry-Rose sang and Shy-Blue stripped and Gideon was gone. Who was Gideon, anyway? Cherry-Rose was crashing high, high, higher, and higher. When the lonely crept in and the not-enough was too much, and the Blue Fairy was off answering other wishes for other mannequin-ghost girls, "The pixie-dust is," as Cherry-Rose said, pursing her lips at her mirrored reflection, "close enough." There just wasn't anything to wonder any longer. Pleasure Island took it all away.

After all, didn't she have everything she needed? A microphone, an audience, an endless supply of pixie-dust, a bed, a mannequin-something under a snake eating his tail all wrapped up in the bluest sky-blue, Shy-Blue eyes. Every night, a full-moon-ritual night.

Day number … whatever … of a three, five, or six-day good time.

Time meant nothing here.

"Shy. Shy. Shyyy. Dammit, Shy-Blue, look at me. Do you remember when we used to play 'I spy'?"

"Stop. Stop it. You … you always do this when you're high."

"I'm not high. You're high."

"You are *so* high. Don't even lie. Remember? Mother says something bad happens if you lie."

"Don't. Do not! I told you. Never. Never. Never ever mention her to me."

"Fine. Whatever. Just pull it together; we have a show in like ten minutes."

"I might be high. But I'm not too high. Am I? Like, can you really tell? Is it bad, bad? Stand over there, back a little. Okay, now tell me. How do I look?"

"Uh ..." Shy-Blue shrugged.

"Damn it! My lips *are* turning blue, aren't they?" Cherry-Rose dabbed at her lips, trying to touch up the red of those icy, popsicle-stained blue edges. "Shy ... Shy." Cherry-Rose spoke into the mirror. Shy-Blue, I spy with my little eye ..."

"Ladies, Shy-Blue, you're on in five minutes."

"Five minutes?!"

"Something blue ... Shy, come on ... Shy, kiss me."

"Pull yourself together."

"Like last night. Like when Johnboy was there. Like when no one was looking in the cottage. Like under the covers."

"Cher, if John could see you, he'd pull out our seams. We promised. No more today. We said we'd stop before you could see the blue. But look, look at yourself. Brother John is going to kill us if we can't get it together," said Shy-Blue to the Cherry-Rose in the mirror.

"Hmmm, Brother John, he wouldn't dare," said Cherry-Rose, still examining the blue lines that edged her lips. "Do you think anyone will notice? What does it matter anyway?"

A voice broke in from the other side of the door. "One minute. Shy-Blue, we need you behind the curtain in one minute."

"Cherry-Rose! D'you hear that? I have to go. You have thirty minutes. You gotta be ready to go on in thirty minutes. Drink some water, K?"

"Kiss me."

"Come on! I'll see you behind the curtain in thirty minutes. Be there." Shy-Blue gave a wink as she exited their dressing room door.

Thirty minutes.

Time slowed behind the door.

Cherry-Rose found herself a lonely stranger in the bright lights of her makeup mirror. "Thirty minutes," she said just to say something to the blue-shot version of herself on the other side of the glass … just to make sure she too was real.

But thirty minutes behind that door … Time stopped here.

*Click. Mic on.

"One dances, the other, she sings, NO HEARTS, NO STRINGS! Let's hear it for Shy-Blue!"

In the Throes

CHERRY-ROSE wasn't sure how, but she was there waiting for her cue, dressed and alone, standing in pitch black just off stage watching Shy-Blue dance like a flame, watching Shy-Blue move like the shadows that danced all muted and distorted on the backstage wall. The wall where the penetrating light dove and turned and threw its beastly nightmare shapes. *Salvatóre? Wolf? Marybelle?* The light summoned the shadowed forest ivy, and it crept and climbed like it was charged with mother-cottage magic. Cherry-Rose stood in her perfect *playing dead, playing too high, playing so high that everything seemed too real and if I don't move you can't see me* pose. The ivy reached and it stretched and it called her name with its legion-clicking vermin.

Mother?

"Cher—Cherry-Rose." Shy-Blue appeared next to Cherry-Rose, naked and wet from the heat of the spotlight.

"You in there, Cherry-Rose?" Two arms shook two shoulders, and Cherry-Rose gave her the playing-dead lean.

No heart!

Cherry-Rose nodded blankly toward Shy-Blue, her face split by the light peeking through the slit in the curtain.

"You've got this," said Shy-Blue, moving side stage just in time.

No strings!

*Incoherent screams

"Yeah, I've got this," Cherry-Rose said to the rising curtain.

"Cherry-Rose!"

"Honey and gold. Gold and … and—"

The horns ripped through the intro: "I've Got the World on a String." It was her song, again. Always. She sang it a hundred times. No, it was their song, just like *they* wanted, whoever *they* were, out there outside the edges of the spotlight's telescoping heat. She had done this intro a hundred times. Feigning helpless marionette. Arms outstretched. Head bowed. Palms turned up. Feigning fabled wooden boy of Fontainebleau, a nod to her lessers rotting out there in their woodpile. Feigning crucified savior of love and lust while the whole audience, every beast of every form, of every sex, collectively imagined giving her the rood. *Oh, to be a nail in that invisible cross*, thought those beasts. *Oh, to be the rood.*

The room sighed and breathed with Cherry-Rose. Everything beneath those lights that cast their stars on the ceiling slipped into silence, waiting for the words to fall from those cherry-red, lipstick-stained lips, only for the first time ever, the first in a hundred and one "World's on a String," they didn't. Cherry-Rose missed her cue.

Things like this could happen during a live performance; professionals know what to do. Wait … reset … hit it again. So, the cymbals crashed again and the drums rolled on again and the trumpets rose again, and Cherry-Rose …

If you had been to any of the shows on Pleasure Island at the famed Beneath the Stars and the Deep Blue Sea, you would have seen Cherry-Rose grab that mic and call and tease the crowd as she might a lover. You would have seen her slink and move her hips with the beat, reeling the crowd in from the dance floor to the edge of the stage. If you made it to the end of the show on any of those nights, you would have seen Shy-Blue tease out from behind the slit in the soft red velvet curtain just behind the encore marionette Cherry-Rose. You would have seen Shy-Blue wind herself around, through, and beyond Cherry-Rose. You would have witnessed the pinnacle of the mannequin-ghost-dance ritual that transformed words into action—arms, legs, lust, love—that twisted and tormented the audience, that sent them into frenzy.

But, had you tickets to tonight's show, if you saw Cherry-Rose feign strung-up marionette, arms outstretched, all timed with the pulling notes that rang out from the brass in the pit, you would have heard silence when Cherry-Rose should have sung. If you had keen eyes, you might have actually seen it happen. It was like an invisible hand cut all the invisible strings that held Cherry-Rose just so. In a flash, you would have seen the mannequin-doll, who never needed those strings, begin to falter. You would have seen it on her face, the moment she wished for strings. And you would have seen her twin blue-shot Jupiter eyes rolling in protest—rolling, going, gone, making bye-bye eyes as she hit the floor.

Next, you would have heard a collective gasp from the crowd, then silence from the band, then a scream as a robe-clad Shy-Blue ran to the not-so-playing-dead doll on the floor. Last, as the curtain descended, you would have heard the voice from behind the spotlight say something like, "Beneath the Stars and the Deep Blue Sea regrets that we must ask you to …" And if you stayed to listen for gasps and screams emanating from behind the red velvet curtain, you would have heard not the magical rain of honey and gold but the great grumble of the crowd as they made their way toward the exits to find other suitable means of unsuitable distraction.

* * *

The hard slap of the floor was medicine that shook Cherry-Rose back to life. She gasped for air as she attempted to right herself. Cherry-Rose was a sick underwater fawn. Her limbs could no longer support her body. Flat, face down on the hardwood, she flailed as her arms slid out from beneath her torso, once, twice … her black, matted mane fell over eyes that spun wild with storms of swirling pale-blue; hair clung to her blue-stained, cherry-red lips that ran red and dripped long, thin, glistening strings of drool. She felt all beast on the forest floor, drained, gutted, split open, torn open. She could feel claws raking through her abdomen, pouring her warmth out of every willing hole. She was doe breathing her last labored breath and this was the forest floor beneath the stars and the deep blue sea; and this was the last unbreakable promise that the forest had to make, it was the *die* that came soon after eat and fuck.

Cherry-Rose could feel the ivy behind her eyes doing what it was made to do. It swam over her fabric and crept inside her seams, it was rope and anchor, and she sank hard. Drowning in the ivy, she felt hands, Brother John and sister Shy-Blue hands, reach down through thick heavy leaves to pull her back to the surface. No, they weren't trying to save her; they were pushing her down, down, deeper and deeper under the ivy, under the soft earth until it gave way to the deepest bluest sea. She kicked and thrashed and shook and trembled; she puked pale-blue something like an imaginary beast with a funeral-birthday on a dream-island shore. Full of water, full of death, nearly drowned, nearly dead. Drowning. Dying. Black. Everything went black for a moment; *time meant nothing here.* Black, as her salty wet poured out of her eyes and her nose and her mouth, grunting like a doe who was being torn in two.

"Huuughhh, huuuughhh, huuuuughhh."

* * *

Beneath the stars, beneath the sea … deep, deeper, darker …

Somewhere beneath the waves, Cherry-Rose felt the cool embrace of black leather as she sank. Down, down, down beneath the waves, light pushed through the watery sky to reveal a forest of ghosts of sisters mounted and displayed. Down, down, Whale hands thrashed her about, pulling her to the bottom of the sea. Down. From somewhere beneath it all, Cherry-Rose heard voices speaking in their underwater other-side-of-the-magic voices. Feeling paralyzed, like that pink-ribbon-day when she lay face down in the clearing—seeing, hearing, feeling everything, but somehow unable to move. The clearing became sofa, sofa the bottom of the sea, and Cherry-Rose was helplessly waiting for someone to pull her back to the living side of the magic.

"You fucking bitch," growled a voice behind two neck-gripping hands. "I warned you. I warned all of you. How dare you embarrass me like that." Hands pressing soft fabric deeper into the cool leather sea.

"And you, Johnboy! What were you thinking? John? … John? … Johnboy! You know the rules," said the voice from somewhere above the black leather surface.

From beneath the waves, beneath the hands and the hurt, Cherry-Rose could make out another voice … It was Snake-Eating-His-Tail saying that he warned them. That he couldn't stop them. Couldn't stop Cherry-Rose. The voice that was Snake said he was sorry, but they wouldn't listen.

Somewhere behind the voice that was sorry, Cherry-Rose heard another someone who was panting and crying and begging. *Has to be Shy-Blue*, said the Cherry-Rose from beyond the dream, finally returning to state the obvious: *We can't breathe enough to pant, nor beg.*

"And you," the choking hands must have said to the begging voice. "How dare you? Do you know what you are? Nothing. You are nothing without me. Trash. A filthy whore-doll that your mother threw away. Do you think I need you?"

Then the voice behind the choking hands softened to say, "And you, Johnboy, Brother John, King of the Roaches. They wouldn't listen? … That must have been a difficult spot. If only we had rules to prevent this sort of mess."

Even beneath the sea, Cherry-Rose could hear the Whale voice pretending.

"Great performance, Johnboy. Well done. Do you honestly think I don't know what you've been up to? Trying to take what is mine? I hope it was worth it."

Cherry-Rose felt the hands loosen. Let go. They were gone, and Cherry-Rose could open her eyes enough to see Whale hitting Shy-Blue and Shy-Blue hitting the floor.

"Johnboy, how long have you been working for me? Three years now? I've told you ... I've told you over and over, because if anyone understands temptation, it is me. I do know how hard it can be. I do ... have I not been clear?"

Brother John did not answer.

"Johnboy, I'd say ... we have two simple rules. One, we do not touch what is mine. Two, the blue is not for the talent. I did remind you, didn't I?"

Cherry-Rose did not hear Brother John answer because he didn't. She heard fabric twisting. She heard Shy-Blue's feet kicking at the floor. She heard twigs snapping. She heard animal howls.

Cherry-Rose could see Brother John standing with his arms behind his back, his head down, the crown of his pompadour hanging over his mask. Shy-Blue's face pressed into the floor. Whale behind, twisting her arm to make her scream.

Cherry-Rose heard the Whale speak again. "I warned you. Didn't I, Johnboy? I told you what would happen if you took from me. Cherry-Rose is mine. You are mine. That damned Gideon, wherever the hell he's hiding, mine." Whale stroked and gathered Shy-Blue's hair and added, "And Shy-Blue here, all mine, aren't you, baby?" He pulled her hair to turn her face up to his.

Whale stood upright and moved to his desk. "You know, Johnboy, it feels like we're starting over."

Drawer opening.

"We have to start over. We do, don't we?"

Drawer closing.

"Too much is too much and we certainly have had too much."

Filling a glass.

"And two ... two dolls when all you need is one ..."

Taking a sip.

"Johnboy, we can't let Shy-Blue come between us, can we?"

Glass shattering against the wall just behind Brother John.

"And since we're starting over ... would you like to do the honors?"

Cherry-Rose could see Shy-Blue, face down, squirming at his words. With her one good arm, she pushed against the floor to sit up on her knees. She was kneeling before Brother John, who was standing perfectly still with his eyes closed.

There was motion behind the desk. Cherry-Rose could hear the Whale on the move.

He called again as he crossed the room. "Oh, Johnboy, you already know how this ends. Let's not make this any more difficult than it has to be."

Whale *click-clicked* a gun. Hard metal against soft Shy-Blue hair.

Shy-Blue stood and ran to Brother John. "Please, please. John … John, I." She threw her one good arm around Brother John. He, his one free arm around her as she pressed herself onto his knife. "John … I love …" Cherry-Rose couldn't hear the words, but she saw them on her lips.

Shy-Blue fell to her knees holding the knife buried where it lay.

Cherry-Rose didn't want to see anymore, but she couldn't stop watching. Brother John gathered Shy-Blue's hair. If Shy-Blue was aware, she didn't seem to care. She was holding herself together. Trying to keep whatever spilled from her abdomen from spilling. Brother John stroked her hair, "Shhh, shh." Shy-Blue's head fell into his thigh. "Shhhh." His left hand slid into his back pocket; then a knife slid down the back of her neck.

Cherry-Rose tried to scream, but the only sound came from Brother John. "I love you too, Baby Blue."

Cherry-Rose couldn't scream. Her voice was lost to another deluge of pale-blue sea water. Again, she poured the sea out onto the floor.

"Don't worry, darling, I haven't forgotten about you," said the voice kicking through Shy-Blue's crumpled shell, "but we have rules, and we must address our grievances as they have presented themselves."

"Now, Brother John, my dearest Johnboy, you do know the price. You do, don't you?" The Whale paused, allowing it to sink in. "Will it be at my hand or theirs?" The Whale motioned toward the silent horde of Roaches that crowded the hallway just outside the office door. "Them or me? You have been so good to me these last few years. The one last courtesy I can extend to you is this choice."

"Quick does sound nice, but if you don't mind"—John paused behind a soft, sad smile—"I'd like it to be one of the boys. I kinda feel like I owe it to 'em."

"As you wish."

"Well, boys," said Brother John loudly. "Shall we get ourselves to the courtyard? Mr. Hale requires a little privacy."

In the doorway, Cherry-Rose saw Hammer, Fire, Three Nails—seven—nine more waiting.

Brother John took off his jacket, placed it over Shy-Blue, then nodded to Hammer as he walked through the door.

For My Blue Fairy

"SORRY about the wait, baby doll," said the Whale, riding over the cresting arm of the black sea.

Cherry-Rose flailed, trying to push against the crush, but sank.

"Seems I wasn't enough for you, huh? But don't you worry, we can fix this." The beast rolled his sleeves up his arms. "All that is left is for us to right the last of all these wrongs." The Whale slid closer. Breath stinking like the must of rotting soil. Arms everywhere, Kraken driving, Leviathan swarming, everything sinking beneath the stars and the deep black sea.

Drowning, Cherry-Rose didn't have any words for the beast. However, the Cherry-Rose beyond her dreams found *her* words.

Something about all those twisted Marybelle lessons, the night of fuck and feathers, something about bargaining with beasts on full-moon nights, something about finding a way.

You can't fuck this away. The words echoed through her body as if it were hollow.

Away … Away … Away.

I'm finding it difficult to … focus. We are in pieces.

Falling apart. Literally.

Kraken and Leviathan turned and pulled at soft fabric limbs.

Disjointed.

Unhinged.

Loose hanging limbs feeling like they belonged to no one lay lifeless, held down by Whale hands. A mannequin form feeling all papier-mâché, fragile, brittle, buried, covered, surrounded, tied down, and anchored to this diving Whale.

Falling, beneath the stars. Sinking, beneath the deep black sea. Pressure building behind her eyes.

Cherry-Rose saw the ivy in her mind climbing, cresting, rolling. She was at the bottom of the sea, caught up in the wash of the cherry-cordial dream; the light, the night, the room, the Whale pouring into the splitting shell, and Ivy came to sing her a sleeping song. *Dormez vous, dormez vous, Cherry-Rose, Cherry-Rose ... ding, dang, dong ... ding, dang, dong,* but the Cherry-Rose from beyond refused to let her sleep.

Time to wake up.

*   *   *

Where is my Blue Fairy? thought the Cherry-Rose in the mirror on the ceiling. *Has there always been a mirror on the ceiling?* thought the Cherry-Rose below the mirror.

The upside-down cherry-cordial Cherry-Rose inquired, "Penny for your thoughts?"

Taker.

　　*grunt

Keeper.

　　*thump

Why is there always a keeper?

　　*huuuughhhh

It was all honey and gold for a time, wasn't it?

　　*thump

Oh, thumping Whale beast, how did it come to this?

　　*grunt

A wish upon the moon? A star?

*sweat

My Blue Fairy?

*drool

The beast lost himself to the thump, grunt, sweat, and drool of the frenzy. He was all wet hide, all over Cherry-Rose. All monstrosity. All beast and blur and pounding blood; slick sick—skin and fur and man.

The Cherry-Rose in the mirrored ceiling was on the verge of laughter. She had been here before—was it once a month, a week, a day on this same sofa sea? She didn't know. It didn't matter. Time meant nothing here. Besides, after the sea rushed in and Shy-Blue's insides rushed out, it was different. No. Before. It'd been different since ... he ... since Gideon left. Her inner dialogue continued to spin as her eyes welled at the twisted comedy of her life.

A sprinkle of pixie-dust? Another fairy tale? Why did she do this to us? To me?

Who were those moon stories really for? Me or her? Those fairy tales? Her fairy tales. Was any of it real? I'm not even real, thought Cherry-Rose beneath a pained and awkward smile.

Breathe, baby doll, said the wolf that rocked her chair behind the mirror.

Exhale, said the deer that hung over the sofa.

Where is my Blue Fairy now? said the cherry-cordial upside-down doll who began to recite lines from her host's journal.

I was sewn together. Remade. Reborn. A plaything. A quilt of a person. A gathering of pieces. Cut by pattern. Tied with a red bow at the base of the neck. A lonely woman's wish. A spirit abandoned in a lump of rags and yarn. Evicted from the sky. Stolen from the moon and the stars. My Blue Fairy left me here in this shell of thread and fabric. To ...? What? To answer a mother's wish? To fulfill her dream? To fulfill a family curse? To make a mannequin dance and sing? For what? So that we could learn how to be ... to be ... a real girl? A good girl? A proper mannequin-ghost girl?

Seen, not heard. A proper playing-dead girl. Yes, Mother.

Remember, don't blink when you are playing dead.

Make a wish.

See? See? A living-corpse doll can learn to be a good girl.

The cherry-cordial upside-down doll made a note: *when we have time, we must be sure to write this next passage.*

~ ~ ~

I hate you. I hate you and this fucking Beast crushing me. I hate you, Beast, for pretending to care, I hate myself for believing in you, and you, Mother, and your family magic, and you, Blue Fairy, for bringing me halfway to life. For leaving me stranded here, leaving me to … to … be nothing more than a plaything; honey and gold. Gold and honey. It always comes back to that, doesn't it? But break it down even further, beyond honey … further, beyond gold … further and what's left. It's all … eat, fuck, die. Do I get to die again? Do I? That comes next, doesn't it? This is the you-know-what that comes after … isn't it? Whatever … we all know what comes next.

~ ~ ~

"Alright, baby, we're all fixed up now."

*grunt.

"D'ya like that, baby doll?" The Whale panted.

Why does he always ask? Cherry-Rose thought beneath her disgust.

"*How was that?*" She repeated the words to the mirror on the ceiling. It reflected a cold cherry-cordial stare. Her features began to melt into one another, blending and twisting with the light and shadow. She could feel the question vibrating, echoing out from her core, building from her feet, growing until it broke through her body, shattering her frozen cherry-cordial stare. *Dormez vous, Cherry-Rose. Are you sleeping?* sang the cicada inside her head. *You can't fuck it away,* they chirped as she imagined putting all her disjointed parts back together—arms and elbows and knees and thighs.

You can't fuck it away …

Away.

Away.

Away, they chirped until the echoes in all her almost-bones in her almost-body became one.

"AWAY!" Her fists struck the beast as the word exploded out from behind her lips. And in an instant, the beast drove into her again, but this time with the back of his hand. This time, across her face.

"Tsk, tsk, tsk," Whale clicked. "Dolls mustn't ruin the fun. Don't you know by now, baby doll, they're supposed to make the fun?" His words turned up all sick and sweet as he wiped his bleeding snarl. "Remember, darling, you are the toy and I am the boy and this is Pleasure Island. You are just another something I got in trade for pixie-dust. I pull the strings and you get to be what you are: a sewn-up, wind-up toy. You are just another whore-doll."

The Cherry-Rose in the mirror watched as the heart tattooed between her breasts rose and fell. She remembered Violent-Joy pressing the needle and ink into her skin. *It really was beautiful. Yes,* thought Cherry-Rose, *I am more than my pieces. More than a patchwork-doll. More than the Blue Fairy's mannequin-lover. More than the Whale's toy. More than anyone's mannequin-whatever.*

There was something before the songs and the striptease dances, thought Cherry-Rose, staring hard at her cherry-cordial reflection, *something before the pixie-dust and the Pleasure Island orgies. There was something ... wasn't there? Something before Pleasure Island. Something before the honey and gold and the gold and honey. There was ... there was the forest.*

Cherry-Rose started to laugh.

*Laughing

"You think this is funny? I'll show you funny."

"It is funny because I'm not even real. And who knows? Maybe you aren't real. Yes, that's it, you aren't even real. Whale, you can't take anything from me."

The Cherry-Rose in the mirror continued to laugh.

"Oh, I will show you what's real, darling; I *will* swallow you whole."

As Whale pressed his hands in and around the soft flesh of a mannequin neck, Cherry-Rose heard the song of the moon, the song of the cicada in summer. She heard a million scratching voices calling from the twigs and ivy of her mind, and she gave them what they needed; she wished a new wish.

As the Whale-made beast, Cherry-Rose felt something new beating behind the tattoo on her chest and she began to sparkle pale-blue. Her eyes, her cherry-red lips, her fingertips, all sparkling with pale-blue electric glitter. And the ground shook, and then the walls quaked, and the vermin on their shelves and the birds under glass began to dance and fall onto the floor. *Yes, yes.* The Cherry-Rose beneath the choking hand could feel what she hadn't felt since she last closed the door on the cottage; this was her magic. She could feel that she was shaking the room, and her magic wanted nothing more than to free those other mounted sister-beasts. She heard Connie Francis, she saw spoons bending, she saw clocks winding, records spinning, books flying open, and nails. A wall of nails in her mind. The nails began to twist and bend, no … she began to twist and bend the nails; folding, bending, pulling, and the heads of the beasts that decorated the walls began to creak and quake.

*kerrack

First, the bear over the doorway hit the floor with a crash, but still the squeezing hands squeezed. Then the fox fell near the bookshelf. *Poor, poor Shy-Blue*, thought the girl glowing pale-blue. But the squeezing hands did not waver. In fact, they squeezed all the harder to match the rising, blue-sparkling, cherry-red smile that seemed to defy their fate. As the hands tightened, Cherry-Rose trembled and shook all the more, and her pinecone-heart rattled, her tattoo-heart leapt, her eyes narrowed, and her teeth bit, and her cherry-red center flowed down her chin, and when she tasted her own blood, she smiled all the more.

Nails … bending … folding.

Just then, the antlered deer above the couch tumbled down to pierce the side of the Whale. The beast writhed and moaned and howled and sent his red onto the black sea of the sofa. Cherry-Rose spilled onto the floor. She crawled to the side of those dead, sky-blue, Shy-Blue eyes, and she pulled at the switchblade that Brother John left for her, shimmering between Shy-Blue's belly seams. Two hands overhead, Cherry-Rose dove into the wounded, fumbling beast and plunged the knife deep into the Whale's neck.

He sank down, down, down, deeper, deeper, darker, darkly into his own pool of red.

Panting, glowing, dripping with Whale-red, Cherry-Rose pulled herself up to the Whale's desk. Searching. She found paper and pen. "For my Blue Fairy."

She spoke the words as she wrote, "*There will be pain. There will be blood. There will be death. There will be fire,*" and she set them alight.

IV

Flying Up Moon

A Daughter's Wish

STANDING on the hill where stumps were once trees, where crow once traded secrets for thread, Cherry-Rose stood facing the forest. She thought of how the trees did their job. Upon hearing footsteps, they bent and stretched to block the sun so that those who might be unsure about entering the forest wouldn't. She thought of how the ivy too did its job. The path into the forest was entirely gone. Ivy had covered those worn and rough open patches; covering all the earth scarred by Marybelle's trips to market.

"Good day, Forest. Hello, Ivy. It's me, Fawn-girl."

There was no answer, but the trees gave her sunlight; and although she didn't think she needed it any longer, Ivy gave her the path.

The walk was long but quiet. Birds were silent, deer were silent; bear and wolf lay low—only Ivy rustled; its snakes slithered, its cicada sang, and its roaches chirped.

Cherry-Rose knew these songs and she was not afraid.

When she made it to the clearing, she was pleased to see the ivy held its ground at its edge. "Why, thank you. What a nice surprise," Cherry-Rose said. "So, you knew that I'd be back?"

Only cicada answered.

From the outer edge of the clearing, not yet moving beyond the ivy ring of the forest, Cherry-Rose observed the cottage sitting perfectly quiet beneath the tree-lined hollow sky and thought, *It is still strange to see the cottage from this point of view … from the other side.*

She stepped into the clearing cautiously, as if she were waiting for something to drop out of the sky, as if her steps might stir the voice that begged her to run, as if her footsteps might awaken Ivy, or maybe the dead. The Cherry-Rose beyond her dreams was silent, and Ivy did not stir, and the earth did not swell with restless, rising, reaching hands. Nothing but twilight fell out of the sky.

Cherry-Rose crossed the clearing and remembered a cottage once full of life.

Dead or happy. "I've been dead. I'd like to be happy."

Time had flattened the burial mound she had made long ago. *How long was I gone?* Daisies grew tall here now. *A year?* Round buttons like the sun held onto petals who shone like fat pale faces to reflect the moon. *Two? Long enough for these weeds to mark the grave. This seems right, though, doesn't it? Daisies.*

She paused for a moment and considered taking a bouquet inside but remembered how the daisies' roots were fed.

Cherry-Rose went to the garden where wild strawberries were left to rot between tufts of marigold, where tomatoes climbed and were pecked clean on their trellis walls, where onion grew unchecked. She traced where thick hairy vines left squash, some ripe, others fat and split, all swarm and fury, full of tiny black ants who wound their way through the mad, wild marigold. The garden was alive but overrun with those musty orange blossoms.

"Taking over, are we?" asked Cherry-Rose as she bent, seam-ripper in hand. She cut the flowers at their base.

Cherry-Rose moved to the center of the clearing, marigold in one hand, the other hand open, palm facing up as if to support the sky. She shut her eyes, drew a long deep breath, and whispered a wish as she began to twirl.

"A new beginning." At the words, tears that she no longer had a reason to hide rose and fell. Tears upon tears as she twirled, tears upon tears as she spoke the words over and over. Words and tears tumbling upon the musk of marigold and the scent of honeysuckle, over and over, into the pink of the western sky and the blue of the east—musk for the rising moon, tears for the setting sun.

When there were no more tears to twirl, when there were no more words to give, Cherry-Rose slowed and opened her eyes. She found herself standing still before a veil of trees; the world exactly the same, but somehow entirely new—brighter, clearer. She could see black birds hopping at the edge of the clearing. She could hear the stream bubbling in the distance far beyond the soft ever-rattle of the too many almost-uncle parts. She could hear the click, click, clicking beneath the ivy, hooves upon ivy, velvet upon bark. She could feel the crush of hidden eyes upon her, the weave of ivy vines crawling over the forest floor. Forest; she could feel Forest and its forever promise humming beneath the twilight moon. Forest and Forever … and she knew—she was home.

Evermore

CHERRY-ROSE propped open the door, opened the windows, and placed the marigold over each threshold. She lit two candles on either side of the mantel, put "Ju Ju Hand" on the record player for Violent-Joy and Peaches, Sprinkles and Mojave. Next, she danced a wild "Passenger" dance for Fae, Rey-Rey, and Siouxsie; she stomped and cried "Pissing in a River" for Jasmine, Daisy, and Scarlet. And when she got it all out, good enough for now, Cherry-Rose made tea with the sage and lemon she carried in her satchel. She sipped and rocked in the chair that wore the grooves into the floor. Here she read Yeats for Shy-Blue. A red thread held its place at *The Second Coming*.

She thought of Gideon and wondered where he might be. She thought she might love him, but she wasn't quite sure, for the love she had always known was built with cages, shaped like doll house diorama, was contained in jars with tight tight lids.

Cherry-Rose recalled the sound of Gideon sliding down the wall, the anticipation of his morning call rapping on her wall. She remembered waiting every morning to tease and torment him as he sat just on the other side, holding back her response until she was certain she had colored his face red. He never knew, but it was she who waited for him. Every morning, she waited perfectly still to hear him open the door from the courtyard, to hear his boots land heavy in the hallway, to hear his sigh escape as his back slid down the thin wall that kept them apart. She'd lie in her bed and revel in the sweet waiting moments.

On the morning after Gideon's lemon-tree goodbye, she remembered waking with a start. She slept heavy but dreamed she was awake enough to hear his boots, his sigh.

How long was I …?

She knew he was gone, but hoped he wasn't. In and out of dream for a moment, and she began to wonder if he was actually there, and if again, she had left him waiting there too long. *No time for games*; she leapt out of bed and burst through the door. She found the hallway was empty of all but a book.

A Yeats anthology. Cherry-Rose found his words on the title page:

Cherry-Rose,
You are in here somewhere. Everywhere. Evermore.
Love,
~ gid

The book fell open to "A Prayer for my Daughter." She remembered reading it twice, once for the rhythm and once to wonder at what sort of poem Marybelle would have written for her.

Once more the storm is howling, the door to the courtyard opened, *And heard the sea-wind scream upon the tower*, his boots were quiet that day, *Hearts are not had as gifts …* at the wall. Sliding … *self-delighting*, *self-appeasing, self-affrighting …* She remembered all those mornings, all the morning-ritual nevermore almosts, all the maybe tomorrows, all her dark-side-of-the-door dreams. Now more than ever, she could feel him on the other side; breathing, sighing; whispering unintelligible words as his finger traced the page.

She remembered when the game began to change for her. She surprised Gideon one morning. She waited at the door, waited for the boots, his back to slide down the wall, and just when she thought he might begin his tap, tap, tap, she leaned out the door.

"Hey, how long have you been waiting there?" Gideon asked.

Forever, she thought.

"Who said I was waiting for you?" she said and laughed. "Just lying about, reading some poetry. Heard something is all."

"Is that right? Well then, *I have spread my dreams under your feet ...*"

"Hmm, I don't know that one. I could use a clue."

"No clues. That's cheating."

Cherry-Rose recalled the lemon-tree goodbye and how, through streaming tears, she found that he had written that very line in her journal.

"Hey Cher–"

"Yeah?"

"Nothing. Never mind."

"What?! No, no, no. There are no never minds."

"It's just that it's fucked up to say out loud ... I've been thinking, it's like everything you and I have been through, separately and together, to be here ... right here ... I don't know that it could have happened differently. I guess I mean, despite it all, despite everything, or maybe even because of it, either way, I'm really glad I met you."

The memory made her scratch her heart tattoo.

"I can't believe I forgot." Cherry-Rose jumped out of the chair. "Where is it?" Seam-ripper. Mirror. Fingers over the seam that edged her heart tattoo. Cherry-Rose cut the threads and emptied the broken heart purse she kept hidden inside her chest. She pulled out a tiny blue feather and placed it in her hair, just behind her ear. Then she pulled out the note that a blue-shot version of herself hid away. *That* Cherry-Rose couldn't bear to read the words that this letter might contain. She remembered wanting to burn the letter, to forget that it ever existed. She knew who she was when Gideon wrote the letter, and if she read those words then, the words that she imagined, words of pain and hurt, it would have been worse than any words spat by Marybelle. And if they weren't words of pain and hurt, if they were words of longing and love, even worse. Much worse than the obsession, possession, hate, and spite of a mother, worse than a wolf's claw to the abdomen.

She remembered dreading the fangs that this letter might contain. She had wanted to hide from the hurt and the pain. She wanted to turn all the lost opportunity that it represented into fine gray ash at the bottom of a ritual jar. She wanted to burn it like she burned all her wishes. She reasoned, *What could it hurt? If it is full of pain and hurt, it already came true. If it is full of longing and love, perhaps it becomes all the truer for me never having read the lines.* But she knew even then, even all high on pixie-dust and ritual-fire fantasies, that one day, maybe, some other version of herself might like to know these words.

How long has it been since Gideon left? She couldn't remember; *too long, but not that long.* "Wrapped in red thread. Nice touch. Did I wrap this? Did he? Red? Really?" She unwittingly tucking the thread somewhere in the folds of *Sailing to Byzantium.*

The Cherry-Rose beyond the dream told her to breathe.

*Breathe.

Dear Cherry-Rose,

I am sorry. So sorry for all of this …

I feel like we might have known each other in another life. I feel you in my bones, under my skin, I feel you in the night when I chase away all the noise in my head. You are there like a dream holding me together so I don't break apart and drift off into oblivion. Sometimes I feel like our souls were made of the same broken star, like we were supposed to find each other to right whatever cosmic wrong separated us in the first place. But here, now … in this life, I feel like we just missed each other. Like we were either born too late or too soon, or too something; either way, our spirits seem to be just slightly out of sync. Like we might have to try again in another life, in another way. There are just too many things wrong with this story. Too many wrongs to right in this life …

I think I love you, Cherry-Rose. I know I do. I love you, Cherry-Rose. But no matter how much I love you, I know that there is nothing I can do to fix whatever it is that is keeping us apart. I don't give up easily, or ever, but I also know that my time here is up. I can't stay and I can't ask you to leave ... and this, me being hurt and clingy ... all emo, isn't giving you what you need. My needs would only push you away. So, this is it, Cherry-Rose, this is me trying to do what I know is right.

Whoever you are, whoever you were, or will become, know this: I know you best of all, Cherry-Rose. You certainly are more than all your pieces.

And someday, if not here, then on other shores, I will find you, and when I do, I won't walk away so easily. One mustn't fuck with the stars.

To Other Shores, Cherry-Rose.

xoxo

~ gid.

p.s. Do you know *Mad Girl's Love Song* by Sylvia Plath? I feel like she wrote it for us ... but maybe I made it all up inside my head.

*Breathe.

The warm honeysuckle breeze poured through the front door. It filled the cottage and called her to the clearing. The flying-up moon was there, rising, just touching the top of the trees, just about to peek out into the open sky. Cherry-Rose lit a fire in the clearing ring and sat on the stoop of the porch to breathe in the honeysuckle, to watch a dancing moth, to wait for the climbing moon, to feel the full weight of the night coming down. She could feel him out there in the electricity of the night, in the poetry that moved the flame, in the song that moved the moth. She watched the fire slide with the breeze and she dreamed of riding the smoke that sailed to those other shores—titan, bear, wolf, ghost-girl, lover, loved. The fire crackled and spat as she read the letter again and again and again, and when she finished, she folded the letter, wound it with its red thread, and said to the fire, "These wishes aren't for you."

When the flying-up moon reached its peak, Cherry-Rose lay down beside the fire. Pure and true, she made an entirely new wish. She didn't write it down, for it wasn't for paper and it wasn't for fire. She didn't even whisper it to her Blue Fairy. This one was hers and hers alone.

* * *

Cherry-Rose closes her eyes and imagines full-moon mirages spilling out over a gentle sea. Each swell makes a new moon, and she names them as they roll. "The Lightning moon, Corn moon, Lynx moon. The Black Cherries moon." Gentle waves rolling.

Fireside in the clover and the earth that edge the firepit. Legs swept up slightly. Dress tucked between knees. Hands in imperfect prayer under ear, under neck. Letter lying in the palm of one hand. Fingers of the other hand on letter.

Tonight's moon, forever rolling ... "Flying-Up moon."

Cherry-Rose opens her eyes and turns over onto her back. Letter over hearts, hands over letter—funeral-birthday pose. Eyes to the moon, beyond; to the stars, beyond. She gives her wish to the Cherry-Rose who watches beyond her dreams. She gives her wish to the Cherry-Rose who, while she sleeps, keeps watch on those other shores.

Cherry-Rose breathes in the night and thinks, *I have poetry and music; honeysuckle and fire; the moon and the stars ... and this is enough for now.* "This *is* enough for now."

Epilogue

ONCE there was a time when the Blue Fairy's magic flowed through Forest; it nourished the soil and the mist of the clouds. It flowed through the smoke and the fire: titan, bear, wolf, doe, lover, loved. Every beast, every beast everywhere. Here, even here there was magic, even here in this humble cottage so far beyond the village that it has now been forgotten by most, so deep in the forest that it is part of the forest. Even here where long long ago a lonely daughter wished for her happily-ever-after ... even here where it was found by Cherry-Rose.

Under a Glass Jar

ON THE funeral-birthday table, there was a jar. Inside the jar, there lived the burnt and black edges of a wish cast seemingly from another life … something about other shores. Beneath that jar, between it and the funeral-birthday table, there was a small scrap of paper. Cherry-Rose had forgotten all about it, but some time after she danced all her dances, after she made the fires by which she read Gideon's letter night after night, after she realized she'd had enough for now, she did remember putting it there. It was a clue for her probably not-dead, possibly unhappy sisters—something about being found at Fontainebleau. The jar, who for the last few weeks became base for long white candles as their flames flickered and their wax flowed, sat unmoved until this very day when she decided that she would keep the old ways. Until she decided that she would set the funeral-birthday table for the ascending Hunter's Moon.

Cherry-Rose moved the jar to the mantel, placed a new candle inside, lit the wick, and held her note over the flame. She watched the paper take the flame, and as its blackened edges curled, she saw that the words weren't hers at all. "Hollywood ~ G."

Milton Keynes UK
Ingram Content Group UK Ltd.
UKHW042308101024
449571UK00013B/103/J

9 798350 734157